I0680973

THE BIG MITT
a novel
Erik Rivenes

Copyright © 2014 by Erik Rivenes. All rights reserved.

No part of this book may be reproduced or utilized in any form or by any means, electronic or mechanical, including photocopying, recording, or by information storage and retrieval system – except in the case of brief quotations embodied in critical articles and reviews – without permission in writing from the publisher.

This is a work of fiction. Names, characters, places and incidents either are the product of the author's imagination or are used fictitiously, and any resemblance to actual persons, living or dead, business establishments, events, or locales is entirely coincidental.

ISBN: 978-0-9773471-3-1

Published by
Trampoose Press
P.O. Box 587
Beaverton, OR 97075

Cover design by James T. Egan, Bookfly Design
Book design by MC Writing Services

The BIG MITT

a novel

ERIK RIVENES

"*The people who were left to govern the city hated above all things strict laws. They were the loafers, saloon keepers, gamblers, criminals, and the thriftless poor of all nationalities. Resenting the sobriety of a staid, industrious community, and having no Irish to boss them, they delighted to follow the jovial pioneer doctor, Albert Alonzo Ames.*"

LINCOLN STEFFENS
THE SHAME OF MINNEAPOLIS
McCLURE'S MAGAZINE, JANUARY 1903

CHAPTER 1

$\mathcal{S}$HE AWOKE WITH A WILD SCREAM locked tight in her throat, and fought to choke it back with short, hard bursts of breath. Her body froze with fear, the terrible fear of not knowing.

Where was she?

She tried to shake out the fogginess, to clarify her surroundings. Her face was damp and she tasted the saltiness of sweat on her lips. She moved her arm to wipe it off, but realized with horror that her hands were tied to a bed, and she was half-sitting, half-lying against the headboard. Then she remembered where she was, and the realization of her situation forced a deep, reflexive sob to shudder through her body.

The room was bone-gnawingly cold, and already her dream of her warm, childhood feather bed was fading into a haze. But the taste of it still lingered, both delicious and bitter.

After a few minutes of desperate tears, her head was clearer. She kicked off her blanket and looked at the greasy, stained sheet she sat on. Her sunless legs stuck out from underneath her gown, nastily bruised with shades of blue and black.

Her surroundings were sparse. There was only the bed, a bureau, a mirror and a chair. It was dark, except for the bright-gray light of a winter sky, which shimmered tauntingly through a little window. Squinting through the frosted glass, she could barely make out a snow-dusted church spire jutting over the building next door. The church bells were ringing, and she wondered why. Then she heard the sound of gunfire outside, and it made her flinch. New Year's Eve, she remembered. Perhaps this is why she was alone. Men were too busy celebrating at parties and saloons to come looking for her. But she knew they would still come, once the excitement of the midnight bells had passed, once they had drunkenly congratulated each other on making it to the first day of 1901.

The cords around her wrists weren't completely tight, but not loose enough to slip her hands through, either. She remembered now that she had tried to free herself before she fell asleep, and the bindings had eaten her wrists raw. She tried again anyway, this time with a frantic urgency. The pain made her grit her teeth, tears again streaming down her cheeks, but she couldn't get her hands loose. The cords were tied to two posts of a rough wooden headboard, cracked with old paint. She wrapped her hands around the cords, pulled, and felt the headboard move forward and the mattress shift under her body. Again, she pulled, and she felt the strain against the frame. A flash of hope leaped inside her, and she thanked God that the bed was cheap and poorly made.

She heaved her body forward, bringing the headboard almost to her back. It splintered with a loud crack and the top of the frame fell against the wall and onto the floor with a thud. She lurched backward and then forward, finally coming to a jolting halt with the headboard lying on top of her. She took a deep breath and slid her legs to the side of the mattress. Someone must have heard me fall, she thought, panicked. She had to free herself soon, because they would definitely come, and if she were found in this position, obviously attempting escape, she would be brutally punished. That, she was certain of.

Her body was small, and she was thin, but she wiped away the panic with a deep breath, feeling the strength return to her shivering muscles. She glanced around the room, her mind racing as she searched for something to help free her.

The mirror. She thought that if she could find the physical strength to pull the bed frame forward with her, she might be able to break the glass, pick up a shard, and somehow cut the cord with her tied hand. It might work, but it would take time, and she suspected that was in short supply. She tried to stand up and drag the headboard too, but she discovered with a groan that the far end was still connected to the frame. She was still trapped, lying between the bed's boards with her feet splayed out on the floor, pinned under the heavy wood.

Then she heard a floorboard creak. It came from just outside, in the hall. She saw the flicker of the gaslight under the crack of the door, and then a shadow choked the light. She struggled feverishly with the frame, bending her thin arms back until her muscles seared with pain. With a great burst of furious force, she tried to twist the headboard's stuck side loose, and she felt it give way a little. But she just couldn't get enough leverage with her hands behind her.

Whoever was behind the door seemed to have heard the noise. The knob turned, and she stifled a cry. Perhaps she could kick him. That's what she would do. Surprise him with a smash to the groin and leave him quivering on the floor. But what then? She would still be stuck to this bed. Too much noise, too little time, and after whatever beating and rape she would certainly endure, she would be bound much more tightly from now on.

The door pushed open, spilling light onto the floor. She squinted and braced her body, but heard a whispered voice instead of the shouts and curses she feared.

"What happened? What happened?" Ollie asked, disbelief on his face. "Did a customer do that to you?"

A warm wash of relief enveloped her when she saw his slender frame in front of her. His familiar mop of curly brown hair sat dirty and uncombed atop his head, and he smelled as usual of wood smoke and penny cologne. Ollie was the only male in the house with a sliver of kindness in him. She wrote this off to youth, for he was barely fifteen years old. It was probably just a matter of time before his gentle inclinations twisted into something more horrible.

"You have to help me, Ollie, please." She shook her hands to show him her predicament.

He wiped his forehead with a soiled square of cloth from his pocket, and glanced back into the hall. "Jesus. I'd be slit from ear to ear if I helped you."

"Emil is going to do worse to me when he finds out," she said. "Is he downstairs now?"

Ollie shook his head, eyes large.

"What about Higgins and Pock? Are they downstairs? Are they anywhere in this house?"

Again, he shook his head. His ear was fat and swollen, no doubt from a recent beating. He looked positively frightened, she thought. She could understand that.

"Well, Ollie, that's good. Do you have a knife? You've got to cut me loose, and quickly."

"They're out, but they'll be back soon. Went to shoot at the moon and have a drink at Carroll's, they said. Celebrate the New Year."

"Do you have a knife?" she repeated.

He nodded, and pulled a small pen blade from his pocket. He moved forward and held it to the cord on her right wrist. She was trembling; afraid she might shake so much he would slip the blade into her hand. He stopped, however, and stared intently into her eyes. He swallowed hard with his next words. "I should just go get Emil. He'd probably give me a dollar for that. A whole damn dollar. I know he won't hurt you. I heard him say you're his favorite."

Her heart dropped, but she sucked her breath in and spoke in her softest, most soothing voice. "You know what he will do to me, right? You think this is bad? He'll be all liquored up when he comes back, Ollie. And when he's drunk he's a monster. Use your imagination and then multiply it a hundred times. You've got to free me." She paused, trying to figure out how to articulate how grave her situation was. Then she remembered.

"You know about captivity yourself. The man you've told me about."

The words hit him hard. Ollie swayed back as if being struck. He froze at some dark memory, and a moment later it snapped. His face melted with sympathy, and she could see he finally understood.

"Yeah, he'll be drunk all right, and hopping mad too."

With a look of resigned determination and the deft motion of an expert thief he cut the cord off her right wrist, and then jumped nimbly over her body to free the left. She touched her injured wrists instinctively, and Ollie's eyes widened when he saw the gore. She reached out, touching his cheek, and he smiled. "Thank you, Ollie," she said, and then pulled down her gown, suddenly aware of her bare, brutalized legs.

"Awww, it was nothin'," he said, looking down quickly at his feet, momentarily shy. "What do we do now?"

"We've got to free the other girls. Get them out. Now's our chance."

"Just you and me?" He shook his head in disbelief. "Minneapolis ain't so big. Emil's got guys everywhere. He's got plenty of dirty cops paid for, too. We can't just parade a gaggle of girls through the snow. The bulls'll pick us up quick, take us to jail, and then sell us back to Emil. He'll work you extra hard to pay that back. And as for me, he won't need me anymore, I reckon." He formed his hand into a gun, held it to his head, and imagined his demise with a whimper. "And we don't have no cush. I don't, anyway. Do you?"

She pulled her bottom lip back with her teeth. Might as well tell him, she thought. If he doesn't help me, then it won't matter anyway. With care, she stood up, wobbling slightly. "No money now," she said, as she rubbed her legs. "But I've got someone who has, and a raft of it too."

"How can that be? You're just a—"

"Yes," she interrupted, "we both know what I am. But I know people, people from my old life."

"Really?" Ollie replied dubiously. "Is it that Ace fella?"

"I can't say, but please, just trust me."

"It'll be suicide trying to sneak Trilly and Edna out in the middle of the night."

He was right, of course. She couldn't put anyone else in harm's way, especially the two other girls in Emil Dander's employ. Better to leave, fetch the money, and then come back for them. First, though, she needed to find a way out of this miserable hole. "You're right. Just me then. I'll figure out what to do about the others later. Now go downstairs, Ollie," she ordered. "I've made a lot of noise. Make sure I haven't disturbed the house."

"Okay," he said uncertainly. "Then what?"

"Give a whistle," she said, slipping on her only pair of shoes. They were so old that her big toe poked out from the end of one.

"What kind of whistle? Like I was looking at a pretty girl?"

"No, not that kind. Something cheerful. What's that song you like to sing? That popular one you heard at the vaudeville?"

"You mean the 'Bluebirds of Broadway'?"

"Yes, that one. And act like you're in a good mood when you whistle it. It's New Year's, after all."

"Right." He grinned slightly. "Miss Mabel Johnson sings it. I've seen her four times at the Dewey Theater. She's the sweetest peach I've ever laid eyes on and dead swell built. I wish I could see her up close some time."

She leaned forward, and kissed him on the cheek. "Ollie. Stop talking. You need to go now. Before they get back. Check the house, and make sure the way is clear. Whistle that tune and I'll be ready."

"What happens if someone comes? Should I whistle something different?"

She thought for a moment. 'Nearer My God to Thee,' she said firmly. "I need to get ready. Go."

He nodded, and flashed her a quick smile. "You sure are brave. Braver than me, anyway. And beautiful too," he added sheepishly. He took off his jacket and handed it to her. "Take this, please. You don't have nothin' warm to wear 'cept that flimsy gown. It's too cold for only that."

She took the jacket and put it on. "Thank you," she whispered, holding back a flood of overwhelming gratitude. First, he frees her, and now this. Moments of kindness such as these were rare in this place.

Face red and avoiding her eyes, Ollie ran to the door and slipped through, pulling it shut behind him.

She tugged his jacket tight over her thin shoulders, examining herself in the cracked mirror over the dresser. An emaciated, tired corpse is all that's looking back at me, she thought. She sighed and pulled open a drawer in the battered nightstand. One final thing to take with me. The drawer came out completely and her fingers reached behind to where a small groove had been cut in the nightstand's back panel. Her hand clasped her prize, and she held it tight and with some relief.

The stickpin's value was obvious. It was about an inch and a half long, gold, and embedded with four small but spectacular rubies. She pulled up her gown and gently inserted the pin into the hem.

Satisfied, she had nothing to do but wait. Five minutes passed without the signal, and then ten. She heard noises downstairs, distant and muffled. At one point she thought she had heard some footsteps, but then no more. The anticipation was excruciating. She moved to the filthy window and wiped the pane with her hand, removing soot and frost. It was one of those exquisite winter evenings, where the fresh snow reflected the city's lights into the night sky. She brightened at its beauty, but also knew she would be easy to spot once she tried to make her way through the neighborhood to freedom.

More footsteps coming down the hallway sent her heart leaping into her throat. They sounded dull and heavy, perhaps work boots. She balled a fist knowing she probably wouldn't come out well from this, but was sure and determined to kick up a row. She put her body against the wall next to the door, thinking if it were Emil, he'd still expect her to be tied submissively in bed. In his confusion she could slip out past him and make a run for it.

The footsteps stopped, just beyond the door. Straining her ears, she made out raspy, forced breathing. Perhaps it's just some randy old reveler, she thought, and wondered how he would react to find a woman behind the door who didn't quite meet his expectations of an obedient whore. Slowly, the door handle turned, and her body stiffened with dread. Back went her hand, ready to punch his hallowed jewels if necessary.

And then she heard it. The agreed-upon tune, whistled low. A voice feverishly whispered, "Open up. It's me, Ollie. Nothin' to worry about."

She smiled and threw open the door, and a massive paw flew into her face, cracking her nose and sending her crashing to the floor. All went black for a second or two, and then as her eyes focused though the searing pain, she saw Higgins's hulking form standing over her, rubbing his reddened right hand.

"Ain't no porcelain face on you, dearie." He smirked. "That actually hurt a little." His breath reeked of dog-cheap whiskey, and when he smiled his usual leer he showed a stunted row of rotting teeth.

"Where's Ollie?" she managed to ask, sniffing as blood ran from her nose onto her lips.

"He spilled his chicken-shit little guts!" Higgins laughed. "Pock took him to the basement. Figured we should wait till Emil comes back before we rip his stringy limbs off. You know, I don't get to many shows, but I saw a vaudeville last month with that song in it." He whistled a few bars. "That damn tune is gonna be stuck in my head now for a long time. Looking forward to tellin' this story to the boys down at the saloon, though. Crazy woman thinks she's gonna fly the coop, and instead I come in and mangle her face!" He tilted his head back and guffawed. "Ain't life like a big old ball of sunshine, dear heart?"

She nodded solemnly, and with all her might, rammed her fist into Higgins's crotch. Her aim wasn't perfect but it did the trick. He keeled over in agony, falling to one knee and bellowing like a branded cow. She was momentarily stunned, not at the writhing mound on the floor, but at her own mettle. Her struggle to free herself from the bed hadn't completely drained her strength after all.

His thick fingers reached out for her, but his slowed speed was no match for her desire to cut dirt and rip out of the room. His body still blocked the door, but she clambered over him, falling into the hallway. Pulling herself up, she closed her eyes for a moment and then opened them, adjusting to the gaslight's glare and her path to escape. The wallpaper's stained and faded pattern of blue and pink flowers seemed to blur, then focus, and then blur again. At the end of the hall, a door led to the stairway. Her chance at freedom went one flight down to the main door. Higgins's voice had diminished to a low moan now, and she looked back at him with horror. He stumbled after her, half crawling, half walking, and staring at her with frenzied, bloodshot eyes.

If he catches me, guaranteed I will never see the light of day again, she told herself. She rushed to the staircase door, pushed it open and leaned back, wanting a few inches of leeway in case Pock or another of Emil's hired men were lying in wait with a baseball bat or crowbar. When no one appeared, she leaped into the stairwell, slammed the door, and bounded down the steps, two at a time. She held her gown high so she wouldn't trip. From above, she heard Higgins scream down at her, barely coherent, a din of jumbled curses. Her blow had certainly made its mark, she thought with a short, grim smile. A just punishment for the ass, beating on a girl like that. Her smile widened as she reached the bottom, and a short hallway leading into the kitchen. It was quiet here, for the moment. She knew Higgins would soon come lumbering down the steps, furious enough to kill her right where she stood. The girls above were probably awake too, but too terri-fied to leave their rooms. Edna would be scared, anyway, but she could imagine Trilly attempting something as daring and foolish as this.

Opening the kitchen door, her nose wrinkled at the linger-ing stink of the burned potato soup that had been dinner. Worn cupboards lined the walls. A cook stove crouched in the middle of the space, a faint glow flickering from the firebox through the air-vent. A flour barrel sat in the corner, and with some grunting she managed to spin its bottom until it rolled like a heavy coin to a stop in front of the hallway door. She took a moment of satisfaction from her barricade, hoping it might buy her a few extra minutes.

The back door was locked, and from the inside. She knew why, of course. Trying her weight against it, she felt it give a little. Hitting it with her shoulder, she felt the wood bend. After a third attempt didn't break it, she stopped to catch her breath and decide what to do. Cans of sugar, salt and flour lined the counter, so she used her arm to fling them aside, hoping a key might reveal itself. She shot a glance over her shoulder as she scoured the kitchen's mess. He should be down by now, she thought, banging on the door and calling her "bitch" and "whore" and whatever else in his vocabulary filled in for a woman. It was silent, though, and the silence scared her even more. She reached underneath the little table, groping for any crevice a key might fit in.

And then she found it. Her fingers curled around the key and she pulled it up, triumphant. Throwing herself at the door, she fumbled the key into the hole, turning it and flinging the door open. Her heart pounded with the thrill of freedom. The room upstairs had been cold but the air outside was far below freezing. It hit her hard in the face and she buttoned up Ollie's jacket with numbing fingers. Snow was falling lightly but lay thick on the ground, wind-swept drifts that looked like white waves frozen in mid-movement. As she stepped outside, the door slammed behind her, sending icicles from the eaves cracking and spearing into the snow.

The path had actually been shoveled, to her surprise. The yard was small, bordered by a rough wooden fence, about ten feet high. A forlorn tin-roofed shed stood in the corner, snug by the fence, eerily glimmering from the winter light. Trying her best to keep her shoes from crunching on the thin film of snow, she gingerly followed the path to the corner of the house. Caution made her stop and peer around the corner. She threw her body back when she saw the dark figure approaching. It was Higgins. She caught a cry in her throat and turned. Frantic, she considered going back inside and locking the door. Or should she run for it in the other direction? There was no way to avoid him. She'd get only a few steps in the thigh-high drift before he'd reach her and finish her there. Without time to deliberate she squeezed herself flat against the house.

Higgins was broad chested, big-bellied and taller than most. He reminded her of a troll in a fairy book that had frightened her as a child. After an instant's contemplation, she realized she might use his size to her advantage. He turned the corner and stopped, leaned forward with his big forearms against his knees, and attempted to catch his breath. "Goddamn dirty bitch," he whispered.

Slowly, he sucked in the icy air, wheezing like a broken accordion. As he stared at the ground she watched his eyes register her footprints. His gaze followed them up until he looked her cold in the face. The surprised gasp he made amplified into a yelp as she wheeled her leg to kick him in the meat of his calf. He went down fast, big arms clawing at the air to prevent his rendezvous with hard ice. Still, he ended up face down on the cement walkway, a fat pile of moaning flesh. The gown she wore had caught on her leg, and now she too fell, right on top of him. He roared with anger and she desperately slapped at his head as he strained to grab her.

"Get off me, you penny whore!" he yelled, spit and frost flying from his mouth. She was small match for his muscle, but still scratched and clawed at his face and neck, drawing lines of bright red blood with her fingernails. With brute strength he turned her over as she kicked and screamed, until his heavy body lay on top of hers. She felt his chest crushing her, and fought to catch her breath.

"I don't care how much tin you earn for him," he said, and threw her arms over her head. They slapped limply against the wet ice, and then he held them down with his hands. "He's not going to care a lick what I do to you now, because I made sure you stayed right here." Tears spilled down her face. She turned her head to avoid the stench of his foul mouth, so close to hers. He laughed and forced a kiss on her. She felt the bristles of his unshaven chin against her cheek, and tasted vomit in her throat.

"Hell, I don't even feel the cold now, dearie," he laughed, and he let go of one of her arms to unfasten his trousers. He was excited now, and hummed a chipper tune, something about the month of May. It was a song she'd never liked. Now she hated it. As he fumbled distractedly with his belt, she used her free hand to feel through the snow, finding nothing but clumps of hibernating grass in her fingers. Higgins struggled with her gown next, trying to force his way through the fabric. She wondered how, in the middle of winter, a man could take off his trousers on icy pavement in the middle of the night and find any joy or arousal. The weight of his body against her was staggering, but she still, desperately, sliced her fingers through the snow, ignoring the crushing pain and hoping to find something, anything, she might use for a weapon. He tried to kiss her once more and she moved her mouth away, so he grabbed her cheeks in his fat paw and held her head still so he could slam his skull into hers.

A bright burst of light filled her vision, followed by blinding pain. Her eyes adjusted to his hideous, ogling mug, still trying to stick his tongue into her mouth. The fear was choking her now. She threw her head from side to side, banging it on the pavement in frustration as ice slashed at her cheeks. He laughed, pulled out his prick, and tore at her clothes, in a vile dash for the finish line.

With a sudden burst of fury, she tried pounding on his back. His hand swatted her arms away, bouncing them against the slick concrete and back into the snow.

There, she thought. She had no more go. Nothing left to fight with. Let him do what he will with her. She released her fingers from tight fists, spreading them out into the soft snow. And then she felt it, dancing along her fingernails. She stretched her hand and clasped the thick, jagged icicle, still buried like an unbroken sword deep in its snowy sheath.

"If you weren't Emil's favorite, I might just ask you to be my girl," he grunted. She responded with a sweet smile and brought the icicle up in an arc and then down into his neck with every ounce of her strength. Most of it shattered, but a dagger-sized splinter punctured his skin. He howled with pain, grabbing the back of his neck in bewilderment. She still held a piece of the icicle and used it to hit him in the jaw. He rolled off her as he pawed at his face. More voices now, coming from somewhere in the house, and a light flared up in the kitchen. A window on the upper story opened, and she heard Edna's scream.

Higgins wiped the blood from his neck and tried to push himself up. She was faster, and cut a dash through the heavy snow towards the shed. Somehow her legs lifted. She fell down but struggled back to her feet. Her front half, face and tangled hair included, was white with pressed snow, but she fought forward, not daring to slow for fear of losing her momentum. She'd lost her shoes in the scuffle with Higgins, and could barely feel her feet as she clambered onto an ash barrel and forced herself to the shed's roof. Knifing through the snow, her fingernails scraped on the tin as she scrambled up the incline, slipping and scratching until she reached the fence. She willed herself to stand up and touched the top with both hands. There it was, the Church of the Redeemer. An orange glow still shone from its windows, and she ached for the safety of its sanctuary.

"Good lord, aren't you a sad sight." The voice was soft, and sweet with sarcasm. The hair on her arms stood straight, and her throat went dry. Her grip on the fence suddenly weakened, but she managed to turn and locked her eyes on his. There was Emil Dander, standing over Higgins. Beside him hovered Pock, as rat-like as usual, holding a rifle in his dirty hands. "Come on down from there, love, and get back into the house. You must be chilled to death standing in this wind. I'll have Pock wake the cook and get some hot water on the stove." Dander lit his handsome grin and stretched out his gloved hand to beckon her towards him. Pock, chuckling, lifted the rifle and pointed it at her.

Her gut told her to scramble to the top and ignore him. Leap to the alley behind and scream until her throat was raw and her lungs gave out. Risk taking a bullet, or breaking an arm or a leg, just to never have to kiss him again with his dry, rough lips. But the rifle's barrel glinted from the kitchen's light and Pock's expression told her he probably wouldn't miss. Perhaps reason might work with him? It hadn't ever before, but she had an advantage, she hoped. Shooting her atop a fence was something he must want to avoid for fear of witnesses. Even in the depths of a slum, there might be witnesses. She decided, in desperation, to try and make her case.

"I-I-I'll never set foot in that house again, Emil!" Her voice sounded weak and unsteady, and she heard Pock snigger. "I can't go through another night there."

"Now why would you ever say something so hurtful, my dear? You really cut me to the quick. Break the heart of the man who has treated you so well."

"That's a bald-faced lie, Emil. I'm not going to let you make another nickel off of my misery!"

"Misery? You have warm food, a soft bed and protection from those who might harm you. Come now, and be rational. Let's go back inside and talk by the fire."

She could barely contain her fury at his condescension. With a deep breath she summoned her strength. "I'm through with this life, Emil. I've had enough. Let me return to my family, and I promise I will never mention this to them. You have my word."

"Your word," he scoffed, "is not to be trusted. Climb down from there and get back into the goddamn house. Starting the New Year with foolery such as this makes my blood boil."

"No! Emil, no!" She felt like a rat caught with a lantern, about to be strung up by her tail. Dander would punish her with crushing savagery if she returned to him, and she had no intention of returning. She would jump now, indifferent to the fall, rather than into his arms. "I'm not coming with you, Emil. Shoot me if you feel you have to, but know that my grandfather will come for you if you do. He'll find you and make sure you pay for this."

Silence. She could sense that he was thinking now, contemplating the best course of action. She took advantage of his withdrawn stare to look up towards the sky and watch the soft flakes fall like a thousand white stars. The wind suddenly picked up, stinging against her bare skin. She could taste the snow as it landed on her lips. Then, a movement in one of the house's windows stirred her to attention. She recognized

Trilly immediately, but also the dull stare in the girl's eyes, utterly vacant despite the scene unfolding in front of her. *My God. This life has left her completely soulless. Get out of Minneapolis and go home to your family and never, ever look back.* She aimed a reassuring smile at Trilly, trying to break her trance. But seeing no emotion there, she turned her eyes again to Emil Dander, who looked grimly back. Sweet words would come from his lips no more, she now knew. Her threat had sealed her death, and she could see it from the ominous cast of his face. She watched him motion to Pock, who, squinting along the rifle's sight, cocked back the hammer and aligned the barrel with her head.

"What a sad end, I think," Dander said. "She was never much to gaze upon, but there were always plenty of men willing to pay handsomely for her." Pock nodded agreement and sneered. A glint of remorse flickered in Emil's eyes, but died as quickly as it came. Pock was a deadeye with a rifle, and it would be easy to explain away the gunshot on New Year's Eve. As long as she fell within the confines of the yard, no one would be the wiser.

She knew there was nowhere to go for her except over the fence, to take her chances on the fall. If she was lucky and her legs didn't break, she'd run to the church's front door and beg for help. Someone was there, after all, ringing the bell. If she was going to go, it had to be now, before Pock pulled the trigger and it was over. She whipped around like a whirlwind, grasped the fence once more and pulled herself up. Throwing her leg over, white and exposed in the pale night, she heard the gun discharge. It sounded crisp and sharp in the biting cold. *Perhaps it might miss me,* she thought with a speck of hope, but then she felt a numb sensation, surprisingly warm, splayed through her body, making her shiver with ecstasy. She ignored the odd feeling and willed herself over the fence. For a brief, precious moment she paused to look up at the church's full figure, wrenchingly beautiful in the stone-gray light, a picture postcard of serenity if she'd ever seen one. Then, she felt her body begin to fall, and the night went to black completely.

CHAPTER 2

*I*F EVER A PLACE COULD BE BOTH spectacular and vile, it was Minneapolis. It was a city just past puberty, still gangly and awkward, but brimming with exuberance over the fortunes a new century might bring. It was a place that saw brick skyscrapers rising at a rapid-fire pace, sometimes ten stories high and outfitted with the latest glass elevators, shimmering skylights, and towers that speared into the sky. Giant department stores ate up city blocks, and Eastern banks competed to build the most elaborate Gothic representations of their importance and power. Wedged precariously between these grandiose beauties were dingy shanties and ragged clapboard lush-cribs, surrounded by dirt yards and worn wooden sidewalks. Drunks and vagrants stumbled through their alleys and across their stoops. The gleaming corporate facades were meant to declare to America that Minneapolis was on the rise. This was certainly true if one believed these buildings equaled civic achievement. Even Saint Paul, which once rivaled Minneapolis in population and wealth, now kowtowed to what was becoming obvious. Minneapolis was on the verge of declaring victory in their age-old cosmopolitan battle. Businessmen, however, leaving the enormous lobby of one of the great wonders west of Chicago, Nicollet Avenue's legendary West Hotel, stepped into muddy, half-paved streets and the horrid stench of spilled garbage. Wheeler-dealers of choice Minneapolis properties propelled themselves into a league of millionaires, but jostled for walking space with gangs of pimple-faced ruffians and world-weary immigrants. This was Minneapolis, half boy and half man, full of innocent eye-opening wonders, but beating under the surface with the heart of an untamed animal.

Detective Harmon Queen, proud member of the Minneapolis Police Department, believed with his very soul in this wild contradiction of high and low. He listened respectfully to the old-timers who pushed down watery beers and yearned for the good old days, telling wistful stories of their first arrivals. How fifty years prior it had been a ramshackle little town filled with rough roads, small, unpainted houses and limestone rubble littering the landscape. Steamboats ambled up the Mississippi River, and well-heeled passengers delicately stepped into the mud alongside frontiersmen and farmers, to try their hands at making a fortune in a town in its infancy. Eventually the population grew, streets and avenues were planned, and a man named Pillsbury brutally harnessed a once magnificent waterfall's power, creating a flour-milling empire that finally put the city on the map. While he hadn't lived that story, Queen felt as though this seedy gem of a city's pulse pumped through him. He was the same as his beloved Minneapolis. A crack of a smile flashed under his thick mustache as he breathed in the sweet aroma of a filthy town. But he quickly looked around, to be sure no one saw this display of undiluted love that they'd certainly never understand.

Confident he was clear of staring eyes, Queen loosened his tie a little. The quiet New Year's Day morning was relaxing him, despite the chill. He really had no need for caution, because any of the crooks he might meet seemed to automatically sense his approach. Perhaps they would shoot a furtive glance his way or look uncomfortably at their shoes as he passed. On a typical day on Hennepin Avenue, the part of thought, there would be some hard feelings out there, adding to the old man's already formidable list of enemies.

The question that most concerned Queen, however, was about the man who would control the entire city police force. Col. Fred Ames would soon be appointed as police superintendent. He was a dour, uninteresting man, opposite in every way from his delightful older brother, Doc. In every precinct house in Minneapolis, cops were discussing the matter, laying bets on what the mayor's sibling would do once he took charge. They argued over whose heads would roll into the ranks of the unemployed, and who would survive only to freeze their bones on another winter patrol.

And despite Doc's confidence in his brother's abilities, the man had a dubious past. Particularly scandalous were some of the rumors that had come from the Philippines, where Colonel Ames had served with the 13th Minnesota Regiment only a couple of years before. His name had splashed across the front pages with words like "coward" and "incompetent" attached to his conduct. Queen didn't know Colonel Ames nearly as well as his brother, or the minute details of the scurrilous stories, but he suspected the colonel had his own agenda and intended to see it through.

Queen also knew where he stood with Doc Ames. They'd been friends for years, including past Republican terms when Queen was forced from the city payrolls and back to work as a private detective. Col. Fred Ames was another matter entirely. Queen and the colonel were civil to each other but had never shared a drink or a genial conversation. It was always business. Both brothers knew Queen's value in getting Doc elected, but Queen wasn't so sure Colonel Ames would do him any favors once the new administration took hold.

His head still hurt a little from the night's festivities, and he cursed under his breath that the streetcars were running slow. Still a good couple of miles away from his house, he picked up his pace, even as he passed a collection of colorless hovels that sat on a block notoriously known as Hell's Half Acre. He'd been here before on many occasions, and even walked a beat through its crooked paths once or twice. It had a reputation from far back as a slum and an eyesore; a place even veteran policemen shied away from if given a choice.

"Help, someone get the police! I need help!"

Queen whirled around. His hand instinctively went to the handle of his pistol, tucked in a holster under his jacket. The voice was urgent, but wasn't coming from the block's worst section. He continued down Third Avenue and turned left on Eighth Street, towards the Church of the Redeemer. Eyes squinting, he marched forward, searching for the source. Despite his age of forty, he was in fair condition. Still, as he increased his speed to a fast jog, he felt a little sting in his lungs. He heard the shout again coming from an alley, and within a few steps he found Officer Merriam. The blue-coated patrolman was crouched in a small open lot, white with an inch of fresh snow. The snow's beauty veiled the grime of rough, slanted shacks and piles of decaying wood. It made the drab landscape almost romantic, like a woodcut from Harper's magazine. Then he saw the young woman under Merriam's scrutiny, and the pool of blood around her head. Brown, bent sunflower stalks lay crumpled beneath her thin body.

"Is she alive?" Queen huffed as he drew close. Merriam looked up. His bell shaped hat lay in the snow by his knee, and his forehead glistened with sweat.

"No, sir. I can't find a pulse, and she's ice cold." His eyes were wet. He roughly wiped them with his sleeve, avoiding Queen's stare.

"Pretty girl," Queen said. "Even with a broken nose."

Merriam's face was flushed. "What should I do, Mr. Queen? I mean Lieutenant...er...Detective?"

"I'm all of the above. Go get the coroner," Queen replied. "And by the way, what are you doing calling out for police help, anyway? You *are* the goddamn police. She wasn't going anywhere, for Christ's sakes."

"Yes, sir. She just looks so lonely lying there. I just thought—"

"I already told you, Merriam. Go."

The patrolman nodded and dashed off.

Queen bent down to examine her. He was struck again by how lovely she was, despite the deep bruises on her face and legs. Not even a pair of shoes to cover her chalky, pale feet. Barebones thin, and scantily dressed for this weather, except for a coarse, frayed boy's jacket, he noted. He gently held up her head, unbuttoned the jacket's top three buttons and pulled back the neck of her gown. He found the source of the blood, a bullet hole, just above her left breast. It's a shame that a girl could be done in this way, he thought.

He stood up and examined the fence and her position. The front of her gown was caked white, and by the looks of the deep snowy imprint next to her body, she had fallen on her front side prior to being shot. He glanced around, searching for tracks. The snow was untouched around where she lay, except for his and Merriam's powdery prints.

A sound startled him. He looked up, and saw a little boy behind an ash can a few feet away, no more than seven years old. He held a chunk of ice like a weapon in his mittened hand. "Is she dead?" he blurted.

"What the deuce? Why are you out here by yourself?"

The boy took a step forward, straining around Queen to look at the girl.

"Do you know anything about this?" Queen asked.

He shook his dirty face and dabbed at the yellow slime that hung from his nostril.

"Well, stay out of my way. Your mother should be ashamed of herself, letting you out alone like this."

"She's sleeping. I didn't have nothin' to do. Jus' wanted to play."

"Play somewhere else. Something bad happened here. You shouldn't see."

"Too late. I already did."

"Did you see what happened to her?"

"Naw, not that. Just seen the body. I also seen a white cloud. Middle of the night, I guess."

"A white cloud in the middle of the night, you guess, huh? Were there fairies dancing on it too?"

"I seen it, I swear. Right over there." He pointed to the end of the fence, close to church property. "Over a man."

"You saw a man?"

"From my window. I sleep right there." Queen looked up at the rat-trap house next to them.

"What time?"

"After midnight. I just heard somebody shoot and I looked outside."

"What did he look like? Tall, short, fat?"

"Don' know."

"And you saw her laying on the ground and didn't tell your ma?"

"Ma drunk too much booze last night. No point in trying."

"You're an irresponsible little snipe, you know that?"

"To hell with you, Mister."

Queen scowled at the kid until he retreated back to the ash can. He considered shooing him back home, but wasn't in the mood to tilt with a tot.

He bent down again and took one of the dead girl's delicate hands in his. Dark raw rings circled her wrists, and her fingernails were uneven and chipped. Gently, he turned the hands over and pulled a small splinter from under a nail. He looked up. The fence was tall and unpainted. His eyes scanned for loose boards, thinking perhaps she had found an exit through the fence, but it seemed well built. Then he glanced to the top. There, farther up than he could reach, was a piece of fabric, fluttering in the breeze. He looked at her gown again, and found the tear. What had she been doing up there? Did she get the splinter from the fence? He walked its length until he found a crack and peered through.

"This is your idea of crack detective work? Peeping through knotholes?"

Queen turned and saw fellow cop Chris Norbeck walk up next to him. His old partner had his hands thrust deep in his coat pockets and a cigar in his mouth. He was grinning madly.

"Damn, if my hands don't feel like they're gonna fall off. Forgot my gloves at home this morning." Norbeck looked down at the girl and pushed her leg a little with his shoe. "That skeleton-bone wag-tail looks dead."

"Now why would you call her that?"

"You'd rather I call her a whore?"

"I'd rather you shut your pan and let her be." He stared hard at Norbeck, challenging him to say more. Norbeck knew better and lowered his head a little in deference. Queen didn't like Norbeck much for a number of reasons, besides the obvious one, which was that he was an outright ass. First, Norbeck grinned like a leering baboon at the most inappropriate of times. Second, he had a queer habit of winking knowingly, at everything and everyone. The third was the most difficult to ignore. Weeks ago, a doctor had told Norbeck he was suffering from acne rosacea. The red, veiny rash had spread across his face and deformed his nose into a bulbous mass. It looked to Queen like the bottom of a sack of potatoes too long in the cellar. Norbeck was overwrought with worry about it, and had even knocked around a handful of men who had dared to mention it in conversation. Every day Norbeck slathered a smelly ointment obsessively over the affected parts, prescribed to alleviate the maddening itch. The doctor had claimed that drinking made it worse, but Queen wasn't sure if Norbeck was so wracked with fear to cut that important part of his life out cold.

Queen pointed at the top of the fence. "She must have climbed up something on the other side, to escape from what we both know this house is known for."

"And she almost made it." Norbeck flashed his insufferable grin.

"Almost."

"So do we go in and arrest him?

"Arrest him? Who?"

Norbeck pulled out a revolver from a holster under his coat and pointed at the house. "Emil Dander. Who else coulda' done it?"

"Put that away. I thought your goddamn hands were cold."

"Danger has warmed them."

"Well, tell danger to unwarm them and shuck that gun."

"Come on, Harm. I ain't Catholic, but I'm pretty damn sure Dander ain't no saint. He did it, and we both know it."

"So he just shoots his own girl? She's worth more alive than dead."

"Maybe he was drunk."

"Maybe you are."

"Maybe I am," Norbeck laughed.

"Let's see if Dander is home. Perhaps we'll catch him at breakfast."

"He leaves a girl dead by his back fence and acts like nothing happened? I'll bet you a dollar he's flown the coop."

"Well, let's go see."

"He's got a few bad fellows working for him. Maybe we should send for more officers."

"I thought you just said you didn't think he was there."

"I don't, but we should still watch our step."

Queen looked disapprovingly at Norbeck. "Stay pat if you want, and watch the girl. It's a good place for you. I'll go alone."

Norbeck rocked on his heels and scratched at his face. "I ain't afraid. But somebody should wait until the coroner comes."

"Kid, where are you?" Queen shouted. The boy crawled out of a broken box, and walked over to the men.

"I thought you told me to go 'way," he said with defiant, puckered lips.

"Yeah, but you obviously didn't. Here's a nickel. Make sure no one goes near her until more police arrive. Can you do that?"

"Hell if I can't. But my ma says you're nothin' but a stupid bull and I shouldn't even be talkin' to you."

"Watch that language," Norbeck snapped, "or I'll slap that filth right out of your mouth. Bulls are what riff-raff say. We're detectives."

Norbeck trailed behind Queen and they went back down the alley to Eighth Street, turning back onto Third Avenue to the face of the house. It was certainly a misfit on this block. Two storied and brick, it stood out like a whore's pimple against the moldering shanties that surrounded it. The front fence was far shorter, and made from iron. A decorative gate barred the entrance to the front yard.

"Usually there's someone on the other side to let people in," Norbeck said. "A kid named Ollie last time I was here. Don't look so cozy, does it?" He chuckled to himself and withdrew a hand from his pocket to shake the gate. "Locked up tight. Anyone there?" he shouted. No one answered. The window curtains were drawn, and the house appeared dark and dead.

"Look at the footprints leading out of here," Queen said, pointing to the ground. "Big boots and women's shoes. I'd say three men and two women." He followed the prints to the street, where they disappeared in a wagon's track. He walked back to the gate and kicked it hard, but it made no movement. "I guess we'll just have to go over, then."

Norbeck groaned. Queen was the older of the two, but capably climbed to the top, put his leg over, and jumped. He landed on the other side standing up. It hurt a little in his knees.

"Can you unlock it from that side?" Norbeck asked with a wink. Queen ignored him and trotted up the path to the front porch. He climbed the stairs and knocked on the door. "This is Detective Harmon Queen of the Minneapolis Police," he announced through the thick wood, knowing already that no one would answer. He tried the knob, but the door was locked tight. Norbeck came hobbling up behind him. "Stand back," Queen said. His kicking leg was sore, so he used his shoulder instead, and heaved it hard against the door. It opened with a crack of breaking wood.

"Jesus, Queen. We can get a patrolman to do this kind of work. We should be saving our strength for collars," Norbeck groaned.

"Dander isn't here, and the sooner I know for certain, the quicker I can go home and sleep," Queen replied. They went through the door and into a small hallway. It was decorated with floral wallpaper and dark wainscoting, and a narrow staircase with a polished mahogany banister ran to the second floor. The stink of cheap perfume hung in the air. "You mouse around outside and in the basement. I'll look upstairs." Norbeck pursed his lips slightly and then nodded.

Queen climbed the staircase, listening for sounds from above. Nothing. He slipped by the door at the top and into the hallway. The rooms were open as he went by, and he was disgusted at their filthiness. Grimy paper peeled from the walls and cobwebs clung in ceiling corners. The shabby furniture looked barely usable. Dull shadows from the morning light crawled over the rough floors, and made the lack of any color or life strikingly bleak.

Emil Dander, for all his gentlemanly airs, ran a low-grade operation. Queen had been in this house before on occasion, not to sample the wares but instead to collect fees as part of official city business. The two men weren't friends, and Dander had never done anything to personally rile him, but Queen found the house's entire business offensive. Perhaps it was because he had grown up in a family of sisters and couldn't fathom an existence like this for the women in his life. Gambling, drinking and opium dens did not offend his own morality, but something about a brothel made him seethe if he considered it for too long. Dander was nothing more than a slaver, a far cry from the more elegant madams in the city's tenderloin districts. I'll see he never owns a business like this in Minneapolis again, he thought. I should have paid more attention to this before.

He saw more blood at the entrance to the last room and stepped in. The bed was in shambles, caved in on itself. There were bloody ropes tied to the posts, ropes that had likely made those deep gashes in the dead girl's wrists. This was a miserable existence for a young girl. Something must have led her to believe she had a decent chance to escape. That, or she just couldn't take it anymore and was desperate enough to risk her life. Everything culminated in a confrontation here. Had she finally had enough from a pushy customer who made her snap? Or had Dander or one of his hired thugs discovered her trying to escape? He got down on one knee to examine the blood on the floor more closely, wincing as he heard a crack in his right knee joint. There in the splatter was an enormous handprint, made by a much bigger hand than the dainty one he had examined outside. He felt a twinge of satisfaction in the guess that whoever confronted her here had fallen to the floor in a tussle, and he hoped she had extracted a little revenge for her suffering. Queen stood up and walked to the window, looking out. His eyes flicked from the Church of the Redeemer's steeple to the fence the young woman had fallen from. Beneath it was a shed, and he could see from the disturbed snow where she had scrambled across the roof. He looked down, closer to the house, and spied Norbeck carefully examining the ground for clues. He pushed open the window and called down.

"Shake up anything?"

Norbeck shielded his eyes from the snow's glare and looked up. "There was a scuffle down here," he replied. "At least two people were rolling around on the ground. I can see where she ran to the fence, and right there," he pointed to an indentation in the snow, "she fell. Probably scared witless over whoever she was running from. And here, too, more footprints. Two pairs of men's boots, same shape as the ones we saw out front."

"Do you see anything strange on the ground? Dropped or out of place?"

Norbeck fished out a wet pair of women's shoes from deep inside a snow bank. "These must be hers," he replied, holding them up high.

"Fine. What did you see on your way through the house?"

"The kitchen opens to the back door. Someone tried to make a barricade with a barrel of flour. Most of the cupboard doors were open and the floor was a mess."

Had someone been packing food for a hasty departure, or had they been looking for something? That thought reminded him to make a thorough search of her room. He closed the window and walked back to the bureau. He opened the drawers, but they were empty. He eyed the broken bed and lifted its splintered frame as best he could, looking under it and the mattress and even peeling back the soiled sheets. What little she had, she must have taken with her. Literally the clothes on her back. Her anguish must have been excruciating, and the thought of her being forced to endure the whims of monsters made his stomach churn.

Queen exited and moved down the hall, glancing into the adjacent room. The window was slightly ajar and a draft chilled the air, so cold he could see his breath. He walked over to shut it and then paused, eyes widening slightly in realization. Dander would lie of course, as would his henchmen, about having anything to do with the murder. The girl in this room, though, could easily have been witness to what he suspected might have happened. When he finds her, he thought, things will clarify.

He went back down the staircase and stood at its foot.

"Norbeck! Did you check the basement?"

There was no response, so Queen stepped into the room to his left to investigate a little more. It was dark and the curtains were drawn, and he pulled them back to let in a little light. This was the parlor, a small waiting area with simple furniture and a worn rug. On a typical business night the women would descend from their rooms above to greet and mingle with paying customers. Unless they were bound to beds like dogs, that is.

Back into the hallway he went, and then to a larger room on the right. In a respectable home this might have been a dining room, but Dander had transformed it into something one small step up from a saloon. A bar lined the wall, and a battered piano sat in the corner. Paintings of nudes, distastefully done, hung from the walls. Stepping over sheet music scattered on the floor, Queen examined his surroundings. All signs pointed to a hasty departure, and Queen had his suspicions about where that might be. Dander had saloon-owning friends who would hide him, but if Dander were smart and really had something to do with the girl's murder, his best option would be a fast train out of town. Traveling with a retinue of toughs and painted-cats would slow him down, but if anyone was arrogant enough to try it, it was Dander.

"Look what I found in the basement," Norbeck said. Under his arm in a tight grip was a skinny, scared-looking boy. Norbeck shoved him forward, and the boy caught his balance, sized up Queen, and eyed the door in one wary, lightning glance. Queen was impressed with the kid's instincts, but stepped between him and the exit.

"What's your name, son?"

"He said his name is Eddie, but it's not. This is the Ollie kid that manned the gate and ran errands for Dander's bunch," Norbeck said.

"Well? True?"

Ollie nodded.

"My name is Queen, and this is Norbeck. We work for the police. Have you heard of us?"

The boy just looked at them. He was breathing heavily and his eyes darted between the two detectives from under a tuft of tousled hair.

"So what were you doing in the basement?"

Silent, his eyes finally focused on Queen.

"Well, son," Queen said calmly. "Here you are, in the devil's own den. Problem is, the devil seems to have taken a holiday, and left you behind to rot. Now why would he leave you behind?"

Norbeck shook him a little, trying to rattle out a response. None came.

"You don't trust us, isn't that right? Well, that means you're a smart young man. You've seen us here before, taking money from your boss. You think that makes your boss and us good pals? Makes us boon companions?"

That made Norbeck chuckle. Queen gave the boy his best honest-cop smile, and continued.

"We need to know where he went. He's in trouble, and your best recourse is the two of us at this moment. Forget anything you ever saw before. One of the girls that worked here is dead, and we're trying—"

"What did you say? Who is dead? Which girl?" Ollie's face went pale. "Where? What's her name?"

"Her body's outside. I'll take you to her in a moment." Tears streamed down the boy's face. He sniffled and wiped them away. "What were you doing in the basement?" Queen asked.

"I freed her!" Ollie cried. "Oh, hell, this is my fault, ain't it? She was good to me, and she asked me for help. I told her not to go, but she went anyway." His face contorted at the memory. "These men that came here did awful things to her. To her and the other girls. I tried to help 'em when I could."

"I'm sure that's true," Queen replied. "So what happened after you let her go?"

"I was supposed to give her a whistle, a code, you know? Higgins caught me as I was practicing it. He figured it out fast."

"You wouldn't think that by looking at the fat asshole," said Norbeck.

"He threw me down the steps. It hurt, but I'm fine. 'Relax,' he told me. 'I'll be down in a little bit to pull your arms from their sockets.' It was pitch black down there, but I got lucky and found an axe. I was waitin' for him when I heard the gunshot."

"Just one?"

Ollie nodded. "Then there was shouting in the house. Lots of walking around. I figured they'd gut me or somethin', but either they forgot, or didn't care." He paused, grief filling his face again. "Take me to her."

"Should I bind him up?" asked Norbeck.

"Are you going to run?" Queen asked the boy.

He shook his head. "I got nowhere to go. I wanna see him pay for this. If you catch him and string him up, all I want is to stand in front as he drops and swings."

All three trudged back to where the girl lay. The coroner's wagon was already there, a couple of the coroner's assistants standing by to retrieve her body. The boy Queen had left to guard her had disappeared. Queen groaned when he saw reporters from the *Journal* and the *Tribune* jotting notes in their books. Ollie burst into tears when he saw her. The reporters looked up; their scribbling intensified.

"Can you move them back a little?" Queen asked Norbeck. "Gently. Remember what happened after the Leonard Day murder? The *Journal* reporter claimed you shoved him into a dirty puddle."

"Yeah, I remember," Norbeck mumbled. He straightened his tie, rolled his eyes, and slunk towards the newspaper men, who licked their pencils in anticipation of his arrival.

Queen pulled Ollie by the sleeve and spoke in a hushed, gruff tone.

"So, what's her name?"

"Maisy. Her name is Maisy."

"Maisy what?"

"Just Maisy. Don't know her last name."

Queen squinted. "I thought you were friends. She didn't confide in you?"

"I never asked her, and she never told. She don't know mine, neither. All the girls just go by first names here."

"Did Emil Dander want her dead?"

Ollie stared at him, shocked. "Well of course. She's dead, ain't she?"

"That's true. I want to know why, though. She was making money for him. I can't believe they thought she'd outrun them, dressed like this, in this weather."

"Yeah, that's true. I never thought of that. But who else might have done it?"

"Well, tell me about the men who paid to visit her. You said they did horrible things. Can you think of anyone in particular she was afraid of?"

"Some of them who come here are pretty mean, but Mr. Dander never let them clout the girls. Other things, yes, but not anything to leave a mark that would hurt their looks."

"Did she have anyone special that she talked about? A regular customer?"

Ollie scrunched his brow. "Sure. She saw lots of men. Important ones, too. A judge I recognized from the courthouse –"

Queen put up his hand to stop what was about to come. "I don't need a list of any law-bending muckity-mucks to complicate my life. Just tell me if there was anyone who seemed overly affectionate, or showed unusual behavior towards her. Said queer things and such."

"Well." The boy took a moment to collect his thoughts. "I can think of one. He seemed awful bughouse to me, whenever he came around. All jittery and shaky and nervous when he talked."

"What did he look like? What was his name?"

"Tall, and wears glasses. Never told me his name, but she called him Ace. She said he was waiting for a big inheritance. I think it was a crock of shit. He was just feeding her a story to make himself look important."

"Where can I find you if I need to talk to you again?"

"I've got friends who sell papers at the train station. They all know me there."

Queen pulled out a couple of dimes and gave them to the boy. "Keep on the lookout for any sign of Dander or his party. Come find me at City Hall if you hear anything. I work there."

"Yeah, I know," said Ollie. He looked back at the girl, who was being lifted up by the coroner workers. One of them grunted as her leg slipped out of his grasp, hitting the ground. "I'm glad I gave her my jacket. She looks a little warmer with it on, even though she's dead," Ollie said.

"That's yours? Nice of you to give it to her. When did you do that?"

"Just before she ran out. You can let her keep it, if you don't mind." He sniffed up a trickle of snot running over his upper lip. "You'll find out her whole name, and tell her parents, right?"

"Did she mention parents?"

"She said she was from North Dakota. Her dad or granddad is a sheriff there, she said."

Queen raised his eyebrow. "Really? Did she mention a town?"

"Something funny sounding. It started with an m. Like 'minuet,' maybe."

"Minot?"

"Yeah, that's it." He paused to think. "That should make it easier for you, shouldn't it?"

"It should." He took out his notebook and a pencil and wrote it down. When he looked back up Ollie was already gone, darting down the alley. The boy pivoted and disappeared between two particularly vile looking shacks.

"Son of a bitch," someone said in an exasperated voice.

It was one of the workers who'd carried the girl to the wagon. They were struggling with her gown, which had snagged on the door. The bigger of the two had dropped her head and torso in the snow. A hoot came from the *Tribune* reporter, standing back a distance under Norbeck's watchful eye.

"What do you think you're doing?" Queen roared, incensed. The attendant saw him coming and stepped back, mouth agape to see the notorious Detective Queen charging him like a starving terrier after a rat.

"Sir, sir, I'm sorry, sir." He held up his hand. "I stuck my finger on something sharp." Queen could see it was bleeding, but it didn't mute his anger.

"Where is Keeper Walsh? He should be supervising this."

"Away with his wife's family for New Year's holiday."

"And when will he return?"

"Later today, sir, is what we were told."

"Will there be a surgeon to examine the body? Will the coroner be there?"

"I'm not sure, sir," the worker said, backing up farther as Queen stood over the girl. The detective picked her up gingerly from the snow and placed her into the wagon.

Queen tucked her gown around her legs to cover the bruises. Then he called Norbeck over. "When you're done with those two reporters, follow the body to the morgue. I want to know what kind of bullet they shake up."

"Jesus, Queen. You order me around like you're my boss. We're both lieutenants, for god's sake." His awful smile scrunched up the red bumps on his face.

"I've got the inside track on who's staying and who's going, and let's just say that you're not a goddamn shoo-in, Chris."

"What does that mean? Who told you that?"

Queen sighed. "Never mind. Just do what I say. Tell those two not to write anything about this yet."

"That's like telling a thirsty Irishman swimming in whiskey not to open his mouth."

"Tell 'em it's a personal request straight from the mayor-elect."

"So what's this about me not keeping my job?"

"I know you hustled hard on his campaign, but you know just as well as I do that everything is up in the air right now."

"But who told you?"

"Just things floating around. Nobody has officially told me anything. Forget it, Chris. It'll all be sorted out soon. Go do your job."

Norbeck trudged back to deliver his news to the reporters.

Queen gave one last look at the girl as the coroner's assistant shut the wagon door. I'm going to try my damnedest to find the person who did this, he thought. The facts would seem to put Dander at the top of the suspect list. He didn't see Dander as the type to actually commit a murder, but giving the order was another story, and he had plenty of hangers-on who could have pulled the trigger. Maisy had obviously been attempting to escape, and from his examination of her living conditions he didn't blame her. From Ollie's account, Higgins had probably been after her, and might have followed her to the back yard. Queen could see it all playing out in his mind. She had climbed to the very top of the fence, she was shot, and she fell, probably dying with the final, terrible thought that she had failed and Dander had won. He shook his head.

Dander could have her killed in a moment of rage, but he was a meticulous and calculating man, and he valued his business and the money he was making. Queen couldn't believe he'd be so stupid, unless his anger was so consuming that he went insane for a brief, terrible moment.

Or, could there have been someone else entirely, a shooter who had waited in this snow-covered filth, ready to blast to heaven a girl running for her life and frightened out of her wits? Perhaps, but it would depend on whether Maisy was facing the house or her freedom when she was hit. And if she had been killed from the alley, then what was the motive? A spurned lover? The only motive he could think of was jealousy. Someone head over heels for her, who couldn't bear sharing her with the rest of the city. But even that would mean an incredible coincidence. What would be the chances of a lover just happening to be strolling along the alley on a moonlit walk in Hell's Half Acre when his beloved decides to escape? She'd seen plenty of men, he was sure, but Ollie seemed pretty confident that one particular client deserved a closer look. However, finding a man nicknamed Ace would be tough going. If he was as high-strung and panicky as Ollie claimed, using his real name at a house of ill-repute, even to the woman he supposedly loved, wouldn't have been a smart decision. He would start by assuming Ace was intelligent, and wait to be convinced otherwise.

The wagon lurched forward and headed down the alley. Queen was tired out, and suddenly felt the strain of the last couple of days wallop his body. There was too much to do, however, for the sleep he knew he needed. His thoughts turned towards his meeting with Doc at the end of the week, and suddenly he felt a pang of nervousness. Months of pandering and bribing and back-slapping in union halls, warehouses and back rooms of saloons for the chance at promotion, and it might all come down to solving this murder. He had stuck by Doc Ames for as long as he had been employed with the police department, and had defended him, often with his fists. And, if the new Mayor was going to do what Queen suspected he would with the police department, he'd need someone trustworthy to handle the changeover. He buttoned up his coat at the sudden wind, and thought about the possibilities. There was green to be made, and he savored the idea.

And then he noticed it, sticking out of the trampled snow. It was shiny, and wrapped in a bit of the silk fabric from the girl's gown. It was what had snagged in the door and pricked the morgue worker's finger. He bent down to pick it up.

Slowly, he held the stickpin up to the light, grimaced with understanding, and put it in his pocket.

Oh hell, he thought.

CHAPTER 3

"*W*HAT THE DEUCE?" QUEEN MUTTERED AS he stepped into the anteroom of Doc Ames's medical office. The room was in complete chaos. Men crowded together, leaning against walls, sitting on chairs and tables, smoking cigarettes and conversing loudly. A few passed flasks with quick, sly movements. He'd arrived a little early for his appointment, wanting to get a good long glimpse at the general character of the job hopefuls. After a few minutes he felt his suspicions were proving true. There were just as many crooks and thugs waiting for their turn with the old man as there were regular-looking men. Probably more so by the looks of it. He stared, stunned, when he recognized a couple of fellows he had collared only weeks before idling in a doorway. One of them turned and locked eyes with him, and then quickly turned away, lowering his voice and pulling his hat down over his face. Another man he recognized as a burglar, a well-known thorn in the side of Minneapolis detectives for years, actually walked up to him, chuckling nervously, and extended a hand. Queen was so surprised he just about took it. Instead, he scowled, scaring the fellow white. There were cops already on the force waiting there too, and Queen turned his attention to the ones he knew best, giving them brief words of encouragement and even a forced, friendly smile for a few. He'd been to some of the precinct stations over the week and knew how petrified many of the officers had been after receiving their invitations to meet with Doc. From police captains on down to the beat walking patrolmen, there was widespread confusion. Some had gotten requests to meet with the Mayor-elect, while others had heard nary a word. No one knew what these invitations meant, and everyone had their own ideas about what the new administration would bring.

Queen went to stand by himself. He pulled his own flask from a coat pocket and drew a nice long sip of whiskey, trying to banish his anxious thoughts and let the past week's worries ebb away. It had been busy for him, and while he had managed to file his reports on the girl's murder, his follow-up on Emil Dander had led to exactly nothing. He had searched the gang's regular haunts, but was met with shrugs or empty expressions. Saloonkeepers knew Queen could make a living hell for them, so for the most part he believed their exclamations of ignorance. Still, even those he didn't trust a mite managed looks of confusion as he strode behind their bars, showed his badge, and shook them around a little.

He'd also sent a telegram up to Minot, but had been disappointed after he received a curt response from the local sheriff, who claimed no children and wished him good luck. After this dead end, Queen had referenced a gazetteer for the possibility of other similar-sounding North Dakota names, but found none that he thought might have caused confusion for Ollie. He figured finding Dander and the girls traveling with him would reveal her identity faster than sending messages to every little town in North Dakota.

He put the flask back in his pocket, and felt the prick of the stickpin on his finger. He'd already examined it a good dozen times since he had found it. The stickpin was encrusted with rubies and a little rich for his tastes, although admittedly he knew nothing of fancy jewelry. He continued to finger the pin, obsessively running his thumb over the jewels. Queen had seen this piece before. The problem, though, was that the man who owned it was almost six years dead, hanged by the state of Minnesota.

Queen and Harry Hayward had crossed paths many times. They'd frequented the same billiard room at the West Hotel and even made some underhanded money together. Their relationship had been one of shared masculine amusements, but also of mutual accommodation. Hayward had had an uncanny ability to straddle the line between the classes. His parents were wealthy, and he included as his companions some of the finest sons of gentlemen in Minneapolis. Likewise, he had fancied himself a criminal genius, and aspired to create his own wealth through whatever means was required, since his parents had long before stopped funding his excessive lifestyle. Queen had found Hayward's balancing act between worlds beneficial for solving the city's crime, but also for lining his own pockets. From Hayward's perspective, Queen was there to help him out of a jam when he got into things over his head. Never had Queen imagined though, in all of his dealings with Hayward, that he would be capable of murdering a young woman.

Her name had been Kitty Ging, and her innocuous occupation as a seamstress masked a seamier story that shocked even the toughened detective. The newspapers had uncovered every gory and titillating detail, of how Hayward had seduced the homely girl and persuaded her to let him take out a life insurance policy against her. Blinded by love, she'd readily accepted, in part because he had promised to fund a sewing business for her, but also because he was charming and handsome. He'd also convinced her he was part of a shadowy underworld gang, and was about to let her in on its criminal plans. This promise is what he used to lure her into a carriage on a snowy December night, for a ride around Lake Calhoun and a supposed rendezvous with his mysterious cohorts.

Hayward had always been a scoundrel of the highest order, but his plan to have her shot by the driver—a dimwitted assistant named Claude Blixt—and left to die was as devilish as the darkest night. And what he'd done afterwards was damnably pompous, marching down to the mayor's office to offer his help in investigating the murder. The only person he knew in Minneapolis as conceited and smug as Hayward was Emil Dander. Queen didn't doubt that Dander would also murder someone if he were pushed to it. Both were dandies and dudes, and the one thing they had in common, which soured Queen's stomach, was that they preyed on young women with no remorse.

Queen clearly remembered the stickpin in Hayward's tie when he'd visited him a few nights before his execution. Hayward had been smug and indifferent to the end, insisting on wearing formal evening clothes for his date with the scaffold, which he'd even asked to have painted red. The ruby-encrusted stickpin, he laughed to Queen, would match perfectly.

So he knew where he'd seen it before, and was positive they were one and the same. Hayward had even told him the pin had been specially made for him in the weeks prior to his execution. He just couldn't figure out how it went from the necktie of a dead man into the seam of a dead prostitute's dress.

The gaslight above his head flickered and he looked up distractedly.

"Doc needs to fix that, I reckon."

It was Norbeck, who had slipped up beside him with his usual snake-like skill.

"None of us know anything yet, Chris. I'm guessing I'll get the news on the returning detectives soon."

"Don't worry about that," Norbeck said, grinning and picking at his ear. "I'm to stay on. I'm officially an Ames detective."

"How in the hell do you know that?"

"I found Dander, Harm. This afternoon. Slugged him once or twice and then dropped him in a cell. Him and that bastard Higgins. Took me and four men to do it, too. Higgins went off his chump when I hit his poor old boss."

"Where was he?"

"Holed up in the basement of the White Elephant Saloon. Right across the street from City Hall, if you can believe it. Dander's got one goddamned swelled head, I'll say. Get this. He had the nerve to tell me my grammar was used up. Ain't that a kick in the ass? That's when I knocked the spots off him."

"Were the girls with him?"

"No, not a one. I figured you'd want to squeeze their hiding place out of him yourself." Norbeck's face went cold sober. "Queen, you think he thinks I'm some kind of inferior to him? I'm an appointed police officer, for Christ's sake. He tries that highfalutin language around me and it puts me on my ear!"

"Ignore him. He's a fop. What about the bullet that killed the girl? Did you visit the coroner?"

Norbeck perked up, reached into his pocket, and held out his hand. Queen took the bullet, trying to ignore the sweat from Norbeck's palm, and examined it.

"It's a .45-70 cartridge. This isn't from any side arm."

"Nope," Norbeck replied. "It came out of a rifle. I seen Coroner Williams come out to look at the body himself. He was going to put it in as evidence for the inquest but I borrowed it. You know what kind of rifle it came from?"

"A Remington or a Sharp, most likely. You *borrowed* the bullet?

"I'll bring it back later today. No one'll be the wiser."

Queen cringed slightly. "Give it to me, Chris. I'll do it. Did you find any weapons on Dander?"

"Him and Higgins both had pistols on 'em, but nothing that would fire a bullet like this."

"But Pock is still out there."

"I've never seen that little freak carry a rifle, though."

"So that means he doesn't goddamn have one?"

"Why the hell are you so 'specially sore today?" Norbeck asked.

"So how do you know you're to be kept on?"

"Both Doc and his brother the colonel seen me, and the colonel told me himself. He congratulated me on catching Dander and told me I was the kind of detective the mayor needed on the force." Norbeck's blotched face glowed a greasy pink, and he lifted his chest proudly.

Queen burned inside when he heard this. It wasn't that Norbeck wasn't qualified, but he'd assumed all along that he was going to be named Chief of Detectives and this dampened his already questionable mood. It should be his job to pass news along to subordinates. That's what a chain of command is for, isn't it? He hesitated, forced a smile, and then shook Norbeck's hand.

"You're a good fly-bob, Chris. A decent detective. They made the right decision on you."

Norbeck's mouth went open, and then he grinned, but it wasn't so much a leer as an appreciative smile. "Nice of you to say so, Harm. I didn't expect it, but nice of you to say so."

Queen stiffened uncomfortably. He wasn't in the mood to have a warm moment with Chris Norbeck right now. "So," he said, "You've just been in to see the colonel?"

"Yeah, that's right."

"In good temperament?"

"I guess. He liked that I collared Dander."

"That's good, then. When I'm finished here, Chris, I'm going to go talk to Dander myself."

"I figured you would, Harm. He's being held at Central Station." He gave Queen one of his weird winks, which made the prior moments of goodwill fly out the door. Queen wanted to slap it right out of him, but held himself in check. "But when I told the colonel you were going to question Dander, he told me to tell you not to. Not yet," Norbeck continued. "You should speak to the colonel first."

"Is that so? The colonel said this? Not Doc?"

"No, not Doc. In fact, Doc didn't say much of anything while I was there, except to congratulate me. Kind of strange, eh, Harm? The old man spits fire in front of voters and reporters, but in there..." He pointed to the office door. "He let his brother do the talking."

"He doesn't have to pass orders to me through you." Queen scowled. "I've got a goddamn meeting with them in five minutes."

Doc Ames's door suddenly opened, and Queen and Norbeck watched Michael Ryan walk out. A big broad-shouldered Irishman from the second ward, he was beloved by the University of Minnesota students he engaged with along his beat. He wore a sad little smile on his face and shook his head, and a few of his friends rushed up to him to ask him what happened.

"Now boys, it's nothing for you to be concerned with," he exclaimed, wiping beads of sweat from his forehead. "I'll venture the good doctor knows what's best for this city, and he's decided that it doesn't include me."

"What?" cried one distraught cop. He ran up to Ryan and put his hand on his shoulder. "That can't be! You're Mike

Ryan! Not a more honest officer in Minneapolis than you! What does this mean for the rest of us?"

"I hope for the sake of those two girls at home, Allan," Ryan said, "that you'll get to keep your salary. Now if you'll excuse me, boys, I don't feel much like lounging around here today." The other waiting policemen surrounded him with words of condolence and somberly escorted him out of the room.

"Holy mother of God," Norbeck said, grinning widely at Queen. "Damn it if I'm not glad I passed muster. They're taking the entire police force and turning it upside down and inside out!"

"Christ, stop that smiling, Norbeck. The other men can see you. This isn't supposed to be funny."

"Sure, right, yeah." Norbeck forced his mouth into a frown. He paused for a moment, and then spoke softly. "I'd better go see how he is. That'd be the right thing to do, I figure."

"Yeah, do that. I'll wait here and smoke a cigarette."

Norbeck slid in behind the procession, and Queen proceeded to light his smoke and boil with fury. Shit, he thought. What are they doing laying off the likes of Mike Ryan? He was a man who was respected by everyone, and even Queen grudgingly admired him, although they were opposites in every possible way. Queen got newspaper stories written about him whenever he got soaked on liquor and into a brawl. Ryan was the kind of officer who'd climb a tree to rescue a homeless cat, or scold a crook who offered him money to avoid arrest. While Queen didn't trust a cop who wouldn't take a bribe, he also knew that papers opposed to the mayor would have a field day with Ryan's firing. What was especially unsettling, though, was the feeling he was having now about his own prospects. Just moments ago, he had been concerned with a promotion to Chief of Detectives. Perhaps he had been fearing the wrong thing. If a man like Ryan could go, everyone was fair game. Especially someone like himself, whose reputation didn't exactly shine in influential circles.

"Detective Queen!" Mayor Ames's portly personal secretary, Tom Brown, came jostling his way through the hall, and the job seekers cleared him a path. The din of excited talk lowered to a whisper at the recognition of Queen's infamous name, and he even heard a low whistle come from somewhere in the clusters of men. Boy, I want to wring some necks, the detective thought, as he eyed both them and the man who came down the corridor to greet him. Brown met his look and hurriedly waved his hand. "The Mayor will see you now, Queen."

He followed Brown to the office door, where a police officer stood guard. Queen knew Fred Connor well, and nodded to him. Connor stepped aside, opened the door, and raised a good-humored eyebrow back in acknowledgement. He was one of the few colored policemen in Minneapolis, and Queen had heard Ames meant to make him his personal bodyguard. Looks like it's true, he thought. It was hard to question his choice. Connor was a crack cop, a pugilist, and not someone to tussle with lightly. Everyone knew the old man was well protected with Fred Connor.

Doc Ames sat behind his desk, smoking a cigar, and chatting with his brother, who was sitting in a chair next to his. The mayor stood up to greet Queen when he entered.

"Hello, my boy! What a night it is, what a night!"

Ames spread a handsome, weathered smile under a thick gray mustache and heartily extended his hand, pumping Queen's arm half off with enthusiasm. "So much work to do, Harm. Choosing men for a police force is challenging work. But," he inhaled deeply, contentment on his face, "We must pick the best, brightest and strongest! No more mucking around with second-rate men, I say."

Colonel Ames rose and also held out his hand. "Hello, Detective Queen. Thank you for making it down here tonight. I know you're busy doing important city work."

"I would never turn down an invitation from the most popular Republican in Minneapolis."

He knew how to humor the old sawbones. Doc Ames threw his head back and chortled gleefully at that. "Three terms as a Democrat, and the fourth a Republican! Never would I have dreamt of a victory snatched from within the ranks of the enemy party!"

Colonel Ames had a drawn, thin, clean-shaven face with pointed features. He wore a blue sack coat with three stars on its collar, which he brushed absently with his hand. "And we now have the opportunity to do great things for this city and for your legacy. A last, beautiful dance that will ignite the sentiments of the people of Minneapolis."

"What hyperbole, Fred," Doc said. I'm most pleased to have firmly stuck a pin in that bloated head of ol' Mayor Gray. Trouncing him has been a veritable highlight of my career, I say."

"You must be excited about the inauguration tomorrow night, sir," Queen said.

"Excited? I suppose so. That daft idiot Gray certainly made things difficult for me." His face turned dark. "You must have read about it in the rags, Harm. As a mayor elected by the people, I thought it only appropriate that the inaugural ceremony's venue should be large enough to hold the throngs of well-wishers."

"I agree with you, sir," Queen said.

"The owner of the Bijou Theater tendered us the use of his building, but Gray put an end to that," the colonel explained. "Despite the Republican caucus of the new City Council agreeing to it."

"That begrudging little dolt!" Doc was seething now, his face tight and red. Queen had seen this transformation more times than he could remember. One minute an affable gentleman, the next a bellowing boob. "The joists in the third floor have shrunk! The damn building is thirty years old! Too many people on the council floor will spring the joists out of place and the whole floor will cave in. It'll send a hundred people to their deaths!"

"Alonzo," his brother said. "The city engineer did an inspection of the floor and determined it safe."

"But even so, I have thousands of well-wishers who will be denied an opportunity to see me sworn in! The Bijou auditorium is much more spacious and comfortable."

Colonel Ames nodded in agreement. "And unfortunately the city side of the new City Hall and County Courthouse is still unfinished. We must make do with what we have."

"Christ, I'm looking forward to getting rid of the lot of them."

Queen took that as an opportunity to speak. "Can I expect to continue on the force as well, Mayor Ames? Seeing as how you are cleaning the house."

The mayor looked amusedly at Queen. "You're never much fun without some scotch in your belly, Harm. Help yourself to some." He motioned to a bottle labeled Dimple Pinch Blended Scotch Whiskey and a glass on his desk, and Queen poured himself some. He took the barest of sips and then set the glass down. It went down like liquid silk, but far too high for his nut, and he wasn't about to let them watch him enjoy it, either.

"Thank you, sir. Again to my question –"

"Of course, Queen, goddammit, why wouldn't you?" the doctor exclaimed, slamming his fist on the desk. "Why the hell wouldn't you? You delivered allies and votes for me. Not to mention personal favors. You're a crack fly-bob to boot! What would make you question that?"

"I saw Mike Ryan come out of your office. There isn't a more popular man on a beat, sir, than him. If you can axe him, I don't know who is safe."

"Well you, for one."

"Yes, sir. So you said."

"And I mean it. Listen. Sit down." Queen found a chair and obeyed. Doc took a drink from his glass, and leaned forward. His pause was drawn out and dramatic. "I mean to make this police force more fully representative of the population. We need people from all walks of life. All backgrounds."

"So it's because he's Irish?"

Ames spread his hands affably. "I don't have a prejudiced bone in my body, Harm. I've got bigger things to think about than Mike Ryan. I'm going to set an example for the city of Minneapolis, and the entire country!"

"My brother is beloved by everyone, Detective Queen," Colonel Ames added. "From civic leaders and businessmen to the tramps and down-and-outers. We want officers who encompass the entire scope of humanity."

"I see," Queen replied. He was starting to understand the full implication of the Ames brothers' plan. Doc had never thought highly of the Irish, and was sore that a couple of their political leaders had fought against him during the election. Slashing their influence in the Police Department was the first step, although he hardly thought Mike Ryan was a political threat.

Doc Ames gave Queen a grandfatherly smile. "You look pensive, Harm. We've all worked hard through this campaign. I need people who will continue to hustle for me. This is politics. To the victors go the spoils. It was the same for Mayor Gray, wasn't it? Don't tell me you haven't benefited from your time as a policeman? You were with me in my third term. I know full well that you've been well compensated for your labor. I want officers on the force who will answer to me, and who won't be afraid to bend the rules a little to deal with certain Minneapolis industries that need a firm hand. You do understand, don't you?"

"Yes sir, I do. It's just that some of those men holding up the walls out there are bona fide criminals that I've had a part in putting away. Working with them every day –"

"Will be challenging, yes, I know. You're up for the challenge, though. You're loyal to me as well; that I know with every fiber of my being. That brings up another thing." He looked a little warily at his brother.

Colonel Ames put up his hand. "If you don't mind, Alonzo, let me give the news to Detective Queen. There has been speculation about the Chief of Detectives position. Newspapers have thrown names around, including yours. You are aware of this, right?"

"Of course, sir." He felt the pulse in his neck start to pound.

"Anyway, to be blunt and straight to the point, Detective Queen, we've decided not to make that position available to anyone now. I'll assume the responsibilities in addition to my job as police superintendent."

Queen clenched his fists. He felt his face flush. He'd considered the possibility that he might not get the promotion, and he had put his feelings on ice about it when he considered the far worse possibility of being demoted or even fired. But he still felt an enormous sting of disappointment hearing it straight from Colonel Ames. *I should be grateful I still have a job,* he thought to himself. *So why am I so hot under the collar?*

"Damn it, Harm. You look crestfallen! Look, we're not ruling it out in the future, and I still need you to show the new detectives the ropes." Doc patted his hand comfortingly. "You're our man, only not on paper right now. Perhaps in the next few months we'll consider it again."

"Yes, sir." He rose from his chair, and Doc stood up as well. "You're welcome to stay, Harm, and offer your advice as we size up our new men. Two hundred pounds average, that's what we're looking for. I want no man less than six-feet two-inches for our drill squad. Every man, woman and child on the streets of Minneapolis needs to feel laid up in lavender, as secure as a baby on a teat, and picking prime physical specimens will guarantee this. Apple pie order, I say."

Six-foot-two? Most of the officers he knew weren't over five-foot-seven, Queen thought. Ol' Doc was dreaming up much bigger men than the city could produce. This was typical Doc Ames, though. He always had difficulty living up to his grandiose promises.

"No thank you, sir. I have to go down to the jail to question someone," the detective replied. He knew what was coming but didn't care.

"Detective Norbeck filled us in, assuming you're referring to Emil Dander," said Colonel Ames. "The courts will take care of him, this I assure you."

"As you know, I'm not mayor officially until Tuesday." Doc Ames leaned forward, his eyes sparkling. "I just want to say that I think you and Chris are doing a crack job on that case of the murdered prostitute. Low-browed criminals like him, shooting up girls, are not something we need, to turn citizens against the law-abiding resort owners who properly pay their fees."

"Frankly, sir, I'm not one hundred percent sure that Emil Dander did the murder."

"Of course he did, detective. It was his house and he certainly makes the obvious culprit. When she tried to flee, he shot her. Respectable resorts gain a black eye when sordid situations like this reach the public ear."

"You're right, sir. The facts and motives so far, without question, point to Emil Dander. It's just that I think there was a witness to what actually happened."

"Really?" asked Colonel Ames, staring at Queen over his glasses. "Who?"

"One of the girls who worked for him. Her room would have given her the perfect vantage point to see everything."

"And where are these prostitutes now? Detective Norbeck never mentioned them."

"They weren't with Dander at his arrest. If he knows where they are, I can get it out of him."

"Why would he tell you where they are?" asked Doc, with a wry look on his face. "From everything I've heard about this Dander character, he's a bit smarter than that. He won't help put the final nail in his own coffin."

"A good point, sir. He's got to be sitting in that cell right now contemplating the possibility of his own execution. And if he doesn't cooperate with me after I explain to him how this young woman might help clear his name," Queen held up his hands as if to surrender, "it's a sure sign he's responsible for her death. But on the other hand, his eagerness to help find her would point to his innocence."

"That makes good sense." The Mayor-elect nodded. "What do you think about this, Fred?"

"I think that you don't need to concern yourself about this," the colonel said, "with the inauguration around the corner. Let the detective do his job, brother." Colonel Ames opened the door, and his secretary came in. "Tom, would you kindly wait until I return before bringing in the next prospect? We haven't eaten for a while. Perhaps you can send for some steaks from the West Hotel?"

"Very good, Colonel."

The police superintendant eyed Fred Connor, who stood near the door with a watchful expression and arms crossed. "Can you go in and talk to him, Connor? He's partial to your company." The bodyguard nodded and slipped in. He winked at Queen as he passed, and Queen returned with a smile, despite his foul mood.

Colonel Ames turned to Queen. "Please follow me, detective." Queen followed him past the staring eyes in the waiting room and into the hall. "We need to speak privately," he said as they walked.

"Is this about what I just said?"

"Among other things. Let's go in here." He pulled out a set of keys, and unlocked a room. As they entered, Queen noticed a young man sitting in a chair, reading a book. He wore spectacles and a silly, enraptured look on his face. The book fell out of his hands when he stood up to meet them.

"Detective Queen, I'd like you to meet Tom Cahill."

"How do you do?" the man said. He was barely taller than five feet, with muscular arms and a thick neck. Queen could usually size up a man with a glance, but was struck by the oddity of this fellow.

"Middling," Queen replied stiffly. He turned to Ames. "Who is this?"

"We've hired new detectives, and this is one of them. You're to take him under your wing and show him the job."

"Frankly, sir, and no disrespect, but I'd like to decline. If you're requiring teams now, put me with Kensington or Hall, or Norbeck at least. He annoys the hell out of me, but I'm used to him anyway. I'd rather not be encumbered, though, if I have a say."

"My brother told you that acting as a mentor will be a major part of your job from now on. We have other plans for

Detective Norbeck. I'd appreciate you accepting this without argument."

"I'd appreciate it as well, Detective Queen," Cahill chimed in buoyantly.

Queen wheeled towards Cahill, who stumbled backwards in surprise.

"Do you have any policing experience?" Queen growled.

"Well, n-no sir. I was in the Army, though. I served under Colonel Ames."

"What rank did you hold?"

"I was a private, sir."

"He's a crack shot, detective."

"Most of what we do isn't shooting. Being a fly means knowing how to sleuth. He's going to find himself in some rough situations, and he needs to be quick with his tongue and his fists. It's not often that I've had to use my pistol."

"Regardless, he is now a Minneapolis detective."

"If you say so, sir." Queen was rankled beyond words, but held his tongue.

"Something else. Tom, do you mind leaving the room now? I have private words to speak with Mr. Queen."

Cahill nodded solemnly. "Of course, sir." He gave Ames a sloppy salute, and left.

Ames turned to Queen. "This matter of the dead prostitute. I understand your suspicions, and appreciate your diligence, but this needs to be kept close to the vest. Once I take official command of the force, I'll deal with this personally."

"There were reporters at the house when we found her."

"And you haven't read about it this week, either. Fortunately, they work for newspapers sympathetic to the new administration, and will remain silent."

"What about Dander? Word will spread soon that he's been arrested."

"Yes, of course, but it won't be for murder. He'll be tried and convicted of serving alcohol without a liquor license."

"He paid the license. I collected the money myself."

"Some kind of kidnapping charge, then. Those girls were inmates, and in a far worse situation than any woman working in a legal brothel in this city. I don't want Mayor Ames to be embroiled in a murder case, because we can't afford public sentiment to turn against this kind of business. Both you and I will lose our livelihoods if it happens. There is money in this, as you know, lots of money. There is also a line between murder and everything else. A murder poisons the whole pot. Women's societies will call for our heads if this gets in the papers. But they'll make the mayor a hero if he helps to break up a kidnapping ring. Can I be any clearer on this point?"

Queen gritted his teeth. "No, you are very clear, sir."

"What's wrong, Detective? This cold demeanor you portray with me is unlike you, from what I've heard."

"What have you heard, sir?"

"Congenial, companionable. You've made many friends in Minneapolis who have kind words about you." Ames's teeth bared into a thin smile.

"I've friends, like everyone, and enemies like everyone," Queen said. "More enemies than most."

"But your friends swear by your trustworthiness and agreeable nature." He paused for a moment, and glanced at the door. "Mr. Cahill and I had that kind of relationship in the war. We had and have a mutual trust. I want that with you as well."

Queen wondered what the hell kind of relationship a colonel has with a private. "I just don't like men going around shooting young girls." He felt his anger rising as he spoke. "How do I explain to her parents when they ask what happened? How is it possible to hide this?"

"We're not hiding what happened. We're just not talking about it. Have her parents come forward yet?"

"I haven't found them."

"Do you really think, Detective Queen, that you will? I'd wager they already believe her dead."

"If she were my daughter I'd want to know what happened."

Colonel Ames shook his head and opened the door. "Let it be. We have enough to worry about without a murder that instigates torch-carrying mobs. I need to go now. See to it that Mr. Cahill is given proper preparation when he's official-ly salaried this week. And please..." He stared intently into Queen's eyes. "No more of this. We shall see that Mr. Dander is punished. I'll personally make sure he's crushing rock in Stillwater Prison by the end of the month. It just won't be for murder."

"Is there nothing more I can say? I think if I explained to Mayor Ames what I believed happened, he might see the light."

Queen caught a momentary flash of malice in the colonel's eyes. Then Ames gave Queen a loose pat on the shoulder, like a master to his obedient lap dog. "I speak on his behalf, De-tective. Let us start our professional relationship off on a good foot. From now on, he will not need to know anything from you, or any of the other detectives, about any police matters. I know your history together is long, but I will be his filter and only pass on the most necessary information. And please keep this conversation private from Cahill. I don't want any distractions from his training."

Queen could barely contain his fury. Not only was he being told not to investigate the girl's murder, but there was now a gatekeeper between him and the new mayor. And he was being handed the leash to the colonel's pet. He willed himself to give the most perfunctory of nods in response, and found himself pushing past the colonel and out into the corridor. In a half-dozen long strides he was out the door and into the cold night air. The winter sting froze his lungs as he inhaled deeply. He walked quickly, not wanting the Cahill kid or anyone else following him.

It was late, at least 10:30, and the stars glittered seductively in the low ebony sky. Queen saw members of a bicycle club on the corner, preparing for an evening ride. Bicycle clubs were all the rage in Minneapolis these days, even on the most bone chilling of winter nights. A group called the Flour City Cyclists rode at midnight from their clubhouse at 18th and Park to Fort Snelling and back, often with groups of revelers sending them off on their slippery adventures.

This was a pack of high-school aged youths, and the five of them stood next to their bikes, joking together and trying to hold cigarettes in their mittened hands. Electric streetlights glowed comfortingly, and as Queen buttoned up his ulster he began to relax, especially the farther he walked from the source of his anger. He'd made up his mind to interrogate Dander as soon as Colonel Ames had told him not to, and figured all the activity tonight might distract attention from him, should he decide to make a little trip down to the jail. A final swig from his flask convinced him that a stop at a saloon first might loosen him more. From Doc's offices at 54 Third Street, Queen went west along Third, turning north on Hennepin towards the city. Few people were out now, and light snowflakes began to fall, glistening under the streetlamps' soft cones of light. His hands were already getting cold, so he removed his gloves from his coat pockets and slipped them on. He listened for the familiar clang behind him, ready to hop aboard a cozy streetcar and find some place to let his frustration thaw. He figured a drink or two and a sandwich would energize his spirits, and a midnight visit to Dander and Higgins would serve as dessert. Even if the administration decided to prevent a murder charge from seeing the light of day, he was more determined than ever to find out if there was really another killer.

A roar of laughter made him whirl around, and there were the members of the bicycle club, rowdily whizzing by him. One particularly obnoxious dummy even heaved a pop bottle at him, but it landed with a soft thud in a snow bank nearby. They all tittered at the near miss, congratulating the boy on his guts. If I had any way to catch up with that mush head, I'd put him in the hospital, Queen thought.

"These young kids now. No respect for anyone."

Queen recognized the voice. The man stepped out from the shadow of a house, and walked towards him. You look like you've got an axe to grind."

"Did you follow me, or are you a happy Minneapolis homeowner now?"

The man chuckled, and stopped at the sidewalk. He was dressed to death in a flash suit and overcoat with a stylish top-piece cocked on his head. He lifted his coat slightly, revealing a pistol snug on his waist. "Just wanted you to know that this isn't a social call."

"Now is not a good time to talk, Jack," Queen said. "If you've come for green," he patted his pockets, "there isn't any."

"Of course I know that," the man said. "Why would you be walking down the street with three hundred dollars that isn't yours?"

Queen pulled out his own gun, and pointed it at the man's chest. "I've been through hell this week and to say I'm not incensed to the point of shooting you dead would be a lie."

The man let his coat drop over his gun. "It's such a pleasant night for an evening stroll, wouldn't you say?"

"So it's just a coincidence that you are standing like a hobgoblin in some stranger's front yard as I walk past?"

"Of course not," the man said, laughing. "Mr. Kilbane wants to know when he should expect to be paid back. You are to tell me, so I can tell him."

"I've got some things I'm working on. I wish I could tell you I was flush with cush, but I'm not. Gray stamped down on our side business to avoid prying reporters when the election started. You know that. We've had this conversation before. And, like I said before, once the new mayor takes over, there will be plenty of honey in the pot to share. Enough to pay you some interest even."

"Interest? You're missing the point, Mr. Queen. When you come to Saint Paul to make a mouth-bet and don't have the green to cover it, then it's me that has to come into this stink hole town to find you. Mr. Kilbane wants your absolute assurance that you have a plan in place for squaring your debt."

"Of course I do."

The man smirked. "And does it involve becoming the head of the detective squad? Because I've heard that you've been passed over for that promotion."

Jesus, Queen thought. News travels fast in sordid circles. "Forget that for a minute. Mayor Ames has faith in me and that job will come with a little more time. I've got the ear of the mayor, Jack. Tell your boss not to worry about it. Give me two months, and you'll have it all back, plus fifty more."

"Again, Mr. Queen—"

"Call me Harm, why don't you?"

"Are we friends now?" the man asked. His eyes blinked with mock surprise.

"Whatever you want to call it." Queen replied. "I just don't like the formality."

"When you've paid my boss back," said the man, "then we can drop the etiquette. Until then, I prefer Mr. Peach." He gave a little shrug. "I won't feel so bad, then, if I have to kill you."

"What the hell, Jack? You think it's a good idea saying things like that to me? I've got goddamn connections. I've got friends in the Saint Paul Police Department who will make yours and Kilbane's lives absolutely bleak. With even a mention of something like that."

"Come now. We both know how Chief O'Connor hates you. You're mentioned in the Saint Paul papers almost as much as the Minneapolis ones, and not with admiration. The one thing you have right now, that makes you valuable, is your connection to Fred Ames."

"Is that so? Tell me why?"

"My boss wants a private meeting with him. And you are to arrange it."

"Why would I do that?"

"Because you are indebted to us. And not just monetarily."

"That little thing is long past, Jack. I'll pay you the three hundred, plus fifty, and then we're square."

The man's pistol was pressed against Queen's neck before he had a chance to take a breath.

"Chuck it up."

Queen dropped his gun in the snow and put up his hands.

"You don't know what kind of miserable evening I've had, Jack. This is making it a hell of a lot worse. If I had a swallow or two of gut-warmer in me it might be funny, but right now I'm more than a little sore."

"You have two weeks to pay us the green and to arrange a meeting with Police Superintendent Ames."

The end of the barrel was warm on his frozen cheek, and when Jack Peach pulled back his revolver's hammer, Queen decided his odds had changed, and might require slightly softer tactics. Slightly. "What kind of meeting should I tell him it is? Are you planning a fat donation to the Washburn Memorial Orphan Asylum? All those snot-nosed little monsters swimming across the river to get into Minneapolis are one hell of a strain on our local charities."

"It's a financial matter, all right. Tell him that if they ever consider retiring early, Mr. Kilbane will happily contribute to their retirement funds in return for some small favors. Understand?"

Queen was up against the wall, so he nodded. Jack Peach lowered the gun and tucked it back into his pants.

"Are you through?" Queen asked. "I've got somewhere to be."

"Just a few seconds longer."

"What else do you want?"

A streetcar passed by, rattling along its track, and Queen cursed under his breath.

"You really need to walk more," Peach chuckled, relishing the detective's irritation. "You're old and out of shape." He patted Queen's belly and walked back into the yard, disappearing into the night.

CHAPTER 4

"*R*ISE AND SHINE, LIEUTENANT QUEEN!"

He forced open his eyes, saw Tom Cahill standing over him, and sent his fist into his face. Although not hard enough to break anything, the impact still made the kid stumble back a step. Queen got out of bed and stumbled too, realizing the booze from the night before had not yet worn completely off. He was stale drunk. He cupped his hand over his mouth, and the stench of his breath made his own head feel light. I need a toothbrush, he thought. Cahill's nose was bleeding, and Queen grabbed a sock lying atop the bed stand and shoved it in his face.

"That should plug the dam, kid."

"I-is it clean?"

"What? You want me to smell it? The hell if I know. Probably. What time is it, anyhow?"

Cahill put the sock to his face, and then pulled out his watch to check. "Ten past one."

"In the *morning?*"

"No, it's early afternoon sir. I was told to fetch you for the inauguration. It starts at two and Colonel Ames says he wants every able-bodied officer not on a beat to come to City Hall."

"Have you even been sworn in yet?"

"Tomorrow, sir. But Colonel Ames counts on me. He told me specifically to get you."

"Who let you in?"

"Your sister. She said she tried to wake you earlier, but you wouldn't budge. When I told her it was especially important, she agreed that I should try."

"Remind me to tell my sister that if she ever sees your face at our door again, not only to lock it, but to board it up, too."

Cahill's mouth hung agape. With a heave, Queen pushed his way to the hall, and then the washroom, realizing as he stretched his tired legs that he had worn his suit to bed. He unbuttoned his trousers, urinated, washed his hands, and began to scrub away with his toothbrush. Cahill came up behind him to watch, holding the bloodstained sock to his nose. "You should brush slower than that, sir."

"What?"

"Slower. You're gonna wear out your gums doing it like that."

"What I do with my gums is my own business." He had no time for claptrap conversation like this. "Go back and tell the powers that be that I'll be there when I've changed my under-wear and taken dinner."

"I'm to accompany you."

"To change my goddamn underwear?"

"Of course not, sir. I'm to accompany you to City Hall for Mayor Ames' oath."

Grumbling under his breath, Queen briefly contemplated picking up Tom Cahill by the seat of his pants and scruff of his neck, carrying him down the stairs, and tossing him onto the stoop. Be rational, he told himself. Control your temper. You've had a night of heavy drinking. This miserable feeling is fouling your mood to the point where any little offense against you might really make you do something you'll later regret. Taking it out on your boss's shining student isn't the best way to get yourself an invitation to the Ames Christmas dinner.

"Colonel Ames also wanted me to tell you he appreciates your willingness to listen to orders."

"What does that mean?"

"He was positive that you were headed out last night to Central station to talk to Dander."

"How does he know I didn't do just that?"

Cahill smiled brightly. "I followed you."

"Really."

"Yes sir. Straight to the nearest saloon."

"And you sat and watched me all night?"

"I did, sir."

"It must have been an enlightening way to spend an evening."

"You'd be surprised."

"Why is that?"

"You pitched into some college boys. They were ready to upend you, too."

Queen rubbed his head, trying to extract the memory. "I don't remember that."

"Luckily there were some cops there and they stopped you from getting drubbed."

"I guess that was fortunate for me." A half-bottle of Cooke's Pennsylvania rye whiskey sat on the edge of his bureau, and he pointed at it and pulled his flask from the inside pocket of his jacket. "Here, fill this for me." He handed it to Cahill, who gingerly took it and unscrewed the top, taking a whiff. "I need a pick-me-up."

"This isn't exactly top shelf stuff, is it?"

"Have they told you what you're going to be paid?"

"$780 a year, and the salary is more than enough for me to live on. I don't have many expenses."

"Good for you. I happen to live the life of an adult."

He realized as soon as he said this that his appearance spoke otherwise. He looked like hell, and reeked like the inner bowels of hell.

"You know what you are?" Queen asked. He crossed his arms and stared coolly at the kid.

"Well, I'm not sure what you mean, sir."

"You're a milkshake."

The boy looked confused. "Why am I that?"

"A milkshake is a sport whose idea of a hot time on the town is an afternoon at the soda fountain sucking through straws."

"Is that because I don't get drunk like you?"

"Exactly. A real man drinks and knows how to have a good time. You haven't even separated from your mother's tit yet."

Cahill said nothing, but his cheeks burned red. He focused intently on pouring the whiskey into the flask's small opening.

"Keep working on that. I'm changing my clothes and then we'll leave together." Cahill looked up and nodded. What a rube, Queen thought smugly, as he pulled a fresh suit and shirt from his closet, walked into the hall, and then dropped the clothing on the floor. When he reached the front door he saw his sister Estella appear, wearing an apron and a concerned look on her face. She held up her hand, about to say something, but he put his finger to his mouth. "I'll tell you about it later," he said apologetically, grabbing his hat and coat from the rack. "I need to do something important, and I need to deal with it, *alone*."

The Second Precinct Police Station, known to all as Central Station because of its location at 671 Central Avenue, was a dreary, unremarkable brick building wedged between others of the same ilk. To one side of the building, a large open doorway revealed a driver scrubbing a police wagon with a dry brush near the horses that pulled it. Queen entered through a steel-arched door, and passed Sergeant Krumweide at the desk. The sergeant barely looked up, intently penciling notes into a record book. It was quiet, and Cahill had evidently been right; most of the officers and staff who would have normally been milling around had left for the inauguration. Others, who wouldn't be coming back, had emptied out their lockers. They should have gone home, but more likely ended up in nearby dives and doggeries to drown their sorrows and plan for their next careers.

There were cells on the first floor, and Queen decided to check those first, before going up to the main floor, which housed more men and the women's ward. The circulation on the first floor had always been poor, but especially so in the winter when windows were locked tight. It led to an excruciating stench that permeated everything, from the worn walls to the crumbling concrete floors.

"Here you are," Queen said with grim satisfaction when he reached the cell where Emil Dander sat. He hadn't had to look far. "You look cozy behind these bars."

"Good afternoon, Detective Queen. I'd been told you were planning to call on me." He stood up and walked towards the cell door. Higgins snored on a bench nearby.

"They should have separated you two," the detective observed disapprovingly.

"If my earthly journey ever gives me the chance to peruse the precious annals of Minneapolis police lore, I guarantee that you, Detective Queen, would go down as the most acrid, depressing representative of law enforcement in its contemptible, comical history."

"I don't have time for this, Dander, so I'd appreciate you answering my questions directly and promptly. None of your goddamn slang-whanging bluster today."

Dander rubbed his jutting chin and lit a hyena smile. "I'm sitting in this rancid cell without the slightest gleam of knowledge as to why I'm here. But whatever you desire from me, I'm extraordinarily pleased to oblige."

"Whatever reason you have for wearing that stupid smirk on your face, it can't be nearly as bad as the possibility of you hanging for murder."

"And who is this most unfortunate that you're accusing me of extinguishing the life from?"

"I told you not to talk to me like that. You know what happened. Christ, you abandoned your house before the girl's body had even turned cold." Queen grabbed a bar with each hand, leaning into them. "And I need to know where the other girls are. The ones who *mysteriously* disappeared."

"Not to worry. They're safely tucked away."

"Did you do the murder? Or are you as innocent as a newborn babe?"

Dander gave an exaggerated shudder. "Please do not mention babies in my presence, detective. I don't find children useful or interesting in the slightest. Whenever one of my girls mentions her month has passed with no blood, my nights are awash with tosses and turns."

"Jesus, don't you understand the situation you're in right now?"

"I certainly understand it." A lock of black hair fell over his eye, and he pushed it from his handsome face. His expression turned serious. "I would never have touched a golden hair on her fair head, detective. She was my favorite, amongst all of my consorts. My muse, my love. Did I threaten her that evening? Regrettably, yes. She was threatening me as well, though. A threat far worse than mine. She was defying every rule I had laid down! Betraying the trust I'd put in her!" A tear ran down his cheek. "My beloved Maisy, plucked from the countryside like a fragile flower, and deposited to me for safe-keeping."

Queen had had enough of this drivel. He reached through the bars, clutched Dander by the throat with one hand, and with the other held his shirt to keep him close. He squeezed Dander's throat. Dander sputtered and spit and his eyes bulged wide.

From the bench, the hulking Higgins rose and moved closer. "Le' go of his gutter chute, Queen!" he bellowed.

"Step back," Queen threatened, "or I'll call every man in this station who's not taking a shit into your cell to slog you down into a fat, bloody pulp." Higgins froze, his veins bulging in his thick neck, and massive hands curled into fists. Dander's face was turning blue, so Queen loosened his grip a little to watch him scratch at his throat and catch his breath to speak.

"W-w-what are you trying to accomplish by this? Release me!"

Instead of being gentle, Queen thought a rough push might highlight his point, and it sent Dander backwards into Higgins's arms. "Now sit down, both of you, and listen to me." Higgins stared with intense hatred at Queen, but Dander just straightened his jacket. They sat on the coarse wooden bunk along the wall and Queen continued, grabbing a bar in each hand to help steady his words. "I think you two are as rotten as they come. You prey on innocent young girls and keep them against their wills. If I'd had even an inkling of the kind of business you'd been running I'd have stopped it long ago. However, despite how I personally feel towards you, my intuition tells me you may not have had anything to do with this. You've always come across to me as plotting, but not impulsive. Killing someone who makes you money wouldn't be smart business. Wouldn't you agree?"

Dander gave a nonchalant nod and picked at his finger.

"So, if it wasn't you, who was it? Don't act smart with me at this very important moment for you. I want straight answers or I leave this cell now, and you won't see me again until I bring you a lovely bouquet of flowers the night before your execution." Queen smiled inwardly at this lie. Evidently no one had yet told Dander that there would be no murder investigation while Colonel Ames was making the decisions.

"I am telling you this with the utmost respect, Detective Queen," Dander explained with a placid expression. "I haven't the slightest idea who would murder her. I'll admit that I attempted to coerce her from flight with the threat of a bullet, but I never seriously had any intention of doing so, for the reason you so aptly stated. As far as others who might harm her, she had clients who frequented her room regularly, but none I would deem dangerous."

"What about a man named 'Ace'? What can you tell me about him?"

Dander laughed. "A jittery wisp of a man. I don't think he'd even have the strength to lift a weapon, let alone pull a trigger."

"He was especially taken with her."

"She was a lovely girl. I was smitten as well."

"I saw the conditions she lived in," Queen spat. "I don't believe for a goddamn minute you cared about her."

"I'm sure I could never convince you of my feelings about my Mopsy, but I had them just the same."

"Mopsy? That's rich."

"Again, despite what you think, I wanted no harm to come to her." He ran his fingers through what little pomade he had left in his hair, slicking it back with his fingers and then delicately wiping the grease on Higgins's sleeve.

"So you are saying you actually want me to find out who did this?"

Dander stood up. His eyes were moist, and he dramatically pulled out a handkerchief to dab them gently. "However you feel about me, Detective Queen, I want you to find the bastard who shot her. I'll give you money if it helps your investigation. I don't have it here with me, of course, but I can connect you to people who do. Hire private detectives if you have to, but know that cost is no concern."

"I'm glad you are so cooperative, although those crocodile tears don't hold much weight with me."

"They're nothing of the kind. Just tell me what you need from me."

"I need to know where the other girls you had locked up in that house are hiding."

"Ha!" Dander threw his head back and chortled. "You want to deprive me of my retirement fund?"

"What good are they doing you here? Once you're tried and convicted of murder, they'll be the smallest of your concerns."

"I'd think, despite your rather beleaguered face, that women would be falling all over you, Queen, with your penchant for authority. Women like men with power. I'd expect you to do much better than with one of my runaways."

Queen gritted his teeth. "The girl whose room was next to Maisy's had the perfect view to the alley in back. If it wasn't you, as you claim, then it'd behoove you to tell me where they are. One of your girls was a likely witness to the killer. Where are they? This might your only lifeline left, Dander, so out with it, quickly."

"This must be some kind of dirty cop trick," Higgins blurted out. "Don't tell him."

"Why?" asked Queen, as he lit a cigarette. "Because your sniveling pal Pock might be with them?"

"He ain't!" shouted Higgins. "He's somewhere you ain't never going to find."

"Give us a rest," Dander said. "You're in no intellectual position to engage the detective."

"Don't tell him, boss," Higgins pleaded.

"You'd better tell me," Queen warned, "if you want to live to see 1902."

Emil Dander sighed, and pulled a bit of paper out of his pocket. Reluctantly, he handed it to Queen. "The fellow you mentioned before, named Ace. Regrettably, I do not know his last name. A secretive soul, he is. I do, however, know, with one hundred percent certainty, that my ladies are with him."

"And how do you know this with such pin-point accuracy?"

"My employee Pock followed them there. He's watching them and just waiting word from me on whether to take them back into our possession or not. I figured there wasn't any harm in letting them be, for now. They're safe with that weak-nosed ninny. Do you happen to have a spare cigarette?"

Queen ignored him and took the paper to read. "I suppose it would be too much to ask your rotten little friend to take a piece of mail out of his box to find out what his real name is?" Dander shrugged. Queen glowered back and continued reading. "This is an address in Bohemian Flats. I thought this dandy had money. What's he doing living in a cesspool like that?"

"Living discreetly?"

"Probably something you should have done. Norbeck said he found you at the White Elephant, just a stone's throw from City Hall. I took you to be a little more up to dick than that."

Dander shook his head, slightly embarrassed. "A brief lapse in judgment. I'm partial to their chicken salad. It's absolutely exquisite, but it proved my undoing. Like the mythical Pandora's box, I simply couldn't resist—"

"That's enough," Queen grunted. "I warned you about talking stupid. What are the girls' names?"

"The ones they were legally born with? I'd like to think that besides their benefactor, I'm their protector too. Divulging that information would certainly jeopardize their future safety. Haven't we already seen what a crazed lunatic with a gun can do already?"

"Their goddamn names."

Dander bowed dramatically. "As you wish. Anything for the grand champion of the distressed and downtrodden. Edna Pease and Trilly Flick."

"And which of those girls had the room next to Maisy's?"

"That would be Miss Flick, detective."

"And Maisy. Is that her real name?"

"Certainly. Maisy Anderson, to be completely compliant with your questioning."

"You wouldn't lie to me about that, now, would you?"

"As you said yourself, you are my best chance at freedom, detective. I tenderly submit to you."

"Where did she come from? I need to tell her family about this."

"We never discussed her past. She wanted to start a new leaf, and I was willing to leave it alone."

Queen gave a wry, disbelieving smile. "How is it that the errand boy knows more about her past life than you? Let me guess how much you really know. You 'found' her as she stepped off of the train, wide-eyed and in wonder of the big city. She told you about her hopes and dreams for a new life. Then you seduced and enslaved her."

Dander curled his lip, but forced it back. "You'll never, ever know of our relationship. She was the only woman who I've ever truly loved."

"So you owe it to her, then, to tell me where she came from. She'd want her parents to know, Dander."

"If she told me, I don't remember. True love can enhance, but often dilute true memory."

"You said before that you plucked her from the countryside. So from that little slip I can narrow it to outside a major town."

"She had rural charm. My assumption."

"If that's the game you want to play, I have other things to attend to now," Queen said, taking a puff from his cigarette. "I'd pray to God, if I were you, that I'm able to resolve this in your favor. Also, if I were you, I'd send word to the idiot that works for you to stay out of my way."

"Of course," Dander agreed. "Pock will not impede your visit. And will you require any of those funds I mentioned before? If it helps grease the hinges of this cell door, I'm delighted to contribute."

"The hell if I'll take any of your dirty money for this."

"Which implies that you'd take my dirty money for something other than this?"

"Screw off, Dander. You and your dough-head friend can sit here and rot in this cell until Christ Almighty returns to earth and sends your pitiful asses to hell, for all I care. And don't think I don't know why you won't tell me what Maisy's name is, or the name of her hometown. Her pop is a sheriff, and when he gets word about this, he's going to find you and beat you down terribly. And by damned if I'll feel an iota of sympathy for you, because you deserve it for what you did to her, even if you weren't responsible for her actual death."

If anyone could pull off a charming smirk, it was Dander. "Gracious me! We don't want the infamous Detective Queen to lose his ongoing battle with his uncontrollable temper, now, do we?"

With a well-aimed motion, Queen tossed the burning cigarette into Dander's face. He yelped and fell backwards as the
glowing embers scattered into the air. "That's the first wise
thing I've heard you say today, Dander," Queen said, and he
turned and walked out of the cellblock.

Sergeant Krumweide looked up this time as Queen passed
him.

"Another busy day at Central?" Queen asked.

"Most of the work has fallen on my shoulders today."
Krumweide had red hair and a chubby face, with untrimmed
side-whiskers crawling from his cheeks. Queen had known
him for years and trusted him. They were different ranks, but
skipped the formalities.

"I'm not supposed to be talking to a certain prisoner today,"
Queen said. "But I did anyway."

"I'm far too busy to watch for plainclothes detectives slipping in and out of the jail."

"You know that doesn't sound good, August. You're the
keeper of the gate."

"Not my fault Fred Ames cleared out the police station to
fatten the audience for Doc."

"So you and I are the only ones here?"

"No. There's a driver in the stable, and the matron and
cook are here too. A couple of officers on the second floor.
Oh, and another detective is here, looking for you."

"Who?"

"Never seen him before. Short and broad shouldered. Said
he's new."

You've got to be joking, Queen thought. Doesn't he have
anything better to do than play tag-a-long? "Where is he
now? Taking a piss on someone besides me?"

"He was going to come and find you, but went down to the basement, into the tramp room, instead."

"Why the hell would he do that?"

"Said he wanted to see what it was like down there. I told him, don't bother; he'll be seeing more than he wants to soon enough."

"Sergeant! Come down quick! These men are rioting!" a voice echoed from below.

Queen sighed. "The jailer's gone, too?" he asked the sergeant, looking around.

"All gone to the inauguration."

"Well, I guess that leaves me."

"Do you need help?" Krumweide asked, with a tired look that said helping Queen was the last thing in the world he wanted to do.

"No, I know how to handle hobos."

The tramp room was always active this time of the year in Minneapolis. Once winter came, most hobos jumped on the quickest boxcar out of Minnesota and rode it into warmer, sunnier climates, but a handful stayed. Inevitably, when the temperature got unbearable, many of them would find a way to get themselves collared, because warm meals and a dry roof were much more desirable than an empty stomach and a snowdrift for a bed, even despite the basement's rank, moldy stench. As he reached the bottom of the stairs, the din increased and the voices sounded raucous, but Queen stopped when he met Cahill, evidently on his way back up for help.

"They look like they're gonna do something bad to one of their own," Cahill said. "We need to stop it."

"You followed me here to the station?" Queen asked testily. "You plan on reporting every step I take to Colonel Ames now? Is that what your job is, Milkshake?" He grabbed a handful of fabric close to Cahill's throat to emphasize his anger.

"No sir. I just thought you might need help. I didn't want to go without you."

"You're a goddamn spy, that's what you are."

"I'm trying to do what's right," Cahill replied, his eyes showing hurt. "I'm barely on the job and already I have found myself in a difficult position, wedged between my commanding officer and my partner."

"We're not partners," said Queen, letting go of his collar.

"Regardless, sir. I'm trying my best, and I think we should help this man out. He's surrounded by enemies."

"Did you say something to them already?"

"I told them to leave him alone, but they just ignored me. I thought about opening the door to let him out, but didn't want them all overrunning me and escaping."

"You know they want to be here, right?"

"What?"

"It's their choice. If they don't have money for a lodging house, they opt for jail instead. They're not going anywhere, especially since it's almost mealtime. You want a real riot? Try to separate a hobo from his goddamn food."

"But listen for a moment," Cahill said. The sound was loud, men banging with tin cups and plates on the bars, jeering and cursing.

"If this is what I think it is, it won't get violent," Queen said.

"Kang'roo court is now in session!" came a loud, enthusiastic voice, followed by catcalls and applause. An utterly miserable moan from what had to be the most wretched creature in existence followed the declaration. Queen made sure he was still hidden in the shadow of the doorway, but stepped out to get a better view of the proceedings.

"What are they doing?" Cahill whispered.

"Just what they said. It's a mock trial. They call it a kanga-roo court. Something hobos do to pass the time."

There were at least forty men in the large holding cell. The station's basement smelled even worse than its main floor, as the stench of sweat and dirt from the unbathed hobos mixed unpleasantly with the uncirculated air. Mold seemed to slither over the walls, and its musty stink added to the already un-bearable odor. The tramps in the room seemed oblivious to the state of their surroundings, however. They'd made a small clearing for the man, who had a look of complete agony on his worn face. He wore a battered stovepipe hat and an oversized coat and pants, and was being turned in a circle by a couple of genial-looking fellows. The rest of the tramps in the large, communal cell were a dirty, motley collection of shapes and sizes, but didn't appear at all ill-tempered to Queen.

"State your name," said a thin, bald, bearded man, evident-ly the ringleader and judge for the bunch.

They stopped spinning the hobo, who floundered to main-tain his balance and stand up straight to face his accuser. This, of course, elicited a fresh round of jeers and hollers.

"QUIET!" The man shouted. "This is a serious affair! This ain't no time for playground antics!" The men around him turned somber-faced, some looking down at their shoes, shuf-fling their feet and ashamed.

"Your name," he repeated.

"Milwaukee Jim," the hobo replied with a whimper.

"And how do you find yerself in kang'roo court?" the man asked.

"I wished I knew," said Milwaukee Jim. "We've always been friends, Slim. Why do you got to go and do me this way?"

"You said you don't have a red cent on you," said Slim. "However, Yankie over here said he heard you jingle when you walked. Wha' does you plead? Guilty or not guilty?"

"Not guilty," Jim mumbled.

"Yankie, I appoint you the court searcher today. Are you willing to be searched?" Milwaukee Jim nodded weakly.

Yankie, a pimple faced youth not more than nineteen, padded up to the accused. "Sorry, Jim, but this here is a serious thing. Pull out yer pockets or I'll have to do it for you."

Jim reached in to his right pocket. "There's a hole in this one," he said, and pulled it out to show the group.

"And the other one?" Slim asked sternly.

"The other 'un," Yankie said with an anxious voice.

Slowly, Jim went for the second pocket. The eyes of his fellow hobos bored into the movement of his hand, and a low hush enveloped the room in anticipation of what treasure might be revealed. Jim moved his fingers about dramatically, poking in the corners.

"Drat, Jim. You're too slow by miles," Yankie said. He pulled Jim's hand out, put his own in and felt around. "There's nothin' there, Slim. I figure he's innocent!"

"I saw him hide money in a shoe before!" a voice called out. "Search them!" Slim nodded to Yankie, who sat down on his haunches and pulled off one of Jim's shoes, turning it over and shaking it to no result.

"Now the other 'un," said Slim. Yankie did as he was told, and shook the second shoe, dramatically this time. Out tumbled the coins, clinking onto the concrete floor.

"I knew'd it!" Slim cried, as the crowd gasped in wonder. "How much is it?"

Yankie counted it out. "Thirty-six cents, Slim."

"You know boodle ain't allowed, Jim," said Slim. "Money in here goes to the whole group. I can't believe you was holdin' out on us."

Milwaukee Jim took off his hat and gripped the brim, wrenching it about a little. "My mother is holed up with a terrible sickness. She needs this medicine, you see –"

A voice piped up from the crowd. "You told me last week, Jim, your mother's been passed on for ten years now!" The hobos all looked at each other, and let out a giant whoop of laughter, some falling to their knees with tears in their eyes. Even the bald-headed Slim couldn't help but crack a smile.

"We all know how good you are at talking some poor farmwife out of a mug of coffee and a piece of apple pie with your sob stories, but do you really think you can pull the wool over the eyes of yer fellow travelers?" Slim asked. Milwaukee Jim stared sheepishly at his feet, still twisting at his hat brim. "I hate for this to happen to you, Jim, but you've got to be punished. You've been found guilty. The travelers' law must be enforced!"

"Why do they call themselves travelers?" Cahill softly asked Queen.

"It probably sounds more dignified than 'filthy flea-bitten tramp.'"

Cahill shuddered. "Shouldn't we stop this? This is not a proper court of law!"

"Don't see the harm in it," Queen replied. "More honest than some courtrooms in Minnesota."

"So, what'll it be, Slim?" Jim asked forlornly.

Slim tapped his finger to his mouth. "Let me consider it. My first idea was to have you pace the floor of the cell one hundred times a day for the next thirty days, but there's too many of us in here bein' winter and all. I've got an idea. Anyone here like washing their own dishes?" Slim asked the group. Almost in unison, they shouted various versions of no. "That's settled then. Mr. Milwaukee Jim, I hereby sentence you to wash every man's breakfast, lunch and supper dish in this here booby room for one week. That, and hand over your shoes, so ya won't hide no more boodle in 'em."

Milwaukee Jim let out a long sorrowful sigh, while the other hobos cheerfully slapped him on the back and congratulated him on his misfortune and then each other on their own turn of good luck.

"Put it in the tobacky fund," Slim decided, handing the money to Yankie.

"A tramp hates work more than anything in the world," Queen explained, shaking his head in disapproval. "He'd probably rather be released into a rail yard packed with armed railroad detectives before being told to pick up a plate and a towel and make the effort to put the two together. Looks like things have been resolved peaceably, kid. Time to go wish Doc good luck."

"That doesn't seem fair to me," Cahill said, looking at Milwaukee Jim, who was now sitting on the floor, slumped against the bars. "It's cold down here. He needs shoes."

"Look at them," replied Queen, as he pulled out a cigarette and lit it. "They're all friends again. If you want to go and spoil their little game, then do it yourself."

Cahill took a deep breath, cleared his throat, and marched into the area in front of the tramp room, turning everyone's eyes to him. Someone farted, and laughter erupted.

Christ, he looks uncomfortable, Queen thought. This will definitely be an entertainment.

"Now listen here, fellows!" Cahill cried. "This man needs his shoes. You're under the roof of the Minneapolis police department, and you can't go around taking someone's belongings in a pretend trial!" The hobos looked suspiciously at him, and murmured in low tones to each other. Slim came to the bars and extended his hand through to Cahill, who reluctantly shook it.

"Hello, good sir. You speak with the authority of an officer of the law. How can I help?" Slim asked with a pleasant smile.

"I told you my name before, when you ignored me and accosted this poor fellow instead."

"We got our own set of rules and it suits us just fine. No offense, young man, but why should you care? He ain't hurt in any fashion. Well, maybe his feelings, perhaps, but those will mend in time. Ain't that right, Jim? C'mon over here and tell the elbow yer okay!"

"Elbow?" Cahill asked.

"Sorry about that sir, just some slang we have for gents like you. Detective, is what it means."

With a set of slouched shoulders, Milwaukee Jim came forward, and forced a big grin. "Don't worry about me. I s'pose I'll survive without a pair of shoes, although ..." his face dropped dolefully and he gave a long sniff, "they were a gift from my daughter. She gave 'em to me the last time I saw her, just before she fell hard to melancholy and had to be sent to an asylum." The men around him snickered under their breaths.

"A real tear-squeezer," Slim said.

"If that's true, give them back to him," Cahill demanded.

"Anybody see Milwaukee Jim's shoes?" Slim turned and shouted. The hobos all looked around and scratched their dirty heads. "Yer welcome to come in an' search yerself, young man. But would you mind reminding the cook about supper first?"

"I saw you take them from him!" Cahill shouted, puffing up his chest. "I demand right now that you hand them over."

"Or what?" shouted a voice from the back.

"Or ..." Cahill thought for a moment. "I'll turn you all out. Onto the street. Before supper is served." The room gave a collective gasp of anguish. Slim's jaw dropped slightly, but he picked it right back up and gave a little smile. "No need for something like that, sir. I'm sure we can find them if we just search hard enough. Anyone back there have any luck yet with Jim's shoes?"

An arm immediately extended out from the crowd holding a dangling pair of shabby shoes. Slim took them delicately, and then handed them to Jim. "Just as fresh as when they last parted from yer feet," he said.

"There," Cahill said, with satisfaction in his voice. "That wasn't so hard. Every man deserves the dignity of a pair of shoes, I think."

"Now that I've pondered it, I'd say I have to agree," Slim said.

"And I," said Milwaukee Jim. His smile revealed more black holes than teeth as he put his shoes back on with a flourish, and he winked with gratitude at Cahill.

"I'll go remind the cook now about your supper," Cahill said, which was met with a gush of verbal approval from many of the hobos, including even a small smattering of applause. "If I come back down here again, though, and see poor Jim here missing his footwear, I'll make good on my promise."

"No doubt you will, sir," said Slim. Cahill turned back towards Queen, barely able to contain his elation. Queen rolled his eyes as they walked up the stairs.

"Now that you've saved the blistered feet of a tramp, I guess you've reached your pinnacle."

"Yes, sir." Cahill beamed, trying to keep up with his short legs.

They got to the main floor, and Queen stopped, panting slightly from the exercise. His eyes were on fire and burned into Cahill. "I've got to know something from you, right now."

"What is that, sir?" Cahill sucked in his breath at the detective's intense stare.

"If you want me to show you how I do things in Minneapolis, you need to swear to me that you won't go to Colonel Ames with every little detail of my business. You said you felt torn between Ames and me, which is fair, and something I understand. But know this: you have to pick a side. There's no way of playing both. If it's Fred Ames you choose, I don't care, but I want you out of my sight because I will not have you telling him where I drink, play cards or go to Sunday church. I'll quit the goddamn force and become a private detective again before taking that nonsense!" He held up his finger, warning him not to interrupt. "You think I have a temper? You've only seen the tip of the iceberg with me."

Cahill nodded, eyes wide.

"So what's this special relationship you've got with him? Here you are, suddenly on the police force, and a lieutenant? Not a patrolman, or even a sergeant." He leaned in to Cahill's ear. "What's going on between the two of you?"

"Detective Queen, no disrespect intended, but I can't give you details of what happened in the Philippines. It's very complicated, and involves high-ranking officers in the military. Much higher than the Colonel."

The last thing I need is for Commodore Dewey to come steaming up the Mississippi in a bloody flotilla looking for me, Queen thought. Navy politics, however, was not what he really suspected was going on. What other reason could there be for someone like Colonel Ames to take this doe-eyed chucklehead under his wing, except that they were involved in some nefarious, underhanded affair?

"Well, if the two of you are backgammon bunkies, I'll find it out," Queen finally said.

Cahill's mouth opened, stunned. "That is preposterous! Nothing of the kind, sir! I-I like girls! Very much so! How could you think such a thing?"

"Well, I can't think of anything else. What could a lowly private have done for his colonel that would get this kind of reward? You must have something on him."

"You read the papers, right?"

"Of course. The 13th's lively stepping was captured on the front page every damn day you were there. I do remember this: Ames got conveniently sick and was carried out of harm's way just as the fighting was getting hot. People said he faked his illness because he was a coward and wanted to go home."

"He really was sick. I was his orderly, and with him most of the time, so I should know. He had severe dysentery, and officers with him were convinced he'd die if he didn't leave the island right away."

"He was also accused of mishandling the Battle of Santa Maria, isn't that correct? He sent reinforcements from one battalion to another, and the weakened one was attacked and defeated?"

"There is much more to the story than that. But yes, he feels beholden to me for my assistance in sorting through things afterwards."

"What things?"

"I told you, Mr. Queen. I can't tell you."

"But you believe in him? Is he capable?"

"Very much so." Cahill nodded vigorously, to emphasize his answer.

Queen grunted. No point in pushing him further, he thought. This was enough information for now. There were others on the force he could question, if need be. The kid seemed sincere, and he hoped for a day when he could trust him, but that day still seemed far away.

"I won't make you pledge your allegiance to me, Milkshake. You need to sort out your loyalties on your own. But I won't let you snitch on me, either. Are we understood?"

"Yes," Cahill replied in a hollow voice.

"Fine, then." He spotted Sergeant Krumweide, sipping something suspicious out of a tin cup. "Krumweide, is that driver doing anything out there besides scratching his family jewels?"

"What, do you need a wagon for something?"

"Colonel Ames needs us over at the inauguration."

"You and the whole damn force. Everyone but the over-looked desk sergeant." Krumweide took a large swallow of his drink. "Sure, go ahead, and toast the old coot one for me."

While Milwaukee Jim was fortunate to be wearing his shoes, his pride had been swallowed and shit out an hour prior, when Slim had given him the soapy water and told him to start washing. The tramp room's occupants were in the midst of a marvelous time, closely watching him scrub their plates, spoons and cups and pointing out when a spot of beef stew or a crumb of bread had escaped his rag. "When yer finished with that," one wit exclaimed to a symphony of guffaws, "you can wash my ass!" The mood was good-natured and festive for everyone except poor Milwaukee Jim. And one other.

This other man sat in a dimly lit corner of the cell by himself. He was perhaps the only one in the room who hadn't gone there willingly. His hair was greasy but carefully combed, and he had recently been clean-shaven, although three days in Central Station had interrupted his meticulous control over his whiskers. The clothes he wore fit well around his lean, sturdy body, and had once been very fine, but now were dotted with patches, like a quilt. A bowl of stew and a chunk of bread sat next to him, untouched, and his arms were folded in his lap. Even though the room was busy and humming with conversation, he didn't listen or look, but just stared straight ahead, deep in concentration. Occasionally his mouth would move, as he recited words to himself, meant only for his own ears. The other hobos in the room kept their distance, because he had a reputation that frightened them beyond belief. Here they were safe in numbers, but any one of them, if confronted by this man on the streets, would run away, as fast as his legs would carry him, even dropping their precious bindles of food in flight.

His lips tonight were trembling more than usual. They were fleshy, and if a fellow traveler had any guts at all, he might have dared call his face fishlike. He had a small nose, beady eyes, and high forehead to complement his features. No one would ever call him ugly within listening distance, and even the most superstitious hobos wouldn't mention his name without a three-state head start on an express train. As for him, though, he didn't care what others thought. He deemed very few things in the world important anymore. The world's joy had long since disappeared for him.

There was, however, something on his mind that needed attention. He had two prushuns waiting out there for him. One that would soon do his bidding, and one that had temporarily escaped his grasp. Both were very important, but for different reasons. The police wouldn't hold him much longer, he knew, and once he got out, he would find them. One to love, and one to destroy.

CHAPTER 5

A COUPLE OF INCHES OF SNOW had settled over the area north of Bemidji where Dix Anderson had his little farm. He didn't bother with a shovel or snowshoes, but just strapped on his boots with the fur lining and crunched out into the gray and white dawn to the barn and the coop beyond that to feed his animals. A cow, a sow, six chickens, a rooster, and his horse Charlie, along with a hot mug of coffee, kept him busy most mornings. Just beyond a stand of birch on the barn's far side was a half-acre vegetable garden, and he'd been pleased the prior fall when his corn and string beans had come out almost untouched by birds and vermin. Even the cucumbers, which he'd never had much luck with, were a record harvest for him. Mrs. Ingebritsen had told him how beautiful they looked when she made a special trip to help with the confounding job of canning.

Nothing had been easy since his wife had passed the year before. The summer had kept him busy and had forced his mind to focus on other things, but the lonely winter had put him under a cloud. He struggled with everything, from cooking simple meals to caring for the wooden floor Martha had always so painstakingly scrubbed. He'd never paid much mind to how she did it, but now that she was gone he felt he owed it to her to try and keep it the same, and he'd racked his brain trying to remember the proper procedure. Did she use ox-gall to remove the stains first? She'd made homemade lye from wood ashes, but he couldn't get the recipe exactly right. In the summer she'd sand the floors, but what had she done that prior winter when sand was hard to come by? All these things made him miss her in a heart-aching kind of way. Mrs. Ingebritsen told him there were oils he could buy from the store that would make it easier on him and his bad back, but he held on to the way his wife had done it because he thought it would make her happy, wherever she was.

Anderson had avoided Bemidji since his wife had died. He hadn't wanted the painful small talk he knew would go with every trip to town. He winced internally whenever he heard "How are you holding up?" from concerned acquaintances. Talking about painful things was not a practice Anderson got an ounce of relief from, so he'd been surprised at how much he relished a visit from a family friend one day. Schmidt, the old German who ran a hardware store in downtown Bemidji, had knocked on his door on one of that winter's more bitterly cold nights. He brought a handful of letters. He also thoughtfully produced from his saddlebag a bottle of good brandy and a pile of newspapers, both the *Bemidji Sentinel* and the *Saint Paul Globe*. After they took care of the horse and warmed up old Schmidt in front of the kitchen stove, they drank the bottle over good-natured conversation about local gossip and state politics. Rural free mail delivery hadn't come to his neck of the woods yet so Anderson was grateful to the German for suffering a miserable ride just to provide him and a few other neighbors with their letters.

With a hearty wave, Schmidt left the following morning, carrying a jar of coffee and some bacon sandwiches Anderson had packed for his ride. After he watched him trot down the road, through the flurry of white snowflakes dropping from the stone-colored sky, and eventually out of sight, Anderson sat down at his kitchen table, with his own mug of black coffee to read his mail. His long curled mustache, white with age, touched the inside of the mug as he drank, staining the hairs. Once, his wife would have chided him for his careless-ness, and gently wiped his mustache clean with the apron she always wore around her plump waist, but now he was left to his own mannish, absentminded ways.

He thought he'd get through these miserable letters of condolence first, of which he'd had more than enough for a lifetime. One was from an ancient aunt he barely knew, now living in San Francisco. She'd met his wife only once, and evidently the news had taken a while to reach her, but the old lady, who had to be close to a hundred now, still wrote poetically about the passing of time and love lost. He put the envelope aside to save the return address, and threw the card and letter into the little fire in his cook stove. He followed this pattern for the next three letters, all of which were from people he hardly remembered. It wasn't that he didn't appre-ciate the thought behind their contents. Picking up a pen and paper takes time, and he accepted that the sentiment behind them was genuine. It was just that he couldn't connect to them, because they really couldn't understand what he'd ago-nized through.

These people, well intentioned as they were, hadn't both-ered to write her a letter when she was alive, and she might have appreciated hearing from them. God knows she had written plenty herself, and not just the Christmas cards she mailed with regularity every October. They hadn't been there with him when he found her, at the foot of their bed, a clean sheet still clutched in her hands, dead of what the doctor said was a heart attack. He still had blueberry on the corners of his mouth from the piece of pie she'd cut for him a few minutes before when he heard an awful crash just above him. She was a heavyset woman and he tried his best to lift her from the floor and lay her on the bed, but his back gave out at the strain and he had fallen too. They'd laid there together for an hour at least, him weeping, and her eternally silent.

No one outside of a few friends from town had been at the funeral either, at the little Methodist church, as the minister said his words, or in the procession that led them back here to the farm where she was buried under the shade of the birch trees near the garden.

A knock on the kitchen door interrupted his thoughts. Schmidt was standing outside, next to his horse, and handed him a piece of folded paper.

"I forgot about this, Dix," he said, pulling his mitten back on. "This is a message from Sheriff Roy. He asked me to pass it to you."

"Thank you for coming back. Important?"

"Didn't tell me. Just asked me to deliver it if I could."

"Well, fine, Rolf. Appreciate it."

"Oh, sure. You said the Berg farm was just past that hill with the big jack pine that fell over, right? Take a left there? I've been to their place before, but everything looks different with the snow."

"That's right. That your last stop?"

"Yep. Back home after that."

"Well, thanks again."

"Any time, Dix."

He didn't watch Schmidt ride off this time, but instead went back into the kitchen and sat down. He took a long drink of coffee as he unfolded the note. It had gotten wet, and the ink had smeared the writing on the bottom corner, but he was able to make it out.

Jan. 3rd

Dix Anderson:

Hope you are well, old man. I received a telegram today from a Sheriff Eagleton in Minot, ND. He wants you to get in touch when you can. Come by the office when you're in town to send the wire. I will buy you lunch at the Gem.

Sincerely,
John Roy

Anderson put on his glasses and read it again. It said Eagleton's wire had arrived January 3rd, but for the life of him he couldn't remember what the date was now. He hadn't replaced the 1900 calendar that hung raggedly from the kitchen wall. It pictured a gigantic buck with massive antlers, courtesy of Bemidji Steam Laundry, which he hadn't recalled ever patronizing. Something else his wife had taken care of that he had now let slide.

The letter was curious to him. Had it been just a few days ago that this telegram arrived? Perhaps it had been even a week ago or more, for all he knew. And what on earth did Eagleton want anyhow? It'd been three years since he'd lived in Minot, and hadn't heard from him since then. They had departed company amicably, and he had trusted Eagleton would do a solid job as sheriff after the election. The voters of Minot had rightly chosen someone younger than Anderson, and he understood their motive. He was long past his ability to chase sling-shot wielding delinquents through back alleys. He couldn't imagine what the sheriff needed from him now, though. Perhaps advice on an old case?

He suddenly realized it was getting chilly, so he piled up wood inside the stove, and opened the door to the parlor where he had moved his bed for the winter. The heat from the kitchen could reach him there until late into the night. The sun went down early in January, and he liked to make decisions by the sun. Winter meant less to do, and sleep seemed to be a logical way to fill the monotony of the evenings when his eyes began to get blurry and hurt from reading by oil lamp. Every moment was heavy to him, and everyone precious to him dead or gone away, so time meant little. A clock on the shelf had sat silent for months, and spiders wove strands of web behind it. Even his back betrayed him. Once strong and flexible from years of herding cattle as a cowboy during his youth in the Dakota and Wyoming Territories, it announced itself sporadically through bursts of intense pain and hideous creaks and crunches.

The light was low in the west, so he struck a match and lit his lamp's round wick. In the sitting room, he set the lamp and the matches on the little table next to his favorite armchair. He took a quilt draped over Martha's rocker and a cup of hot water from the tea kettle on the stove to sip on, and finally settled down in his chair, feeling the tension from his body ease and the pain in his back dissipate. His thoughts turned back to the letter and to Minot, and his prior life. When he and his wife had first arrived there in 1886, it was a tent town, final stop on James J. Hill's Great Northern railroad extension. He remembered vividly the conductor shouting "Minot, this is Minot North Dakota, prepare to meet your doom!" as the train ground to a stop. While he and Martha had exchanged smiles at the declaration, they quickly discovered that it was as rough and tumble a town as they'd ever set foot in. Anderson had decided to hang up his star and go into private business, and they opened a little cafe to feed hungry railroad workers. They'd come alone, as their only daughter Minnie and her husband Pete, employed as an insurance man in Chicago, had no interest in following them. Anderson didn't blame them. He'd been a lawman of one kind or another for over forty years, always in the west, and Minnie had begged for fancy dresses and big cities since she could first talk.

When their granddaughter was born in 1880, he'd still been a marshal in Colorado, and they'd spent weeks traveling by foot, horse, wagon and finally train to Chicago to witness her first months in the world. Martha was overjoyed at the birth, and asked him if they could stay longer. Perhaps Anderson could find a job as a police officer or detective in the city? The railroads hired their own detectives. She'd wondered this out loud in hopeful expectation, barely able to contain her excitement at the possibility of a permanent reunion with her daughter and now granddaughter. Guilt twisted into his heart like a rusted screwdriver thinking about their conversation, and how he'd explained to her that they absolutely needed to return. The town required it. Criminy, now he'd even forgotten the town's name, but he could still remember, as clear as any memory he had access to in his thick stupid head, the look of grief in her eyes as she silently nodded back to him, yielding. She had been a good, good wife.

Six years later Minnie and Pete both died of typhoid fever, and he and Martha had gone to fetch Maisy. Anderson brushed over the memories of heartache at his daughter's death. Too painful to contemplate now, in the comfort of his armchair. He sipped some hot water and closed his eyes, willing forward happier thoughts. Maisy was the apple of his eye, and she had helped ease the crushing pain for both of them, with a sweet dimpled face and golden hair that streamed like a river from some mythical land. He and his wife had been living in Minot when she arrived, but quickly bought a house in the country to give her space to run and play. By this point Anderson had sold the cafe for a tidy profit, and agreed to stand for election as county sheriff. He'd make her pancakes on Sunday mornings before church and she'd come downstairs, rubbing her sleepy eyes and smiling like the world was the most amazing, exhilarating, wonderful place imaginable. Despite Minot's raw pulse, she grew up unscathed by its bawdy existence. She seemed to draw the best from the town, its passion and earthiness and ribald energy, without letting it corrupt her soul. A single exquisite light in a colorless world's vast emptiness was how he saw her, every moment of every day she was in his presence.

When she'd decided to attend the University of Minnesota, he felt two things: a grandfather's incredible heart-bursting pride, and a lawman's wariness. He supported her desire to expand and explore, but Minneapolis was a big city, and he wasn't so sure traveling that far away was necessary.

"I'm a little over-protective, I know," he admitted to her one afternoon, as they took a walk along the lane near their house. It was fall, and the golden waves of billowing wheat surrounding them would be threshed soon. The air was fresh and cold.

"I'll go straight to the campus," she laughed, and reached out to grab his ample, callused hand. "I'll be safe in the girls' dormitory. There are strict rules about those things. When I do visit the city, I promise I'll only go with a respectable chaperone."

"How will you know he's respectable?" he asked, the words feeling gravelly in his throat.

"It will be a lady, I'm sure!" she reassured him brightly. "They've got teachers and others to do those things; employees of the school! Please try not to worry about me, Grandpa!"

She squeezed his hand tighter and he knew he was helpless against her arguments. Containing a soul like hers would be near impossible, and it grieved him and gave him joy at the same time.

On the day she'd finally left, both he and Martha were at the train station to see her off. Martha was crying and so was Maisy, and they all embraced. He remembered the bounce in her step as she climbed the steps to the car, and her eyes, round and excited, as she turned to wave one last time. She'd promised to telegraph when she got there, after she settled in to her dormitory. He was supposed to wire her money for tuition so she could register for classes, and he waited at the Western Union office most of the day for a message that never came.

He sent a telegram to the University of Minnesota, and the clerks in the dean's office were equally perplexed. They'd sent someone to meet her at the depot but said she never got off of the train.

Stop thinking about this, he told himself, or you won't sleep tonight. He drained the last bit of water from his cup. He was quite warm, and decided to spend the night in the armchair instead of having to get up and irritate his back. He reached over to extinguish the lamp and settled back in, humming Vivaldi's *Spring*. It always soothed him and reminded him of budding trees, fat flowing creeks and singing birds. Anything to remind him of life instead of death.

A loud knocking on the door the next morning brought him into consciousness. He rose slowly, taking special care to make no sudden movements. Once straightened out, he strode briskly to the door. More visitors in two days than in two months, he thought, as he pulled the door open. A good-sized man in a fur coat and slouch hat stood in front of him, his thick brown mustache caked with frost.

"Hello, Dix."

"Hello to you, John."

"May I come in?"

"Certainly," he said. "I'll make some coffee."

"That'd be great."

In the kitchen, as the man took off his coat and hat, Dix put more wood in the stove, bending with great care. "Sorry it's a little cold in here. I fell asleep."

"And I'm sorry to rouse you, Dix. I wouldn't have come if it wasn't important."

"I figured so, John. Let me get this made before we talk about what you came here to talk about."

Sheriff John Roy was a decent man, and had been enforcing the law nearly as long as Dix Anderson had. They'd swapped uncountable stories together when the Andersons had first arrived in Bemidji. Roy liked to tell him he was glad he could count on a fellow Indian-fighter should the Chippewa decide to come crashing down on them from the deep hardwood forests. Anderson had never fought an Indian in his life, at least not the kind from a Fenimore Cooper story, but they had laughed together nonetheless. Now here was John Roy in his kitchen again, but from his humorless expression, he knew whatever he had to say wouldn't be a light quip.

"I'm not sure if I should wait, Dix."

"Well fine, then. Say it now." Anderson put a plate of gingersnaps on the table. "Help yourself with these, too. The coffee will be ready soon."

"Got another wire from Sheriff Eagleton in Minot, where you were sheriff. He seems like a good man."

"Definitely a hard-working fellow. I thought he joked around too much sometimes when he was my deputy. But he was always the first out the door when trouble was brewing."

Roy's face was somber. He shifted in his chair, and seemed to will himself to look into Anderson's eyes. "This is hard news to bear. But I figured I was best to tell it to you." He wiped the palm of his hand over his mouth. "Eagleton got a telegram from Minneapolis. A second time, after I sent the message with Schmidt. It was from a detective down there by the name of Queen. He said he found Maisy."

"Where? How? How could it be?" Anderson felt his body tremble, and gripped the wooden table top with both hands.

"She—she's dead, is what he said. Didn't say where or how. Says you can contact the city morgue to arrange to have her brought back." Roy looked down, and rubbed his brow roughly.

Dix Anderson sat silent, holding the table tight, as if to keep it from sliding across the kitchen floor and into the wall. His knuckles trembled and he tried to contain every last ounce of despair from exploding into the air. He'd presumed she had died, but hearing the words, and *now*. Two years after she went missing? And all the time, she'd been in *Minneapolis*? He could have looked harder for her. She had still been some-where in that city. Had she even been abducted to begin with, or had she started a new life without telling him and Martha? Roy continued to stare down at the puddle of gritty snowmelt underneath his damp boots, not knowing what to say or how to act. The coffee began to boil over, hitting the hot stove with a hiss, sending up puffs of steam. Roy leaped up, grateful to have something to do with his hands. He grabbed a towel, removed the gurgling pot, and poured cups for both of them.

"Perhaps we both need a drink instead," he said. "Damn, Dix. I am so sorry to have to tell you this."

Anderson released his grip on the table, letting his arms drop to his side. "When are you going back to Bemidji?" he finally asked.

"I only came to see you."

"Give me an hour to take care of the animals, and pack a bag. I'll swing by the Bergs on our way out and ask him to look after things here."

"You need to go to town to sort out bringing Maisy home?"

"No," Anderson said, his eyes welling. He got up, walked to a kitchen drawer, and pulled out a thick, worn leather belt, and two holsters holding matching Colt .45 revolvers. The morning light made them glisten and gleam as he drew each out, examined it, and then returned it to its home. Slowly, his hands moved, behind and around, and strapped the belt firmly to his waist. The guns rode high on his hip, the way he'd worn them for forty years.

"I'm going to Minneapolis," he replied.

No rest for the wicked, Queen thought, as he dropped the coins into the man's hand. He sat himself in the driver's seat and took the reins, feeling the jerk. He drove out of the livery stable onto Hennepin Avenue. It was a nice little rig, with an exposed seat in the front for the driver and a companion, and an enclosed compartment in back where he'd put the girls. He'd paid for five hours of its use and figured it would be plenty of time to take care of his task at hand. The livery owner had suggested a sleigh, but he preferred a buggy's wheels, even though patches of ice and snow still covered the cobblestone pavement.

The sun hadn't quite yet risen and the day was just beginning on the streets of Minneapolis. Dawn had enveloped the city in a soft purplish glow. A light dusting of snow the night before capped the tops of the street lamps and the awnings of shops he passed. He maneuvered around a wagon full of coal stuck in a gaping pothole, and tipped his hat to a couple of factory girls walking to work, bundled up in thick scarves and coats. The rich aroma of fried steak filled his head as he passed by an awakening restaurant, and it made his stomach growl. When was the last time he'd eaten? A plate of steak and eggs would really taste like a deuce right now, but the sooner he finished this, he reminded himself, the better. He tested the reins a bit, and the horse responded well, making a smart stop as a sleepy-looking night watchman plodded across the street in front of him.

Bridge Square loomed ahead, once the city's prominent commercial district. He could make out the back end of City Hall as he veered right onto Washington Avenue. The wedge-shaped limestone building sat where Hennepin, Nicollet and Washington Avenues met, and sputtered out at four stories high, with a central tower adding a little extra height. Doc complained bitterly about City Hall whenever he had a chance, rightly declaring it was much too small, poorly ventilated, and a tinder-dry fire-trap ready to bring the building down on itself at the single strike of a match to a cigarette. Others agreed, and a newer City Hall, combined with a courthouse and offices for Hennepin County, was going up a few blocks away. It was partly finished and the Fire Department had already moved its offices there, but the mayor and police were still stuck in this muck hole. Christ, why couldn't the Fire Department have stayed, he wondered? Who better to deal with a fiery inferno of burning aldermen jumping from windows? On second thought, ridding Minneapolis of some of its aldermen might not be the worst idea in the world. He found himself containing a smile at the thought.

Queen's buggy rattled down the avenue for three blocks. He yanked his horse to a halt at Third Avenue, directly in front of Milwaukee Depot. This was Minneapolis' central train station, built just the year before, still sparkling new and sharp as a tack. It was tastefully designed, built of brick and three stories high, with graceful arched doorways and a truss-roofed train shed extending out of its side. The most impressive feature, however, was a 100-foot clock tower, crowned by an elaborate cupola, standing majestically above the depot and staring boastfully over the far-reaching city.

He waited, watching as a few passengers from an early train straggled out the depot's front door. A couple of boys waving newspapers ran up to a plump, jolly-looking older gentleman wearing an expensive suit and a top hat. They exchanged brief words, and the man reached into his pocket, smiling, and bought papers from both.

"Chilly morning, huh?"

Queen recoiled as a face appeared in his view, in all its weird, leering glory. How does he slip up like that? He motioned to Norbeck to get in.

"Morning, Chris. Had your regular breakfast of liquid courage yet?"

"Nope, not yet. You?" Norbeck winked a bloodshot eye as he pulled himself into the seat next to Queen.

"I don't drink this early. Usually."

Norbeck sniggered. "Neither do I, then."

"Are you trying to imitate me?" asked Queen. "I'm terribly honored."

"Why the hell would I do that?"

"Don't know. Just seems that way sometimes."

"If I want to stay up all night at saloons, I don't need you to show me how."

"Fair enough," Queen replied.

Norbeck took his ointment out and delicately dabbed it over his nose and cheeks. "So where are we going this fine winter's day?" he asked.

"Couldn't you have done that before?"

"I can't help if it feels itchy."

"You look like some specter belched up in a séance."

"What's a séance?"

"You know. Those bughouse spiritualists who think they can talk to the dead and raise ghosts from graveyards."

Usually Norbeck took great offense at blatant mockery, but this morning he just grinned. Queen never knew whether his good humor was genuine or not, and was no more enlightened today. The ointment, the acne, and his big set of yellow choppers combined were a ghastly sight.

"Boo," Norbeck said.

Between the hunger pains and Norbeck's face, Queen felt his stomach turn. He stepped up from his seat, lowered himself to the sidewalk and turned towards the station.

"Where are you going?"

"Pipe down and try not to wake up the city. I see someone I might know. It'll just take a minute."

Queen crossed the street to where the boys were sitting on their bundles of newspapers. As he got closer, he recognized the shorter one and called out.

"Ollie!"

As Ollie looked up, Queen saw a flash of fear in his eyes. The other boy, sinewy and rough looking, wore a look of malignant derision under his scruff of wild orange hair. Queen doubled his stride to reach them before they could tie up their papers and run.

"What's got you so scared?" the detective asked, huffing up to the two. He aimed the question at Ollie, but carefully watched the older boy from the corner of his eye. The boy was chewing on a cigar stub, wore a coat three sizes too big and crossed his arms defiantly. Queen thought the kid's stare might burn a hole through him. Ollie shoved his hands hard into his pockets, staring down at his brogans. He looked like a tortoise, with his wool cap pulled down tight over curly brown hair.

"Does this guy know who I am?" Queen asked Ollie.

Ollie looked up, glanced quickly at his companion, and then nodded his head once.

The detective turned to the orange haired boy. "What's your name, son?"

"None o' your business anyway."

"Well, if you're not going to be friendly with me, then get the hell out of here. I don't have time for you right now, or I'd spank your freckled bum and haul you down to a Central cell for insolence."

The boy's face sizzled with fury, and he spat his little cigar nub out onto the sidewalk. "Put me there, I don't give a damn. I'll just get out."

"Listen, I have a matter to discuss with your friend, here. If you know who I am, then you know I have a reputation of pounding down men who prevent me from doing my work. You're not even close to being a man yet, but I'll make an exception for you because you're a snot-nosed little son of a bitch." Queen lifted his fists like a pugilist and glared at the boy.

"Ha," he said, his voice breaking slightly. "My name is Mc-Cartan, and my pap was Patterfeet McCartan. He knocked out twenty men, includin' Lou Knockabout in Kansas City. If he was here he'd break your nose and smash your ears."

"Well he's not, so scram."

"He can stay," Ollie said.

"No, he can't," Queen replied.

"If you want to talk to me, then he stays."

"Why? Is this fellow part of the gang you told me about?"

McCartan curled his lip into a snarl and he turned to Ollie. "You told him about our gang?"

"I just told him he could find me here. Nothin' else."

Queen leaned in towards the orange-haired newsboy. "He told me a lot. He told me you were the toughest gang of boys in Minneapolis. He said, Don't mess with this McCartan fella either. The worst delinquent in the city."

"The city? Ha! Try the state. I spent three years at the Red Wing Reformatory. And as for our gang? We're the toughest in Minneapolis, and we're just gettin' goin'."

"I don't know about that. I've seen plenty of bad ones. What do you call yourselves?"

"Ain't gonna tell you," McCartan said, smirking at his secret.

Queen scratched his chin thoughtfully. "In some circles I'm considered the best detective in Minneapolis. Did you know that?"

"Sure," said McCartan. "What of it? That don't scare me."

"Well," Queen continued. "Every great detective needs a nemesis. An enemy as smart as he is. Have you ever read Sherlock Holmes?"

Ollie mouthed a "Yes" as McCartan shrugged indifferently.

"He's from England, and every so often he knocks heads with a devious criminal called Professor Moriarty. I've got some of the stories at home, too, if you're interested in reading them."

"He can't rea –" Ollie started, before McCartan gave him a shove in the head.

"Maybe I will," the orange-headed boy said, puffing up his chest a little. "I like to spread out around the fire at night with a bottle of Duffy's Pure and a newspaper sometimes. I even got some copies of the *New York World*. I think them Yellow Kid pictures are super."

"If you truly are the mastermind behind a great gang," Queen asked him, "Then what does it matter if I know its name? If you're as cunning as you suggest, then you have nothing to worry about."

"Well, all right then," McCartan answered, his eyes betraying an idea dawning in his brain. "I guess there ain't no harm. We're called the 'Don't Tell Gang,' and don't you damn well forget it. I figure we'll be a thorn in your side 'fore you know what hit you."

"And how many are in your gang?"

"Four of us now." He lifted a dirty hand and counted each out on his fingers. "Me, Dirk, Spindle and Ollie. Oh, and Ollie's brother, when he's old enough anyway. That'll make five."

Queen's brow furrowed. "You've got a brother, Ollie? Where does he live?"

"Not in the boat with the rest of us. At home with my ma."

"Awww, hell," McCartan said, flicking his finger against Ollie's ear. "Don't tell him where our hideout is. I'll bet the perfesser didn't tell old Sure Lock Homer where he lived, did he?"

A locomotive whistle blew, and Queen looked up at the sky. It was starting to get lighter now, and he needed to hurry. "Listen, Ollie. I need your help. It's about your friend Maisy. That's my rig across the street, and I need you to come with me. We have to get down to the flats right away."

"Maisy?" Ollie's face dropped. "I'll go. Do you mind, Mc-Cartan? There's still a pile of papers settin here."

"Is this about that dead girl?" replied McCartan, his eyes growing large. He sniffed and wiped his sleeve against his pug nose. "My poor ol' ma was in the same line of work, and died from getting strangled in her sleep. If you're as good a bull as you say, go find who did this and bring 'im here. I'll stab him one straight and then a give it a little twist for dear ol' Mother."

"You brought your gun?" Queen asked Norbeck, as he returned to the driver's seat. Ollie scrambled over him and wedged himself between the two detectives.

"Of course." Norbeck looked at Ollie and laughed. "I recognize him. Are we gonna stop somewhere for ice cream sodees?"

"How many bullets do you have?"

Norbeck's eyebrows lifted. "You've got us doin' somethin' dangerous, huh?"

"We're going to get those girls of Dander's. Emil handed the address over to me yesterday."

"I thought the colonel told us not to get our noses into this."

"He did."

"Oh." Norbeck scratched his head. "Okay."

"The thing is, that creepy little rat Pock is going to be nearby, I think. I'm going to talk to this Ace fellow, but I need you to guard against Pock."

"What's the kid for?"

"Do you want to deal with these women if they're hysterical?"

"Well, it'd be like going home to my wife."

"If they're acting all bughouse, you can handle it, right?" Queen asked, turning back to Ollie.

"They trust me, if that's what you mean."

"Do me a favor and don't tell me any more," Norbeck said. "I'm glad you asked me to come, and all, but I don't want no trouble with Ames. I don't have a long leash like you do."

"Good, because I don't feel like talking."

As they bumped along, Queen mulled over the prior afternoon's events. He and Cahill had gone back to City Hall, both to make their presence known to the Ames brothers, and to witness the inauguration festivities, which were as colorful as expected. Crowds surged through the corridors, taking every available foot of floor to witness the goings on. Some stood three deep on desks and even on the railings for a glimpse of Mayor Gray's abdication and Doc Ames' triumphant assumption of the executive chair. Ames gave Queen his usual broad smile and firm handshake when they met, but had only a moment for him. The new mayor was far too preoccupied basking in the adoration of the masses to give any one person more than a few seconds of his illustrious presence. Queen noticed Ames's bodyguard Fred Connor moving fluidly alongside him, keeping a respectful distance but ready for any uncomfortable situation. Fred Ames was there too, of course, having his own conversations with businessmen and aldermen, always focused and never quite happy. Cigar smoke choked the air. The voices and laughter were merry and wild. Despite the chaos, however, everyone was quite courteous and mostly sober. Colonel Ames's edict that all available officers on the force show up as security turned out to have been a tad over-cautious. Most of the cops just milled around in their smart blue uniforms, performing monotonous functions like ordering the occasional clown down from atop a banister.

Queen lost Cahill at his first chance and visited the tele-graph and telephone desk, where he found Operator Jones leaning back in his chair and stuffing himself with a celebra-tory chicken sandwich. On a typical evening Jones would both operate the telegraph and man the telephone, taking reports and emergency calls from patrolmen at police boxes scattered through the city streets. Tonight most of the patrolmen were here, and business was slow. He dragged the man up into the proper sitting position and gave him a telegram to send. Queen knew Dander had probably fed him a false name, but Ollie had identified the town as Minot and Queen thought it was worth another shot. After brushing bread crumbs from his fingers, Jones tapped out the dispatch with expert speed. Queen got lucky with a message two hours later. Sheriff Eagleton knew a Maisy Anderson. She was the granddaughter to the former sheriff. Yes, he would pass word on to him that she was dead and to contact the Minneapolis police department for arrangements. Queen had considered sending another dispatch to ask Eagleton for more information about Maisy, but he didn't want to keep the operator banging away on his telegraph all night. Better to wait for the return message he knew would come, inevitably, from this Dix Anderson.

He continued taking advantage of the party around him by slipping into the basement room where case files were kept, to try to learn more about Maisy's disappearance. The paperwork he'd found was scant on details. She'd traveled to the city as a University of Minnesota freshman but no one could remember seeing the girl on the train or at the station. Evidently Sheriff Anderson had immediately come to Minneapolis and curried some favor, which had led to an investigation. But there hadn't been much they could do without witnesses. Dozens of girls went missing every year in Minneapolis, and in his report the detective in charge speculated that she had just decided not to get off, but kept going, probably to Chicago or New York. Queen scoffed when he read it. Every good policeman knew what happened to many of these missing women; they were abducted and forced into prostitution. Dander had said he'd seduced Maisy, but he'd obviously been looking for innocent young women fresh off the train to snatch and enslave. Whether she'd fallen for his good looks and sweet tongue, or had been lured away with some other promise or lie, it had been one hell of a horrible moment in her life. Anger boiled inside him as he replayed the imagined exchange in his head. How Dander had probably offered to show her around the city or carry her bags, or give her a ride to the campus. Probably the first time she'd ever encountered a lecherous snake like Dander, oozing with oily charm, a sharp suit and that deceptively handsome face.

"Christ, Harm, watch where you're going!" Norbeck cried.

He pulled the reins back hard and the hack jolted to a stop, just in front of a woman and her baby carriage crossing the street. He tipped his hat apologetically, but she glared and furiously pushed the carriage past him.

"What is she doing out for a promenade at seven thirty in the morning in the month of January?" he grumbled.

"You want me to drive?"

"We're almost there."

"Which is where?" Norbeck asked.

"The Mississippi flats. Here's the address." He handed Norbeck the note. "I haven't been down there for a while. You know where it is?"

"109 Mill Street, huh? Well, once we get down to the bottom, there are only three main roads through. I'm pretty sure it's near the bridge."

"Which one?"

"Washington," Norbeck said, as he made a final dab and screwed the cap back onto his ointment.

With a flick of the reins, they picked up speed and made their way toward the Washington Avenue Bridge, which spanned the Mississippi River. When they got to the foot, Queen slowed down to make way for a clanging streetcar heading east toward the University of Minnesota. The revered school on the opposite bank comprised a handful of majestic buildings that hugged the top of the bluff.

"That's the way down, see?" Norbeck said, pointing to a dirt road that veered to the left, just before the bridge.

"Yeah, I know where it is," Queen replied. Looking down, he could make out much of the road through the skeletal snow-smattered trees. "Christ, it is steep." He climbed down to get a better view, buttoning his jacket. "It's in poor condition," he remarked, looking up at Norbeck with a shake of his head. Ollie leapt down like a cat.

Norbeck stood up from his seat and peered down to get his own view, grasping the frame for support. "I don't think we can make it down in this rig, Harm." He hopped out and tugged on the hackney's wheel as if to test its durability.

"We're going to have to leave it here," Queen agreed. He turned to Ollie, who had already taken a few steps down the path. "Hey, kid. I need you to stay here and watch it."

"You're joshing me, aren't you? Who would boost this prime piece of garbage?" he asked. Norbeck laughed at this one.

"These girls will need a ride out of here. I don't want to take a chance of it getting stolen."

"What about a trolley? They run right past here."

"We don't want any attention. If Dander's man is creeping around here, he might try and follow us. A streetcar is predictable."

Ollie crossed his arms. "This isn't why I came. I want to help find whoever killed Maisy. Also, if you don't remember, I've met Ace before. I told you about him, for crying out loud. Why doesn't *he* stay instead?" Ollie jabbed his elbow at Norbeck, who looked up from picking at one of his scabs, surprised to be included in the conversation.

"I don't want a surprise from Pock, and Detective Norbeck's armed."

"Well, who are two men against an ambush, anyway?"

Queen sighed. "Come on, kid. I'll owe you one. We'll be back in a heartbeat. I'll buy you lunch and dinner and an ice cream sundae."

The light in Ollie's eyes brightened. "I'll tell you what. You have a deal, but only if you agree to this. I want dinner at Coffee John's. The whole works. Oysters, clams, steak, and a fat baked potato in a bowl of butter. And a nice bottle of fancy red wine."

"You are how old?" Queen asked suspiciously. "Certainly not old enough to drink. In case you've forgotten, I'm a Minneapolis police detective. A lieutenant. You think I'm going to buy you booze?"

"I'm fifteen, but I won't tell nobody."

"Do you know how many cops eat there?"

Ollie licked his lips, and thought for a moment. "No wine. But I want enough food for my whole gang, all four of us." He spit in his palm and stuck out his hand. "And my brother. And my ma."

"How much cush do you think I have? Do you think I've got silver dollars falling from my ears?"

"Fine, I'll be seeing you around then," Ollie blurted out, and he turned and started for the streetcar stop.

"Wait just a moment," Queen said, his hands on his hips. Ollie halted and squinted at him coolly. "Here's the deal," Queen continued, "and as a man who's spent more than his fair share of time at gaming tables, I know that I've been thoroughly fleeced. You and your friends'll get dinner, but it'll be packed up and given to you outside the restaurant. You can have a picnic under a lovely January moon, or just take it back to your boat hideout and scarf it down there. Take it or not, but I'm not shaking that hand."

"All right. Deal!" Ollie replied brightly. He could barely contain a smile as he climbed back onto the buggy's front seat and put his feet up on the harness.

"Jesus, Harm, Coffee John charges too much for them oysters of his as it is. Multiply that times six!" said Norbeck.

"Forget it, Chris. Let's go."

They began their descent of the hill, which was even steeper than it looked and plenty icy. There were a series of twists and turns, and Queen had to brace himself twice with his hands as he fell backwards on the slick ground. Norbeck wasn't having any better luck, and his face knotted as he concentrated on each footstep.

"So if we find these girls, how are we going to get them back up this hill?" he asked Queen.

"I'm wondering that myself. Christ, will you look at that?" Norbeck looked in the direction of Queen's gaze to see a file of men trudging up the road opposite them. Each carried a lunch pail in one hand, and many held a shovel or toolbox in the other. All wore coarse clothing and work caps. "It must be their boots," Norbeck muttered.

As they closed the gap between them, the first man in line, sporting a thick black beard, stared at them suspiciously. He waited until he could speak directly across the slippery roadway. "What are you two fellers doing, going down to the flats?" he asked. As he stopped, the men behind him ground to a halt as well, all looking at them warily.

"We've heard the ice fishing is good this time of year. Just want to see for ourselves."

"Dressed in suits and with no fish poles?" The man put down his lunch pail and lifted his shovel menacingly into both hands. "Just 'cause we live on the flats don't make us stupid."

Queen smiled. "What are you going to do with that?"

"There's a dozen of us and two of you. My wife and children are down there. These fellas too. I want to know if you're goddamn rent collectors or not."

Might as well tell them, he thought. He pulled out his badge and held it out to the man. "We're police detectives. I'm Queen, and this is Norbeck. We're looking for someone who lives on Mill Street. 102 is the number. At least that's what we've been told. He goes by the name of Ace."

"Mill, huh?" the man asked, narrowing his eyes. "Should be right up against the Washington bridge column." He turned to the men behind him. "Ain't that the old Svoboda place?" Grunts of confirmation rolled through the group and he looked back at Queen, confident of his identification. "There is a man living there, all right. He keeps to himself, and acts all queer and nervous, like he don't want nothing to do with the rest of us."

"That's him," said Queen. "Another question, if you don't mind. There is a second man we're looking for. Give 'em a description, Norbeck."

"Looks like a five-and-a-half-foot rat, come to earth especially to screw with us."

"Christ," Queen said with a disapproving shake of his head. "A little more detail would be nice."

A shaky hand shot up from the group of men. "I seen him," he said. "All shifty-eyed, and with a pointy nose. He had holes all over his face." He shrugged a little and pointed at Norbeck. "Not like the sores on his—more like pockmarks."

"And hence the name," Queen confirmed. "Where was he?"

"By the garbage dump. It sits right in front of the house. Most of the houses. He was darting around a couple of days ago. My kids were picking through it looking for stuff to sell when he popped out and scared them half to death."

Queen had forgotten about the dump. It was one of the biggest in Minneapolis. Multiple tons of garbage were brought there every day, left in pits by the river's edge. The stench wasn't as bad in the winter, of course, but during the summer he remembered how much the levee stank of rot.

"He must be sleeping somewhere," said Norbeck.

"There's a few abandoned places around," offered the black-bearded man. He had grown more relaxed in his stance, and leaned on his shovel. Obviously relieved that we're not looking for money, Queen thought.

"You can try asking one of the pickers," the man continued. "They'd likely help you if he's still nosing around."

Queen nodded. "How do the garbage carts get down this steep slope with the snow and the ice?"

"When it's like this they use other dumps. They come every day in fair weather, and even in winter whenever the road is safe. Speaking of this road, I've got something for you that might help," the man said. He reached into his pocket and pulled out some heavy sandpaper. Attach this to the bottom of your shoes. Nail it if you can, but a piece of twine and a tight knot will do in a pinch. It'll help the walk back up."

Queen nodded his thanks. "Appreciate your help. If you ever need any favors from the police, come and find me. I'm a man who always returns a good deed for another."

"Kind of you. My name's Hare." He introduced them to the others, and they amicably parted company.

The next bend allowed them an excellent view of the levee. The flats were a ramshackle community, houses of all shapes and sizes. The ones closest to the water were the worst built, shanties barely held together with driftwood and nails. In the houses elevated farther from floodplain and closer to God, the owners could afford stone foundations and chimneys and real plank siding. No one, though, would ever claim this was a well-to-do part of town. While it looked as Bohemian as its popular name "Bohemian Flats" suggested, Queen had heard from the patrolmen who worked this beat that of its twelve hundred or so residents, most weren't actually from Bohemia. A collection of Czechs, Germans, Poles, Scandinavians and the Irish lived poor and packed-in lives, in special fear every spring that the Mississippi might rise higher than it should. Whenever the thaw sent the river over the levees, it forced them to collect and carry their sparse but precious belongings to higher, dryer ground.

When the detectives reached the bottom of the hill they picked their way through the collection of shacks. Many were shoved so close together there was barely breathing room for the junk wedged between. A few high wooden fences offered the inhabitants some vestige of privacy. On a side street approaching the river, Queen looked up at the campus on the opposite bluff. That is where Maisy had planned to attend school, he thought. And now we're looking for answers to her murder just a stone's throw away, in a wretched slum built next to a garbage dump.

"This way," Norbeck said, as they paused at a slightly wider street. "This is Mill. Should be that one, right there." The concrete column of the Washington Bridge loomed over the house, casting it into a blurry shadow.

"Any sign of Pock?" Queen asked, looking at piles of trash strewn everywhere. Old shoes, broken bottles, tobacco stems, leather straps and stable refuse littered the riverbank and all the way up to the front doors of the first row of houses. Women's bustles, high heels and hoops discarded by garbage carts sat next to rotting apples and old rags. A handful of thinly dressed children walked slowly through the waste, carrying ominous-looking sticks with hooks on them. One used his hook to yank up a piece of rotting wood through the film of snow, and together the children lugged it to a wagon. A bent old man tried to help them lift it, but all seemed to struggle in slow motion. It was as if the cold, dull morning was caving in on them and they hadn't had enough breakfast to spark a scrap of energy.

"Let's make this fast," Queen said. They stood at the door of a miserable hovel, with number 109 crudely painted on the front step. Queen noticed smoke coming from a metal pipe on the roof, and rapped on the door. Norbeck cupped his ear and leaned in, listening intently.

"I think I hear 'em movin' about."

"Open up! We're police detectives," Queen shouted. "Now, or I toe your door!"

After a moment of arguing and a woman's stifled half-scream, they heard a lock snap open, and both men instinctively pulled out their guns. Queen felt the nerves in his neck twinge with anticipation, and a sudden barrage of thoughts flooded his head. If Pock is in there, he's going to be armed to his rodent teeth. Could this be some kind of elaborate ruse that Dander had planned to trap them? He reached for the knob but it turned from the other side, and suddenly the door flew open. A tall bespectacled man in a grimy robe stood before them, with his hands stretched to the sky.

"Egads! Don't hurt me! Don't hurt me! Whatever you do, don't hurt me!" he cried, and then dropped to his knees and gave a pathetic moan.

"Son of a bitch," Queen said.

"You know this nervous Nelly?" Norbeck asked with a shake of his head.

"Yeah, I do," he replied, putting his gun back into his holster. "It's Harry Hayward's brother, Adry. This is the far less famous Hayward brother, the one who didn't swing. Get the hell off the floor, 'Ace.' And put some clothes on."

"Th-th-thank you, Harm," Adry stuttered, pulling himself up and awkwardly drawing his robe tight over his pale, hairless chest. "Whatever you say. Come in! Come in!"

The inside of the house wasn't much better than the outside. The rot of wet wood permeated the air, mixed with the odor of burnt bread. Queen noted several pallets on the dirt floor, covered with thin blankets, and a rusty stove in the corner. Adry moved towards a pile of clothes on the floor, and dug around before pulling out a pair of trousers and a shirt, and started clumsily putting them on.

"We heard women in here, Adry," Queen said. "Where are they?"

"Yes, yes!" Adry exclaimed. He buttoned his shirt and pulled a pair of limp suspenders up over his shoulders. He smoothed what little hair he had back from his tall forehead, finally gesturing to a door along the far wall. "Another room. Girls, come out! The cavalry has arrived!" His eyes bulged as he shouted.

"Damn if we will!" called out an angry, high-pitched voice.

Adry gave a sheepish smile. "You'll have to excuse them. They may be in a state of undress, as I myself was." He wiped his fingers over his waxy, pencil-thin mustache, and tapped his toe nervously. "Girls, please, get yourselves presentable and come out at once!"

"I don't get this," Norbeck said. He pulled his finger over a layer of grime on a rough-hewn wood table and wiped it on his pants. "You pay hard-earned cush for top-of-the-line whores and you live like a pig in a pen?"

"My needs are few," Adry said with an embarrassed grin. "But I do like to provide my... shall we say, my libido, with proper nourishment."

"A nice little arrangement for you, Adry," Queen said as he stepped through the litter on the floor toward the shut door.

"Tell me, are you still paying Emil to use these girls as whim-whams, or is he paying you to keep them safe?" He shook the doorknob. It was locked, of course.

"It's not like that at all, Harm. They came to me on their own accord. I know you've come about Maisy, as well." He shook his head dolefully. "You've probably heard stories about the two of us. I did love her, you know. If you're considering me as a suspect, search my house. I own no weapons. I could never hurt a hair on the top of any young woman's head, and especially that poor sweet girl."

"And you gave her this?" Queen pulled the stickpin out of his pocket and held it into the dusty light. "She had it sewn into the hem of her gown."

"That was mine," Adry said with a pathetic nod. "She was carrying it with her when she was shot? How tragic."

"It was actually your brother's. He was going to be buried wearing it. Funny how it should end up in your possession."

Adry swallowed hard. "Yes, I took it. I decided it wouldn't do anyone any good under six feet of soil. And with his reputation, I assumed that grave robbers would eventually pilfer him of every article of clothing and strand of hair on his head to sell as souvenirs."

"I remember a lot about the trial, Adry. Harry had tried to enlist you to help him kill Kitty Ging, hadn't he? He called you a weak-willed coward. You'd considered it, hadn't you, helping to murder her? Brotherly loyalty? The promise of greenbacks? You were even collared for the crime, if I recall correctly."

"No!" Adry cried. He'd been anxiously wrapping his hand around his suspenders, and gripped them tight as the accusation touched him. "It was a sweatbox confession they tried to wring from me, but I stood firmly by the truth. It was proven in a court of law that I had nothing to do with it! My brother was a heartless fiend. He used me to try and deflect suspicion from him. He even accused me of being insane! *Off my rocker!*"

"But Harry had asked you to help him?"

"He asked me if I was willing to kill a woman for $2,000. I said I was not willing to kill anyone." Adry pulled up a chair and sat down wearily as he continued. "He said it was easy to do it, and nobody would be suspicious of me. He said it would be easy to kill her while driving in a hack, and if need be the hackman could be killed too. After that he suggested getting her drowned in a lake, but that looked too much like suicide and he gave up. Then he wondered how she would fall if he took her riding in a buggy and it should strike a boulder, whether he could get her body to fall out, or maybe get her tangled up in the lines and have the horses run away."

"He confided all of this to you, but didn't push you any harder to help him."

"I told him it would be an awful thing to kill a woman. Eventually he said he was through with me, that I had no nerve."

"And you have no nerve," Queen said.

"I have no nerve," Adry confirmed. He sighed pitifully. "I'm not a killer."

"So," said Queen. "Where were you on New Year's Eve, Adry? The night that Maisy Anderson was murdered?" He squinted his eyes intently at Hayward. "Don't flub-dub me, either. The last time you were questioned by detectives you broke down like a three-wheeled wagon."

Adry hung his head low. "I was with my wife, at home."

Norbeck threw his head back and guffawed. "You're a real weasel, ain't you?"

"If you want to know who killed her, ask them." Adry pointed to the door behind which the girls were hiding. "They saw everything."

"And you're a fool for getting yourself wrapped up in this. You've always got a way of bringing trouble to yourself." After trying the knob again and feeling its empty wobble, Queen felt his temper begin to surface like a freight train from a dark tunnel. "I've no damned time to fool," he said, as he banged on the door. "Come out of there!"

"Screw!" came a voice from inside, shrill and furious.

And then a gun fired, the crack echoing sharply against the bluffs, and the front window splintered. Queen whirled around, saw the sharp hole and the cracks through the glass, and then followed the bullet's path to the door he'd just tried to open. The bullet had bored into the plank, plowing clean through. Adry dived to the dirt floor, hands clasped over his ears, and crawled frantically under the table on his knees and elbows. He cowered underneath, softly sobbing. Queen and Norbeck crouched low, revolvers in hand. One of the girls was screaming from behind the wall.

"It came from the river," Norbeck said.

Queen gave Adry a soft kick at his head. "Is there a rear exit?" the detective asked sharply.

Adry peeked between his hands at Queen. "Yes! Yes! The back room has a door. But you have to get past those screaming whores."

Queen nodded grimly. "Fire a couple of shots out there, Chris. Show 'im we mean business. I'm gonna bust this door down."

Norbeck gave a furtive wink and threw a heavy can of coffee through the window, expanding the hole into a chasm. He jumped up and pulled his trigger, aiming at the piles of garbage fluttering in the frozen wind. Queen stood and smashed his shoulder against the door, easily breaking it, and stepped through. His heart was pounding as he scanned the dark little room. Then he felt the intense pain of something smashing into his back. He staggered to a knee, but threw himself around and caught the board with his hand before it came down onto him again. Staring at him through the darkness was a stunningly pretty young girl, with blazing brown eyes, dark brown hair, and an acorn-shaped face. Her lip was curled like a cornered cur's might be, teeth ready to tear his throat into pieces. He tried to yank the board from her miniature hand, but she was deceptively strong, and tried to pry it from his, too. Their fury was equal, but he was stronger. He twisted the plank from her grasp, throwing it against the wall. The girl stepped back, eyes seething and scouring the room for anything else she might turn into a weapon.

"I need to leave from the back," he huffed.

"You shot at us!" she shrieked, moving towards a figure in the corner. It was another girl, who had a look of absolute horror screwed onto her face. They clung to each other, dressed in meager men's nightshirts, probably Adry's, pushing themselves back against the wall, so frantic and fearful that their bodies rose up inches from the strain.

Queen felt a stab of sympathy for them, and suddenly forgave the wild one for the throbbing pain where her blow had landed. "It was Pock," he said in a low voice. "Dander's henchman. He's been watching this place, and now, for whatever reason, he wants to kill you, or me, or all of us. I'm going to go get him."

They stared at him with eyes that looked pasted open, unblinking and unmoving. He unlatched the lock on the rear door, slowly pushing it open. A cascade of light came pouring in, and he saw their faces better. The girl he had tussled with was definitely beautiful, and the new light gave her an angelic sheen, highlighting a pair of lips that were delicate and full. The other girl was homelier, with a pointed witch's nose and a slight overbite, and she was far from smiling now. Queen figured she might be a little more becoming in a happier moment.

"If you want to live, don't leave this place. Hide yourselves. I'm a Minneapolis police detective, and I have a partner in front. We're going to take you somewhere safe." The girl with the pretty face blinked once, in the barest acknowledgement. He paused, straightened his tie a little, and stared at them as they stared back.

"I'm not here to hurt you." Their tear-stained faces calmed, but their breasts heaved with emotion under their thin garments. The silent girl in the corner was shuddering. What the hell else am I supposed to say? Queen realized his shoe was untied so he bent over, fumbling with the shoelaces before pulling them tight. Finished, he stood up, awkwardly tipped his hat and turned for the door.

"Wait!" the fiery, lovely girl cried. He turned back to her.

"It was *him*. Pock killed Maisy." Her face was hard and resolute.

"And you saw it? Are you absolutely sure, miss?"

"I'm sure. She tried to get away and he shot her. On the fence. I saw everything from my window."

He stood silent for a moment, searching for the truth in her eyes. Finally, he gave a brief nod and ran out.

CHAPTER 6

T HE MEN IN BLUE HAD FINALLY seen fit to release him, and the time was right. Idle talk filled the crowded cell, and while he never, ever partook in conversation with grown men unless necessary, he liked to absorb information in his own way. Word had spread quickly about the goings-on in the wretched whore-mongers' house in Hell's Half Acre. He gleaned from his cellmates' banter that the bastard pimp had been captured and was being held now, just above them, with possible murder charges under way. That meant his prushun was free and roaming the thoroughfares, and he knew it was the opportune time to act. By divine luck a guard had arrived that night to release him, leaving him free to complete his task.

The dirty ragged men had parted from his way like the waves of the Red Sea as he strolled out into freedom. A policeman had given him back his haversack, which he now wore strapped close to his body. The breeze was bitingly cold, but he needed the sensation to feel alive. Very few things awoke his senses like the weather did. It could blast the internal rot away with a single gust and make him feel pure and young. The sharp wind made his manhood flow strong and thick.

He'd known for weeks where his prushun lay, but it had disappeared now, which meant more difficulty for him than he wanted, but he wasn't worried. Death and birth were natural cycles, and though he had to end the life of the first, it would make way for the blossom of new innocence, which he needed close to him, to cradle, and to live.

His destination this morning was the depot, and he walked with long strides, ignoring those he shared the sidewalks with. Occasionally someone would take pity on him, as he trudged down the road, offering him a ride on the back of their wagon, but he always preferred to walk. Things with hooves and wheels put him on edge. They took away his control, and above all else, he despised losing control. There was rarely anywhere so important he needed to be that would require him to use anything but his own two legs. In rare situations, he'd take a train with the other tramps, but always picked a place close to a door or between boxcars. He needed to get off in his own time, as he saw fit. He'd heard stories of hoboes getting locked in cars and trapped for days, and this was a fate he wanted no part of.

As he marched toward the depot, he took a piece of candy from his bag and sucked on it. It was a chocolate bon-bon, not his favorite, but it was sweet, and most importantly gave him a surge of fire through his body. The sugar crystallized his mind into sharp clarity, which he needed to complete his sacrifice. The manna of babes had to flow within his veins to accomplish the inevitable, sacred act.

Oh merciful God, he thought, laying his eyes on a figure sitting on a bundle of newspapers. There is my divining rod, and it will show me the way. He watched and waited, focused on the figure's movements, as it moved with its papers from person to person. Sometimes it took money and sometimes it spit on the heels of those who ignored it. It was much too old for him, he thought. He preferred the ones that shone of innocence, and this one, with its garish orange hair and spotted face, did nothing but provoke hatred in him. He could be patient, though, and continued to wait until the pile of papers began to disappear. Once they were gone, he knew he needed to act swiftly, and he placed another piece of candy into his mouth. This one had a strawberry filling, and he liked it much more than the last. As he sucked the last of the chocolate coating off his fingers, the figure began to move, and he did with it.

It jaunted down the avenue like a dirty little whore. He picked up his pace to make up the ground, watching for the perfect moment, when no one would see. For three blocks he followed, edging closer to it, but still kept back far enough to avoid notice. He examined the prints it left behind in the snow; toes curved in like a stunted pig, and tasted bile in his throat. These imperfections were created by God as evil on earth, but *he* was created by God as its antidote, and would scour its face clean at the proper time. He watched it bump into a man walking the opposite way, lifting the wallet from his pocket as smoothly and fluidly as fresh cream poured from a bucket. Half a block later, it turned into an alley, and the moment revealed itself.

When he rounded the corner, it was sitting on a crate, counting out money, the wallet already discarded on the ground. This appeared to be the only way into the alley; a fence blocked the other end. Another sign from the Lord.

Its face was concentrated on the bills laid out on its lap, and it cackled gleefully, full of its own putrid cleverness. The filthy harlot didn't even look up at him until he stood by its side. His broad shoulders blocked most of the alley's width, but it didn't seem afraid.

"What the hell do you want?" it said with a sneer. "You'd best be off, trout-face, and staying away from me. My whole gang will be here soon. Let me alone and go bother someone else."

"You took that man's money, young chap," he said with a smile. "Aren't you old enough to do a day's worth of honest work?"

"Look at you," it taunted. "You're a goddamn hobo. Don't talk to me about real work 'til you done some yerself. Run off, 'fore the 'Don't Tell Gang' come a-callin' and you get the beating of your smelly ol' life."

"How old are you anyway?" the man asked. "You look to be no more than twelve."

"You goddamn asshole!" it shouted, leaping up. "I'm seventeen years old. Old enough not to be scared of nothing, especially a rotten trampity-tramp like you." It reached into its sock and retrieved a sharp little job-jab, brandishing it with a vicious smile. "I stuck a man straight through his wrist once when he tried to hit me. I brung this knife down faster than he could lay his blow."

The man had had enough with the games. He swung his fist much, much faster than this whore had ever seen, and smashed it across the face, spraying teeth and blood into the brick wall. It went down in a whimpering heap, its face too heavy and cloudy to lift. It tried to talk but nothing coherent came out, except the gurgling of more blood, dribbling out like an invalid at a sanitarium dinner. It weakly waved its arms back, as though it were out for a morning swim, which made him feel uncomfortable to watch. So he leaned down and put his thick leg over it's back and shoulders, pinning them to the ground. Closely, quietly, he whispered into its ear.

"The one called Ollie. Tell me where it is." He pulled a rag out of his bag and pushed its mouth open, wiping blood and another tooth out. "Where?" he repeated.

"I d-don't know," the whore croaked, straining its head up to look the man in the eyes. "Never heard the name."

"Listen to me. You look like a boy who knows all the other little boys in the neighborhood. This one is of particular importance to me. Do you want me to pull the nails from your fingers, one by one? Or cut your ass into pieces and cook them over a fire?"

It shook its head violently, and he could feel its body tremble under his weight. It was gasping for air, limp and battered by his threat. It seemed to contemplate its situation for a moment. He caught the strain and agony on its face as it struggled over what to do. Finally, it began to talk.

"He went with a police detective. They were gonna go find some girls. Down to the flats." It groaned from his weight and made a feeble attempt to twist free, but they both knew it was useless. "You know about the flats?" it finally choked in a whisper.

The whore's little job-jab was a few inches away from its hand, and he reached over to pick it up. He twirled it in his long fingers. It clicked against his uncut, broken nails.

"I know of the place," he replied. He sighed inwardly, and felt a strange twang of melancholy ripple through him. It wasn't supposed to be this easy. He had divine tools given to him by a vengeful God, and it felt shameful to use them with such laxity.

The grubby little pig opened its mouth, involuntarily because of the pressure, and the lines between its teeth were still stained with a thin red film. Its gaping mouth looked like a vile vessel for the anti-Christ's dirty work. It made him sick with disgust to look at.

He laid the job-jab on the ground, and reached into his bag, withdrawing a claw hammer. Lovingly, he ran his fingers over the smooth wooden handle. A gift from his father when he was sixteen, and the only material memory of his childhood, it had seen him through long hours of day labor and soft nights of bliss with his pliant, lovely prushuns. The end was whittled to a sharp point, his own personal alteration.

He needed a test. A test of his transcendent gifts. He wrapped his hand around the hammer's grip and held it over its writhing head. Whether it chose to cry or not was none of his concern, but only to rid the earth of one more open wound.

With the force of muscles born of a thousand fights, and a brief, shivering rush of pleasure, he stuck the handle of the hammer down into the back of its neck, slowly and carefully, until it came out the other side and met the dirt.

There was a small yard behind Hayward's wretched house, and Queen passed out its back gate and through the little alley until he was under the bridge's shadow. The supporting column was much wider than he was tall, and stood stoically like a concrete monument to the floodplain's gods. He circled around the column and toward the river, searching for a glimpse of Pock. I should have tied some of that sandpaper on my shoes, he thought. He hadn't slipped yet, though, even jogging at a brisk pace.

His fingers were beginning to feel slick with sweat, and he paused in the darkness behind the massive bridge support to shove the gun into his holster and wipe his hands dry. He patted his pockets for his gloves, but they were gone. He was breathing hard and the cold air turned his exhalations into tufts of icy mist. I've barely made it out the door and I'm already used up, he thought, but there was something about a chase that excited him, too. All the problems plaguing him seemed less important when he was defending himself and others against a gun-wielding villain. Let me catch my breath and try to convince myself how insignificant they are. He'd suffered the indignity of being denied a promotion by Doc

Ames, and it gnawed on him. It wasn't Doc, though, who made the decisions. The colonel was firmly in control and didn't trust Queen, despite everything he'd done to prove his loyalty to the new mayor. This led to the mystery of Maisy's murder, and Colonel Ames's refusal to have it properly investigated. Doc had given a thousand and one campaign speeches about his firm stance on crime and the importance of swift justice. But the first violent crime on his watch was being swept under the rug, and it made Queen furious. Then there were his own financial issues, and the debt he needed to settle to get a mick crime lord from Saint Paul off his back. What else could go wrong in his life? He could die right here, for one. He could be dropped with a bullet in the head and left to die in a garbage dump. It would certainly solve all his worries. And wherever he ended up, be it a bright flowery field in heaven or the burning pits of a fiery hell, it would be a damned sight warmer than Minnesota in January.

Another crack reverberated under the bridge. He drew his weapon again and peered out of his hiding place, looking for the shot's origin. He didn't have a view of the house, as the concrete pillar stood firmly in his way, but he could see the river and much of the trash on its snowy bank. He knew Pock was hunkered down behind some pile of muck waiting for a clear shot into the shack. He wondered whether that last gunshot had come from Pock or from Norbeck, and where it had been aimed.

A layer of ice stretched nearly across the river, but he saw it thin out as it met the flux of black moving water in the center. The Mississippi's current was deceptively strong underneath. He'd been called out on duty more than once for suicides off the Washington Avenue bridge, and it was always an exhausting job to find the bodies once they'd been sucked under and swept down river. Distraught students during finals time sometimes felt enough pressure to prefer an icy plunge into oblivion over facing their parents' wrath. Then there were the children playing too close to the edge who slipped in, and the occasional boozed-up tramp camped on the bank, who by accident or malice found himself flailing for his life in the murky, treacherous depths.

Queen carefully stepped out from his cover, examining the bleak, frosted landscape for some sign of Pock. A lone bird circled some edible garbage on the river's edge, and he heard voices and a streetcar's clang above him on the bridge, seemingly close yet a world away. All signs of activity on the bank had ceased; the child garbage collectors and the old man must have vacated the dump quickly once the first gunshots ignited the air. One less thing to worry about, Queen thought. He watched the bird land between a broken crate and a pile of fat burlap sacks that were oozing their foul innards onto the ground, probably dated food from a downtown restaurant. The bird stabbed its beak at one of the bags, and then suddenly flapped its wings frantically to scoot a few feet away. The glint of a black rifle barrel poked out of the stack of sacks, and Queen was relieved that it was pointed at Adry's shack and not him.

He crept forward, hunched down, heedful of where he put his feet as he kept his eye on Pock's hiding place. There was no danger of him being in the rifle's line of fire, he figured, because the burlap sacks were firmly packed around the little prick like a cocoon. It would simply take a stealthy prowl around and behind the gun barrel, and the capture would be quick.

His shoelace was untied again, both ends flapping on the wet ground. As he bent down to retie the knot, he noticed his fingers weren't sweating anymore. Just knowing he had the upper hand was starting to slow his heartbeat to a more or less natural pace. For good measure, he took a couple of deep breaths to bring himself back to a semblance of composure.

To err on the side of caution, he chose a wider loop around, making absolutely sure he wasn't spotted from the side. But as he picked his way through the rubbish, he realized he could be seen from the shack's broken window. Christ, I hope Norbeck gets a good view of me and doesn't think I'm Pock. I'm taller and fatter and don't look like something from the sewer, so he should have the sense to not fire at me.

Another pop shattered the silence, and he whipped around to see where it came from, just in time to see splinters fly from the shack's door. I need to get him before someone gets hurt, he thought. He tried to move faster but it was tricky, maneuvering around the intermittent pockets of refuse and odd obstacles. Every foot forward was another adventure. He passed a decapitated rocking horse lying sadly on its side. With the next few paces, he found himself stepping ungracefully over a smashed baby-blue crib with a ragged blanket crumpled up inside.

He finally reached the point where he had to head back towards his prize. Each step had brought him closer to the river's edge, and he grew unsure whether he was standing on firm ground or thin ice. A cart stood directly between him and the heap of garbage hiding Pock, and he moved toward it, less cautiously now, confident in his situation. Fortunately the way was clear, and he sprinted to the cart without apprehension, gun drawn and spirits high. The cart was the perfect cover, piled up with a tangle of broken furniture, the morning work of the children he'd seen earlier. There were plenty of cracks to see through, and he viewed the object of his desire, the stinking stack of burlap sacks, wiggling and heaving from his foe's little body squirming inside. He crouched down to think. Maybe he has to piss, and he's having a hard time re-

moving his trousers. The thought of this cheered him completely. I'll walk right up behind, point my pistol at the back
of his head, tell him to throw his weapon to the ground and
order him out. He'll be sharing a cell with Dander and Higgins
before lunchtime.

Queen steadied himself with a hand on the cart's wheel.
He readied himself to move, said a quick prayer to his dead
mother, and threw himself up and forward, using the wheel as
leverage to give himself a little momentum. The cart creaked
and rolled backwards under his grip, and dropped on his foot
before he could pull it away.

He let out a groan as he fell backwards, landing hard on
the packed snow and splaying himself out like a stranded fish.
With a push of his elbows and a groan he sat up, and then
managed to stand. His muscles strained as he shoved, pulled
and rocked the wheel with every ounce of his strength, but
it made no movement. Hoping for the tiniest give, he found
himself even trying to swear it into submission through a
vile, whispered stream of curse words, but the only effect that
had was to frustrate him more. The stubby wooden wheel
had found the very rut where his foot stood and trapped him
securely under the cart's weight. His ankle was slightly bent,
and he went down to a kneel, tugging at his shoe and hoping
to slip his foot out, but the ice burned at his fingers and he
knew after a minute of digging that it was no use. He was in
a bad box.

More sweat now, and it felt clammy against the chill of the
wind off the river. He heaved himself up and stared again past
the cart's cargo and in Pock's direction. Most of the sacks
had been pushed aside, and he could see a couple of slushy
footprints in the pool of slime forming on the ground. He
looked around for his gun, and saw it lying a few feet away,
just beyond a brown, broken liquor bottle.

Backwards he fell, stretching to reach his weapon. His fingers clawed above his head and into the ice, but he wasn't even close to touching it. With his foot trapped he could only lie on his back, sprawled and flailing like an overturned turtle, but he bent his head onto the ice and stared at his gun, coveting its black barrel and brown handle grip.

He felt as helpless as a baby in a crib as Pock stepped around the corner of the cart and stood above him. It had been awhile since he'd seen him, but nothing had changed except the disgusting state of his clothes, now coated with swill and caked with bits of bluish meat. He still hunched slightly, and wore his thin little French-style mustache over an ever-present sneer. God, Queen thought, blinking his eyes against the sky's brilliant white, he had really gotten himself in the soup. It was going to take some quick thinking to climb out. Pock was brandishing the rifle, and Queen thought back to his conversation with Norbeck about the weapon that killed Maisy. The bullet had come from the same kind of gun—probably the very same gun that Pock now held in his claws.

Queen managed a smile. "Fancy meeting you here. You must feel right at home amongst the garbage."

"Fancy meeting you here, without a soul to see." Pock wiped his nose with his skinny forearm, and pointed the rifle at Queen's head.

"Your boss is a jailbird," Queen said. "He's got bigger problems right now than a couple of scared wags and a skulker who jumps at his own shadow. What gives?"

"As long as I get paid, I follow orders. Nothin' more to it. I'm supposed to keep meddlers away from old pointy prick and the whores." He curled his mouth up into a ghoulish smile. "So far, so good."

"And now you're in trouble with the Minneapolis police department. You've got to be daft, shooting at cops. How far in life do you think you'll get making damn-fool decisions like that?"

"If I kill you, and then your pal inside, who would know?"

"Every detective and sheriff in Minnesota will hunt you down if you kill me."

Pock laughed. "I heard you ain't supposed to be working on this case anymore. I'll wager nobody even knows you're down here." Queen's mouth dropped slightly in surprise, and Pock's eyes brightened when he saw it. "Everyone underestimates ol' Pock, but I'm a sneaky son of a bitch with my ears to the ground. And if you think your partner is any match for this here Remington Rolling Block, you've got more than a screw loose, copper. I've got the upper hand, and don't you know it!"

So that was Dander's plan after all. He had required a payoff, but Queen had assumed it was all about getting out of jail, not the thrill and satisfaction of murdering a police officer. Pock had orders to finish them off quietly, in a place empty of witnesses.

"So how do we proceed?" Queen spread his hands.

"I don't know," Pock shrugged. "I guess just kill you and be done with it."

"Like you killed Maisy Anderson? You're holding the rifle that did it, too, aren't you?"

Pock glowered at Queen. "Somebody else did that. We were trying to scare her silly, yeah, but the bullet came from somewhere else. The hell if it was me."

"Quit with your goddamn lies! You did it!" Queen snapped. His eyes flashed darkly at Pock. "You did it under Dander's orders, and you pulled the trigger. I've got a witness that saw everything."

"You ain't got nothing except a couple of breaths left," Pock sneered.

"I've got a partner who isn't going to let you out of this levee alive if you use that thing on me."

"Ha!" Pock's greasy, matted hair clung to his forehead. He reached into his pointed nose, flicking something out with a blackened nail. "Everyone's heard about how hopping mad you get. Must be a real pisser for you to be on your back looking up at me like this."

More insults aren't going to do me any favors, Queen thought, and he took a deep breath. Reel it in. He lifted his hands over his head, as if to surrender, and felt the cold hardness of the liquor bottle's neck lightly brush his finger. He managed a smile. "No point in me getting mad, or you either. I'll admit you've got me at a disadvantage, but I've got other things you might want. Cush, for instance."

"Don't move!" Pock yelled, tensing his arms as he held the rifle's aim at Queen. The sound of his words seemed to travel through his nose and come out in a nasal sputter. "Not even a twitch, copper! God, I hate coppers!"

His finger trembled around the trigger, and Queen watched his hand intently for movement. If he shoots at me, he'll hit where he's aiming. I might try moving to the left or right, but my chances are nil to none. A half-dozen ideas flew through his head about how he might avoid being murdered in a garbage dump, but none seemed to have any promise of success. He looked again at Pock's twitching trigger finger, and then at his bloodshot eyes. He scanned down to the rifle's mechanism, and saw the hammer was pulled back, ready to fire. But something looked odd, and it didn't register for a second or two. But when it did, he almost instinctively slapped his forehead.

Hellfire. Why didn't I see that before?

"The breech block is pulled back. You don't have a round in your chamber, idiot," Queen said matter-of-factly, and wrapping his hand around the neck of the bottle, flung it forward.

Its jagged bottom hit Pock squarely in the face. The bottle hung for a moment, glass embedded just over his left eye and a good portion of his forehead, and then fell, exposing deep red gashes. The little rat shrieked and whirled around, dropping the rifle and clutching the wound.

"NORBECK!" Queen shouted at the top of his lungs. "NORBECK!"

Attempting to see through the blood streaming from his forehead into his eyes, Pock rubbed them furiously, all the while twisting and turning and howling. He stumbled and tripped on a broken dress hoop, fell, and stumbled back up, disoriented and bewildered. Queen heard the shack's door slam shut as he pulled himself as close to standing as his trapped foot would permit. In the corner of his eye he saw Norbeck, and to his surprise, Hayward, close behind, running towards him.

Perhaps Pock could sense their approach too, because he let out a yowl and began cantering, off-balance, into the heart of the garbage, toward the ominous Mississippi. He pitched back and forth as he ran, once crashing to the ground after slipping on either ice or trash. He sprang back up as if possessed by a demon, whirled around blindly, and started running again.

Norbeck was panting when he reached Queen. "Holy hell," he said quietly as he watched Pock, still clutching his bleeding forehead with one hand, flailing the other wildly in the air. "He's going straight in."

"You want to stop him?" Queen asked grimly. "Go ahead."

"Nobody could," Norbeck murmured, his grin wide and toothy, mesmerized by the show unfolding before him. Adry came huffing up behind him, opening his mouth to speak, when he saw Norbeck's stare. He followed it to Pock, now caterwauling in a pitch so high it threatened to summon every dog in earshot.

"Jesus, both of you, help me get this goddamn thing off my foot," Queen sputtered. They snapped to attention and ran to his side.

"On the count of three," said Queen. "One. Two. Three!" The wheel groaned forward as they strained and shoved, and Queen pulled himself free. He turned his ankle and felt some mild pain, but knew he was lucky it wasn't sprained or broken.

"Would you look at that moon-calf," Norbeck said admiringly, already in rapt engrossment again at Pock's exertions. "Who'd a thunk a little gore could put someone off his trolley? What a sight!"

Closer and closer to the ice's edge Pock staggered, bumping, slipping, tripping and spinning his way past the dump's boundary and onto dangerous footing. The opposite bluff, high and imposing, looked to Queen almost like a monster's gaping mouth, welcoming Pock in anticipation of a feast.

He was standing now on the brink of the ice, a step or two away from the rolling black waters. Queen wondered what was happening in his head to cause him to act in such delirious fashion.

"Christ," whispered Adry. "Why isn't it breaking?"

"He can't be more than ninety-five pounds. Any normal-sized man would already be catfish food," Queen said.

Then, suddenly, Pock stopped cold in his tracks, streaks of frozen blood clinging to his cheek. His eyes grew large as the situation clarified, and he wagged his head, as if to shake out the clouds that had suffocated his brain. As he slowly turned, a look of terror began to register on his face. The ice was cracking around his feet. He looked at Queen, Norbeck and Adry, almost pleadingly, and then leapt forward, with the intent to save himself, but instead slipped and sprawled on his belly. A gigantic fissure ripped with a loud snap directly in front of his head, and he grabbed the edge of the ice as it separated from its host. For a moment he lay suspended, and the ice floated serenely into the current. Pock wasn't smiling, but he wasn't frowning either. He just stared at Queen with a dumbfounded expression as he glided away from shore.

Then the slab of ice Pock clung to began to slant back. He clawed for a handhold but the ice was too slippery. As the floe tipped backwards, Pock slid like a shot into the Mississippi, caught in the undertow. They watched for a few moments, Queen half-expecting him to surface like a bedraggled rat, but no one surfaced. Pock was gone.

"The case is closed," Queen told Norbeck, as they plodded up the hill to the buggy in their sandpaper-wrapped shoes. "The little weasel denied it, but one of those girls saw him shoot her."

"Was it the sweetie face? She sure is a looker," Norbeck replied, with a wistful glance in her direction. The girls walked a few paces behind, huddled under blankets and clinging to each other. "Doesn't she look like this?" He pulled a bent cigarette card out of his pocket, and showed the picture to Queen. "Maisy was a bird, but I'll be damned if this young flower in our care isn't truly heaven-sent."

"You carry around garbage like this?" Queen questioned disapprovingly. "I never took you for a cigarette fiend or a sparrow-catcher either. What a lucky woman your wife is."

"Ol' Johnson, from Third Station, gave it to me. Before he got fired, that is. He had a stack of them in his desk that he looked at while he ate his roast beef sandwich. Every day the same goddamn sandwich."

"Isn't that interesting," Queen said, looking back casually at the girls. Adry had confirmed their names as the same ones Dander had given him. The one who'd bashed him with the board was Trilly Flick, and when he told her of Pock's demise she'd cursed the man's name with words he'd rarely heard come from a woman's mouth. After she emptied out her emotions he'd felt a twinge of comfort to see her soften a little. As she'd gathered her sparse belongings for their departure from the flats, she smiled at him for the first time. It was sweet and beautiful and intoxicating. It gave him a slight thrill to think that he had come to her rescue and given her a taste of the vengeance she seemed to desire. Whatever terrors she suffered under Pock's hand he could only guess, but from the look of gratitude she'd given Queen, it had not only closed the door on the matter, but slammed it shut and locked it tight.

The other girl, Edna Pease, still hadn't said anything. She wore a look of permanent dread stamped on her face, as if the sky was about to burst into flame and set her on fire. Queen had tried to talk to her, but Trilly pulled her away, almost obsessively protective of her friend.

Adry had been overjoyed to see them go, as the morning's climax had filled him with a level of panic that overwhelmed any carnal happiness he'd now be missing. He even whistled a tune as he directed their departure from his hovel. When he stuffed the girls' hands with money, Queen didn't protest in the slightest, and even momentarily felt an urge to force Adry to hand over every penny he possessed for their troubles, and a little to him too. The girls were already out the door, however, and he didn't want to prolong the situation any more. There would soon be more than enough of the long green to be made, and shaking down the pitiful Adry Hayward didn't seem so heroic at that moment.

Queen had arranged a place for them to stay and he knew they'd be well taken care of until he could figure out a more permanent home. He planned to find legitimate work for both of them, and it pleased him a little to think he'd see more of Trilly in the future. A short buggy ride to meet his friend, followed by a trip to the girls' new quarters, would tie up this last loose end. Then he could move on to running the detective squad and getting things ship-shape for Colonel Ames. He was ready to deal with Sheriff Anderson as well, grateful he could hand him some consolation about his granddaughter's death with the news that her killer was dead.

Dander and Higgins were another story. They had a court hearing scheduled soon, Norbeck had told him as they climbed the hill, and were likely headed to Stillwater once convicted. He hoped they got nice long sentences and found breaking rock in ankle chains a charming change of pace from kidnapping and raping girls. And if he ever found himself with business in the prison, he might make another visit and introduce their faces to the butt of his gun.

They reached the top of the hill, and Queen saw the buggy sitting right where they had left it. Good old Ollie, he thought. The horse whinnied in anticipation as it saw the group, and stamped its feet nervously.

"Come out of there! You'd better not be sleeping!" Norbeck called out loudly. "I've had enough of the flats to last the rest of my life. Christ, my legs are sore," he added as an afterthought.

"Where are you, kid?" Queen shouted. The buggy's windows were glazed with frost. Maybe he had nodded off, and steamed up the windows with his breath. He reached for the door's handle and pulled it open, ready to jerk the kid awake so they could get going.

Empty. Where in God's name did he go? Queen glanced at the seat, and then saw something on the floor. It was dark and round, and he carefully picked it up, but it was mushy to the touch. Why is there a warm piece of chocolate candy on the floor, he wondered? It couldn't have been here very long or it'd be frozen into a chunk of ice. If somebody had stepped on this the livery owner would have charged to have it cleaned. Kids and their candy.

"You got to see this, Harm," he heard Norbeck exclaim from the other side of the buggy. There was trepidation in his voice, so he limped around to see the focus of Norbeck's concern. He stopped cold when he saw drops of blood on the patch of trampled snow just slightly beneath the rig. "Look there," Norbeck said, pointing to footprints coming from the woods near the road they'd just walked up. "Somebody came up here from those trees. Right here, and then up to the road. I don't see Ollie's prints, though. The windows are fogged up so it couldn't have been too long ago." He scratched his head, and wore a concerned expression. "I teased him and all, Harm, but I liked him too."

"Ollie!" Queen yelled, as he looked down the avenue. The Washington Bridge was bare, and he could see clearly to the other side. Not a figure in sight. The other direction, towards the city, looked quiet as well.

Edna gasped at the name, and Trilly looked wildly at Queen. "Did you say Ollie?" she cried, and rushed up next to him to see the blood and footprints for herself. "Is it the same Ollie we know?"

Queen nodded solemnly and tried to keep balance as she lunged at him, grabbing his lapel and falling to the ground. "God, no! He found him!"

"Who found whom?" Queen demanded, pulling her back up. "Do you think someone took him?"

She bit her lovely lip, and nodded. "And if you don't get him soon, Detective Queen," she blurted, eyes welling with tears, "he's as good as dead."

Queen grasped each girl's hand as they stepped over the red-dotted snow and into the buggy's compartment. "What's this man's name?" he asked.

"Don't know his name. Never seen him," Trilly replied, rubbing her eyes and leaning closer to him after settling in.

Her exhaustion was gaining advantage over her emotions. Despite his seriousness, Queen couldn't contain a shiver as he felt her near him. She placed her hand on her neck, and he found himself stealing glances at her delicate fingers, then back to her soft, ethereal face. So opposite now to the fiery soul who had tried to smash his back into pieces just an hour before. She was like a pendulum, swinging from extreme to extreme, and he couldn't help but feel arousal in each wide motion.

I need to focus on the task at hand, Queen reminded himself. Enough of these fantasies.

"Why would you think Ollie's in danger?" he asked.

"The blood. The tracks. Plus, this man from his past that scared him crazy, but he wouldn't say more'n that. Just told me he was very bad, and lived far away."

"And why was Ollie so afraid? He never mentioned anything to me about running from anyone."

"He always clammed up when I asked him more about it," Trilly said. "Ollie told me the reason he took the job with Emil was 'cause he felt safe workin' for him. He figured if the man ever came back, he'd have Emil and Higgins and Pock between himself and him."

Trilly's lower lip trembled and Queen found himself gazing at it, to the point he realized he was only half listening to what she said. He silently chastised himself for his weakness, and at the same time wanted to comfort her, tell her Ollie would be okay. But there were too many questions about what might have happened to him for him to say it honestly. Speechless, he just looked at her with sympathy, and gently shut the door.

CHAPTER 7

NORBECK HAD DECIDED TO CATCH A streetcar back to headquarters, having pressing business with another case, so the buggy ride to the outskirts of south Minneapolis was quiet. Both girls fell back in their seats and went to sleep almost immediately after Queen snapped the reins. The soothing jostle of the rig's movement cooled Queen's nerve, although he was still preoccupied and perturbed over Ollie's disappearance.

Not only had he been baffled by the girls' reactions to Ollie's name being mentioned and the trickle of blood in the snow, but their answers to his detailed questions had been frustratingly vague.

Now he turned the buggy onto Cedar Avenue, trying his best to avoid the rough holes so the girls wouldn't wake to an unpleasant bounce. He had a friend in south Minneapolis who would take care of them until he could figure out a more permanent solution to their predicament. The city was fully awake, and wagons, carriages, streetcars and people all vied for space. Gloomy winter clouds were being pushed aside for sunshine, and while normally his mood would brighten with a welcome flash of blue sky in the depth of winter, today it didn't.

After some time to ponder, he wasn't so sure Ollie had been kidnapped. It didn't seem such a stretch for a carefree kid like Ollie to get bored or distracted. He'd certainly shown concern for the girls' welfare, but he was still a boy, and frankly lived the life of a wild animal. Wandering the streets, living in abandoned boats, and running with a gang didn't exactly instill a sense of responsibility and stability. Queen didn't think the blood in the snow was from any life-threatening wound, either. A few droplets from a cut or a bloody nose could easily explain it away. As for the footprints, they could have been from anyone. When he had time, he would go back for a visit with McCartan to see if Ollie had surfaced. Ollie might even be with him now, plying more newspapers, or maybe at his hideout with his friends. Possibly even back home with his mother and brother. It wasn't to say that this mysterious figure Trilly talked about didn't worry him more than a little. But with no name or information, following up on that lead seemed like a long and twisting road, especially as he wasn't convinced Ollie wasn't holed up somewhere safe.

As they continued south, the street lost its pavement and turned to dirt. Buildings were no longer packed together and the sky broadened in front of him. The air was fresher too, and he breathed it in, a welcome change from the thick city smoke behind them.

He turned onto 42nd Street at a grove of poplar trees, and the quality of the road decreased considerably. The buggy ride became a series of jolts and lurches. The girls awoke, rubbed their eyes and moved to the windows, entranced by the sun-lit, rural surroundings. Queen could only imagine how long it had been since they'd been out of the city and sensed quietness. This would be a good place to give them some rest, and he completely trusted the man he was about to deliver them to.

The detective pulled the horses to a halt, climbed down from his seat, and opened the buggy's door. Again, he gave each girl his hand, and again he felt a tingle when he touched

Trilly's soft fingers. Whether she also felt it, he couldn't be sure, but she was smiling as she stepped down. Edna's eyes were still wide and afraid, and she scanned her new surroundings with apprehension. Queen had yet to try questioning her with any vigor. He wanted to be sensitive to her recent trauma, but also began to wonder if she'd experienced too much suffering to endure the world around her. His attempts to speak with her were met by a face that tensed up to the point of rupture. He made a note to have a doctor visit, to check not just their general health, but Edna's odd behavior in particular.

They had stopped in front of a one-and-a-half story house. Its front door was flanked by modest windows, with an attic window at the peak. It was built of wood and surrounded by a dirt yard, patched with snow. Out the door came Queen's friend Peder Ulland, beaming happily, his blond hair thinning and his head bare to the cold air. The door banged shut behind him as he strode forward.

"Dat fella isn't boddering you, is he?" Ulland called to Trilly. She looked up, smiled, and shook her head. Queen and his friend shook hands vigorously.

Queen and Peder Ulland were about as unlikely a pair of friends as he could imagine. The Norwegian was truly kind and selfless, a far, far stretch from the greedy backroom wheeler-dealers and immoral riff-raff Queen was forced to deal with as his daily routine.

The two of them had met ten years ago, when Peder, working as a trade union leader, and had helped organize against John Pillsbury and his B Flour Mill. Objections by workers over abuse by an unpopular foreman named William Horner had set the Packers and Nailers union to strike. To build their case, Peder had hired Queen to investigate Horner's background. In 1891, Queen had been between salaried jobs, and with a partner ran a private Minneapolis detective agency. Eager for work, Queen had dived headlong into the job, and had uncovered some unflattering facts about Horner's past: enough information to resolve the issue two weeks later, when Horner was transferred to the A Flour Mill and the union was satisfied. From that point on, Queen and the Norwegian had built on their friendship, each getting something from the other that was missing from his own life. Queen thought Peder, deep inside, enjoyed the company of a scoundrel, and even lived a bit vicariously through the detective's crime-fighting stories. For Queen, it was simple. Peder, and especially his sister Karoline, calmed him and made him feel normal. And nothing was better at untying the knot of frustration and anger that perpetually twisted in his stomach than Karoline's sweet, generous spirit.

"You don't know how you're helping me out, Peder," Queen said. "I owe you a big debt on this."

"Vell, you've helped me out more times den I've helped you," he replied, placing a hand on each of Queen's shoulders. "I'm pleased you've brought dem here, Harm." He looked at the girls, and then back at Queen with a sly grin. "I know you've got a big heart underneat dat hard frame, but you vouldn't be doing dis for any odder reason, vould you be?"

Queen frowned slightly. "What are you implying, Ulland?"

Peder threw back his head and laughed. "Never mind. You're doing the right thing, and I'm pleased to see it. I'll make you vun of us yet."

"A member of the Socialist party?" asked Queen. "We've debated this before. I don't involve myself in politics." Unless they're a means to a personal end, he thought.

"Harm, I'm not a Socialist, although I must admit I sympathize vit dere cause. By one of us, I mean an organizer. Dere are plenty of trade unions and charities who could use a sympathetic ear vit da new mayor, and dat could be you."

"Peder, outside of my friendship with you and your family, I have no interest in pitting myself on one side or another of these issues. My job is to solve crimes and keep the peace. Not laying my head on Jim Hill's main line for a chance meeting with a locomotive."

"My vork is yust as important as yours, Harm. Immigrants are being abused every day in dis city. Vimmen and children are de biggest victims and suffer far vorse den you or I." Peder took a breath and wiped a bit of saliva from the corner of his mouth, which always formed when he was adamantly arguing his cause. "Ve need to create a permanent place vere dey can go to escape from dere miseries. Have you heard of Jane Addams in Chicago? I visited her Hull House last year and vas impressed at da vork she's doing vit da poor."

"Do you have time for that?" Queen asked with a little smirk. "Aren't you busy already with all the Norwegians moving into Minneapolis?"

"Ya sure, of course. Lots of 'dem, for sure. Danes and Swedes too. Most of dem don't speak a vord of English ven dey arrive. Dey need yobs and a place to hang dere hats, and I try to help as best I can."

The girls had moved closer to them during their conversation, and Trilly took her opportunity to speak. "We're to stay here?" she asked.

"Yes, miss, my humble home. Velkommen."

She looked warily at Queen, and then back at Peder. "No offense, Mister, you seem like a nice enough fella, but we just came from a house not much smaller than this, trapped with a love-starved louse. Frankly, I've had about enough of an arrangement like that."

Peder bowed slightly, smiling gently. "I vork in Dania Hall. Dat's vere my office is, vere I help young ladies and many odders get back on dere feet like you. Dat's vere I'll stay ven you're here, so don't vorry. I've got a comfortable little cot to sleep on for myself. My sister vill get you vot you need."

"Karoline is here?" Queen said with surprise. He felt his face warm at her name. "I thought she was back in Norway."

"She vas on her way, as far as New York, but she decided to return," Peder said. "She heard about the vinter cholera epidemic and vanted to assist."

"Where is she now?" Queen said, more quickly than he should have. Trilly looked at him with a bemused expression and a slightly cocked head. "I mean, it would be a smart thing to have her here to see to their needs," he continued. "She's had experience in these situations."

"What kind of situations?" Trilly asked combatively. "Seeing after sad little whores? Well, let me tell you, Mr. Queen, that I don't need a caretaker to watch me! I may have had some troubles in my life, but that don't make me no degenerate!" She gritted her teeth and looked at him defiantly, but her fierceness seemed to make her only more beautiful. He wanted to tell her how scandalous it would be if she used that language within earshot of regular society, but he didn't have the heart to do it. He doubted that Peder cared, and frankly he was used to much worse, but it was still jarring to his ears from the mouth of a woman.

Peder looked amused. "Karoline vill be back in da afternoon. Let me take you to vere you vill be sleeping." He turned to Trilly and Edna. "Ve can pour a hot bath for you too, if you'd like."

Edna nodded her head emphatically, and reached for Trilly's hand.

"Do you have any bags to carry in?" Peder asked. The girls shook their heads.

"You vant to stay for some coffee, Harm? You can vait for Karoline if you vant to."

"Thanks, but no," he said. He suddenly felt very odd, talking about Karoline in front of Trilly. "This rig is rented, and I have to get it back, and I've got lots of work to do. Give her my regards, and tell her I'll call on her in a couple of days. We can catch up then."

"Ya, vell sure, Harm. If you need to talk to me, you know vere to find me, too." Peder motioned for the girls to follow him, but Harm put his hand gently on Trilly's shoulder.

"Can I speak to you for a moment before you go in?" he asked her.

"Sure," she said, giving Edna a tender push towards Peder. "Go on, I'll be right there."

Edna nodded, seemingly comforted, and silently walked to the house.

"Let's talk over here," he said to Trilly, and led her to the buggy.

"What the hell are you going to do? Profess your undying love to me?" she laughed.

"N-n-no," Queen stammered. He put his hand in his pocket and touched the tip of the stickpin. He had decided not to give it back to Adry, at least not yet. He pushed it into his finger and the prick brought him back to focus. "I don't think that would be appropriate," he managed.

"I'm only joshing!" she laughed. Then she suddenly narrowed her eyes, a glint of suspicion igniting. "What's wrong with you?"

"Nothing," he replied. "I just wanted to confirm what you saw the night of Maisy's murder. You watched Pock kill her? You saw it? You're sure of it?"

"Yes, like I already said. Dander was there, too, and he talked to Maisy before it happened. But my window was shut and I couldn't hear what they said. I saw Pock put up his gun, the long one. What do you call it?"

"A rifle."

"Yeah. Point the rifle at her and shoot."

"Do you think Dander might have given him an order?"

"How the hell should I know? Do I look like a Davenport brother? I ain't no medium or nothin'. Go ask one of them famous ones, if you're so inclined."

"So you don't know if it was planned. Only that Pock raised his gun and shot her off the fence."

"Yeah, that's what I saw."

"Would you testify to that in court? If it should come to it?"

"If it means a final end to your goddamn questions, I'd say so."

"Fine. Thank you." His words were curt, although he wanted them to come out softer. She was riled now, her cheeks red with excitement, and he wished their parting might be more amicable, but he didn't know how to make it so.

"I'll come back around in two days, to see how you're doing," he finally said.

"Yeah, I heard that from before."

"Right." He suddenly thought of something, and reaching into his pocket, pulled out a roll of bills, counted out three dollars, and held them out to her. "You and Edna need new clothes. Something respectable. Take this. Tell Karoline your size, and she can buy some for you when she has time."

"I got cush. Right here." She pulled a small purse from underneath a fold of her dress. "It was the least that asshole Adry Hayward could do after what he got from us."

"Well, you can have this too."

"For what?" Trilly steamed. "So you and this Karoline woman play father and mother to us? Have a laugh over how you cleaned up a couple of whores and tried to make them look respectable? Well to hell with you, Detective Queen!" She took the money from his hand, and tossed it into the air. Queen stood dumbfounded, not knowing what to say. Then she crossed her arms, threw up her nose and stormed toward the house. Peder met her at the doorway with a smile, but she pushed passed him and out of sight. His friend waved meekly at Queen, shrugged and closed the door.

Is it too early for a drink, or a goddamn dozen? Queen picked up the wet bills, folded them and put them back into his pocket. He uttered a sigh so low and forlorn that he surprised even himself.

With mindful concern for his back, the long-built Dix Anderson stepped off the smoking train, under the trestle, and into the chaos of the Minneapolis depot. The city's rank air walloped him like a brick in the head and forced a cough. He carried his bag, which he'd bought an extra ticket for just to keep it next to him.

He was tired from his ride, and from his thoughts. Guilt and despair had racked his mind the entire way. He'd had nothing better to do than to stare out the window, preoccupied with the days ahead and with past regrets.

Now that he was here, he knew he needed to muster his energy and ready himself for the onslaught of Minneapolis. The city reminded him of a woman he'd met once, long ago, before even Martha. She'd been a ravishing beauty, stunningly skillful in the art of cajolery. However, a terrible illness had overcome her, and she'd died as a tumor had savaged her insides at seventeen. He could sense the decay, here as well, just underneath the surface. Somewhere, somehow, Maisy had gotten lost in it, and paid for her misstep with her life. He vowed, again, as he had a hundred times since he'd ridden from his farm that morning, that he would discover the cause of her demise, and exact vengeance.

As he strode through the bustling crowd, his get-up immediately drew stares and gaping mouths, but he paid them no mind. There were a handful of reasons for the attention paid to him. For one, his white mustache was old-fashioned, sweeping across his face and naturally curling at the corners. He was also a good six inches taller than most of the mass of travelers he walked through. As he had been a lawman in the West, he wore clothes befitting his past, including heavy boots, a wide-brimmed slouch hat, and a long Mackinaw coat, which went down past his knees. It was made from old three-point trade blankets, bright red with black checks, a far contrast to the sea of black and brown coats and suits worn by the Minneapolis men around him. He cared very little for material possessions, but the coat was special to him. He'd received it at one of his first jobs, working for the Hudson's Bay fur company at fifteen years old. He'd already reached his six-foot-four height when he worked in the Canadian forests, carrying packs of fur on his back. No one batted an eye in Bemidji, as the pattern and color were a common sight in the north woods, but here in Minneapolis he stood out like the Eiffel tower in a cornfield. He'd had the coat through countless scrapes, and while he'd closeted it when he retired as a sheriff, something moved him to take it out again for his journey to Minneapolis. Perhaps it was the comforting familiarity of the wool, snug over his shoulders, or the way it made him feel like an individual up against an ocean of sameness. And also, a more important reason. It hid the two Colts that sat tight on his hips.

His old friend had agreed to meet him, and true to his word, he was there. Martin Baum was looking intently at his watch, and then up to the board that displayed departure and arrival information, when Anderson approached him.

"Martin," Anderson said. "Glad you could find the time to see an old badger like me."

"Anything for an old badger," Baum returned, with his mouth turned up in a sideways grin. He was much rounder now than Anderson remembered, and wore a brown suit that was fraying at the trouser and sleeve cuffs. His collar was worn and greasy, and even his derby hat had seen better days. Despite his clothing, though, and his sagging, tired face, he looked genuinely pleased to see Anderson. They went back a long way together.

"Happy New Year, Dix. How was the ride in?"

"Tried to sleep, but nothing came of it."

"It's good to see you again," Baum said. The two old friends walked together through the depot and out into the cold. Fat flakes drifted lazily down through the evening air, trying their best to cleanse the dirty, icy sludge marred by hundreds of sets of footprints.

As they made their way to the street, Anderson spotted three young boys sitting on the curb, all crying and looking miserable. Hurried passengers moved around them without taking a second glance. As Anderson and Baum approached, their eyes widened at the sight of the towering sheriff. One was chubby, with pasty, tear-stained cheeks. The second was rail thin, with dark hair and olive skin. They looked to be around twelve, Anderson thought, but the third boy couldn't be older than six or seven. He was a cute looking little shaver, with pink cheeks, pinched by the wind, and blueberry eyes, which stared at him like he had just flown down from the sky.

"What's got you so upset?" he asked the little one, gently bending to look him in the eye. The child stuttered a little as he examined Anderson's guns.

"Are th-th-those real, Mister?"

The plump boy smacked his friend on the shoulder. "Don't talk to no strangers, Petey."

"Well," Anderson said, giving him a wink. "Between you and me, no. I just wear 'em for show, to scare the bad men away."

"They don't shoot?"

"Well of course they do," Anderson said, smiling. "Just not bullets."

"Then what?"

"Whatever you want. I'm partial to strawberries and marshmallows."

The chubby boy wiped his tears away with his arm and gave a little grin. "I'm partial to 'em too! Is that why yer mustache is so white? Covered in marshmallows?"

"Aw, skittles, you two," said the dark haired boy. He stood up, eye to eye with the bent Anderson. "We got scads of friends around here and I'll shout if you keep talkin' to us. Just go away."

"I'm a sheriff," Anderson said.

"Yeah? Then where's your badge?"

"I don't have a badge."

"See?" cried the dark-haired boy, his eyes flashing with triumph. "A fake sheriff."

"Sheriffs carry stars, young man. Not badges." He reached into his pocket and pulled out a silver star, bent on one point, but polished to a silver gleam. They oohed in unison, and the dark boy sat down, bedazzled by its beauty.

"That sure is swell, Mister. You ever mix with In'juns?"

"Come to blows? Never."

"Oh." The three boys were uniformly disappointed.

Anderson's back was stiffening, so he wiped some snow off the curb and gingerly sat down next to them. "You keep crying like that in this weather and you'll make enough ice for a pair of skates."

"Pshaw, Mister," said the littlest boy.

"It's getting dark. You should go home."

"We're waiting for someone."

"For who, partner?"

"Just someone."

Baum bent over and wagged his finger. "You can't loiter here, none of you can."

The dark-headed boy moved between his friend and Baum, his small fists raised and ready to scrap. "Scram, why doncha? You like goin' around pickin' on kids, huh? Are ya willing to take a pop on the nose, grand dad?"

"None of that is necessary, young man," said Anderson. His back already hurt in this position, and he needed to stand again. With hands in the dirty slush for support, he tried to lift himself up, but his body wouldn't go. It just wouldn't go. He tried again, straining to stand, and suddenly the three boys had rushed to his side, pushing him up with all of their strength. He held onto their small shoulders, slowly easing up to his full length. Getting old was a hard hard thing, he decided.

"Much obliged, young men," he said, feeling in his pocket for coins.

"No sir, we don't need that," Petey said, with a little sniff and a wipe of his nose. "But if we ever need a sheriff with a strawberry gun, then you can owe us, right?"

"That's a mighty fine deal," Anderson said.

"You're welcome to stay with me," Baum said, as they continued down the sidewalk. "I'm lodging in the city. You can sleep on the floor in my room, or get one of your own near mine."

"Thanks, but I've engaged a room somewhere else. Is there a place we can talk? I can't take too long, and I need your wisdom."

"Of course," Baum said. "We can take a bite to eat and discuss old times and whatever else is on your mind. You must be hungry."

"I am," Anderson replied. He paused for a moment, and looked into Baum's doleful eyes. "And you must be, too."

"A reference to my current state of dress," Baum said, embarrassment flushing his cheeks. "You don't know the half of it."

Baum led the sheriff to a modest-looking cafe across the street. Most of the dinner guests had left, so it was quiet. Anderson ordered steak and mashed potatoes with butter, and Baum a cup of coffee from a shuffling waiter who looked as though the recent rush had about collapsed him. Although the waiter was tired, he still stared at the two uncomfortably until they realized he wanted them to remove their hats. They did, and Anderson apologized. The waiter huffed in return and left.

"I asked you to meet me for your help, so the least I can do is treat, Martin," Anderson said. "A single cup of coffee won't sustain you."

The waiter dropped a plate of biscuits on a table next to theirs, and Baum's nostrils flared slightly as he caught the buttery aroma. "If you insist, Dix, then I won't fight it, but you know I'll have the check at our next meal."

"Fine," Anderson said. Baum flagged the waiter down and pointed at a number of things on the menu. The waiter nodded wearily and went to the kitchen.

"How are you holding up, Dix? With Martha gone things must be difficult."

"More than you can imagine," he said. "I miss her every day."

"I miss my Joanne, too."

"What happened?" asked Anderson. "You mentioned a boarding house. Why aren't you in your home with your wife?"

"She had enough with my drinking," Baum said. He picked up a fork and began absentmindedly wiping it clean with his finger. "About all she could take. I don't blame her."

"Well, being the wife of a police sergeant is difficult."

"I'm not on the force anymore, Dix. I was fired. Thrown out with the garbage. Two days ago."

Anderson raised an eyebrow in surprise. "For true? How could that happen?"

"I had a nice comfortable job in a precinct that doesn't see much action. A good way to spend the golden years, I thought. Old Doc Ames comes in and hires his brother to clean the house. He fired half the officers on the force. *Half*. Remember Swan Walton? He was the captain of the Third precinct under Mayor Gray, and now he's been reduced to janitor in the very same building. Can there be anything more humiliating than that?"

"What in God's name would Ames do that for?" asked Anderson.

Baum looked around to the left and the right, and leaned in. "The con is on, Dix. The biggest con ever, right here in Minneapolis. I know what they're about to do and it's going to be whopping."

"Do? What do you mean, do?" Anderson asked. Plates of steaming food were set before them, and Baum slathered a hot biscuit with butter and thick strawberry jam. He devoured it and started fixing another as he talked.

"Every cop he fired was as honest as the day is long. We're all similar that way. You know I am. Hell, I know I'm old and not quick on my feet, but you know I've always tried to do what's right. You can swear an oath on that, Dix."

"Indeed you are, and you have."

Lowering his voice even further, Baum narrowed his gaze with an intense seriousness. "What I'm about to tell you, I don't know for absolute certainty, but I'm pretty sure of it. I've been doing my own investigative work, just asking some questions. I've got nothing better to do, and have a handful of friends still on duty. The Ames boys replaced us with criminals. Honest to goodness true-to-life swindlers, robbers, bruisers and cheats. Some were yanked right from their cells and into Fred Ames's office, and handed a badge before they left. A sober business, Dix."

"And these friends of yours that are still working in the department have told you this?"

"I don't have absolute proof, if that is what you mean," Baum replied, wiping some gravy from his chin. "But people talk, and these new officers are already blabbing away. Bragging about what they plan to do and how they're gonna use their sway to pad their pockets."

"It could be just talk, Martin. I've seen some crazy things in my day, and I know you have, too. It's just hard to believe that a mayor of a city the size of Minneapolis could pull off organized corruption like this without raising hairs."

"I'm willing to bet on it. A dinner at the West, and that's more expensive than I can afford. I'm certain bad things are going to happen. Call it my lawman's intuition."

"Well, I have some of that too, and I just can't see it. I stopped a sheriff from terrorizing a small town in South

Dakota once, but there were only a few dozen families under his thumb. Pulling it off in Minneapolis, with its industry and the millionaires behind it seems like lunacy. They won't let that happen. Do you think these big bugs will risk their reputations and the reputation of this city and look the other way while shakedowns and cons are going on around them?"

"That's just it," Baum replied. He had a thick piece of halibut in front of him, with a side of buttered carrots, and put a fork full of both into his mouth as he talked. "If the right people are put in charge, no one will be the wiser for it. If they're making lots of green, everyone will keep quiet for a piece of the take."

"Who have you heard is taking part in this?"

"Doc and Fred Ames, of course. Harm Queen, without question," Baum said, wiping his mouth with a napkin. "Do you know him? He's the rottenest goddamn apple on the tree."

"He's been trying to contact me. He's the reason I'm here."

"The hell if he's not. He wired you? Why?"

"Do you remember the last time I was here, Martin?"

Baum nodded slowly. "I do. It was when your granddaughter disappeared." A look of understanding washed over his face. "Oh, Christ, Dix. They found Maisy?"

"So Detective Queen says." Anderson said. Even the mention of her name tore at his insides. "Her body is sitting in the morgue. I'm here to identify her and take her home."

"I'm so sorry," Baum said, his voice cracking into a whisper. "I remember her so fondly as a little girl. She even called me Uncle Martin. I want you to know, Dix, that I have been thinking about her and looking for her since it happened. I made a promise to you that I would watch for her every chance that I got." He paused, blinked his eyes and continued. "Did Queen tell you what happened to her?"

"I got a telegram to come here. That was about all. I plan to see him first thing tomorrow morning."

Baum glowered when he heard this. "Don't trust him, Dix. Don't trust him. There isn't a man alive I trust less than Harmon Queen." He lifted his knife in the air to emphasize his point. "If you start asking too many questions it'll arouse his suspicions and he'll wonder how to get you back on the next train out of town. Whether that requires a gang of ruffians or uniformed officers will be the only question. The outcome will be the same either way."

"I was going to ask you what you thought of him, but you offered it on your own," Anderson said. "I haven't read many newspapers over the winter, especially about Minneapolis affairs, but if what you say is true, this city has problems. Adding one more, like me, won't make a difference."

"Do you know anything at all? Like where she has been?"

Anderson shook his head. "I fear the worst, though," he said.

"The strange thing is, I haven't read anything about Maisy in the papers here. Usually a murder is front-page news. Maybe it was an accident."

Anderson cut his steak slowly, and watched the pink juice pool onto his plate. He was the type of man who chose his words carefully, and opted to endure some seconds of silence in order to say the right thing, the right way.

"I expect to scare up the truth while I'm here. If it was an accident, I'll accept that. If it was something more sinister, I won't. If harm did come to her maliciously, I swear, on the grave of my beloved wife, that I will drop that murderer dead on the street." His face, normally stoic and void of emotion, twisted in agony as he finished his words. It was the pain of an entire family lost and of absolute loneliness. Then his expression dropped back to normal as quickly as it had changed.

He put a piece of steak into his mouth and chewed.

The Coffee John Oyster Grotto sat at 217 Nicollet Avenue, one block from City Hall, wedged between Olson's Dry Goods Bazaar and Heffelfinger's Shoe Emporium. It looked like any other ordinary restaurant from the outside, and the big window by the single door proclaimed its specialty menu item in bold, colorful lettering:

OYSTERS AS YOU LIKE THEM—25 CENTS.

The Grotto's proximity to the city's center of power made it a prime political hangout. Its owner, Coffee John Fitchette, the swaggering big-bellied cook and Ames crony, was a tornado of a personality who ran his restaurant with a mix of bluster and his own life-long political aspirations.

Queen didn't much care for Coffee John's bravado, but understood that his relationship with the Ames brothers was as solid as steel, and took care to maintain a cordial association with him to keep the inner circle harmonious. John Fitchette was an old Yankee veteran of the Civil War, like Doc, and he'd worked tirelessly on behalf of the Ames campaign in every election since he'd first arrived in town to set up his restaurant in 1888. Stories abounded about Coffee John's colorful past, so many that Queen wasn't sure what to believe. He'd seen the picture of Fitchette along with the other grand jury members ready for the trial of Jefferson Davis after the war's end, and he had no reason to believe that it didn't happen. Less believable, but a story that probably explained a lot if true, was that he had been in the Battle of Ream's Station in Virginia, where a shell explosion had shattered the top of his skull, landing him in the hospital and a battle for his life. After an arduous recovery and a piece of his skull permanently missing from the top of his head, friends who knew him before and after said Coffee John was never quite the same. He was ever after prone to uncontrollable fits and impulses that would come careening out to the world around him. Queen had seen these bursts of rage many times himself, but he'd also seen a generous, kind man, whose passions could rise in an admirable way when someone downtrodden crossed his path.

Another reason for Queen to be amicable was a completely selfish one. As Queen was partial to seafood, he enjoyed his open tab and pick of the better oysters, clams, lobsters, crabs, scallops, shrimp and fish that Coffee John kept in a massive ice chest. This was proudly displayed in the front window, in all its magnificent glory for those strolling by to see. He was thinking about a plate of fried scallops when Tom Cahill met him at the front door. Cahill was clumsily cleaning his spectacles with his big farm hands and almost dropped them when he saw Queen approach.

"Lieutenant!" Cahill fumbled to put the glasses on as they met.

"What the hell do you want?" Queen grunted. "Weren't you supposed to be getting trained with the other raw meat today? You should be home in bed and resting your little britches."

"You were to do the training, sir. Colonel Ames isn't happy about it, either. A number of new patrolmen have already resigned, and he's red-hot. He's looking for reasons why, and your name was mentioned in a ten-minute tirade."

"Resigned? Why? Because being a policeman isn't a walk in the park after all?"

"I don't know, sir," Cahill said. "Do you know that the Mayor and Police Superintendent Ames are here now?"

"No," Queen said, swearing under his breath. He pulled out his watch and saw it was later than he'd thought, well past supper time. "Dinner, drinks or dessert?"

"Colonel Ames has been dealing with ex-officers coming to his office all day, begging for their jobs back," Cahill said, peering into the darkened restaurant. "He wanted a respite."

"So what is he hiding here for? Officers quit, and ex-officers want their jobs back. A solution presents itself."

"I think he's tired of listening to their sad stories," Cahill whispered.

Queen didn't see anyone around who might be eavesdropping, but he knew Cahill felt trapped between him and Colonel Ames. Some people are just naturally anxious, he thought. Usually women, in his experience, but Tom Cahill and Adry Hayward were exceptions to the rule.

"Men with perfect police records," Cahill continued, "sick families, no money. We've heard it all today."

"Well, it is the middle of winter and people need coal to keep themselves warm. I'd do the same, I suppose."

"You would?" Cahill asked, a little incredulously. "You don't seem to be the type of man who would throw himself on someone else's mercy."

"What do you know about me?" Queen snapped. "Don't get ahead of yourself. You've officially been on the City of Minneapolis payroll for how long? Days? Hours? We may hold the same rank on paper, but that's as far as it goes."

"Yes, sir, you're right," Cahill said apologetically. He shuffled his feet and looked uncomfortably at the sidewalk. "I'm sorry for that, Mr. Queen."

"Is there anything you'd like to say? Have you resigned as well? What a shame that would be. Well, at least you can go help Pa get ready for the spring thaw and planting season at the family farm."

"I haven't," Cahill said quietly.

It infuriated Queen that Cahill wasn't attempting to defend himself. He was in the mood for an argument and nothing made him angrier than someone who rolled over when he was itching to go at it.

"Never mind." Queen jerkily waved his hand at the door. "Lead the way, Milkshake."

The first floor of the Oyster Grotto was the gentlemen's dining room, simply furnished with tables along one side and a counter with cooking ranges running along the other. Coffee John was busy with his frying pans, his white shirtsleeves rolled up to reveal stout forearms. He wore a grease-spattered apron around his ample waist, and was busy barking orders to a pair of colored waiters standing patiently nearby. Queen followed Cahill to a table at the very rear of the restaurant, where a group of men sat with their coats off, vests unbuttoned, and ties loosened. His eyes immediately focused on the mayor of Minneapolis. Doc had a charisma that made him the center of any gathering, and Queen figured it was his easy smile and bright, penetrating eyes that drew people to him like flies to honey. Always the politician, Doc rose and greeted Queen cheerfully, gripping his cigar between his teeth as he put out his hand. He shook it so robustly that Queen felt his spirits rise in spite of himself.

"Detective Harmon Queen. We've missed you! Today has been chaos, absolute chaos. Glad to see you reporting for duty."

"He came here to eat, I'm guessing," Colonel Ames retorted sourly. He was sitting next to his brother, and remained seated as the other men rose to shake Queen's hand. Tom Brown, the mayor's secretary, offered a quiet hello. Another fellow Queen knew well, Irwin Gardner, who was employed as Doc's assistant in his medical practice, smiled as he greeted him. Gardner was young and good-looking, a tad on the thin side, always jovial, and very loyal to Doc. Across the table were scattered the remains of a hearty meal. A porcelain dish held emptied oyster and mussel shells. Bits of lobster shells and shrimp tails littered butter-stained plates. Drained coffee cups had been pushed aside for a bottle of bourbon and glasses for all.

"How does it feel, Queen, to live a life free of schedules and obligations?" the colonel asked dryly.

"I have been busy on police work today, sir."

"*Really?*" Colonel Ames asked. "And what case were you following up that was more important than training new detectives?"

As tempted as Queen was to tell him that he'd been gambling while drunk in a whorehouse, just to watch Colonel Ames's head explode, he wasn't in the mood to pussyfoot around anyone today. "The Maisy Anderson murder."

Colonel Ames's face darkened. "You've discovered her full name, I see. I thought we were clear that that investigation is on hold."

"There were women in danger, the last of Dander's inmates, and I wanted to ensure their safety."

"And did you?" Doc asked.

"I did. I found them and moved them to a safe place."

"Well, good for you," Doc said with a satisfied look. "Brilliant follow-up. Fred, you need to let this young man up easy. These women might be voters someday. Their movement is picking up considerable steam and it's only a matter of time before they have the right to vote. We must look towards the future, brother!"

"Perhaps," Colonel Ames replied, forcing his mouth into a smile while meeting Queen's eyes in a nasty lock. "That doesn't change the fact, however, that you were derelict in your duties today. You've wanted a promotion to Chief Detective, haven't you? This is far from the best way to get there."

Queen was floored that the colonel was dangling that little carrot in his face. Just two days ago he'd been told the position didn't exist. Now the colonel had the gall to threaten him with something that wasn't even on the table. And this in front of the Mayor and others whose business it wasn't. Was public humiliation his game now?

"You've changed your mind, then, sir? More work than you anticipated? The past two days must have been exhausting." Queen smiled inwardly as he watched Colonel Ames glow red. Doc, oblivious to the sentiment underneath the exchange, snapped his finger for a waiter.

"Bring this man a menu! Harm, you should be rewarded with a good meal for rescuing damsels in distress. I read "A Connecticut Yankee in King Arthur's Court" a few months ago. You know the story by Mark Twain? Damn fine writer he is. If I'd lived back then, or afforded the opportunity to travel back in time, like good old Hank Morgan, I would have enjoyed the age of chivalry quite well, I think."

"Yes, sir," Queen assented, as he sat down. Colonel Ames stood up.

"Alonzo, we have to get back to work. Much to do."

"But we have everyone here! I should say that this is the perfect time to discuss the business we were speaking about yesterday. Getting the old coffers going and all."

Colonel Ames stared at Queen, eyes burning. "Perhaps we should work over more of the details privately before we open things up."

"Nonsense!" Doc cried. "Sit down, brother. The sooner we move forward on this, the better it is, for us, and for the city."

"Very well." Colonel Ames lowered himself into his chair with a thin, forced smile. He poured a drink and handed it to Queen. "Enjoy, Lieutenant. A very fine vintage."

Queen nodded thanks, even though he felt like taking the glass and breaking it over the bastard's head.

"Wonderful!" Doc exclaimed. "Tom. Can you ask John to join us? This little meeting involves him."

Cahill, who had been standing back some distance, seemingly unsure of what to do in the presence of so many of Doc's old friends, was eager to be of use. He trotted over to Coffee John with Doc's request. Coffee John removed his greasy apron, washed his hands, and came to the table. A waiter had anticipated his need and set a chair down for him. The proprietor promptly dropped his massive body into the chair, grabbing a bottle of bourbon off the table for a well-deserved drink.

"Hello, gents. You like the lobster today? Only forty-one hours from Boston. The freshest seafood in the Midwest, by God!"

Everyone knew that the best way to get on Coffee John Fitchette's good side was by complimenting him on his food, and the men at the table made their rounds of congratulations to the beaming cook. He waved his hand modestly, threw his drink down his throat, and motioned for the waiter to bring another bottle.

"We haven't had time for a personal celebration yet!" John boomed. "Fill up the glasses. Let us imbibe a final smile! A toast is in order." He hoisted up his large frame, and the others followed.

"To our esteemed Doctor Ames, now mayor of Minneapolis, but always our friend. There has never been a better or more beloved man in the city, and may he live long and stay mayor for another ten terms!"

The men echoed his sentiment with "Hear, hear," and more drinks were poured around the table, as they again lowered themselves into their chairs.

"Tom, pull up a seat," Doc said. There wasn't any room at the table, so Cahill scooted a chair up behind Queen, who didn't particularly care for this. But he held his tongue. "Where is Fred Connor? He needs to be here, as well," the mayor continued.

"A wonderful thought," Coffee John said brightly, "I think he's a swell fellow, but you know he's colored, Doc. Those of us at the table here don't mind of course, but my other patrons might, and I can't turn away customers on the count of some Negro eating here, as crack an officer as Connor may be."

"I asked him to run an errand for you," Colonel Ames said, cutting off the pass on his brother, who Queen knew was about to say something in his bodyguard's defense. "He'll be back shortly. Let's get down to the business at hand, shall we? Now that everyone is here."

"Right," Doc agreed. "You are the men who have helped me more than any others in last fall's electoral victory." He swept his hands over the table, including everyone present in the gesture. "'To the victors go the spoils,' the old adage says. So too, must they go for our merry little band. I'm an old man now, and I am closing in on shore. God willing, once these two years are over, I'll retire and have some brief chance to smell the proverbial flowers. Access to the garden, however, requires funds. Here, gentlemen, is our chance to provide some meaningful income to supplement the pittances we're paid, for the enormous duties we face as the protectors of Minneapolis."

Queen couldn't resist speaking. He had known this little meeting would happen, but hadn't expected it so quickly, and the mention of greenbacks flooded his head with reminders of his own precarious financial position. He also knew from long experience that certain plums didn't hang long on the tree. "I know the resort madams in the First Street, Main Street, and Eleventh Avenue districts. We're on good terms, and I can easily collect whatever fees you plan to charge," he said.

"This isn't going to be a discussion, so much as a meeting to hand out assignments," Colonel Ames replied, his eyes sparkling with pleasure as he sensed Queen's desperation. "That particular task will be taken care of by Mr. Gardner. Gardner, can you handle that job?"

Irwin Gardner's face stiffened in surprise. "I think so, sir. I'm not a member of the police department, though."

"You are as soon as we swear you in. You'll be made a special officer. Your responsibilities will continue at my brother's office as you help Dr. Clark with patients. This extra duty will be well compensated, and won't take much of your time."

"Congratulations, Irwin!" Doc declared, and the others at the table repeated his sentiment. Queen half-heartedly stood up and did the same, and then flopped back down.

Gardner in charge of graft collections? Queen was flummoxed. Gardner had no experience in the delicate art of collecting fees from madams. It required a quick tongue and a loose smile, but most important, an understanding of the brothel business. Gardner was trained to bandage wounds, not to shake down women for cush.

"Another appointment for which we need an able man is Captain of Police. Someone to work with the new officers, and to make sure that they're appreciative of their new positions. When we considered whom to appoint for this job, we decided on a man who carries weight on the streets of Minneapolis. Someone who has the respect of both high society and the working man." Colonel Ames licked his lips and took a sip of his drink.

This won't be an easy job, Queen thought, but it might have its financial rewards down the road. Every new officer had to shell out a fee for the right to wear the uniform. Getting some of these hoodlums Doc has hired, as fresh fish, to actually dig into their pockets and hand over money will take a lot of arm-twisting. But it was a prestigious position in the department. He had a feeling, as Colonel Ames again looked at him with a half-smile, that this job wasn't coming his way. As a detective it wasn't suited for him anyway, unless Colonel Ames' final coupe de grace today would be to demote him to a beat patrolman.

"There isn't anyone that we know more capable, or more of a man of the people, excepting my brother himself. He's been a loyal Ames man since we first met him. John Fitchette, will you accept our appointment?"

Coffee John bellowed like a bull moose in heat. His eyes were wild with excitement, and he almost threw himself on the Ames brothers, thanking them profusely for their kindness. A smattering of applause filled the air.

"Hot dog!" he cried. "I always wanted to wear a blue jacket. Johnson!" A waiter scuttled over to his side. "We got any champagne?" Johnson nodded confirmation. "This is about the best goddamn day I ever had. Bring it out, and the nice crystal flutes from the back! And don't smear them!" The applause grew a little louder when he mentioned the champagne.

"A good day all around!" Doc affirmed. "You've got something to discuss with Harm, though."

The Colonel's expression turned stale. "This matter hasn't been fully ironed out, Alonzo. I really insist that we wait before we talk about it. There are certain details—"

"I don't think waiting is a good idea. This is something that requires immediate action. I'm a man of action. Do you think that shifty mayor Carter Harrison in Chicago waits before he leaps? I knew his father, you know, before that bullet felled him in his own home. *There*, another reason not to wait. As-sassination. Anything can happen at any time."

"We'll speak now, but privately," Colonel Ames said. Ani-mosity was slithering out of the colonel's pores, and Queen enjoyed the exchange tremendously. "Please excuse us for a moment, gentlemen. We have something to discuss. It will concern you all in due time, but Detective Queen has some preliminary work to do."

"You'll be back for your scallops, Queen?" asked Coffee John, as he emptied the last of his bourbon glass. "I was about to fry them for you."

"I will," said Queen. "And a glass of your fizz."

"Gardner. Can you come too? I think this may require your presence," Colonel Ames said. He turned to Coffee John. "Can we speak somewhere quietly?"

"You're welcome upstairs, Colonel. The second floor is my ladies' dining room, as you know, but it's closed for a repair to the ceiling."

"Do you need anything from me, Colonel Ames?" piped up Cahill, standing at attention.

"No, Tom. Stay here. You'll have plenty of work once this is over."

Queen muffled a scoff. He knew Ames wanted to siphon in-formation to Cahill slowly, acclimate him on how he planned to run his police force. Cahill was an innocent, but loyal to the core. The colonel would break down the boy's morals bit by bit until he created the vassal he envisioned. Queen had a half a notion to take Cahill aside and explain what he was in for. As enjoyable as that might be, though, it would probably get him knocked down to cleaning the jail toilets.

They followed the colonel upstairs to a room much more elegant and feminine than the simple main floor they'd just come from. Queen didn't know much about fine furnishings,

but he'd read the advertisement Fitchette had placed recently in the *Minneapolis Tribune*, and assumed the carpets on the
floor were really from Brussels, and the chandeliers were real
crystal. Expensive sideboards, china closets, Vienna chairs,
hall trees and parlor furniture dotted the large, airy room. The
supreme accent was a Miller grand piano, which Coffee John
hired a pianist to play on the afternoons when ladies' clubs
filled the room with their meetings and refreshments.

Queen felt no sense of dread, but more of amusement, as
Colonel Ames led them to a table. He anticipated the same
manipulative colonel he'd visited with after his meeting with
Doc in his personal office. Once apart from his brother, the
colonel was less inclined to hold back in his opinion. Queen
figured he'd be dealt some choice, explosive words outside
the mayor's hearing range. He wasn't disappointed. Ames
turned on him and the spittle flew freely.

"Jesus Christ, Queen. Do you know how close you are to
being fired for insubordination? I don't give a damn about
how much my brother likes you or what you've done for him
in the past. You're under my command. Do you know what
I would do to you if we were in the Philippines right now?
You'd be stripped down to nothing and digging holes in the
middle of a mosquito-infested jungle. What the hell were you
doing, anyway, chasing whores around this morning?"

"Like I told you, I was following up on a clue."

Colonel Ames let out a sound like a snarl. He was beyond
furious, but fighting to maintain control. Christ, for our dif-
ferences, we are still similar when it comes to keeping it in,
Queen thought suddenly, startled by the revelation.

"You swore to me you would follow orders," Ames
managed to say. Irwin Gardner stood silently by, stunned by
the conversation.

"I didn't swear to that."

"You *need* to follow orders."

Another revelation was dawning on him, one that comforted him more than the last. Colonel Ames despised him, but hadn't asked for his badge, despite Queen's disobedience. If it ever were to happen, it should be right now, but here he was, still a Minneapolis police detective. Queen was starting to believe that he had more leverage than he once thought.

"I killed someone today," he said matter-of-factly. "Well, not exactly killed him. I stuck a broken bottle into his eye and he ran into the river and drowned. It was the man who killed Maisy Anderson."

A low whistle slipped out of Irwin Gardner, and Queen noted that he sounded impressed, which gave him a pinch of satisfaction. Surprise, however, didn't register in Colonel Ames's face as he figured it might.

"You think I don't know already?" Ames replied. He took out a cigarette and a match and lit it with a steady hand, blowing a curl of smoke before continuing. "You visited Adry Hayward, brother of the infamous murderer. One of Dander's lunatics ambushed you and you confronted him. That confrontation led to his demise. He happened to be the shooter of the girl you so desperately want justice for."

Queen lifted his jaw from his stomach. How in God's name could he have gotten this information so quickly?

"When I mentioned I'd found the girls, in front of Mayor Ames, you looked surprised. You're telling me you already knew? Who told you?" Queen asked.

The Colonel's eyes had changed, from ferocity to something steely and cool. "Not your concern. This is a good lesson for you, however. Whatever autonomy you've had in the past is officially dead. I am to be made aware of every move you make. Every report you fill out. Every dribble of shit you produce from that high and mighty ass of yours." He paused, letting his words permeate the air for effect.

Queen wondered if Norbeck had spilled the beans, or if Ames had had him followed. He'd been careful, but not thorough. The idea of Colonel Ames, in the midst of a giant transition of power, tailing him, would have made him laugh earlier this morning. Now, he couldn't laugh if a clown dropped from the ceiling with a bottle of seltzer water and shot it into Ames's big mouth.

"So," Colonel Ames continued. "Your search for the whore's killer can cease now that you've sent him on a holiday to the Gulf of Mexico. We need to turn to the business at hand." Ames tapped the ashes from his cigarette into a teacup on a table nearby. "Generating green is our immediate goal, and Gardner has come up with an idea. Would you please share with the detective?"

Gardner took in a little breath and stepped forward. "Mr. Queen must certainly be aware of this kind of operation already." If he was looking for affirmation, Queen decided he wouldn't give it to him. Gardner shifted a little on his feet. "We don't know each other that well, Mr. Queen, but I don't have, shall we say, a pristine history. Were you aware?"

"On the level, Gardner, I've never given you much thought at all. You've always seemed content mopping up blood after Doctor Ames's appointments."

"Doctor Ames has always been especially kind to me, and encourages my medical studies. Without a father in my life, he's given me advice and support. I owe a great deal to him."

"Did he pull you out of some gutter somewhere?" Queen asked, "Dust you off and put you to work? I've read Horatio Alger before. You don't seem to have quite the same pluck as Ragged Dick."

"I've been determined, especially since he's taken me under his wing, to become a doctor. But I've also been on the wrong side of the law. I've seen some things. We have friends in common."

"Friends of low character? Is that what you're getting at?"

"Friends who have taken part in rigged games. Do you know what a mitt joint is?"

All too aware, Queen thought. "Of course."

"I figured so. We plan to start a few in Minneapolis. I've got men at some of the saloons and gambling houses who are keen to cooperate."

"When do you plan to move on this?" Queen asked.

"Not right away," Colonel Ames said quickly. "All eyes are on the new administration now. The press is scrutinizing every single movement at this early stage. We need to ease ourselves in. I think by summer we should be fully operational."

"I thought you had the newspapers under your weight," Queen said.

Ames eyeballed Queen carefully, as if to determine how much he should tell him. Finally, with a little shrug, he decided to persist. "There is currently a fair level of goodwill towards us. Everyone, except that damn *Minneapolis Times*, is going easy. We're giving the rags plenty to write about and people are excited about the changes we're making." He smeared the remainder of his cigarette into the teacup. "It's all completely superficial at this stage, of course, which is what I … we want."

"Throw them a cookie, and while they're eating it, push a wheelbarrow full of cake right past."

"An ill-sounding analogy, but tepidly appropriate."

Queen barely heard him. He was contemplating the money. Mitt games could be extremely lucrative if pulled off correctly. You needed lots of people, all skilled in their specific roles to make it work, but if the pieces were in place it was a money tree, no question. The general idea of a mitt game required a sympathetic saloon, called a mitt joint; and a steerer, a kicker, an inside cop and of course a dim-witted sucker. The steerer's job was to locate out-of-towners unfamiliar with Minneapolis nightlife but looking for a good time. Businessmen with money were ideal for the role of sucker, and once the steerer found one, he'd befriend him, offer to take him around the city, and ultimately direct him into the mitt joint. The steerer would introduce the sucker into a game, usually stud poker or three-card monte. Everyone at the table was part of the con of course, and the dealer used a trick to ensure the man lost his money. It was called "cold-decking"—switching to a new deck to ensure the appropriate cards were dealt. If the sucker didn't suspect cheating, he'd simply lose his money and leave the joint, and no one would be the wiser. However, if his hackles were raised, the kick would be set into motion. Once the sucker questioned the game's honesty, the dealer would raise his hat. That signaled a man called the kicker, outside the game, to call the local police station. Then this man would take the sucker to meet the cop who was part of the business. Though kindly and concerned, the officer would still ask the sucker if he had a license to gamble. The chances of that? None.

"Well then," the cop would say. "You'd best be out of town."

"What about my money?" a particularly stubborn sucker might query.

"You gambled without a license. Your money is gone. Get out of Minneapolis now before you're in real trouble and have to be taken to jail."

The cop would then take him to the train station and send him off, with any luck never to see him again. That was the racket. It had the potential, under the right guidance of course, to make its players comfortably wealthy within months. This is why Harm Queen had stuck by Doc Ames so long: a payoff to end all payoffs. This was the nearest thing to a jackpot he could conceive of, and he wanted in.

"So, you have steerers lined up?" Queen asked Gardner.

"I know some fellows, but I don't know if they can handle something this big," Gardner replied.

He felt himself soften a little at the sight of Colonel Ames. Whatever slights he'd experienced began to melt away as he realized how important this mitt game was to him. Queen knew, without hesitation, that he was the best man for the job. He had the best connections of anyone in the city and could make a killing for himself and the Ames brothers and anyone else lucky to hang on for the ride.

"I know the best confidence men in the country," Queen said, replying to Gardner's statement, but staring hard into Colonel Ames' eyes. "You let me take care of this, sir," he said, to Ames this time.

This is like selling my soul to the devil.

Ames slipped him that thin-lipped smile, and Queen knew at that moment Ames understood their new relationship. He'd wanted Queen under his command, and now he had him. In any other time or place, Queen would have been revolted at the idea, but now, to his surprise and shame, he was giddily excited.

CHAPTER 8

THE FRONT OF CITY HALL LOOMED before Anderson like a monolith. Not in a physical sense— plenty of buildings in Minneapolis were more impressive—but it stood as a symbol. It represented the law. He respected the law, and rules. They hadn't let him down yet. Life certainly had, and it was punching him in the gut with relentless force again, but he knew the law would prevail in the end. He would find out what happened to Maisy and if there were anything—anything—that pointed to foul play, he would find out. And the law would prevail.

He also found himself thinking about tobacco. Martha had forbidden it years ago, and he'd lost his taste for it God knows when. It had been a long, long while. The desire for a pipe or a plug of chew suddenly overwhelmed him. Something about being here, even under these terrible circumstances, stirred the embers in his belly. Senses he hadn't felt since he was a salaried, working lawman. It was the thrill of the hunt, and it made him feel a step younger. His lawman sensibilities were bubbling to the surface once again, and he admitted to himself, grudgingly, that he enjoyed the feeling, even as it battled with his grief.

A brilliant burst of sunshine lit the morning sky, and the streets were already sticky with wet snow melting in what appeared would be an unnaturally warm day. Anderson walked across Nicollet from the Columbia Hotel, where he had rented a room, towards City Hall, where Nicollet and Hennepin avenues converged. He stared for a moment at Bridge Square, a broad, wedge-shaped intersection, thickly bordered by shops and the Mississippi. The Steel Arch Bridge continued across to the opposite bank, just over Nicollet Island, to the flour-milling district beyond. A streetcar track on the Hennepin Avenue side competed for the road with cabs and wagons.

He'd been here many times, mostly passing through. A few of those times he remembered fondly. There had been nothing but little clapboard houses when he'd first ridden across the old suspension bridge as a young lad with the United States Cavalry. Fifteen years ago, after fetching Maisy from Chicago, he and Martha had stopped in Minneapolis for a few days. The three of them had walked on these very streets, window-shopping and eating in cafes. The emotions they had felt—sadness at losing their daughter, and excitement and relief over rescuing Maisy from being lost to an orphanage—came back now in a dimmed but still palpable memory. Anderson could remember how they'd bought Maisy some licorice from a candy store, still in business, catty-corner from where he stood. They had also gawked at a massive mast that stood close to where he was now, at the crux of the avenues and a dozen feet from City Hall's door. It had towered almost 300 feet and was topped by eight enormous electric arc lamps in an attempt to illuminate the gateway to Minneapolis. They had marveled at it, but now it was gone. For a moment he considered asking someone walking by what had happened, but he knew he had more important things to do.

At the cake-slice-shaped City Hall's blunted tip, he entered through the narrow front door. He stood in a large open room, filled with desks, ringing telephones, and intense-looking men in vests and rolled up sleeves, smoking and clicking away on noisy typewriters. A slight fellow with a big toothy smile sauntered up to Anderson.

"What in God's name are you supposed to be?"

"Pardon me?" Anderson's cragged face surveyed the speaker coolly.

"Is there a new dime museum in town? A circus theater? A Wild West show?" He sputtered laughter and took a long draw from a cigarette. "I'm only kidding, you know," the man said. His eyes sparkled with merriment. "The name's Freddie Bonge, crack rag reporter."

"I'm Sheriff Dix Anderson. Retired." He put his hand out, and the man took it with a sweaty, limp little squeeze.

"What brings you to the hallowed offices of the *Minneapolis Tribune?*" Bonge asked.

"I thought these were city offices. I'm here for a meeting with a police detective."

"You don't say," Bonge said with a chuckle. "The right building, but the wrong door. You can find who you're looking for by taking that door to the lobby. Turn right; go outside and then to the door on your right. Someone there can help you." He pointed past the cluttered desks to an interior door. His mouth moved into a slightly mischievous grin. "May I ask which detective you are here to see?"

"Lieutenant Harmon Queen."

"Is that so?" Bonge twisted at a little pencil shoved behind his ear and gave a whistle that sounded like a plunging artillery round. "Must be important."

"It is. Excuse me, but I have to go, young man. Nice to meet you." Anderson tipped his hat and started for the door, past the staring, grinning newspapermen.

"Wait a moment, please!"

Bonge jogged up to his side. "We've got an 'Out and About' section and I'm supposed to write it this week. We report on the comings and goings of interesting and important people in Minneapolis. My editor ordered me to the West Hotel to cover some British fellow named Winston Spencer Churchill, who's in town to lecture about 'The Boer War As I Saw It.' The *bore* war is more like it, if you ask me," he snorted. "But, *you*, sir, intrigue me. You're wearing quite an outfit and you must have a good story to tell. Will you have time to talk to me during your visit?" He thrust out a business card.

"I don't think so. Not the chatting sort."

"Well, just take this anyway. If you ever want a free lunch, I'd be happy to buy, in exchange for a little of your time."

"I'll keep you in mind, if I ever get the mind to gab," Anderson said, and took the card.

"Remember me!" Bonge cried. His echo followed Anderson as he walked away, and the old sheriff shook his head, slightly embarrassed at the outburst.

"Wait, wait!"

Anderson turned, as Bonge huffed up to him. "Perhaps the mayor's office would be faster. Just through the mayor's reception area is the police assembly room, and beyond that, the detectives' desk. Your Detective Queen will be there. Here, let me show you."

"Fine," Anderson said. Bonge led him through the lobby and out of the building.

As they walked, a shrill honk made them both twist their heads towards Hennepin Avenue. It came from a black-painted open-air vehicle, shaped like a small sleigh, suspended high atop what resembled four thick bicycle wheels. Two men sat crammed together in the seat, trying to appear as regal as possible. The one wearing goggles pushed a tiller to steer, and they veered and weaved around horses and carriages with daring speed. Anderson thought it about the most ridiculous thing he'd ever seen. Hissing and sputtering, the contraption finally slid to clanking halt.

"A horseless carriage, eh? I've read about those, but never seen one," Anderson remarked.

"A *horseless carriage*? They're called *automobiles*! My, you are fresh out from nowhere," Bonge replied excitedly. "Mark my words, Minneapolis is bound to be a hot 'mobile town! There are a good dozen here already. We even have Republic Motor Vehicle Company, which makes the electric type. That one is a steam powered two-seat."

"A damn nuisance, if you ask me," Anderson said with a critical eye.

"Electric, gasoline and steam, and we've got a few of each," the reporter continued, ignoring Anderson's scorn. "An electric brougham, an electric Stanhope, a steam Locomobile, a gasoline two-seat, an electric runabout." He was crossing them off in his head, while gazing at the parked auto like a caged bird at blue sky.

The chauffeur at the tiller hopped down to the icy pavement. He wore a smart looking cap, and placed his goggles above the brim before trotting to the other side. He held up his gloved hand and helped the other, an elderly gentlemen in a black top hat and a trim white beard, alight to the sidewalk. The man radiated pomposity, and as he marched to the entrance the chauffeur rushed in front, pressing past Anderson to get the door.

"This should be good," Bonge said with a sly grin. They followed behind, and entered a well decorated but not especially comfortable waiting room, with some hard-backed armchairs and benches lining the walls. The bearded man had already greeted two other cigar-smoking gentlemen standing in the corner, and they immediately engaged in an animated discussion. A thickset man with glasses scowled behind a desk, and

Anderson presumed he was the mayor's secretary. Above him was a grandly painted battlescape, Union soldiers gallantly holding back a horde of charging Rebels. The man stood up, eyes narrow with suspicion.

"And how may I help you, sir?" The words were curt, as though he had no interest in what he was asking.

"I'm looking for Detective Queen. He's expecting me," Anderson replied.

"This is the mayor's office, sir, not a place for police matters. Please leave and go in through the opposite side."

"This man, Mr. Bonge," Anderson said, pointing to the reporter, "told me the rooms were connected, and I'd have access to the police offices. He works for the *Tribune*, and seems to be in the know." Bonge was already feverishly writing in his notebook, and looked up with a gleeful gleam in his eye when his name was mentioned.

"Mr. Brown," Bonge said, licking his pencil tip, "I'd like you to meet Sheriff Dix Anderson. He's a real-life old-time lawman, probably fresh from Indian country. Tell me, Sheriff, what do you think of the big city?"

"Christ," Anderson groaned.

Secretary Tom Brown was furious. "No press, no press! I'm going straight to your editor, Bonge. These stunts are wearing thin. You need to schedule interviews here. I don't like surprises."

Bonge cleared his throat, and tried to look serious. "Apologies, sir. But I think it would be swell if you'd introduce Mayor Ames to Sheriff Anderson. Two larger-than-life, past-their-prime figures, exchanging wise words from lifetimes of hard-fought experience. Mayor Ames in the political arena, and Sheriff Anderson, with two fists and twelve bullets! Our readers would cry with joy!"

The men in the corner were now attentive, and the white-bearded gentleman from the automobile especially. The thick gold watch hanging from his suit pocket swung as he stepped forward. He cleared the mucus from his throat, eyeing Anderson evenly.

"You, sir, are a damned spectacle, parading around in public like a fool." The men with him nodded their haughty approval. Anderson turned to face him. Men like this were not the kind he chose to socialize with. Under other circumstances, he might ignore the comments, but today he felt emotional. The flood of memories of Maisy and Martha, and the crushing, ceaseless heartache had shortened his fuse.

"Sir, I don't take kindly to pompous jack-asses who don't mind their own business," Anderson said tersely. "Choose not to look at me, if it offends you. I don't care." He straightened up to his full height, a good head above the man who mocked him. It hurt his back to do so.

"I would suggest you depart these premises and find a suitable place for a shower-bath," the bearded man said, eyes bitter and flashing. "I will venture a guess that you are not a married man; otherwise you wouldn't keep yourself in this condition. Or if you are, perhaps your wife may need some basic hygiene lessons to help guide you to cleanliness."

A ripple of laughter. Bonge giggled like a schoolgirl as he wrote, mumbling under his breath about Minneapolis flour magnates. Anderson suspected he was speaking to someone with some status. At this point it mattered little to him. He had no patience for anyone who insulted his wife.

"Sir, this is a place of order and law," Anderson said. His glare was damningly hot. "You are fortunate that I respect the institution of law. I'll give you the opportunity to take your words back, like the gentleman you believe you are. We'll then both go on our ways."

"Now, now!" Secretary Brown was at his side, a hand on his arm. "Please depart this office at once. Take your meeting with Detective Queen from the police entrance, or I will call officers in to escort you out immediately."

"I would advise you to listen," spat the bearded gentleman. "Be fortunate you aren't being escorted to the tramp room, dressed the way you are."

Anderson flexed his hand. A good slap would defend his honor without shattering this buffoon's teeth, he decided. He pulled his hand back, and the man's eyes showed a momentary fear. And then he felt another hand grab his wrist and pull his arm behind his back. The grip was immensely strong and the movement was swift.

"Thank you, Mr. Cahill, for averting this," Secretary Brown said. "Please take him out."

"He's here because his granddaughter is dead," Cahill said. His spectacles were steamed and he was peering over them. "I'll take him through to the assembly room where he can have his questions answered. Please open it for me."

Brown sighed and complied. Anderson felt himself being gently pushed from behind. "Please go, sir. This is for the best."

The restraint was powerful and Anderson knew he had little choice. The door slammed behind them. His arm was released immediately.

"I apologize for that, sir," Cahill said. Anderson turned to meet the voice, and was surprised that someone so short, with a face like a cherub, could possess such iron arms.

"You probably did the right thing, son." He uttered his words with reluctant appreciation, rubbing his arm. "I'm not used to being manhandled like that, but your judgment was correct."

"Thank you, sir. Do you happen to know who that was?"

"Someone important?"

"Yes, sir. It was John Pillsbury."

"Well, that explains his doughy face."

Cahill's face melted from anxiety to a big grin. "It does at that, sir."

The pencil whipped across the paper with almost a mind of its own, as Queen furiously scribbled out numbers. An average haul of $200 per sucker, he estimated, at two or three per night, multiplied by as many mitt joints as they could set up. Plenty of money would need to get paid to all the players in the con, but plenty more would be left over. He leaned back in his chair and breathed a sigh of relief. Even the stale air in his dingy little detectives' office tasted sweet today. It was shared amongst the police force's dozen detectives, each with his own desk. He'd made sure he was alone this morning, as he expected a special guest who required some privacy.

The mitt games would allow him money to pay back Kilbane and get Jack Peach off his back. Peach was an enormous concern to him. While he hadn't seen him for a few days, their conversation still echoed in his head. Jiggs Kilbane wanted a meeting with Fred Ames, and Peach insisted that only this would satisfy his debt. The thing of it, though, was that Queen wasn't so sure he had Colonel Ames's ear yet. At least, not to the point where he could suggest this meeting. Secondly, he was sure, despite their truce, that the calculating rascal would gladly get rid of him if he thought he could get along without him. Why would Queen want to set up a powwow with the two people in the world least likely to be on his Christmas card list? Putting them together might make it worse for him if his name came up. Queen still believed that green, lots of green, could adequately resolve his debt with Kilbane. Why should it be anything else, anyway? He owed

Kilbane money, and would pay him back with money, regardless of what Peach threatened him with.

Still, he grimaced as he thought of Peach, and his way of showing up at Queen's most vulnerable moments. The guy had a sinister reputation and little in the way of weaknesses, as far as Queen could see. He was one of the few men he'd ever met whom he considered an equal. It was hard for him to articulate, exactly, why he thought that. Peach just had a way about him. Slicked-up, well-spoken without being pretentious, and chock full of charisma and guile. What made Queen especially wary, though, was Peach's reputation, like his, for figuring out the angle. Rarely did adversaries find themselves one step ahead of Queen, but Peach was like a ghost, fluttering just out of reach, taunting him to no end.

Peach's boss, Jiggs Kilbane, had none of his enforcer's finesse. He was volatile, short-tempered, and from what Queen had heard, came from a low family in New York's Five Points slum. Kilbane had run with the Irish Whyos gang as a youngster, and risen through the ranks, rubbing shoulders with notorious gangsters like Paul Kelly and Monk Eastman. For reasons Queen didn't fully know—although he'd picked up plenty of rumors about a massive falling out—Kilbane was now comfortably situated on the Mississippi river's east side, preferring to be the biggest toad in the puddle than a bit player in one of New York's sprawling gangland empires.

And Queen understood full well that crossing Kilbane had unfortunate consequences. Last year he'd investigated the murder of an Irish immigrant, found filled with slugs in a tenement basement. They'd caught the killer, but clues had pointed to Kilbane as the mastermind. The dead Irishman had been running numbers and withholding information on the profits, specifically the cut due Jiggs Kilbane. Solid evidence, however, had been in short supply, barely enough to present to his counterparts in the Saint Paul Police Department. They'd laughed Queen off as bughouse. His relationship with the Saint Paul cops hadn't improved much since then.

Queen needed to focus on the present. He had to figure out how the Big Mitt game could operate most profitably. His alliance with Colonel Ames was precarious at best, but while he felt uneasy, he understood perfectly well the area of gray where they were working, and the bigger picture. Murders were disturbing and distracting to the public. The city needed to feel secure so business could go on. He felt the satisfaction of Pock's punishment, and even without a trial he'd sleep well tonight. No question about that, although he knew in the back of his mind that he was justifying his own actions. Emil Dander was a rotten apple, and whether or not he'd given the orders to kill Maisy, he was directly responsible for her being in that terrible position; clinging to a fence with hardly any clothes on a bitter winter's night, taking a bullet that sent her plummeting into the snow. For now, having Dander in Stillwater prison would be enough. For now.

A knock on the door interrupted his thoughts. "What is it?"

Cahill's glasses almost fell off as he stuck his head in. "There is someone to see you, sir."

"Who?"

"Sheriff Dix Anderson of Bemidji."

Queen sighed. He had already heard that Anderson had skipped the formalities of a return telegram, and come directly to Minneapolis, uninvited. He wasn't looking forward to their meeting, but there was no way around it. "Come in here for a moment."

Cahill slipped through the door and gave Queen a weak salute.

"I'm not your superior, number one. And number two, that was a miserable excuse for a salute if I've ever seen one."

"S-sorry," was all that stumbled out of Cahill's mouth.

"Tell him twenty minutes." He put the paper with his figures in a drawer and locked it. From another drawer, he pulled a file at random, removed the papers and spread them over his desk like a poker hand. He'd prepared himself to lie to the old man. It had been a difficult decision, how to explain Maisy's passing to the sheriff. After considering it for a spell, he realized that Anderson wouldn't be satisfied simply with Pock's death. He'd want revenge on Dander as well, and that would make things messy in regards to Queen's new arrangement with the colonel. An accidental New Year's Eve shooting with Maisy in the wrong place at the wrong time was the story he'd decided on, with Colonel Ames's blessing. He felt bad being dishonest to a grieving grandfather, but he really couldn't see a better way to get this all behind him.

Cahill's voice filled the hallway, high-pitched protestations to a voice that was deep but gentle. The door opened and a lanky elderly man stepped into the light, filling the doorway's height. Cahill stood behind him, wringing his hands.

"I told him, sir, twenty minutes."

"That's fine, Detective Cahill," Queen said. He stood up somberly. "Please come in, Mr. Anderson."

The sheriff took off his broad hat, placed it on the desk, and eased himself into the chair. Queen was sure he heard a crack from the man's back. He was struck by the sheriff's appearance. He looked like he had just stepped off the cover of a frontier dime novel.

"Looks like you've come prepared for battle," Queen said, eyeing the bulge of pistol handles jutting out of his long coat.

"Not at all," Anderson said, his low voice warm and calm. "With your permission?" he asked Queen. Queen nodded, and Anderson's long thin fingers pushed back his coat. Deftly, he pulled the pistols from their holsters. Their ivory handles gleamed as the old lawman placed them on Queen's desk.

"Quite a pair of guns," Queen said.

"They were a gift from Bat Masterson. We worked together once or twice before, and I helped him out of a pickle in Cheyenne. Normally I don't go for the flashy stuff, but they've been with me for a while."

Don't go for flashy? The whole get-up was pure looniness, but Queen wasn't offended so much as amused. Something dug out of a dusty box from a different time, when law enforcement was black and white. The old man beneath the strange duds is a fish out of water here. Best to get him out of Minneapolis as quickly as possible.

"You're here for answers, Sheriff," Queen said with a quick smile. He hoped it didn't appear patronizing, but Anderson either didn't notice or didn't care. "I'll answer them as best as I can, even though I'm busy with the work that goes with a new detective force."

Anderson smiled wearily. "Understandable, Lieutenant. Tell me what happened, and show me my granddaughter."

Queen considered asking Cahill to leave, but decided to let him stay. This would avoid any appearance of secrecy, lest it get back to Colonel Ames. There was no reason the kid couldn't watch, though it went against Queen's perpetual instinct to go it alone. Cahill already knew the sheriff had lost his granddaughter to a terrible accident, and his soft demeanor and open sympathy might help blunt the edge for the old man. Queen himself, while feeling equally for the sheriff, had a harder time expressing himself so freely. Having a second officer here might make the situation more comforting for him. It also might be a good lesson on how to handle situations like this delicately, as long as Cahill stayed in the dark about the true nature of her death.

Queen had more than his fair share of experience leading some poor sucker through the motions and out the door. His fears about butting heads with a wily old sheriff had already started to ease once he had fully absorbed his whimsical appearance.

"First, my sincerest apologies for your loss," Queen said. No truth was bent with this statement. He felt tremendously for Maisy's family. "While I don't have any children, I do have sisters, and can't imagine the heartache you must be suffering from at this moment."

Anderson sat quiet. "Thank you, Detective Queen," he finally said, his dry lips barely visible under the mustache. "You were the one who found her body?"

"Yes, it was me," Queen replied.

In the next ten minutes Queen told Anderson the case's relevant facts, starting with where Maisy had been found—that fact couldn't be changed, because too many witnesses had seen the body. Then he assured the old man that her death was nothing more than an unfortunate accident, the result of too much careless celebratory behavior. He left out the details of the fence and the fall, and Dander, of course played no part in the story. Although when he mentioned where she was found, between Eighth and Ninth Streets near the Church of the Redeemer, he saw Anderson bristle. He's obviously familiar with Hell's Half-Acre, Queen thought.

When Queen finished his story, there was silence. Anderson sat back, his elbows tense on the chair's arms, looking down into nothing. Queen gestured to Cahill for a glass of water, and Cahill scuttled out, deep concern furrowing his young face. Minutes passed as Anderson stayed lost in thought. Cahill came and went with the water. Queen was a man of action, never satisfied to just sit and wait, but he felt guilt after he'd concluded his tale. That, along with the deep, forlorn grooves in Anderson's weathered face and sad eyes that seemed dead with grief, made him decide to give the sheriff his time.

Finally, Anderson stirred, shaking and raising his head. He gave Queen a hard fierce stare, eyes blazing. Queen felt himself blanching slightly at the change in Anderson's countenance.

"Take me to see her, please, Detective." The words came out tight and terse. Queen only nodded. Let's get this over with, he thought.

He's lying to me, Anderson deduced, as he adjusted the Colts in their holsters. Anderson had met enough liars in his life to know this Queen fellow was hiding something. There weren't any of the usual telltale signs of dishonesty. Queen hadn't averted his eyes, or touched his face while spinning his story. The detective was firm, direct, and sympathetic at the most appropriate times, in fact so polished that Anderson's suspicions rose with each sweep of Queen's hand, each rise or fall of inflection in his voice. He had received a short and to-the-point explanation of what had happened to his granddaughter, completely and utterly poppycock. Too damn perfect. His friend Martin Baum had warned him about Queen's reputation for bad behavior, but he hadn't been prepared for how skilled he was in the art of deception.

They said nothing to each other as Anderson followed. Walking with gritted teeth, Queen cleared a path through the large assembly room, wanting nothing more than to be done with the prying sheriff. Patrolmen moved out of Queen's way when they saw him approach, and Anderson wondered whether that was out of respect or fear. Baum had warned him about Detective Queen's double-handedness, and he was definitely on guard. Anderson put on his slouch hat as they stepped onto the busy sidewalk.

"The morgue is a few blocks away." Queen said. Anderson's legs were longer than Queen's and in two broad steps matched his pace. "Once you've identified the body as your granddaughter's, we can make arrangements for transportation to Bemidji for the funeral. Normally the Police Department doesn't get involved with matters like this, but under the circumstances, we'd be happy to assist you."

Assist me in getting out of Minneapolis as quickly as possible is more like it, Anderson thought. And why special circumstances for me, as opposed to any other investigation this serious?

"I'll take that into consideration, Detective," Anderson said.

Queen was hailing a cab when Cahill ran up behind them.

"If you don't mind, I'd like to come. I haven't been to the morgue yet." His face turned red with embarrassment. "I didn't mean to sound disrespectful, Mr. Anderson. I hope neither of you mind if I tag behind."

"I don't mind," Anderson said, noticing Queen shake his head in chagrin.

They took the cab for four blocks without conversation, getting out in front of a plain, two-story brick building at 815 South Fourth Street.

"The County Morgue," Queen explained as he paid the driver. "I called ahead and Superintendent Walsh agreed to meet us. He's been eager to confirm identification."

Keeper Walsh was, as promised, there to greet them when they arrived. He was a dignified, good-looking middle-aged man with a brown mustache and an athlete's build. Walsh immediately took Anderson's hand, putting his other hand on Anderson's elbow, and locked eyes with him.

"I am so very sorry for your loss, Mr. Anderson. Words cannot describe. Your granddaughter Maisy was a lovely young woman."

Anderson winced slightly, taken aback at the mention of her name, but also felt gratitude for the genuine sympathy. "Thank you."

"I wish I had been present when she was found. Mr. Queen might have told you I was out of town." He looked to Queen, who nodded confirmation. "Our one and only family holiday. New Year's is typically a quiet time for my line of work. Except for the occasional suicide." Walsh solemnly held his hands behind his back as they walked into what appeared to be a reception room. "I'm sorry the coroner isn't here, but that position is in flux at the moment. In with the old, and out with the new. My time is short here, as well."

"My regrets on that," Queen said. "We've worked together on many cases."

"I think a new change of scenery will do me well," Walsh replied. "I've seen some horrible things. It wears you down after a while."

"We shared the witness stand at the Hayward trial," Queen said. "Remember that? You were called up six times."

"Miss Ging was in the most unfortunate physical state when she arrived," Walsh said with a sigh. "Coroner Spring was here then. When we examined the body, I found her left eye gouged out. I picked up the eyeball, and the bullet that had caused her death fell out of her head. When we looked further, we found that the bullet had entered the back of her head. Dirty work."

Anderson stood, silent and uncomfortable, and Walsh seemed to sense he probably had said too much. His cheeks grew pink and he hung his head slightly.

"My apologies, sir. This isn't the time to reminisce, especially on this particular topic."

From the reception room they entered what appeared to be a poor man's courtroom. Six chairs lined a side wall, a judge's desk stood elevated at one end, along with a witness chair and a small gallery.

"This is the inquest room. Whenever there is the slightest question as to the reason for death, witnesses are called before a jury of six, and a determination is made. Typically, though, it reaffirms whatever judgment the coroner has already decided," Walsh said. "We'll continue to the back, where the bodies are kept."

The bodies were kept in a dead room, Anderson knew, but Walsh was being considerate enough not to say the words. He wasn't, however, yet finished with the matter of the inquest. As a sheriff in a small western town, he'd been accustomed to these duties being conducted by local mortuaries. Rarely were official inquests done—in his own personal experience—but it was interesting that Queen hadn't mentioned any inquest. In a major metropolis like Minneapolis, he thought, inquests were probably automatic. This would need to be settled.

"What was the outcome of the inquest for my granddaughter?" he asked Keeper Walsh.

Walsh looked questioningly at Queen. "Have you discussed this with Mr. Anderson?"

Anderson turned to Queen for his answer. Cahill, standing behind Queen, looked away, to examine some chipped paint on the wall. Queen gave Anderson a reassuring smile, and put his hand comfortingly on the sheriff's shoulder. "Perhaps we should visit your granddaughter now, and review this later, at my office. I'm sure Mr. Walsh is busy."

"You seem to enjoy reminiscing about old times," Anderson said. "Why not a brief discussion about the inquest? When was it held?"

Queen paused for a moment. "There wasn't one," he finally said.

Anderson stared at him hard. "And why not?"

"There wasn't an inquest because the case was cut and dried. It was an accident. Correct me if I'm wrong, Mr. Walsh, but when there is no doubt as to the nature of the death, an inquest is not requested."

"How do you know for certain?" Anderson asked. The questions he had held back in his grief were bubbling to the surface now, giving way to indignation over being lied to. Something strange was going on here, and he wanted to know what it was.

"There are scads of saloons in that part of Minneapolis," Queen replied. "When the clock struck midnight, guns went off like wildfire. Stray bullets flew everywhere. It was a grim, grievous accident. There were no witnesses."

"So did you visit the saloons and question the owners? Find out which patrons went out and fired their weapons? Did you try to match the bullet to a gun? Did you do anything to find witnesses?" Anderson's eyes were cold. "A famous detective like you, one would assume, would get the answers quickly."

"I did," Queen returned. "Rounds were made and questions were asked. Nothing surfaced that added to the case."

"Another question, detective. One that has been bothering me since I got your telegram. Perhaps I should have asked you, back in the privacy of your office, but the moment passed. I won't let it pass again." He pulled on his long mustache, smoothing it out and curling it up. "How did you identify her as Maisy Anderson? Who told you that name?"

"A young boy who had befriended her told me her first name. The sheriff in Minot gave me the last."

"This boy you speak of. What was the nature of their friendship? Can you tell me what she had been doing? How she had made her living? Was she under some kind of duress?"

Queen's eyes grew dark and serious. "The boy who might answer these questions more fully, sheriff, is currently missing. He said they were passing acquaintances. I had a limited time to question him, and now he's disappeared."

Cahill cleared his throat. "Sheriff Anderson, on behalf of Police Superintendent Ames, the department wants to officially offer its condolences. Rest assured, sir, if Detective Queen says it was an accident, it was." His eyes narrowed a little as he glanced at Queen. "He is not a man to cut corners."

I believe that, Anderson thought. He isn't a man to cut corners. He is thorough and calculating, but not a careless man.

"After we finish here, Detective Cahill, I want you to take me to the site of her death. I want to see where it happened. As you may know," he met both Queen's and Walsh's eyes, "my granddaughter disappeared two years ago. Perhaps seeing the surroundings she moved in might help put some of the pieces together for me."

"I don't really know anything about it, sir," Cahill said.

"Don't you think, though," Queen said, a look of deep concern on his face, "that perhaps after a funeral, you might want to rest? Our hands are currently tied with police business and a new administration, but once the dust settles I will personally try to answer those final questions for you. If she was in trouble, I will try to find the people who might have forced her into that position."

"That would be fine, Detective Queen," Anderson said. "I'd rather know sooner, though." He turned to Walsh. "Do you have her clothes and other belongings?"

Walsh nodded. "Yes, we have her things in a locker. She was wearing a silk gown and a boy's jacket. I don't know under what circumstances she lived her life, of course." he blushed again, hesitating. "The dress was quite revealing. I feel uncomfortable mentioning this to you, sir."

Anderson felt his heart sink. That wasn't like his Maisy at all, and confirmed his worst fears. She was never the type of girl who dressed immodestly. Yes, she was high-spirited, but always careful to protect her reputation. The neighborhood she was discovered in, he knew, was called Hell's Half-Acre. He was well aware of its unsavory character, having toured it with Martin Baum the last time he was in Minneapolis searching for her. It was a wretched, stinking, frightening block, and his stomach twisted like a wrench as the pieces came together.

"Tell me what kind of bullet felled her," Anderson asked. "You were with Coroner Williams when you examined her body, right?"

"Yes," Walsh replied. "We extracted a .45-70 size bullet from just over her left breast. It entered her heart, and I believe she died instantly. A mortal shot."

"And from a rifle, I assume." Anderson was parched, and wiped his dry lips with the back of his hand. He wished he'd downed that water Cahill had brought him earlier. "Do men usually bring rifles to saloons here, Detective Queen, on New Year's Eve? I can imagine a pistol, perhaps, tucked into a belt, but who carries a rifle into a saloon in Minneapolis? That seems to be looking for attention."

"That does seem odd," Keeper Walsh agreed.

Queen wore a concerned look. "A valid question, Sheriff. But there are many rough types about in this city, and I don't find that particularly strange. Perhaps someone had come back from a hunting trip, and without time to leave their gear at home before heading out for a drink. There are dozens of possibilities like that one. It doesn't seem out of the ordinary to me."

"Tell me, Mr. Walsh. Is it usually the coroner or the Police Department who contacts family members regarding their deceased?" Anderson didn't care that Queen was standing there. He was now past being polite.

"The coroner's office does that, but we are in transition right now. Detective Queen kindly offered to ease our swamped situation."

Footsteps stomped above them, interrupting the discussion. Keeper Walsh gave a faint, abashed grin. "I live upstairs with my family, and my wife is preparing lunch. She has a heavy step when I don't appear on time. Sheriff Anderson, let us take care of what you came to do."

The three men followed Walsh to the back, into a dark room that appeared to be an annex to the main building. Anderson knew it was the dead room. His eyes adjusted as Walsh turned up a gaslight. Even with the extra illumination, the room felt heavy and somber. Six marble slabs filled the sullen space.

The sheriff had seen his share of corpses in his day, but the anticipation of seeing his sweet Maisy lying on cold marble numbed him from head to toe. His senses slowed as they passed the slabs. Flat, cold and empty. Walsh, in his black suit, took on an undertaker's persona, serene and taciturn. Queen's face was ashen. Anderson's limbs grew weaker as they approached, and he grabbed for support at the slabs he passed. Detective Cahill came up like a dart behind him, reaching out to help, but Anderson waved him away with a shake of his head.

"No, thank you, young man," he said in a low grumble. He needed to pull his strength together, and with great effort, knees feeling like bending branches, he stretched himself up once more, letting go of the support of the slabs.

"Are you well enough to continue?" Keeper Walsh asked, looking alarmed.

"Yes. Let's finish this now."

They stopped at the back wall, by two slabs shrouded in white linen sheets, blindingly white in the gloom. One was fully covered. The other's sheet was turned down, revealing the head of a ginger-haired teenage boy. His bare arm hung limply from his side, fingers smudged black and pointed to the floor. Anderson saw a recognition light up Queen's face when he set eyes on the boy, a quick twist of horror and dismay. The look was there for an instant, then gone. The edge of the sheet, tucked under the boy's chin, was drenched in blood, and his eyes were crossed, as though looking at his own gore from beyond the grave.

"Where did you find him?" Queen asked, his hand cupped over his forehead.

"In an alley near the depot, late last night," replied Walsh.

"How did he die?"

Walsh cleared his throat and looked at Anderson. "It is quite gruesome, Lieutenant. Perhaps right now, isn't the best time for those details. I'd be glad to –"

"It's fine," Anderson said. "Tell him."

With a solemn nod, Walsh continued. "He was impaled, I believe, through the neck. Perhaps with a stake." Walsh pushed the boy's eyelids down with his fingers, to still the expression of frozen torment.

"W-why would someone do that?" piped up Cahill, looking horrified.

"There are dangers in living a life on the streets," Queen said, gritting his teeth. Anderson watched Queen turn his head away. The detective looked genuinely affected by the boy's death, and Anderson, even in his spell of melancholy, was touched.

"Sheriff Anderson," Walsh said.

Anderson looked up. This is it, he thought, the moment his life crumbles into nothing.

"I have written as much of Maisy's information as I know in the register in the reception area. Once we've confirmed identification, I'll ask you some additional questions, fill out a complete report, get the coroner's signature, and she'll be released to you. Her body has been here for a week, but fortunately the weather has been cold. Up until today, anyway. Normally a body is handed over to a mortuary first, but Detective Queen thought it best that we worked directly with you. Out of respect for your past law enforcement background. Do you understand?"

"I understand." He gripped the edge of the slab, and closed his eyes. Keeper Walsh was about to uncover her face. Anderson thought of his granddaughter when he'd last seen her, holding his hand on that sunlit day, readying herself for the big world about to open before her eyes. That's how I want to remember her, with her sweet, ethereal smile, and a dulcet laugh that made everyone around her gay. I'll look for just a moment, and it will be enough, and then I'll return forever to the image of her I adore.

Anderson opened his eyes as Keeper Walsh pulled back the sheet, and the girl's dirty yellow locks fell to the side. The lips on her pretty face were blue, her eyes closed.

The moan he let loose was guttural, a long deep primal release. His knees buckled, and he felt not only Cahill but also Queen and Walsh there to help him. Again, he used his sinewy arms to raise his aged body to its full length.

Finally, he managed to speak. His face was awash with deep, deep relief.

"It's not my granddaughter. This is not Maisy."

CHAPTER 9

A FTER HIS ENCOUNTER WITH JOHN PILLSBURY yesterday, Dix Anderson was in no mood for another one. That morning, with a touch of shame, he had folded up his colorful Mackinaw coat and packed it into his bureau drawer. A look at the *Minneapolis Tribune*'s early edition, delivered at his hotel room's door, and the embellished article about his visit to the Mayor's office by one "Freddy Bonge," brought out his scissors and straight razor. After a good bit of wrangling he managed to completely remove his mustache. Curled remnants of his twenty years' effort sat in the sink and on the floor, white bits of fluff floating through the air and dusting the carpet.

It wasn't embarrassment that led him to it. He'd been called far worse than by Pillsbury, and had heard every name imaginable during his long years. He wasn't ashamed for the way he dressed or how he carried himself, either. In fact, the last time he was in Minneapolis, reporters had written about his quest in a very agreeable light. His outlandish garb and alpine height, along with the tragedy surrounding his visit, had elicited lots of warm-hearted attention. He'd received flowers, cards, and a proposition from the widow of a prominent Minneapolis businessman, which had even made Martha smile. While that earlier visit had been wracked by worry, he'd also felt the city's enormous outpouring of support.

Bonge's article, this time around, wasn't flattering in the least, with no mention of why Anderson was here. Cahill had spoken of the reason as he'd grabbed Anderson's arm and nudged him away. You'd think, Anderson thought, that his presence in town again, compounded by the discovery of a dead girl the police had thought was his granddaughter, and it would be screaming across the front page of the *Tribune*. Instead, he'd been branded a "once formidable, now antiquated Don Quixote" who had gotten in over his head, tilting lances against Minneapolis's greatest leaders of industry with humiliating results: a five-foot-tall policeman pushing him out of harm's way just before being arrested for disorderly behavior and attempted assault. He made a note to himself: no more conversations with reporters. No more unnecessary attention. He was here to find Maisy, God willing, alive, and as discreetly as possible. If that meant packing away his good-luck Mackinaw and slouch hat in favor of a drab gray city hat, suit and coat, then so be it.

The shock of yesterday's discovery was still echoing through his head and heart. Once the astonishment had worn off for everyone in the dead room, Queen had hastily shaken his hand and apologized for the confusion, explaining he was needed elsewhere in the city. Out the door he flew, Cahill close behind, although not before the greenhorn detective offered Anderson some kind words.

"The good news, sir, is that she is still out there! Hope springs eternal!" Anderson wished he could view the world through such rose-colored glasses.

Keeper Walsh apologized, as he had an unidentified girl on his hands. No doubt realizing the work of finding her family would be daunting, he excused himself as well, leading Anderson to the front door. The sheriff assumed from the way his cord had been snipped so hurriedly by Queen, that what little goodwill he had with the police was now gone.

And here he was now, about to rough it alone. What was his next step? Where was he to go? What did he know today that he didn't know two years ago, when he scoured the city for his little girl? He knew somebody knew her name. Someone had heard of Maisy Anderson, and connected it to that poor dead girl, and it didn't seem like such a common name to have. Sure, there were probably thousands of Andersons in Minnesota, but the name Maisy would narrow it down. His intuition told him that her disappearance, and the appearance of a dead girl with her name, were more than mere coincidence.

After a night to sleep on it, he had wished he could have asked Queen about the boy in the morgue who had given the detective such a shock. Anderson wondered if he was the same boy Queen had mentioned earlier in the evening, the friend who had identified her as Maisy.

He could take two directions, he decided. One, he could explore the shantytown where the girl's body had been discovered. Ask questions, describe his granddaughter's face, and see if someone might have some little tidbit of information that could somehow connect him to her trail. Or, there was another possibility, perhaps a faster way to get the answers he needed. A few sips of coffee later, he had decided where he needed to go.

Milwaukee Depot was flush with the flurry of passengers, most looking cheerful as the day's weather was unseasonably warm. Anderson tugged on the outside of his new suit jacket, trying to make it a little roomier, as he hadn't taken the fit into consideration before strapping his gun belt to his waist. It had been awhile since he'd bought new clothes—not since Martha had been there to help him out. He remembered now why she did all the shopping. There was no chance this time of his pistols showing, though. He kept his long overcoat firmly buttoned, and this winter garment was far roomier than the jacket.

The dead boy's fingers had been smudged with newspaper ink, and that was what led him back here. He remembered the teary-eyed newsies he'd spoken with when he'd first walked out of the station, and while he wasn't certain, he suspected now they might have been mourning a friend. A friend in the morgue, stone cold dead, with his throat split open.

Queen had admitted that he'd learned about the dead girl's identity from a boy. It was a long shot, he knew, but he figured those newsboys had as good a chance as any of knowing something about a fellow delinquent, who in turn might know something about his granddaughter. He hoped that the keeper of that information wasn't the boy in the morgue, the one who'd made Detective Queen's jaw drop in shock, but there was only one way to find out.

The cobblestone pavement was clear of ice, but slick and wet from melted snow. He watched from across the street, waiting for the three boys he'd seen yesterday to material-ize from around a corner, lugging their newspapers, but they didn't appear. Perhaps they only sell the evening papers, An-derson thought. It might be a long day ahead.

There were other boys hawking their rags, though, spread out along the sidewalk and trying to outshout each other with titillating headlines, the more gruesome the better.

"Get yer paper, here! Thirty children burned and suffer-cated in an orphan asylum fire in Rochester! Terrible tragedy! Only two cents for the whole story!"

Anderson crossed the street, narrowly avoiding a lemon-colored streetcar and its cursing motorman, and made his way to one of the boys brandishing a morning rag. Enough with the wait, he thought.

"Who sells the *Journal*?"

"You don't want the *Journal*, you want the *Tribune*, sir. Two pennies will give you the best news in Minneapolis."

"I want the *Journal*, son. I've lost all taste for the *Tribune* in the last twenty-four hours."

The boy shrugged, and his oversized cap fell over his eyes. He lifted it up and placed it back on firmly. "Usually the fellas who peddle it are here, but they ain't today. McCartan runs the *Journal* from this corner. Him and his gang of bummers."

"Where would they be, if not here?"

"They got a hang-out at the river. Downstream from the Pillsbury A Mill. McCartan sure brags about it. Says it's haunted by the ghosts of the men who died in the Mill explosion. Don't believe it, myself."

"What is it? A shack? A cave?"

"Supposed to be an abandoned boat. McCartan says it was left by river pirates."

"And this McCartan might be there now?"

"Maybe. Listen, Mister, if you ain't gonna buy a paper, I need to sell to somebody else."

Anderson took a quarter from his pocket and handed it to the boy. "I need to find these boys. Another dollar if you can take me to them."

"You ain't some kind of nancy, are you? You ain't gonna hurt 'em? One of 'em is a tiny little fella. A real sweet kid."

With a quick flash, Anderson showed him his star, which he had pinned to the inside lapel of his new overcoat.

"Whoa, Nellie! That's a neat trick!"

"I'm here to help them. I've met them before. The name of the little boy is Petey. Isn't that right?"

"Yeah, sure. Petey, his brother Ollie, McCartan, Dirk and Spindle. They got a name for their gang, too."

"What's that?"

"The Don't Tell Gang. They're not so tough, though, to be in a gang, 'cept for McCartan, and Ollie a little."

"Take me there, now. Do you have anyone to watch your papers?"

"Yeah, my pal is right over there. Hey Joe! Keep an eye on these, would ya? Sell some and I'll get you the money!" A boy with a battered derby and a dirty face signaled back agreement with a touch of his hat.

"All right, then, Mister. Let's go," the boy said with a firm nod, as the cap slid over his eyes again.

Anderson and the boy took a ten-minute walk to the Mississippi River, and towards the once mighty and majestic St. Anthony Falls, a long ago wonder of Minnesota. As a young boy he'd visited the falls with his parents. Even then sawmills, textile mills and flour mills had surrounded it and tapped it for power. Today, though, the area was vastly different. The Pillsbury A Mill loomed above the dam and a large concrete apron controlled the flow. He cringed inside when the name Pillsbury skipped across his brain.

A sea of mills, powerhouses, warehouses and factories stood atop stone retaining walls and bluffs, all overlooking and drawing power from the churning, roaring rapids. These falls had almost singlehandedly created the enormous wealth that built Minneapolis, enriched its founding families and created untold industries.

They padded silently across the stone arch bridge, built by James J. Hill for his Great Northern Railway twenty years prior. It angled downstream across the river. No trains rumbled across while they moved along the pedestrian side.

Anderson could see the graceful arcs under the bridge below as it curved gently in the water in front of him, but he paid little attention to its impassive beauty. More important to him were his surroundings. He noticed the falls to his left, the University of Minnesota's rooftops to his far right, and the towering Industrial Exposition Building, jutting like a castle over the horizon. He scanned the banks below the bluff, filled with broken rock, debris, and scraggly bushes at the river's edge, hoping for a glimpse of the Don't Tell Gang.

"Down this way!" The boy ahead of him looked back eagerly, pointing down as they rounded the bridge's curving abutment and started down a path that was both narrow and steep. Looking down the bluff to the bank below, Anderson thought that a grappling hook and some rope would make their descent safer, but of course he had neither of these.

"It gets easier, just watch yer step," the boy called out, already skittering down the path like a squirrel, his floppy cap now clutched in his hand. Anderson grabbed branches like ropes to steady himself, trying to keep pace with the speed of youth. His back tightened uncomfortably as he descended, and he could tell his legs weren't reacting as quickly as his mind was telling them to.

With a mounting headache he knew was caused by nerves, he found himself at the river's edge. He looked up at the stone arches almost directly overhead, then the clumps of floating ice. The sun reflected off of them in bursts of blinding light.

"Yer down, Mister?"

"Yes, right behind you."

"Over here, then."

He followed the boy's voice to the left, and saw him standing beside a tangle of logs and brush. Anderson's head was pounding now and his chest heaved for breath, a rotten by-product of old age. Sucking in the cool morning air with long slow draws, he saw what the boy was looking at. A wrecked rowboat sat among the rocks, turned over and propped up with thick branches to form a shelter. The boys he'd seen at the depot the day before were sitting on boulders, attempting to start a small fire with a flint and steel. They looked at him in panicked unison.

"Aw, skittles," the dark-haired boy said. "Are you a copper?" He turned on the boy with the big cap, snarling. "What did ya bring him here for, Pickle?"

"He said he knew you fellows," Pickle replied, dropping down by the fire to blow on the damp sawdust they were using as tinder. "He showed me his star."

Petey stood up "It's you, ain't it?" He smiled wide. "Hello!"

"Hello," the sheriff replied, sitting on a rock with a grunt. He pulled out a book of matches, and handed them to the boy with the corn-fed belly. "You're Dirk, right? These might get the fire lit faster."

Dirk's fat little cheeks wobbled confirmation. "Yep, and Spindle, and Petey."

Spindle crinkled his brown eyes and spat. "No more talkin' to strangers." He put his hands on his hips and tried his best to look menacing. "Who the hell are you? You a truant officer? A guard from the flour mill? I ain't goin' back to school for you or anyone, ya hear me?"

Petey shook his head emphatically. "Don't you remember him, Spindle? The sheriff with the strawberry marshmallow bullets! His mustache and red coat are gone, but it's him, don't ya see?"

Spindle looked him over carefully. "Yeah, you're right, it's him. He got himself a shave. What are you doing here?"

"I came to check on you, and McCartan and Ollie. That's his name, right? Ollie?"

"Aw, skittles," Spindle said to Pickle. "You told him about them, too?"

Pickle pulled his cap over his eyes. "I didn't swear to no secrecy, Spin."

The wind picked up a little, and blew lightly on the fire, sparking the sawdust into flame. Anderson added a couple of twigs and then larger branches to build it up. The wood was wet, and it smoked and sizzled as the fire tried to come to life. "You boys were crying yesterday. It was because of McCartan, right?"

"He's dead," Petey said. "Cold, hard, plum dead."

"Oh golly," said Pickle, and put his hat over his heart.

"Do you know who killed him?" Anderson asked.

"Could have been anyone. Sometimes he talked too high for his nut," Dirk said solemnly. "Lots of people had it in for him. He took care of us, though. He made sure we always ate. Sometimes nothin' but scraps and throwaways, but we still had full stomachs." He patted his belly proudly, and sniffled a little.

Petey edged so close to Anderson that he could feel the warmth from his breath. The little boy's blueberry eyes were extra round. "We're scared, Mister, real scared."

Anderson couldn't think of anything to say. He had poured so much of his heart into his granddaughter these last few days that he wasn't sure if he had enough left for a group of rag-tag street Arabs. He had lived his whole life, though, fighting for people who couldn't defend themselves. And this little fellow was breaking his heart, right here, in this pitiful, tiny shelter they called home.

"You're scared because your friend was murdered," he finally said.

"Not only that," Petey replied," but Ollie's gone, too."

"And you don't know where?"

"Not for certain." A tear trickled down his cherubic cheek. "He just disappeared."

"Well, boys in your position, they sometimes don't stay in one place. Maybe he found a warm bed for the night."

"He's my brother, though," Petey said, biting his lip. "He wouldn't leave me."

"Where are your mother and father?"

"My father's dead. My mother lives a few blocks from here."

"We ain't orphans," Dirk piped up. "We all got homes."

"We just don't like goin' there, sometimes," Spindle added.

"Well, you boys are going to go home now. It isn't safe here."

"It ain't safe at home for me, neither," Spindle answered. "My pa beats me when he's drunk, and he's always drunk."

"And mine's never home," Dirk said. "Travels around, selling stuff."

"What about yours?" Anderson asked Petey.

"I told you, Father's dead. Mother just likes to cry."

"Listen," Anderson said. He looked gravely at each of them, and they stared back with their own grave faces, recognizing the seriousness of his expression. "My own granddaughter is missing, too, and I think she knew either McCartan or Ollie. Did either of them mention a girl named Maisy to you?"

They nodded in unison.

"Yeah, Ollie knew her," Spindle said. "Worked for Emil Dander. He ran a place with women, like a resort, but not so fancy. You heard of him? Emil Dander?"

"Was it in Hell's Half Acre?" Anderson asked.

"That's it," Spindle said. "Ollie ran errands for him. Made friends with all the girls there. Three of 'em in all. He said Maisy got killed." His eyes widened. "Was that your granddaughter? The girl Ollie said was shot by Dander?"

Anderson's insides started to burn. That was Queen's lie. The girl—whoever she really was—had been murdered, and he was covering it up.

"No, that wasn't her. This Emil Dander. Where is he?"

"Ollie said that he heard Dander got caught and is sitting ass down in Central lockup," Spindle said.

Anderson looked at Petey. "How long has Ollie been missing?"

"I saw him yesterday morning, 'fore breakfast," Petey said. "He and McCartan went out to sell papers. Last time we saw either one of them."

Anderson's heart skipped a beat. Could another one of these prostitutes they were referring to be Maisy? Had there been some kind of higgledy-piggledy over names when Ollie identified the body? At the very least these girls might have some information. Finding them would be difficult, though. The city was vast, and full of dirty little hiding places. He wondered if Dander's man could well have nabbed Ollie too, possibly to kill him, to hush him about the girl's murder.

"Do you think you can find my brother?" asked Petey.

"I don't know," admitted Anderson. "Could someone who worked for this Dander character have taken him?"

Petey shook his head. "No, Mister, I don't think so." He crawled underneath the overturned boat and pulled out a tattered book. Anderson took it carefully, as it looked like it was about to crumble into pieces.

"Ollie would leave it here. He didn't want it at home, 'cause he knew Mother would burn it if she found it."

The cover was worn, but Anderson could read its name clear as day. *Ragnarok: The Age of Fire and Gravel.* He'd never heard the title, but he was well aware of its author, Ignatius Donnelly, who had been a recurring personality in Minnesota politics for years. A Congressman, land speculator, populist orator and writer on eccentric subjects. Anderson had avidly followed politics, and Donnelly had played a colorful role for decades in Minnesota. The book's pages were brittle, and he delicately leafed through its contents.

"It's a cracked book," Dirk said. "Real bughouse. Ollie said it's about how a comet from outer space crashed to earth, and set the world on fire. Can you imagine something like that might come flying down out of nowhere?"

It sounded pretty preposterous, Anderson admitted to himself. "Tell me why you think this connects with Ollie disappearing," he said, tenderly closing the book.

"The German." Petey shivered as he spoke, and Dirk and Spindle exchanged dark looks.

"Who is the German?"

"A man who stole Ollie. A long time ago."

"What do you mean, stole him?"

"Talked him into going with him on a train. Told him stories of how he'd take care of him, and promised they'd go on grand adventures. Gave him chocolate and candy and told him there was plenty more."

'So Ollie has been missing before?"

"Yes," Petey replied. "For a long time. That's why Mother still cries. But he came back, to take care of me."

"And this book," Anderson held it up. "Did the German give it to Ollie?"

Petey bobbed his head vigorously and Spindle chimed in. "Ollie said the German told him it was as important as the Bible. God destroyed the world once, and the German thought it would happen again. That book was the proof."

Go on and keep it, Mister. I don't want it," Petey said.

"Thank you," he said, placing it in his overcoat pocket. "I'll return it to Ollie when we find him. Can you tell me this German's name?"

They all stared back, and Spindle shrugged. "He said we should never know."

"But I do," Petey said. "I do."

"You know his name?" Anderson asked. This story was disturbing. There was a certain specimen of tramp who would lure young boys away from their homes, and then threaten them if they didn't comply with their will, dragging them across the country as slaves. Most hobos, in his experience, were harmless, but this particular type was as dangerous as any criminal he'd encountered in his own career. He had heard sinister accounts like this before from other lawmen, but had never come across one himself.

"He would say it in his sleep." More tears streaked down Petey's face, and his big blue eyes were circled red with fatigue. "Gottschalk. His name is Gottschalk. Please, Mister. You got to find him. You promise you'll try?"

"I promise."

"Honor bright?"

Anderson held up his hand in oath. "Honor bright."

Detective Harmon Queen was in a rage. It was a rage that had simmered like a pot of coffee left on the stove too long, burning into a rank, bitter sludge. He was ready to take Emil Dander out of that cozy little cell of his and smash his smug face into a shambles of split flesh, broken bones and lots and lots of blood, courtesy of the butt of his Smith and Wesson Model 10.

He'd thought about Dander through the day, but his duties as a badge-carrying member of the Minneapolis detective squad forced him to wait to relieve his desire for vengeance. A burglary call pulled him to the city's north end almost as soon as he'd left the morgue. Then followed a two-hour meeting with new detectives, which included a stern lecture about how to write a proper report. Finally, he'd been called to a late-night, last-minute audience with Colonel Ames, who demanded to know how Queen's encounter with Dix Anderson had gone. The colonel had gotten a full report from Tom Brown about the sheriff's confrontation with the flour magnate. He was concerned that the city would be abuzz with gossip about the old fool's brush with John Pillsbury once the morning papers came out.

"Damn it, Queen!" he had said, with a smack of his fist into his hand, "Get this ridiculous character out of town! I don't need any embarrassing press, especially in the Mayor's reception room!"

Colonel Ames hadn't blinked when Queen revealed that the dead girl was now officially unidentified again. "Christ, I don't care about that. I told you that. Deal with this Sheriff Anderson and continue with your duties. We have a city to run." Irritating as the colonel could be, though, he was the least of Queen's troubles now.

Once he was through listening to Ames, he turned his focus back to Dander. The lying bastard knew who that girl really was, he was absolutely sure of it. That cheap, poetic "My beloved Mopsy" bunk made him writhe with fury.

As he stomped down the street towards Central Station he heard a piano playing from a cracked window. It was a ragtime number, and its jaunty sound echoed tinnily through the street. He reached for his flask and his liquid fortitude, and took a long deep swig, refusing to let the music cheer him up. The door to the station appeared like a beacon, and he threw it open, stiffening his shoulders when a young patrolman brushed past him. He knocked the kid sideways, and it felt great.

"Sergeant Krumweide." The desk sergeant looked up from his paperwork as Queen hovered over him. "I need to see

Dander and Higgins. Are they in the same cell they were a couple of days ago?"

"Jesus, Queen. You look fit to be tied. What's the matter?"

"Never mind, Krumweide. I'll just go back there myself."

"They're not there."

"Okay, then which cell?"

"I mean they're not here. They're gone. They went before Judge Dickinson in district criminal court early this morning and made bail. Out the door the dirty slugs went, not two hours ago." He shoved the register towards Queen to prove their signatures. Queen stared at the handwriting, Dander's flowery cursive and Higgins's first-grade scrawl.

"Son of a bitch," Queen said. "Son of a goddamn bitch."

"The courts these days," Krumweide said, shaking his head in disbelief. "I know we can't shut 'em all down, Queen, but Dander deserves jail, if anyone does."

I should have been more diligent about this, Queen thought. I've been busy with so many things that I let Dander slip out of my grasp. His arraignment hearing was this morning and I forgot. Queen didn't even know what the charges were. He remembered Colonel Ames mentioning hauling Dander to the bench as a kidnapper, and that was a serious offense. There is no chance he would have gotten bail on a kidnapping charge, with his odious background on full display. Judge Dickinson was notoriously fair in his handling of the law.

"Do you know what he was charged with?"

"Not having a liquor license."

"To hell with that," Queen said. "Was a bond posted?"

"Somebody came in, calling himself a family friend, and said he paid the entire bail. $6,000 for the two of them. The court office confirmed it."

"Family friend?"

"Clean-shaven fellow. In an expensive suit and a sharp hat."

"Two hours ago?"

"Yeah," Krumweide said. He fiddled with the buttons on his uniform sleeve. "I'm sorry about that, Queen."

"Not your fault. Carry on."

Where were they going, and who was behind his release? Queen burst from the station door into the bright daylight, and took a moment for another quick drink. He patted his pockets for a cigarette, but couldn't find one. Christ, I need a smoke to stop the shaking, he thought. His immediate, urgent concern was for Trilly and Edna. Trilly had been in the back of his mind since they had parted yesterday, and he was flummoxed that he couldn't keep her out of his head. She'd cursed him, beat him and belittled him, and her background frankly sickened him, but her pretty little face was wedged in his memory like a dream. The thought of Dander finding her and stealing her away made him desperate to see her and to make sure she was fine.

He waited on the corner for a cab, and thought about Mc-Cartan's quieted, freckled face, and his defiant eyes closed in death. His concern for Ollie had increased a hundredfold since that moment in the morgue. What the hell kind of sadistic lunatic would push a stake through someone's neck? Is the person behind this responsible for Ollie's disappearance, or worse, death? He needed more information about the stranger who frightened Ollie so badly. Once he arrived at Peder's house he would rack Trilly's brain for more information. Perhaps he could even get Edna to talk, once he explained how much danger the kid was in.

A cab rounded a street up ahead, and Queen raised his hand to hail it.

"Don't do that. We need to talk."

Queen turned to see Jack Peach, leaning against the wall, his gentlemanly airs barely able to contain the cold-blooded killer beneath.

"Peach. To what do I owe this pleasure? Is my tie straight? Why do I always feel inadequately dressed when I'm around you?"

"Because you spend all of your hard-earned money on liquor and games of chance, Queen." He smiled a wide smile, and casually handed Queen a flower.

"What's this for?"

"You're going to visit a lady friend, aren't you? I can't do anything about the stains on your shirt or the missing cuf-flink on your right sleeve, but at least a fresh flower for your lapel will slick you up. I believe first impressions ought to be good."

This took Queen by the family jewels with a good-sized twist. How in God's name did Peach know anything about his personal movements?

"Remember that I am a Minneapolis police detective with all the authority in the goddamn world, and you are a fish out of water. Saint Paul is a forty minute streetcar ride away, if you've forgotten where you are."

Jack Peach held his hands up in mock surrender, tossing the flower over his shoulder and smiling like it was his birthday. "There. I've littered on a Minneapolis sidewalk. Arrest me now and appease that false sense of superiority you're trying to cling to. I've got matters to discuss, Queen, and they di-rectly involve you."

"I'm not setting up a meeting between Superintendent Ames and your boss Kilbane, Jack. It just won't happen. Ames is worried about bad press, and if word leaked about the Ames administration sitting down with a known gangster from another city –"

"That has been taken off the table, Queen. And how many times do I have to remind you not to call me by my first name? We're not friends yet. Yet. Let's talk there." He pointed to an alley, and started towards it, hands jauntily in his pockets, as if he had meetings in alleys every day. Queen wouldn't have been surprised if he did. His instincts were usually sharp about dangerous situations, and although this seemed like a natural setup to an ambush, his gut told him it would only be a conversation.

"This should do," Peach said when they found their privacy. The alley was next to a fruit market, and crates were stacked along its brick wall, below a low-hanging fire escape. Peach sat on the bottom step, somehow still looking genteel in his cashmere suit, checkered in the latest style. It was beautifully tailored, and Queen took a moment to grudgingly admire the man's taste. It had been a long time since he'd bought new clothing, and once things settled a little in his job, a fine worsted suit might give him some courage around Trilly.

And then, as he admired the suit, it dawned on him. Krumweide had said a finely dressed gentleman without facial hair had paid Dander's and Higgins's bail. Here was just such a gentleman, alive and well, sitting on a crate before him. What the hell?

"As I was saying, Queen." Peach lifted an apple from an open crate, and wiped it with his silk handkerchief. "We don't require a meeting with your police superintendent anymore. In fact, Mr. Kilbane has generously agreed to settle your debt. Don't worry about paying him back. You are absolved," he said, making a priestly sign.

"Either Jiggs Kilbane has suddenly found Jesus, or you haven't told me the rest," said Queen.

"Mr. Kilbane is Catholic, Queen," Peach laughed. "Catholics don't require the same salvation as Protestants do. I've heard your new mayor isn't particularly fond of the Irish, is he?"

"I wouldn't know," Queen lied. "So, you made a special trip to Minneapolis to track me down, simply to tell me I don't owe your boss any money. Forgive me if I'm not celebrating yet, but I think more is coming."

Peach gave a little smile. "You looked ornery coming out of the pokey. Is something wrong?"

"What did you do with Emil Dander and his no-account thug?" Queen responded.

"I expected you to live up to your celebrated reputation and figure things out a little faster." He pulled a long, ominous-looking blade from inside his coat. "A little too big for cutting apples," he laughed, slicing off a piece. "Would you like a taste?"

Queen ignored his offer. "So you made bail for a shiftless brothel owner. What gives? Why does a bad pill like that matter to you?"

"He matters to my employer," Peach said. He put a slice of apple in his mouth, and chewed, then pulled the piece out with exaggerated disgust. "I must not have cleaned my knife properly." He turned it, examining it with feigned curiosity. "There, see? Blood. It's got an odd metallic taste to it, don't you think?"

Queen stood silent. He wouldn't respond to Peach's pathetic little vaudeville.

"Never muddle your knives," Peach said. "One for fruit." He pulled his handkerchief out again, and wiped the blade dry. "And one for meat."

"And what do you want with Emil Dander, Peach?"

"I'm not at liberty to say. But I am to pass this on to you. Dander isn't your business anymore. Jiggs Kilbane has officially broken communication with you, and trust me, that is a good, good thing. Forget about Dander. That's all." He stood up, tossed the apple to the ground, and brushed off his pants.

"How did you know where I was going?" Queen asked.

Peach shrugged and smiled.

This is goddamn crazy, Queen thought. How is he involved in this? "Tell me again, what do you want with Dander?"

"Again, I can't tell you. The offer Mr. Kilbane has made you is quite fair. I promise you Mr. Dander will not cross your path on this earth, ever again. He is out of your hair forever."

"And what if I go and find him?"

"And what if you do?" chuckled Peach. "What if I make a call on your sister? What if I visit your friend Peder Ulland? You can't keep your eye on everyone, all of the time."

"Do you know anything about the dead girl?" Queen asked, despair rising in his throat. "Does this have something to do with you and your boss?"

"Never mind about that," Peach said. "You've got enough to worry about here." He put the knife back inside his lapel, and straightened his cuffs. "I think I'm going to grab some of those Coffee John oysters before I depart your fair city. Saint Paul has its charm, but the seafood can't be beat at Coffee John's."

Queen felt inadequate in front of Peach, and couldn't find words to respond. The man had come into his city, slapped him in the face, and was now just strolling away as if conversations like this were everyday episodes for him.

To *hell* with the debt release. No one ever tells Harmon Queen not to investigate a murder, and no one threatens his friends.

Except Jack Peach, evidently, who gave him a wry little grin, and then strode away, turning the corner into nothingness.

CHAPTER 10

S OMETHING WAS WRONG, QUEEN KNEW, when he hopped from the cab and saw the broken lock on Peder Ulland's front door. A Shanghai rooster was crowing crazily in the front yard, and it charged him as he walked up the dirt path towards the house. He pulled his revolver as the bird came closer. The rooster must have gotten a good look at the gun because it bolted in the other direction, screaming its anger to the world.

Queen scoured the yard for anything out of place. The snow continued to melt in the mild warmth, and water dripped from icicles on the eaves, but otherwise all was quiet. The driver of the hansom he'd ridden was still sitting in his rig, watching Queen in fascination. Queen gestured for him to drive on, but the driver, wanting a show, refused. Queen groaned an obscenity and cautiously approached the door, which besides being broken was ajar. A feral moan, low and guttural, came coursing from the house and then abruptly stopped. A thousand terrible thoughts stabbed Queen's brain all at once. Three women had no chance against intruders, and the idea of both Karoline and Trilly hurt made his head spin. He cocked the revolver with his thumb, slowly pushing the door open with his foot before stepping inside.

He saw the gore immediately. A huge figure lay on the parlor floor, fat body blocking most of the entrance. Blood seeped from the man's mouth into a tiny pool that trickled into a crack in the floorboards. Higgins had a look of surprise on his face, and his glazed eyes were twisted to the right, as if he'd been caught off guard by something seen too late.

A sagging clothesline hung across the room, filled with bloomers, shirts and other wet, wrinkled garments. There, between a pair of long underwear and a veil-thin bed sheet and slumped back in Peder's favorite armchair was Emil Dander. His throat had been slashed and his necktie and shirt were washed with red. Even in death he was fiendishly handsome, Queen thought with a moment of irritation. The moan came again and it was from Higgins. At least a dozen stab wounds marked his burly chest but it still moved faintly. Higgins's eyes suddenly snapped forward, meeting Queen's in confusion. Queen wanted to ask him what had happened, but wasn't sure if the culprits were still in the house. He thought back to Peach and his blood-caked knife and suspected not. The detective stepped over the large body and crept into each of the main floor's small rooms. Each one, empty.

"Who's here?" he called out. A teapot started to hiss on the stove, startling him a little, the only answer he got. Trilly and Edna were gone, and Karoline as well. His forehead throbbed and his palms dripped with sweat. Goddamn it. Goddamn it. Where are they? What the hell happened?

Queen pushed his way back through the damp clothes to Higgins. He kneeled down and brought his head level to the brute, whose eyes were darting around the room madly. His lips were pulled back, and he wore an expression of intense pain. There would be more if Queen didn't get the answers he was looking for.

"Did Jack Peach do this?" he asked.

Higgins' chest lifted and fell in grunts and wheezes, and he struggled to speak, but his mouth was jelled with blood. The words came out gluey and unintelligible.

"Just nod or shake your head," Queen said.

Higgins nodded.

"Did you come here to kill the girls?"

Higgins shook his head. He gave another terrible moan.

"But you wanted to take them with you?"

A nod this time. He's telling the truth, Queen thought. "Did you see them? Were they here when you arrived?"

Higgins struggled to lift his head, to get closer to Queen's face, and then in an instant his immense hand grabbed the back of Queen's neck like a vise. Holy hell, Queen thought. He was still holding his gun, and raised it to Higgins's head, shaking it slightly under the pressure of the big man's grip. However Queen saw no anger in his eyes. He wanted Queen's attention. Violently and emphatically, Higgins shook his head. Trilly and Edna hadn't been here, and neither had Karoline. Queen exhaled as Higgins released his grip, and felt a wave of relief settle over him. They're fine.

In a last heaving gasp, Higgins let out a whistle that hung for a moment in the air, and then petered into oblivion. Its sound melded into the noise from the teapot, now bubbling and shrieking. Queen got up and took it off the stove. He saw the teacup on a little table next to the forever-slumbering Emil Dander. He had been making himself a cup of tea. Unbelievable.

Queen needed fresh air to clear his head and stepped outside into the sunlight, taking care not to touch Higgins's oversized corpse with his feet. The gawking cab driver was still there in his hansom, but wasn't watching the house now. Behind him was another carriage, and stepping down were Trilly, Edna and Karoline. Lovely women evidently had as much hold on him as they did on Queen. Peder was last out of the carriage, giving Queen a quick wave and a cheery smile.

When Karoline saw the detective, her normally composed face broke into a radiant beam. She ran towards him, holding up her skirt in a lady-like fashion so as not to let the hem drag in the dirt. He smiled back, and was surprised when she embraced him. Not a proper thing for a respectable woman to do, but he enjoyed it nonetheless.

"Well, you are a sight for sore eyes." She said it with barely the hint of an accent. He'd often wondered how she had escaped it, while her brother had not.

"Your brother had mentioned you were returning," he replied.

"Does it matter anyway? I was here all autumn, and you didn't call on me once." Her cheeks were wind-burned, and her shining green eyes sparkled playfully at him. There was a sweet gentleness to her; a grace and presence that put him immediately at ease.

"The election consumed my time, Karoline."

"I know, Harm. Peder followed the papers and kept me abreast. You certainly have a way of keeping the spotlight." She gave a little laugh, covering her mouth with her dainty gloved hand, and then took his hand in hers, patting it gently in comfort.

Queen blushed a bit. He'd had some trouble in a lush-crib last September, compounded by a few too many whiskeys. A Polish laborer had been bragging about his boxing prowess, and Queen, in his inebriated glory, had challenged him to a match of fisticuffs in the street. Queen had taken a single chump to the head, which had ended his night's festivities, and the *Minneapolis Times* had been on the scene to gloriously document the exchange for its readers the next day. Mayor Gray had been furious, and old Doc, of course, had thought it marvelous.

"That wasn't my brightest moment," Queen admitted. Behind her, he could see Trilly and Edna watching them. Trilly looked amused, and suddenly Queen felt guilty. He let go of Karoline's hand, and took a step back.

"Miss Flick, and Miss Pease, good day to you!"

Edna mouthed out a hello, still looking bewildered. Trilly sauntered up, not bothering to keep her skirt from the dirt, and flashed her beautiful smile.

"Detective Queen, come to check on the poor helpless women." She inspected the cab, and then him. "But I don't see any gallant steed out of a fairy tale book. I thought you carried a fat wad of dough? Or are you all busted out?"

First she refuses the cush I offered her, and now she's worried I'm on the cheap, Queen thought. He had no idea what to make of this girl. "I considered a bicycle but the road out here is bumpy," he finally said, and then instantly felt regret at his words. *A bicycle?* What tongue-tied foolishness would he utter next? He looked at both, waiting for a laugh, but neither reacted.

"Karoline is such a lovely hostess," said Trilly, tossing her nose up and taking Miss Ulland's hand. "And Peder was kind enough to take us to the Donaldson Department Store. It sits in a building called the Glass Block! I don't mind ruining this awful thing," she continued, brushing her skirt, "because the new green fabric will make a simply swell looking dress. Isn't it woozy, Karoline?"

"Yes, of course, dear. Brother Peder, can you help these young ladies carry their purchases in?"

"Ya, sister," Peder replied. He had one hand on his hip and held his hat with the other, smiling ridiculously at Queen and Karoline standing together. He gave Trilly his arm and escorted her back to the buggy to fetch Edna and their belongings.

Queen wanted to scratch his head. These two women, both of whom kindled feelings in him, were getting along well, but Trilly was being a queer fish. Then he saw Karoline give him a little wink and a droll smile.

In a low voice she confided, "She fancies you, Harm. Hasn't stopped talking about you all morning."

He didn't know what to say, and shifted uncomfortably on his feet, until finally something came tumbling out. "Well, first off, I can't tell. Second, I'm sure she's confused about things right now. I don't know if you're aware of where she's recently been, but the conditions were dire. Downright horrifying. My coming to her rescue –"

"Peder told me everything. Thank God you've delivered them from danger." She gave him a quick kiss on the cheek, and Queen smelled the faintest scent of lavender. It was delicious, made even more so by the fact that as a young, unmarried woman, she shouldn't be doing anything so scandalous.

"Why is the lock on the door broken?" she suddenly asked, looking over his shoulder.

Queen heard Edna gasp. He looked up to see them all staring at the house. Christ, he thought. Bewitched by two women and he had already forgotten about the grisly wreckage of bodies inside.

"Please," he announced, clearing his throat. "What's inside is not a sight for a woman to see."

"What's going on, Harm?" Karoline gripped his arms firmly, but her voice trembled. "Is there someone hurt? Perhaps I can help them. I volunteer at the hospital and—"

"There's nothing to be done."

"But—"

"Peder!" Queen shouted. The Norwegian was already trotting towards them.

"Vot's da matter, Harm? Vot is wrong vit the door?"

"Karoline," the detective said. "Please, go to the carriage, and wait for me there."

She touched him again, this time grabbing his arm with a working woman's firm strength. He looked at her with pleading eyes and saw recognition lighting hers. She turned and went back to Trilly and Edna.

"Peder," he said in a low, firm voice, once out of the women's hearing range. "There are two dead men in your house. These ladies need to be moved somewhere else."

"Vot do you mean? Who are dey?"

"The men who enslaved the young women in your care."

Peder ran his fingers between his stringy blonde strands. "You are certain dat dey are dead?" he asked.

"I am. I've already been inside. I'll go and get the coroner."

"Yah, a good idea. Vonce things are cleaned up, I vill move the girls back here."

Queen shook his head. "No. I have good reason to believe the men responsible for this might come back for them." He opened his flask without even thinking, and took a long drink. I'm parched with this goddamn ghastly work, he thought, and to compound matters, I'm infatuated with two women, both of whom who seem to actually like me back. Although, he admitted to himself, he had to take Karoline's word on how Trilly felt towards him. Every time he thought he had women figured out he'd get a surprise hurled at his head faster than a Minneapolis Millers fastball. At least keeping them safe, now, was in his power. He could worry about his feelings later.

"Listen, Peder, I can't go to Colonel Ames for police protection because he doesn't give a damn about any of this. We need a new hiding place. Perhaps one outside of Minneapolis, but it can't be Saint Paul."

"Harm, ve mustn't vorry. Do you remember vot my yob is? I'm an organizer. I've got a dozen big Norske men vit strapping arms who vill vatch my house night and day."

"I can't let you do that, Peder. These men have guns. They're professional killers."

"Six of my men ver in da Norvegian army. Dey can handle demselves. De odders are strong as oxen. Trust me, Harm. Dey all love Karoline. She's helped dere vives and children vit everyting from food to clothing to medicine. Dey von't let anything happen to her, or anyvone else in her care."

Taking another half a day to find safe quarters for these young women, as pleasurable as he anticipated it would be, was something he just couldn't do. Their safety would consume him, but his problems were compounding by the minute and time was important. He knew the best way to resolve this Jiggs Kilbane business would be to nip it in the bud, and that meant confronting the rotten bastard in the flesh.

A cry from the carriage halted his conversation with Peder. He looked back and saw Trilly running towards him, hand held high, with a knife in her hand. He stumbled back, as did Peder, and raised his hands in defense. Her eyes were focused on the door, however, and as soon as he realized this, he bolted after her. She was fast in a skirt, blazing fast. She slipped through the door, a few feet ahead of him, and he heard Peder right behind. What the hell is she going to do? What set her off like that?

He skidded to the door and threw it open, feeling it hit Higgins's body with a thump. Trilly was there, smoldering hatred on her face, standing over Emil Dander's seated corpse. She wielded the knife in one hand like some great hunter, and held a clump of Dander's thick black hair in the other. She'd pulled his head back so his blank expression faced the ceiling, and the gash on his neck gaped open. The sticky congealed blood coating his throat had cracked open and streams of fresh blood turned his red shirt redder.

"Trilly!" Harm shouted. "He's already dead! What are you doing?"

"She's yust gone in da head," Peder said in a hushed tone. "Votever he did to her must have been black."

Her eyes were glassy, brimming with tears. She glared wildly at Dander, then at Queen. "The monster," she cried. "Damn him! Damn the monster!" The knife fell from her hand and she fell to the floor, crumpling into an anguished heap. Queen surged towards her, taking her into his arms. He was utterly inexperienced at the art of consolation, especially for a woman afflicted with such sorrow. She didn't pull away, however, and he felt her body go limp in his hold.

"Harm, I'm so glad he's dead," she sobbed.

Once more, Anderson rapped on the door, this time loudly enough to stir whoever else was holed up in the rooms lining the narrow, dimly lit corridor. The smell of burned food and stale piss permeated every cramped inch of the flophouse. The peeling paint and the lone electric bulb swaying from the low ceiling did nothing to instill any cheer in this dark place either. He used his fist this time, and the pounding echoed through the paper-thin walls. The noise was loud enough this time to create a stirring from within. Soon, he heard shuffling feet, and the click of a lock. The door squeaked open, and Anderson heard a muffled voice, gravelly and hoarse.

"Come in, come in."

He followed the voice's instructions, and entered the tiny space. A narrow bed was pushed up against the far wall, which contained the only window in the gloomy room. The glass was cracked and filthy and barely let in the waning afternoon light. A wobbly table and two mismatched chairs filled out the furniture in Martin Baum's little piece of hell on earth.

"How are you, Martin?" Anderson asked. He had to stoop a little to fit under the ceiling.

"I've taken quite ill, Dix. Quite ill. As you can see, I've slept most of the day."

Baum wore only a dirty set of flannels. His skin was sallow and sweaty. Anderson searched the room with his eyes and noticed a half-consumed bottle of whiskey poking out from under the bed frame. "This is a bad time of the year for getting sick. You can't play games with your health. Have you seen a doctor?"

"I don't have the money for that, Dix. The wife has seen to emptying my accounts." He gave a weak smile, and sat on one of his chairs. It creaked under his weight, and for a moment Anderson thought it might break.

"Did you get my messages, Martin? I left three of them with your desk clerk downstairs."

"I've been in bed all day, Dix."

"What is that?" Anderson pointed to an envelope, scarcely hidden under a blanket on Baum's mattress. In two long strides, and before Baum could protest, he was at the bed and had yanked it out. Fifty dollars.

Baum's face turned like a thundercloud. "I guess I'd forgotten about that."

"I don't know where to start," Anderson said, shaking his head with disgust. "Do you know what I learned last night? My granddaughter isn't the dead girl I was led to believe she was. Maisy could very well be alive." He watched Baum's face twist into a facsimile of surprise. He already knows, Anderson thought.

"That is spectacular news, Dix! So you've been looking for her today?"

"I've been looking for information about her. Someone in this town knows who she is, or her name wouldn't have been slapped onto the girl in the morgue."

"Of course you know, Dix, that Maisy was like a grand-daughter to me as well. We wrote each other many times, and I never forgot her birthday. Uncle Martin, I was to her."

Anderson had already had enough. He grabbed the other chair and put it next to Baum's so he could sit nice and close. The stench of cheap booze oozed from Baum's skin, and Anderson found himself trying to blink it away. "Who visited you, and what did they say about me?" he asked, resting his large hand on Baum's shoulder. "I know you've been served a bowl of cold gruel, Martin, and your situation is difficult."

"I'm simply under the weather," Baum replied. He looked down at his lap.

"And that fifty dollars fell from the sky. What kind of stupid fool do you take me for, Martin? Enough of your fimble-famble. I read the newspapers, and I know you do, too. You're afraid of helping me, aren't you?"

Martin looked as though he was about to shoot the cat. Anderson stood up, walked to the corner of the room and picked up a crumpled paper bag, sitting about the other trash. He opened it and held it out to Baum, who took it sheepishly.

"If you're going to throw up your whiskey, do it, Martin. I don't have time right now for this game." He glared at Baum, and watched him sink two inches in his seat. "I must say, I never figured you for a liar. So much for our decades of friendship."

Baum rubbed his eyes until they were red, and looked up at Anderson, ashamed.

"He came this morning. Told me I wasn't to help you or even speak to you while you were in town. Gave me that money as payment."

"Who was it? Harmon Queen?"

"No, not him. I wouldn't deal with that dirty scoundrel for twice that amount. It was another detective. His name is Norbeck. I don't know him well, but he's easy to recognize, with his face covered in red sores."

Glad you're able to draw a line in the sand when it comes to betrayal, Anderson thought. Looking at his old friend's pathetic, shivering form, however, softened his anger. Baum had always lived by a strong moral code, but he was also living in squalor and filth. Anderson hoped he would never have to face the same decision Baum had.

"I hope you feel better," Anderson said. He bent down under the bed, feeling his back burn in the process, and pulled out the bottle of whiskey. He set it hard on the table. "Enjoy the rest of your medicine," he said, and walked out.

It was a bitter pill to swallow, at this late hour, as Anderson had already suffered a difficult day. He had taken the name Petey gave him, Gottschalk, and visited every flea-bitten, rat-infested nook and cranny where a tramp of that ilk might be hiding. Flophouses far worse than Baum's, train yards and empty boxcars, places were he expected hobo camps might be. He'd climbed down under bridges. He'd crawled into filthy blind-pig saloons with two barrels and a plank for a bar, serving two-penny-a-glass watered-down beer. He'd gotten absolutely nowhere in his inquiries. It wasn't that the tramps he approached didn't recognize the name. In fact, he could see real fear in their faces when he uttered it. They just refused to speak to him. Perhaps it was his brand-new city suit and coat, many steps above the ill-fitting clothes the rail riders wore, but Anderson suspected not. It was Gottschalk himself, who seemed to have a ill-boding reputation that far preceded him.

Anderson walked into his hotel's lobby, petered out and stiff from padding the hoof. A large fireplace crackling merrily with flame and some comfortable chairs looked too good to resist, and he let his aching body fall into the lushness of a well-cushioned seat. The proprietor, an elderly woman with a pleasant face, plodded over to ask if he needed something hot to drink. He ordered coffee laced with a shot of bourbon.

Today's work had taken a mighty toll on his old bones, and he'd stopped at a drug store for something to ease the pain. For fifty cents he'd been sold a bottle of Five Drops, manufactured by the Swanson Rheumatic Cure Company in Chicago. The druggist was positive, after a couple of questions, that the sheriff was suffering from rheumatism, and so recommended the medicine highly. As an extra benefit, the druggist told him, it would also treat sciatica, gout, neuralgia, la grippe, asthma, catarrh, croup, backaches, lumbago, headache, toothache, earache, hay fever, liver complaints, dyspepsia, kidney troubles, malaria, heart weakness, paralysis, eczema, sleeplessness, and creeping numbness. The numbness he recognized, but not the physical kind. He had been directed to put five drops into his drink. The doctor had suggested water, but Anderson figured the coffee and bourbon would do just as well. He reached into his pocket for the bottle, but he felt the book, instead.

With nothing else to do, he took it out, and examined it again. It had been read many times, with the pages dogeared, and notes scribbled in the margins. This had been Gottschalk's copy, he assumed, a gift to Ollie for services rendered. Why the boy kept it, with the unnatural relationship he imagined they'd had together, baffled him. It was a strange book to carry around, filled with gloom and doom about the events that led up to humanity's end. He sighed and closed the book, laying it on his lap when his drink arrived. A few sips of this, and I'll soon be fast asleep, he thought. When morning arrives, though, I'll be no closer to the truth than I was when today began.

He felt himself drifting, and as his eyes grew heavy he saw Maisy's image in his head, a little girl, standing on a rock and bent over the edge of a stone well they'd had in Minot, behind the house. She was giggling, and pointing at a duckling that had decided to take a swim in the murky depths.

"Papa, does it live there?" she squealed, her pigtails flopping as she bobbed up and down in excitement.

"I think it is just visiting," he replied, peering down into the blackness. She grabbed hold of two of his fingers and pulled at them. "Papa, it doesn't have a home like us, does it?"

"It belongs somewhere," he replied, stroking her hair with his other hand.

"We need to find its mother and father," she said, her little lip pushed out in seriousness. "It can't be alone."

A hand reached out of the darkness and touched his shoulder. He thought it was Martha, and then opened his eyes. Sadness enveloped him when the hotel's parlor came into focus and he realized where he was. He looked up to see Tom Cahill straightening his spectacles, waiting patiently for Anderson to awaken.

"Sheriff Anderson, I'm sure you remember me."

"Of course I do. It was only yesterday. The young man who wrestled me into submission."

"I apologize again for that, sir. I was trying to help you avoid some embarrassment."

"It didn't seem to work." Anderson smiled gently at the young man, who let out his breath, evidently relieved he wasn't disturbing him too greatly.

"Unfortunately, not. That reporter from the *Tribune* has caused Mayor Ames problems in the past. He somehow got that past his editor."

"Probably because it didn't embarrass the mayor at all. It merely pointed out my presence in an unfavorable light."

"Well, y-yes sir. You seem to have changed your appearance a little, though, as a result."

"I thought it best."

"A smart idea, sir. Anyway, I wanted to find you, to offer my services, as you had asked for them in the morgue. Be your guide through the city, as it were."

"At this late hour? Pardon my suspicions, Detective Cahill, but I have a hard time believing you haven't been dispatched by your superiors to keep an eye on me."

"An astute observation, sir. I would be lying to you if I said that it wasn't true, so I won't. I followed you for most of the day."

"And what did you discover?"

"As much as you did. You're looking for a German man."

"And did I locate this German man?"

"No, you didn't. He seems to be a difficult man to locate."

"Sit down, son." Anderson motioned to the opposite chair, and Cahill sat.

"Can I buy you a drink?"

"That would be most appreciated, sir."

"What will you have?"

"Whatever it is that you have."

He ordered another coffee and bourbon for the young detective, and they sat for a moment, just looking at each other.

"Tell me about yourself, son," Anderson finally said.

"What would you like to know?"

"Where are you from?"

"A farm, outside of New Ulm."

"And you are the only son?"

Cahill looked surprised. "How did you know, sir?"

"Those thick arms of yours tell me you've done a lot of hard work. It was a guess."

"Well, it was a good guess."

"Why are you here?"

"What do you mean, sir?"

"Why did you choose to leave the farm, come to a big city like Minneapolis, and join the police force? You seem like a smart young man. Very considerate. Not exactly the hackneyed image of a police detective."

"I actually fought during the war, sir. I served with Colonel Ames."

"And he looks after you now?"

"That is one way to put it, yes. I helped him out of a fix, and he was very grateful. Told me he needed me here, by his side."

"And he is the one who asked you to follow me?"

"Well, yes, sir. He is more than a tad nervous about you being in town. He says you're stirring up a hornet's nest."

"For someone so loyal to Colonel Ames, you are very honest."

"I don't know how to be anything else."

"Did Colonel Ames ask you to simply approach me and offer your help?"

"He did sir, but he told me not to say why."

"But you already have."

Cahill took his drink and gave himself a long sip. His body shuddered with the shock of alcohol down his throat. "That tastes delicious," he said.

"Guaranteed to keep you awake and relaxed at the same time."

"You were falling asleep, sir, a moment ago."

"I'm an old man."

"Yes, sir. As to your earlier question, my parents taught me not to lie."

"This must be problematic for you as a Minneapolis police officer. From what I've learned here on my visit, deception is part of the job."

"I've noticed as well, but it just isn't my nature."

Anderson shifted in his seat. He felt alert now, and sat up straight. "Why would you want to help me?"

Cahill's eyes watered a little, and he wavered. "I can't imagine losing a loved one like you have, sir. I wouldn't wish that on my worst enemy. When I first talked to Colonel Ames about becoming a detective, I was hesitant. It isn't something I have any experience in. Detective work, sleuthing and all, it seems so strange to me."

"You followed me around town today without me knowing. That shows some skill. I wouldn't be so hard on yourself."

"Probably luck, sir," he said, offering Anderson a little smile. "I happen to be good with a rifle against Filipino soldiers, but other than that … well …" He took another long draft and shuddered again, with less force this time. "After thinking about it for a spell, I figured if I could help people who have suffered some injustice, it might make life worthwhile." Cahill drained the rest of his mug in one long swallow, and awkwardly put it on the table. "I also see you to be someone of high moral character, something I strive to be as well."

High moral character, Anderson thought. He had tried to live his life by doing right, but he also wondered what good it had really done him. He still had trouble sleeping at night. He still suffered, and was still lonely.

As for the young man, he believed what he was saying, but the sheriff knew he would also tell the truth to Colonel Ames. Having him by his side, however, might allow him to control that information, and more important, buy him more time with the police here in Minneapolis. He didn't want to deceive Detective Cahill, but he was desperate to find Maisy.

He sensed that the boy was sincere, and another man with a badge might offer a more direct route to the information he sought.

"Young man, I'll accept your offer of help."

"Excellent, sir!" Cahill grinned, leaned over to shake his hand, and gave Anderson another reminder of how strong the boy was. "Now that we are partners in the matter, can you tell me specifically how this German will lead you to your missing granddaughter? That is the connection I haven't yet deduced."

"If I tell you this, can you swear to me that it won't get back to Ames?"

"Well..." He squirmed a little in his chair. "I can swear to you, sir, that I will not volunteer the information, and I don't plan to see him until tomorrow evening. If that gives us enough time to catch the man, then it won't matter anyway, will it?"

"Fair enough," said Anderson. "I'm looking for a boy named Ollie. He was present at the girl's murder, and he identified her as Maisy Anderson. Something tells me he knows more about my granddaughter. I also believe this Gottschalk character has abducted the boy. I hope one leads to the other."

Cahill sat, stoned-faced and silent, with only a slight movement in his throat. "A boy, you say? I wasn't aware of that, sir."

"Well, talk to Detective Queen about keeping you in the dark on the murder case, Mr. Cahill. That is why I am questioning men in low places."

"I believe I can assist you in finding him tomorrow."

"What makes you think that?"

"Well, sir. The man we seek is a tramp, isn't that correct? We know that to be fact."

"Yes, and a dangerous one at that," Anderson agreed.

"You haven't had any luck yet ingratiating yourself into their society, but I might know someone who can."

Anderson found himself leaning forward. This young man was already surprising him. "You have a friend on the down and out?"

"I'm not sure I'd exactly call him a friend, but I helped him out of a rough spot. His name is Jim, but he goes by Milwaukee Jim. Don't exactly know why, sir. Perhaps he's from there? Or wanted in that city? Anyway, I can visit him tomorrow morning."

"I'll come with you. Where shall we meet?"

"I'm afraid that won't work, sir. He's locked in the basement of Central Station, and they won't let you set a foot in there, I fear. He owes me a favor, though. I'll ask him where he thinks Gottschalk is hiding. He's a popular fellow with his fellow hobos, and if anyone knows a fellow tramp's movements, it will be him."

"Well then," Anderson said, standing up. "We have a busy day tomorrow."

"Where shall we meet, sir?"

"The Minneapolis Central Library, when you've finished with your questioning." He patted his pocket. "I've found a book which this tramp gave to the boy as a gift. It may be nothing, but I want to do some research on it."

"What is the book, sir?"

"A book by Ignatius Donnelly, about a comet destroying the world."

"I know that one. *Ragnarok*, and something about fire and ice."

"*Fire and Gravel.*"

"That's it. Do you want to know something odd, sir?"

"What?"

"Ignatius Donnelly died, sir. He was discovered dead, on the very same morning the girl was found murdered."

Anderson took a deep breath. This was getting stranger and stranger by the moment.

CHAPTER 11

$\mathcal{S}$HERIFF ANDERSON, DESPITE HIS FATIGUE, had stayed awake late on his bed to read the tattered book. Rarely did he read books like this to pass the time, but this one was surprisingly interesting. He awoke the next morning with the light still on and neck sore from being propped up on the pillow.

The boys from the Don't Tell Gang were right on the mark about the comet. The premise of Ignatius Donnelly's book was that a "Great Comet" had come plummeting to Earth, creating a spectacular, fiery cataclysm that destroyed its surface, and produced a layer of stratified rock called the drift in the process. Donnelly wrote in a fairly engaging style, citing geological and archeological evidence, but also delving deep into ancient texts, religions, and mythology to support his theory. Anderson's teachers had taught him that the Ice Age had caused the ancient world's mass extinction, but Donnelly tried his best to debunk all the usual theories—glaciers, ice sheets and tidal waves—as possible reasons, and instead threw all his dice on a flaming piece of rock plunging from the sky.

The book got even loonier at the end when Donnelly proposed that humankind had been destroyed with the comet's arrival. Not just Paleolithic hunters, for which he claimed ample proof, but an actual high-stage civilization, replete with artists, architects, and metallurgists. After this advanced society fell, a tiny group of these people, hiding in caves, were able to survive and ultimately rebuild and repopulate the Earth.

Anderson cringed as he pictured it in his mind: ancient men, women and children, staring up, stupefied, as a great ball of death came hurtling towards them, burning them into embers. That, he thought, would be one hell of a way to go. Who would want to ride out their lives in a cave while the Earth was being ravaged in a fiery blaze, anyway?

He continued to think about the book in the morning's drab chill as he walked over frost-coated sidewalks to the streetcar stop. The title, *Ragnarok*, which meant the "darkness of the gods," or "the rain of dust and ashes," hearkened to humanity's great finale predicted by Scandinavian myth. Anderson remembered bits and pieces of the prose Donnelly used to make his point.

> *Wolves will devour the sun and moon, stars will hurtle from heaven, and mountains will topple down.*

This enormous disaster sounded an awful lot like the Revelation to him. Could someone twist an interpretation out of this book to suit his own desires? Someone unsound, maybe? He'd seen hard-shell Baptist ministers do it to scare folks into making offerings, but they had full use of their faculties, with intelligence and cunning to spare. Anarchists reveled in the idea of such chaos. Any man with a gift for deception might twist these notions into something monstrous. The fact that the book was left in a child's care, given out of some perverse love, made the hair on his neck stand on end. This Gottschalk had already proven himself a master manipulator, using his snake's tongue to snatch young boys from their mothers' bosoms. Men like this were unpredictable, and as dangerous as the Great Comet at the heart of Ignatius Donnelly's text. Dangerous enough to incinerate anyone in their path.

He sat on the sleepy streetcar as it rattled down Hennepin Avenue, under the somber, dawning sky and the cobweb of criss-crossing electric lines that powered his ride. Anderson had considered walking the ten blocks to the Minneapolis Central Library, but his legs were still sore from yesterday's adventures, and decided a seat might save a little strength for whatever the day might bring. After a handful of stops that introduced new, drowsy-looking commuters to seats made warm by the recently disembarked, the car finally reached his destination. He exited gingerly, taking care not to bump his head on his way out. The streetcar clanged once and lurched away, and he found himself in front of a grandiose sandstone building, bejeweled with rows of arched windows that took up a quarter of the city block. It rose a solid three stories high, punctuated by nipple-shaped towers rising regally from two corners. It seemed to speak to the world that it was there, and that nothing would ever move or destroy its impressive, massive form.

Approaching the building's main entrance, a formidable set of squared doors guarded by granite pillars, he noted a statue of what he guessed to be the Greek goddess Athena centered in an alcove directly above the door. Give me a little of your wisdom today, he thought.

I need to find her, and find her soon.

Maybe Anderson had been away from the big city too long, but he found himself dazzled by the city's architecture. The library's interior was splendid, lined with impressive curved doorways leading to a foyer brilliantly lit by skylight. He followed the signs to the reading room, which greeted him with a wave of warmth. A few conservatively dressed women sat reading delicately held books near a large fireplace, piled with wood and blazing brightly. Tables dotted the room's expanse and were surrounded by gentlemen devouring newspapers. The sheriff presented himself at an enclosed counter, where a square-jawed woman with spectacles and graying hair looked up from her work. She examined him closely.

"May I assist you, sir?"

"You may. I am looking for any books you might have about the life of Ignatius Donnelly."

"He passed just last week," she said.

"I am aware," he said.

"Well," she said, sucking in her bottom lip, "We have no biographies of him. Is there something more specific you can tell me?"

"I am trying to interpret this." He placed his Donnelly book on the counter and she studied it carefully.

"We have copies of this. It is a very compelling work. Not six months ago Mr. Donnelly was here, in this very room, discussing it with some other men. It was an informal discourse, something which Mr. Donnelly quite enjoyed."

"Do you know much about him?"

"He was a familiar face to me and we spoke on occasion. His reputation as a lover of books is quite well known. He told me he had three thousand volumes in his personal library." She squinted, suspicion seeming to change her expression. "Pardon my directness, but is there another reason for your inquiry? I hope you aren't trying to gain some advantage with the family."

"That is not my intention at all, ma'am," Anderson replied with an amiable smile. "I'm not a bill collector, nor an attorney, nor an agent of the government. No one who would have any reason to cause trouble to the Donnellys. Just an admiring reader, intrigued by his story, and interested in more."

Her face relaxed at his explanation. "Well, you've heard of his most famous work, haven't you?"

Anderson shook his head. "I'll admit I've read many more newspapers than books in my life. I know of his politics, but not much else."

"He wrote a book about the lost city of Atlantis, about twenty years ago. If you think the ideas in this tome are explosive ..." The librarian cracked a mischievous smile and lowered her voice to a hush as she pointed to Anderson's book. "Then his *Atlantis, the Antediluvian World* would appear downright scandalous. He went out attempting to prove that the mythical city really existed."

"And did he?"

"Well, to many, yes," she said. "He attracted many devout followers with his theories, but as many, if not more, naysayers."

Devout followers. The words stuck to his tongue like flypaper. Ignatius Donnelly was the kind of flamboyant personality who would draw followers like a moth to flame. He had been a malcontent, a firebrand, and a fiery populist in the political arena, his gift for oratory legendary. He'd served as a congressman, lashed out against the gold standard, and even been nominated for vice president under the Populist Party. Whipping up frenzied crowds had been easy for him. Could the mysterious German have been influenced by his politics, as well?

"He was known as the Prince of Cranks, you may be aware," the librarian said, mistaking his silence for rapt attention. "For his outlandish theories. And he was called the Apostle of Discontent for his political beliefs. Neither of those names ever caught on as well as the Sage of Nininger, though."

The Sage of Nininger. Of course. How could he have forgotten? Donnelly had been part of a boomtown bust. He and his partners had attempted to create a utopian community five miles west of Hastings, buying thousands of acres and selling lots at $100 each, way back in 1856. Anderson remembered his awe when he read about this 25-year-old kid from Pennsylvania, who managed to build a town of a thousand people almost overnight and made a small fortune in the venture. Perhaps he had marveled so greatly because he had been the very same age as Ignatius Donnelly. But unlike this young genius lawyer with a penchant for sweet talk, Anderson had been a deputy sheriff with a worn six-gun and an ancient horse. Donnelly must have been on top of the world just before the Panic of 1857 pummeled the economy. And that was the downfall of his town. Nininger had literally risen and fallen in two years, completely abandoned except for one final resident, the colorful Ignatius Donnelly, who refused to leave until the very end.

It had to have been devastating, Anderson thought, for a young family to pack every belonging they had, and travel hundreds of miles across wilderness only to have their dreams dashed to pieces when their property became worthless.

And then, Anderson had a thought.

"There is something, I think, you can help me with, ma'am. Do you have any records of the names of the men who purchased Nininger township lots from Donnelly?"

The woman lowered her head slightly and peered over her spectacles. "One moment, *Ragnarok*, and the next, Nininger? You seem to be a man of changing interests."

"My mind tends to wander without my permission. A symptom of old age, ma'am." Anderson managed a smile. "I try my best to keep up."

"For crying out loud, Harm, you're pushing me too hard!" The slender man with the thin mustache appeared as though he were about to burst into tears. Queen gave him a little extra shove just for good measure as they jostled down the cellblock corridor to the man's new home.

"Quit your complaining, Adry," Queen said in a muted snarl, taking care to make sure there were no eavesdroppers to their conversation. "Why you couldn't just keep low for a few weeks is beyond me. You were first playing house with a murdered girl, the two prostitutes on the lam, and I *still* let you go without bringing you in. Now you're a goddamn check forger? Forgive me if I choose not to handle you with kid gloves." He could feel Adry's arms shaking, worse than a penniless opium fiend. "I am damned disappointed in you, Adry."

Adry flinched as Queen gave him a final push into the cell, and flopped like a rag doll to the floor. "I thought we were friends. Why would you go and pinch me like this? How long will it be before I can get out of here?" he asked, wagging his head a little, as if he was bringing the world back into view.

"That's up to Judge Dickinson. But be warned, no mention of our recent visit to your rotten little house. There is always some jack-assed junior reporter sitting in the back of the courtroom looking for a juicy story, and him writing one because of your slip-up would not make me happy. Do you understand me?"

Adry pitched his way to his bunk and sank down on the mattress, meekly saluting Queen before lying flat, feet hanging over the end. Queen left the cellblock with Adry holding a pillow over his head in anguish, and went back out to the waiting area where Sergeant Krumweide was busy with a mop and bucket.

"Where is the janitor?" Queen asked him. He took out his cigarette case. "You want one?"

"This warm spell has melted the snow, and it's leaking through the ceiling. He's in the basement where the water is two inches high." Krumweide examined the cigarettes hungrily. "Captain Phillips doesn't like the desk sergeant smoking, but he's not here and I don't mind if I do." He selected one and they shared a match. "Isn't that Harry Hayward's brother?" the sergeant asked.

"In the living flesh."

"Doesn't have his brother's looks or his charm."

"He's a nervous sort," Queen replied. "His disposition probably saved him from the gallows. You know his brother wanted him to do in Kitty Ging?"

"A stinking state of affairs that was," said Krumweide. "Speaking of scared-looking fellows, your new partner is here."

Queen lifted an eyebrow. "Tom Cahill? Where?"

"I'll give you one hint," said Krumweide. "Where in this building does the unlimited generosity of Minneapolis taxpayers mean a rent-free life with no need to buy coal or food?"

"You mean he's in the tramp room again?"

"Ankle deep in water," Krumweide replied.

Queen met Cahill coming up the stairs. "I need to talk to you,"

"Good day to you, sir," Cahill replied. He appeared to be deep in thought, but Queen's glare snapped him back to focus.

"What the deuce, Cahill? Are you so charmed by the life of the tramp that you spend your lunch hour with these fellows?"

He shook his head. "No, sir, not at all."

"I don't really want to know what you were doing down there," said Queen. " But I need you to do something for me. Right now."

"What is it?"

He handed him a folded piece of paper, which Cahill opened and read. "This is an address."

"Astute work, young man. I want you to go to that address and guard the occupants of that house."

"Why?"

"The women are in danger, and I need someone I can trust."

Cahill blushed, and gave a little smile. "Well, my goodness, sir. To say that you trust me, well… it means a great deal coming from you. The only thing is, I'm under orders from Colonel Ames."

"To do what?"

"To watch someone."

"Who?"

"I'm not supposed to say, sir."

Queen put his hand on the back of Cahill's neck, and drew him close. The kid's breath smelled like maple syrup, and for an instant he thought about breakfast, something he'd neglected again. "Tom. Who are you following? We've had this conversation before. If we're to be partners, we have to trust each other."

"Y yes sir." He took a breath. "It's Sheriff Anderson. Colonel Ames wants him out of town, and is trying to figure out a way to do it. He says that Anderson is a rabble-rouser and troublemaker of the highest order. I don't see how he could come to that conclusion. He's a decent man at heart."

This is not good, Queen thought. The colonel wasn't doing this the right way. Anderson wasn't a man to be bullied, and the harder he was pushed, the more he would push back. Better just to let the old sheriff ask a few questions, hit some dead ends, and go home. Once his schedule cleared, Queen would start looking for Maisy himself and fulfill his promise to Anderson. Right now, though, his priority was protecting Karoline, Trilly and Edna. Stocky Norwegians were a good start, but he wanted a fellow cop there too, just for insurance. "I know I'm not your superior in rank, Tom, but I want you to trust that I know what I'm doing better than Fred Ames does. I will take full responsibility for Sheriff Anderson's actions. There are women at this house and I need you to keep an eye on them, because they might be in danger. Can you do that for me?" He took Cahill's hand in his. "I'm counting on you."

Cahill rubbed at his eye, holding back a tear. "I can do it, sir. I will do it."

"Fine," Queen replied, satisfied.

"But one thing, sir. He's expecting me to meet him at the Minneapolis Library soon. I don't want to stand him up."

"What's he doing there?"

"He has a book, and wanted to ask some questions about it."

That doesn't sound particularly threatening, Queen decided. Better that than smashing up saloons, or worse yet, using those Colts to stir up trouble.

"Don't worry about that. If I can, I'll send word that you've been ordered elsewhere." Queen fished in his pocket for a roll of bills, and handed one to Cahill. "Take a cab and get there quickly."

Cahill shoved the money into his pocket. "I will sir, but before I do, may I ask you a question?"

"What is it?" Queen asked testily.

"What's a big mitt?"

"Where did you hear about that?"

"Just around, sir. I know the general idea. It's like a giant hand, right? A hand that swoops in and whisks away some unlucky customer involved in a con game."

This kid understands more than I ever gave him credit for, thought Queen with a touch of respect. He's been listening enough to get the gist of the colonel's scheme. He deserves an explanation, especially since I'm asking him to risk his life for the sake of the Ullands and their wards.

"It doesn't mean giving the sucker the mitt after he's been fleeced," replied Queen. "A big mitt is a hand at cards. The fellow who runs the game is a big mitt man. Let's leave things there."

"Are you involved, sir?"

Queen was surprised that he felt a pang of guilt at the question. Instead of answering though, he grabbed Cahill by the shoulders, turned him around, and gave him a little shove forward. He had no reason to feel bad over his collusion with Colonel Ames. It was all business, after all, and he was the only man on the force who could see to it that the game ran smoothly. He would see to it that no one got hurt either. That is why he was important.

"I told you that time was short, Tom. Go, now."

The striped awning above him pattered with frozen rain, and little strips of icicles formed delicately along its edge. Anderson buttoned his overcoat for warmth. He missed his wide slouch hat, and even though this shorter-brimmed homburg fit well, he didn't feel comfortable in its dudish, city style. And then there was this choke-strap, tied around his neck like a noose. His entire experience in this big hot town made him uneasy. Minneapolis was both fascinating and confining, with its mountainous four-story buildings, its avenues packed with people, and its odd mixture of smells and sounds. When he'd investigated Maisy's disappearance on his former visit, he had considered strongly that she might have been whisked out of town by her kidnapper, and her time in Minneapolis short, but now, two years later, he thought perhaps not. She could still be here, stuffed away in some dank basement, or forced into the life on the streets. His eyes were peeled for a sign of his granddaughter at every turn; her yellow hair, the way she bounced on her heels when excited, her tendency to twist her head to the side when in deep conversation. He knew her every peculiarity like the back of his beaten hand.

The streetcar stops were tight with men and women waiting to board, and as the temperature wasn't biting cold yet, he thought he'd hoof it to his hotel. Instead of heading back up Hennepin he decided to turn northwest, and moved through the darkening shadows towards Second Avenue, a longer way home but far more interesting. As he went he noticed the neighborhood gradually change. While he still walked along cobblestone streets lined with canopied brick storefronts, things were dirtier and the occupants less affluent. Street-walkers and night hawks lingered on corners, and tag rags mooned about in alleys as he strode by.

The number of saloons was increasing as well. As he passed each one, he was drawn by the warm light, rowdy laughter and melodic songs. He considered a beer and then decided not. He wanted a clear mind to sort out some of the information he'd gathered at the library that day.

The good librarian had offered to look around through the library's archives, and had come back to the delivery room with a stack of old, musty books, documents and snipped newspaper accounts, all about the failed town of Nininger. He'd pulled out an old advertisement, touting the community to prospective residents, complete with the picture of a sturdy looking steamboat plowing up the river, with "Nininger" displayed proudly on the paddlewheel.

EMIGRATION
UP THE MISSISSIPPI RIVER

The attention of Emigrants and the Public generally, is called to the now rapidly improving TERRITORY OF MINNESOTA. Containing a population of 150,000, and goes into the Union, as a state during the present year. The CITY OF NININGER, Situated on the Mississippi River, 35 miles below St. Paul, is now a prominent point for a Commercial Town, being backed by an extensive Agricultural, Grazing and Farming Country.

He had sifted through the mountain of information until he'd finally found what he was searching for, a bound leather register that filled his nostrils with the stink of mildew. It was a list of everyone who had bought a Nininger lot, and those who'd managed to build houses and live there during its brief, doomed existence. The names were a hash of nationalities, from a wide geographical swath, many from eastern American cities, and even overseas. Among those names was one he had hoped to find: an O.H. Gottschalk, who, accompanied by his wife and two children, ages eight and five, had upended their lives and traveled from New England to Minnesota. As he continued to dig, he discovered in a file a newspaper clipping that shed some light.

NEWS OF YESTERDAY

O.H. Gottschalk, a prominent musician of German-American extraction, has been extended an invitation as Music Director for the new city of Nininger. He is editor of the Deutsche Musik-Zeitung of Boston and one of the finest musicians in America. He is reported to have high prospects for creating the best Musical Department West of New York.

So the Gottschalk family had been important, and Mr. Gottschalk famous in music circles. Donnelly had probably considered it a coup to snare such a respected individual. If, in fact, one of these two children of O.H. Gottschalk happened to be the man he was hunting, then something tragic must have happened to trigger his downward spiral into trampdom. No doubt the family had lost considerable money in their ill-timed decision, and it might have been enough to ruin them. He could see how such family destruction might have led to resentment and hatred, even trickling down to the youngest. But on the other hand, this hobo he chased, the son of O.H. Gottschalk, seemed to obsess unnaturally over Donnelly's work.

So, what did he have here? He had a possible answer to why this hobo had become the man he is now, and a definite connection to Ignatius Donnelly, but not more than that. He still hadn't found the German, and he needed to do that soon, not only for the answers he sought, but also for Petey, who needed his big brother to help navigate through this difficult life. He'd been counting on Tom Cahill for help with that, and had expected all afternoon for the young detective to interrupt his work in the reading room with news about Gottschalk's possible whereabouts. Anderson wasn't worried, but found it odd that mere hours after Cahill had informed him that he was to be the sheriff's tail, he had also disappeared. Most likely the incompetent colonel had realized how ridiculous it was to waste a public-paid city servant, riding herd on a creaky old man. At least he hoped that was how it was. He liked the earnest young tenderfoot, especially his uncompromising honesty; he was similar to Anderson's memory of himself at that age. Straight and true to a fault.

He stopped to look at a saddle in a shop window, and thought about his horse, still stabled in a Bemidji livery, waiting to take him back to his farm. He hoped everything would be just as he left it when he finally returned home. Perhaps, just perhaps, he might have a granddaughter to take home with him. Her bedroom was still as she'd left it, as Martha hadn't had the heart to change a single thing.

He had turned to finish his walk back to his hotel when an eager-looking fellow with long side-whiskers approached him from under a streetlight. He carried a wad of tobacco in his cheek and turned politely, just as he approached, to spit the brown juice in the opposite direction. He was a distinguished looking chap, and his eyes glinted of merriment when he gave a friendly smile.

"Begging your pardon, but have we met before?" he asked. "My name is Billy Edwards. Do I know you?"

"Not likely," Anderson replied. "The name is Anderson."

"A common but stout name," the man said. "Do you have the time, per chance?"

Anderson pulled out his watch. "Twenty-five past six."

"Ahhh," the man cried, looking over his shoulder at the watch's face. "That is unfortunate. I had made plans to meet a friend at the West Hotel for dinner at five-thirty, but I was delayed with business." He winked at Anderson. "The kind of business my wife would slaughter me for if she ever found out."

"I see," Anderson said. In an instant he felt very old. The thought of being with a woman in an intimate way hadn't occurred to him since his wife had died. Those sensations seemed to have gone into hibernation a dog's age ago.

"Say, would you mind keeping me company for a time? I'm venturing my friend has already taken his meal, and I need a bit to eat."

It had been a good while since Anderson had eaten, and his hunger had already been stirred by some of the smells wafting from the saloons nearby. The man might offer him some information about the local resorts as well, since he seemed to know them from personal experience. Maisy could even be holed up in a back room along this street.

"I'll take you up on your offer, Mr. Edwards," Anderson replied. "A thick slice of ham and a pile of salted fried potatoes would go down well."

Edwards chose the Dandelion Saloon, only a block away, for supper. It was a middle-class affair in the typical fashion. A couple of poorly-made lamps splaying dim light swayed from the patterned tin ceiling, its paint yellowed and peeling. A long dark bar with an iron foot rail ran the side of the joint. Over the warped mirror behind the bar hung a faded portrait of George Washington. He probably never would have imagined while living that his fate after death would be to preside every evening over a pack of drunken, crowing men.

Despite the surroundings, the meal turned out to be amiable and surprisingly decent. Anderson had decided to indulge in a single glass of Gluek beer, while his dining companion had thrown down three. Their conversation was general: about President McKinley and the strong state of the Republican party, the notorious Pat Crowe gang, which had evaded capture for months now, and the latest escapades of hatchet-wielding temperance crusader Carrie Nation. Edwards confided his occupation, clerk in a Chicago law office, and explained he was visiting for the week with business colleagues. The sheriff was less willing to speak of his own business, and Edwards, a very polite and genial chap, didn't push or pry. Anderson put his lunch hooks into that ham he had been craving, and the potatoes were nice and crispy, slightly burned on the edges, just the way he liked them. The pleasantries lasted a good two hours, but as the evening progressed, Anderson's mind filled with the tasks still to be done. Morning would come early and he needed to find Cahill to plot his next move. However, he still had some questions to ask his dining companion.

"You'd mentioned before your interest in a more carnal satisfaction," said Anderson, wiping his chin with a napkin. "I don't have an elegant way with words, Mr. Edwards. No finesse, as it were."

"Aha!" Edwards cried. "You wish to accompany me this evening as I continue to peruse the local goods? Find the gratification of female companionship? You are quite welcome to join me!"

"Too old for that," Anderson said. "But curious. Are there many joints like that around?"

"Yes, yes, certainly. Whatever your taste, it can be found, in any of a multitude of tenderloin districts across the city. You are a man of some experience, I'll wager, with your rugged countenance and Western way. I'll bet some young savage girl might be quite to your liking. There are choices for every taste. Older women, girls, men, boys, boys dressed as girls. If your pleasure lies in the Far East, or with a colored girl from the Deep South, there are resorts that cater to every whim and flavor." He licked his chops and leaned back in his chair. "The possibilities are endless."

It tore at his heart to even say the words, to associate Maisy with a place like this. He had no choice, though. He had to know. "I'm looking for a particular young woman."

Edwards raised his eyebrow knowingly and leaned in. "Forward march, Mr. Anderson. Some young rapturous beauty you encountered one evening, and haven't been able to duplicate since. I certainly know the feeling. What is her name? What does she look like?"

"Maisy. Her name is Maisy." His body tightened as the words came out. "Corn-silk hair, and a beautiful smile."

"Maisy, you say?" He rubbed his head in thought. "No, I don't recall a Maisy. A Mildred, yes. Molly, a sweet Irish lass, with searing brown eyes. Plain old May is another, although she can contort herself in ways that make her much more exotic than her name implies. I know a Mai-Yoon, although you hadn't mentioned her nationality."

"Forget it, Edwards. I was just curious, like I said before. We don't need to discuss it further, if you don't recognize her name."

"Certainly. We can drop the subject. I must say, you seem a sensitive fellow at heart, Mr. Anderson. Let's have one more round. It's my shout this time. Name your poison!"

"Thank you for your good company, but I need to go."

"Why, so early?" Edwards grinned, revealing a set of slightly twisted teeth. "While we've established that a good old-fashioned screw is not to your liking tonight, the evening is still young, and I plan to play a few hands of cards at this very saloon." He leaned forward conspiratorially. "I have it on very good authority that a lively game of poker is progressing at full swing in the back room." He motioned with his head to a door just past the bar.

"Would you care to join me? An hour of good fun, and then you can retire with your winnings!"

Anderson couldn't remember when he had last sat down for a game of cards. He once was tolerably good at it, and like his recent desire for the taste of tobacco, something tugged on him, urged him to give it a go. He felt that fire light again, the one that told him to live a little, like he used to, and take a chance or two before his coffin came to claim him. He needed sleep for another busy day of searching tomorrow, but a quick hand or two wouldn't hurt.

"All right, friend. Let's give it a go."

Edwards clapped his hands together once, delighted, and Anderson followed him to the door. The bartender, a reserved, broad-shouldered fellow with a scar on his neck stood behind the bar and eyed them dully.

"He's a big fellow for a barkeep," Anderson said. "Does he do chucker-out duties too?"

"I'd imagine," laughed Edwards. "But this is a quiet little place most of the time."

The bartender came from around the bar and met them. "No guns allowed inside, gentlemen. Either of you carrying?"

"Not I," said Edwards, patting himself for proof.

The barkeep inspected Anderson, who had already hung his coat and hat at the door, and was wearing only his suit and necktie. The pistols he carried were obvious behind the ill-fitting coat, so he unbuttoned it, revealing the weapons. He unstrapped the buckle and slid the belt off, handing the whole thing to the bartender.

"Expensive looking pistols," Edwards said admiringly. "You come prepared for trouble, evidently."

"I like to be prepared," the sheriff said.

They went in.

The night was black and the moon used its curved head like a hook to reel him forward. He felt its tremendous power, letting it sheath him in its ethereal splendor.

No ponderous coat was necessary; he wore nothing but a shirt and pants. The moon melted the ice in his path, and he followed it along the river like a jackal, lithely crawling over rocks, blissful in the knowledge that the night was his.

All was going well, the way he knew it would. The thing he had killed, the one that peddled newspapers, had revealed the location of his first prushun. With that knowledge, it was easy for him to discover the sniveling little freak, in the company of a soldier under the command of despots; an oppressor named Queen. This Queen had picked up his scent, he imagined, but was only a distant threat, he understood, irrelevant at this moment in time.

He had in his sights the sweetest of morsels, a stunning seraph with an angelic face, and it consumed his every breath.

The prushun called Ollie had revealed its young sibling's hideaway hole after an evening's palaver of pain. The process hadn't given him satisfaction, because it had not remembered their eternal pact. Long ago, the prushun had vowed to be ever devoted to him, but breached that oath when he shirked his duties and tried to hide with the flesh-peddler. When he finally found his prushun, weak and oblivious and just outside this Queen's grasp, his fears had been confirmed. It was nothing now but a used and useless toy; dirty, to be discarded as soon as the littlest one entered his fold. Their unity of two, once made with love, was now shattered and sick. The prushun Ollie had refused, at first, to comply with his will, so he used fire to withdraw what knowledge he required. He had only felt sorrow afterwards, the sorrow of a broken heart, and a faint wash of past love that no longer existed.

Once he had his information he found this place with ease, but on this night the space below the bluff was devoid of life. Nothing chose to lay its head under the ice-cold rain. He listened to the low cracking of the frozen river's edge, and the lapping of the black eddies that swirled cold and empty. The overturned boat sat as the prushun had told him it would. He saw remnants of cooking fire, bits of former life, but nothing that moved. The space beneath the boat was small, but he slithered in like a grass snake, looking for a sign, any sign, of his beloved. Other things shared the space, but he held his nose as he passed their belongings, wanting nothing to do with the rotting stench. Only an item touched by his prushun's grace would satiate his hunger, allow him to pass the night softly.

Then he saw it. An exquisite, doll-sized mitten, the color of blood, under a pile of wet leaves. He could smell its scent, and leaped towards it, snatching it with a jump of joy in his heart. So sweet and dear, the scent of an innocent, virgin childhood, before any desecration despoiled it.

He held it, caressed it. And waited.

Anderson had figured it out. He was being cheated. Bamboozled, sucked in, sold, roosted over, rooked, bilked, scooped in. Whatever you wanted to call it, it was all the same damn thing.

They had let him win a few small hands, and then the game had changed. He had missed it the first time, but once the stakes started getting higher, and he began steadily losing money, about two hundred and fifty dollars' worth in chips, he kept a firm eye on the dealer.

The second time, he spotted the dealer cold-deck him.

If there was anything the sheriff was good at, it was bluffing. He was a master at offering no emotions when the situation required it. Certainly this trip had been an exception to this; he had broken down in tears when the angel he'd expected to see on that marble slab was some other unfortunate, instead. But in the working world, he could be as stone-faced as the toughest, coolest hombre in town. He chose this face now, as he observed the dealer, with considerable skill, pull a fresh stack of cards from somewhere under the table and introduce them into the game.

He looked at Billy Edwards, who seemed to sense he was being watched, glancing back at the sheriff over his hand, flashing a little smile. He is the steerer, Anderson thought.

This is a hold-up game, and he was being squeezed like a lemon.

"It's your play," a paunchy, round-faced player to his right said with an impatient stare.

Anderson laid down his hand, which held three queens. "I quit," the sheriff said, void of expression.

Edwards chuckled. "Quit? Come now, friend. You want to walk away with a hand like *that*? This is a serious game, and while we all like a bit of good-natured codding now and then, joking about money maybe isn't so funny."

"No one is codding anyone," Anderson said. He stood up, eyes flashing. "I saw your dealer wrist-twist under the table. This is a bunco game and someone here is trying to swindle me. Nothing but monkey-shines in your little back room."

Edwards held out his hands, as if to bless a congregation. "That's an accusation you sure shouldn't be making, Anderson. We're all friends here, and no one is out to flim-flam you. Even the thought of that is just plain ridiculous."

Anderson shoved his few remaining chips into the middle of the table. "Worthless," he said, burning a stare into Edwards.

"Christ, man. You've got three queens."

The sheriff reached across the table and turned Edwards' cards, spreading them out with his thick fingers. "And you have two kings."

"You've got the better hand!"

Anderson snatched the deck from the dealer's hand and flipped it over. The third and fourth king sat on the bottom. "I know we don't normally see royalty in America," Anderson snapped, "but it seems to have gathered for a picnic in the basement of this here deck."

With lightning in his socks, Edwards moved to block the door, his arms out to either side. "Now, now, let's not get this out of hand. If you can't post the pony it's nothing to be ashamed about. I sure as hell don't carry that kind of cush with me, either. We'll just go down to the bank, bright and early tomorrow, and you can have a check drafted."

"You seem awfully concerned that the saloon gets its money," Anderson replied. "I'll give you credit for one hell of an acting turn, Edwards, but I have it all figured out now. Get out of my way or I'll call for the law."

Edwards was taller than average, but still shorter than the sheriff. Anderson, even in his advanced years, remained tough as old saddle-leather. He grabbed Edwards by his hair, pushed him out of the way, and threw the door open. He heard the table behind him explode with commotion as the remaining players stood up, knocked over chairs, and shouted obscenities.

"Give me my guns," Anderson growled to the bartender.

"Cough up the cush," the bartender growled back.

The saloon's patrons stood up from their seats, mugs of beer in hand, and backed towards the walls.

"Come now, Anderson," Edwards said from somewhere.

"I'm no rube," Anderson said. "Just give me my pistols and I'll walk out of here."

"And go to the police, you said."

Anderson pulled himself up tall and pivoted in a slow circle, surveying any extra dangers to be seen besides the bartender. The barkeep had his Colts now, but they were drawn and pointed at him and he looked hot enough to shoot.

"Hold on, now!"

The front door slammed open, and in walked three men, one wearing a plain suit and derby, and the others in Minneapolis patrolmen's domed hats and blue uniforms.

"What's this? A fight?"

The man's face was covered in a bumpy red rash, his eyes fixed on Anderson. He gave two firm winks to no one in particular, and loosed a repulsive grin. "I'm Detective Norbeck from the Minneapolis police department. What's going on here?"

"The bartender refuses to hand back my weapons."

"Are those his?" Norbeck asked the bartender, who affirmed with a nod.

"Holster those shooters and give them to me."

The bartender did as he was told, and handed the belt over the bar to one of the patrolmen.

"Guns aren't necessary here, are they?" Norbeck asked, to no one in particular. He glanced around the room, noticing a couple of poured drinks on the bar top. He reached over and took one, downing it in a single swallow.

"Now, now, sir," he said to Anderson with a glint in his bloodshot eye. "Let's step outside for some fresh air, and you can explain to me what happened."

"Speak to Billy Edwards. And the dealer, and the bartender. They're all part of a con game, and they've meant to muck me out."

"No, no," Norbeck replied. "Just you."

The detective led Anderson outside. The nearest street lamp was out, and the only light that shone on them came through the window from the saloon's feeble bulbs and a bit of moonlight between buildings.

"You're in serious trouble," the detective said, trying hard to sound sober and severe. "Unless you have a permit to gamble."

"Of course I don't."

"Well, that is a problem. It's an arrestable offense, you know."

"What about the others in there? Have they paid theirs?"

Norbeck's face shone with the barest trace of humor. "Officer Evans, go in there and check all of them who was playing whatever game it was, for registered permits."

The officer nodded and went in. The other cop stood silently next to Norbeck.

"Listen, here," said Anderson, buttoning his coat. "You've got something much larger to worry about than me. Those men inside are running a bunco joint. I was the target tonight, but sharp enough to figure it out. What about tomorrow night, however? Or the night after that?"

"Don't worry about it," Norbeck said with a wink. "You need to fag out of town, now. You're in deep trouble, Mister."

"The hell you say," Anderson growled.

"Go back to your room and pack your things. I'll have this officer escort you. He'll take you to the train and you can be on your merry way." The detective picked a piece of flaking skin from his fat nose and flicked it aside as he spoke. "You had bad luck tonight, and were up against it. Be grateful I don't march you down to the pokey for talkin' back to me."

Maybe it was his growing disdain for the way that law was practiced in Minneapolis, or perhaps it was his plain lack of fear about anything that could happen to him. Of course he wasn't going to go. He didn't care about anything except what he came here to do.

"If you think you're going to run me out of town" he said, "you'll need more than yourself and a couple of officers to do it."

A gust of freezing wind whipped at their figures, swirling a tiny dusting of newly fallen snow on the sidewalk. Norbeck pulled out a nasty looking blackjack from underneath his jacket, and the officer next to him followed suit with a billy club.

"I haven't broken somebody's bones in a good long time," Norbeck sneered. "Now's as good a time as any."

"I can give it out cold as well," returned the sheriff.

It came faster than he expected. Anderson felt the blackjack smash into the side of his head, and another strike on the square of his back by the club, almost in unison. A brilliant white light filled his vision momentarily, and then everything went dark. He threw his fist forward, feeling it make contact with what he thought was flesh, but with only blackness before him he couldn't see who, or what he'd hit. Another blow in his stomach forced the breath out of his body, and he staggered to one knee. A final hard wallop to his side and the sound of cracking ribs, and his hands braced the pavement in front of him. Finally a boot met his stomach from beneath, lifting him inches off the ground and then back to earth in an agonizing thud. A mist seeped through his head, clouding his brain in a numbing, vibrating tingle, and he suddenly felt sleepy. Fight, he told himself. Get up like a man and fight, and then go and find your granddaughter. Except his body wouldn't move, as much as he willed it to. The feeling of sleep suddenly overwhelmed him, and he slipped in.

CHAPTER 12

T HE ASSISTANT MATRON LED QUEEN through the Swedish Hospital's sterile corridor, over freshly scrubbed and polished wooden floors, and through a wide, black-framed door. Six beds stood against each wall, separated by white linen curtains. Queen immediately spotted Sheriff Anderson, as his feet hung awkwardly over his bed's metal footboard.

"He's just too tall," she told him, fret in her voice. "We have a man making an adjustment to another frame in the basement, and we'll get it up to him as soon as we can."

He looked in a rough spot. His chest was bandaged and his face was swollen and badly bruised, rendering him almost unrecognizable.

"Sister Swanson, his nose looks broken."

"It is, Mr. Queen. Five broken ribs, a broken nose, swelling in the left ear, which he may not hear out of again. He came in with a concussion late last night, but has since regained consciousness."

"Can he talk?"

"His pain is such that we've medicated him heavily. It is better that he sleeps, but even awake he wouldn't be much of a conversationalist."

Queen set down the bag he was carrying next to the bed. "I went to his hotel room, Sister, and brought him some clothes. He only had one other set, and frankly they're a bit garish, but he'll probably be grateful not to wear that." He pointed to Anderson's suit, neatly folded on a shelf against the wall.

"Was he wearing a set of pistols when he was found?"

She shook her head, and tucked a lock of gray hair back under her mob cap. "We abhor weapons here, Mr. Queen. We are a place of healing, not violence."

He put his hands up in surrender. "No argument from me, Sister. I was simply wondering, as the detective investigating his case, whether they were taken or not." He grabbed his notebook and pencil from his pocket and jotted down some words to prove his innocence.

"So you are in charge of finding who did this?"

Queen honestly didn't know. He hadn't been to police headquarters yet that morning, and it had been the early edition of the *Minneapolis Tribune* that notified him of the sheriff's situation.

"I expect so, Sister," he said.

"He is an officer of the law, isn't he?" she asked him.

"Yes, as a matter of fact," he replied. "He was, anyway. How do you know?"

She reached into a pocket in her apron, and pulled out his battered silver star. "It was found on the ground beneath him when the ambulance arrived. He seems quite old to be rounding up desperadoes."

"He's just a man looking for someone he loves," Queen said. "Give it to him when he wakes up."

He thanked Sister Swanson, wheeled and made for the door, feeling guilty as hell. He'd promised Cahill to find Anderson, and he'd failed. The old man shouldn't have been knocking around that part of Minneapolis, but he noticed the sheriff's knuckles were swollen, and figured he'd gotten in at least one good blow before he went down. An apology was in order, and although it pained him to have to deliver it, he knew Tom

Cahill was owed one directly. Queen tipped his hat to a gaggle of nurses at the hospital's entrance, and as he put on his hat and coat, felt a tap on his shoulder.

"How proud of you the citizens of Minneapolis would be, if they could read about you visiting sick patients, instead of getting into saloon fights."

There was Karoline, pretty and trim in her striped gown and white apron. She touched his hand lightly, just enough to send a tingle down his spine, but not enough to draw unwanted attention from the hospital staff.

"Karoline. Of course you'd be here. Although I'm surprised. I thought Norwegians and Swedes didn't get along so well."

"Well enough," she laughed. "I'm here almost every day to volunteer. They have a children's ward." Her expression grew serious as she looked him over. "Harm, you don't look well. What's the matter? Is it someone here you know? A friend?"

Queen shook his head and looked away. "Not a friend, but someone I let down."

She reached to touch his cheek. Too forward a gesture in public for her reputation to allow, he thought, and gently moved her hand down. She blushed and looked away.

"Karoline. I can't let you –"

"I know. I'm sorry," she replied.

"I don't mean to upset you, it's just –"

"I understand. Let's not mention it again. I'm sure you have so much to do." Her eyes met his and she gave him a brave smile, but he saw anguish behind their sparkle. "There is a young girl down the hall, named Astrid. She has pneumonia because she had no coat to wear to school. I fear for her life and must go and comfort her, Harm. Please, let me go now."

"I'll come to call on you," Queen heard himself blurt out. "As…as soon as I can."

"If you're serious about that, you must ask my brother's permission first." She smiled again and it was both radiant and sad. "But I saw how you looked at your young ward, Miss Flick. You know how much she admires you, don't you? I would dare say her feelings go even farther than that."

And that is the problem, Queen thought. I have feelings for Trilly. And for you, Karoline. He wanted to tell this young woman in front of him how lovely she was, and how desperately he respected her for her compassion, poise and grace. But he had no idea how to meet her in that elevated place. Deep down, he knew he didn't deserve someone like her to love. He knew with certainty that if they ever were together, she'd quickly tire of him and his wayward ways. His connection to Trilly, on the other hand, was much more real. Like him, Trilly was combustible and acted on impulse. And she needed him, to protect her and love her. Christ, he was confused.

"I don't know what to say," Queen replied.

"She's there now," Karoline said. "Ask her. Go to her."

"I'll go to your home," he finally said. "But it's to talk to Tom. I'm sorry to have surprised you by sending him over, but I figured Peder wouldn't have a problem with an extra guard."

"What are you talking about, Harmon? Who is Tom?"

"Detective Tom Cahill. He went to your house last night."

"I was there last night and this morning. No police officer came to our home."

Queen stopped himself from reaching for his whiskey flask, and instead furiously rubbed his brow in frustration.

"You are upset," Karoline said, worry on her pretty face.

"I have to go," Queen replied. He bowed awkwardly, unsure of how to part company with her, and she returned with a little curtsey and, of course, that stunning, sad little smile.

The police wagon driver bent quickly to threats, Queen discovered. Even idle threats that he never meant to carry out. Queen knew the driver had a nasty opium habit, which would lead to certain expulsion from the police force and possibly family ruin if ever revealed. Queen hated using this information gleaned from low places, but he needed to get to the Ulland house fast, and when he saw the wagon parked near the hospital, he pounced.

Riding through the city, Queen pondered Anderson's situation. Who would do something so violent to him? Had he so quickly stumbled onto information that would put him in harm's way? It seemed hard to believe. He was still carrying his copy of the *Tribune* and scanned it until he found the article to verify where Anderson had been found last night.

Just yesterday, he had handed Colonel Ames a list of men and saloons that might fit into their plans. It took a special kind of criminal to pull off a mitt game, and Ames had been eager to get Queen's recommendations for which local swindlers and bunco artists might be reliable enough to do the job. One of those was the owner of the Dandelion Saloon, on Hennepin Avenue's north side. He had a back room for poker and had worked with Queen on a couple of ventures in the past. He was reliable and, even better, had a dealer who was lightning fast at cold decking. The paper said Anderson had been found at the corner of Fourth Street and Third Avenue, literally five feet from the saloon's door. Could this have been Colonel Ames's doing? His brain smoldered at the very thought of the police superintendent not only attempting such stupidity on a wily old dog like Anderson, but using Queen's own list without his knowledge or participation. He forced his fists open to grip the wagon seat as he stepped down, to keep from slugging the driver out of blind rage.

When they arrived at the south Minneapolis homestead, Queen jumped out with barely a word to the driver, reminding himself to stay calm until he could confront Ames in person and get the truth. He ran up the path, giving a quick wave to the men sitting or standing in the yard. Peder's Norwegian friends were smoking cigarettes and holding shovels, bats and other makeshift weapons. He recognized the largest of them as Big Snorre, a gigantic man in saggy overalls with a fat, pleasant face and a wisp of brown hair on his balding head. He greeted Queen in Norwegian, proceeding to babble on as if Queen were a fellow immigrant from the old country and understood every word. Queen gave Big Snorre a quick hello and pretended not to hear the rest. Big Snorre was a decent fellow, Peder's right-hand man when he needed a menacing presence at labor rallies and political meetings. Peder was a pacifist at heart, but smart enough to know a little muscle standing nearby helped make his case more relevant in certain situations.

He'd barely knocked on the door when it opened, and there stood Trilly, ravishing in Karoline's second-hand clothes. Her eyes lit when she saw him and she laughed to see his jaw drop.

"Karoline let me borrow this, until I finish my own. Too proper for me, isn't it?"

"Not at all. Very becoming, in fact."

"I can tell you like it," she said. "Should I invite you in? I don't know how to feel in these clothes. What's proper and what isn't. Or should I say ain't? I just can't tell no more."

"I'm actually here looking for someone, Miss Flick, and you can leave the door open if you'd like, but I don't think those fellows out there care much what's proper or isn't." He stepped in and she shut the door. The house was neat, the blood had been scrubbed away, and the clothesline stripped clean.

"Is Miss Pease safe?" he asked.

"Upstairs sleeping in the attic. We all get to share a feather bed together. I had my own bed before, but at least I don't have men crawling all over me here."

Queen didn't know how to respond. Just continue with why you're here, he thought, and don't let her know that she is the pink of perfection. This is not the time or place.

"Let's sit on the sofa, for a moment, if you don't mind," he said.

She flopped herself down, looking dejected. "This is dull music," she said. "I thought you might be taking me out for a ride."

"I wanted to make sure that a man named Tom Cahill hasn't been here this morning."

"I don't know him," she said quickly. "It's a hum-drum sounding name too, if you ask me. Say, speaking of names…" She sidled up to him, and he smelled Karoline's lavender perfume wafting from her skin. "What kind of a name is Queen? I've never heard a man called Queen before." Her tone was playful and cutting at once.

"It's English."

"English. I see." She moved even closer now, and the hair on his arms rose as her bosom brushed lightly against him. Even through the thick layers of fabric, he could feel the warmth of her, and her sweet breath as she brought her mouth close to his. He wanted to step back but was transfixed at the sensations overloading his body, arousing him in every sense of the word.

"So what are you waiting for, anyways?" she asked him, batting her eyes.

"What are you driving at?" Queen asked, even though he knew perfectly well what it was.

"Men!" she scoffed. "Don't be coy. I've seen you makin' goo-goo eyes at me, Detective Queen. Or should I call you Harmon, like *Karoline* does?" Her voice dripped with sarcasm as she stretched out Karoline's name.

"I-I came to see about a fellow detective, Miss Flick."

"Well, that's cold coffee for you." The corner of her lip curled into a sneer, and then it was gone, replaced in an instant by a sultry, pouty smile. His every instinct as a policeman told him to get up and leave, but his arousal, even greater now, kept him planted in his seat.

She kissed his neck, and then, finally, his lips. His heart pounded in his chest as he returned her kiss with his. She reached her arms over his shoulders, and he responded in kind, grabbing her waist and pulling her tight. For an instant he second-guessed himself. This was the home of a woman he'd admired – and loved, too – for such a long time, and Karoline might love him in return. But there was no way he could keep this bottled up inside any longer. The anger, the frustration, and the attraction he felt towards Trilly was manifesting itself as cold-blooded lust. Was there love, too? He couldn't tell, and frankly, at that moment, didn't care.

They kissed with desperation, trying to push their mouths closer together, and then he found himself grasping at her skirt. Her body heaved back and forth in anticipation, and she licked at his lips and bit them hard as he undressed her. Then he worked at his trousers, but she was impatient, and tore at them until they were at his knees. Locking their lips again, they fell from the sofa and onto the cold floor, grinding on each other frantically. He wanted to finish before Edna came down, or one of the guards out front opened the unlocked door.

"Christ almighty," she groaned, as they held one another. Her eyes were glazed in concentration, and her beautiful face had collapsed, surrendered, almost in a trance. Her breathing was rough and intense, and he felt his chest heave with hers in unison, her supple, small nipples pushing against the hair on his chest. They were pulsing now, moving like animals, unable to stop. He couldn't hold any more, and he released, gripping his bottom lip with his teeth, and a moment later heard an anguished scream from her lips. They both gave low moans, and then he rolled onto his back, pulling out of her as the fear of discovery filled his head.

"I don't care if anyone hears," she said.

"I do," he replied. He stood, picked up her bloomers and handed them to her, but she tossed them aside like a sullen schoolgirl. He ignored the display, and quickly put on his trousers and shirt. "Are you going to throw a few bills on me next? You think I'm a fast girl, don't you? A *tottie*?" she asked, her face deepening in anger.

He stopped. This wasn't the way to act, but he still knew what they'd done wasn't fitting. So, feeling a stab of guilt, he got down on one knee next to her, pulling the hair from her eyes. He gave her a kindly smile, but forced himself to look into her face and not at her small firm breasts and brown nipples that still stood erect in the cool air.

"I have feelings for you, Trilly, please know that, but I think we're being hasty in all of this." As he spoke, he listened for the inevitable stamp of footsteps from above or a pounding at the door, but none came. Her face softened but she still fought to maintain her glare. "Where are you going?"

"To find Detective Cahill." He stood up, slipping suspenders over his shoulders.

"What for?"

"I need to speak to him."

"What about?"

He stuck out his hand, and reluctantly, she took it, pulling herself up. "He's working on a case, and I want to find out what it is."

"Why do you care?"

Telling police business to innocents wasn't something he ever made a habit of, but he was feeling weak at the moment, and frankly she wasn't innocent at all. It felt good to tell someone the position he was in. She of all people, having lived a life of trouble, might understand, especially as she was plainly involved in the case.

"The girl you knew as Maisy Anderson—that wasn't her real name. Maisy's grandfather came to identify the body, and said it wasn't her. He's been looking for clues to help find her ever since. I believe he may have enlisted Detective Cahill to help in his search."

There, he'd confided in her. She wasn't feeling the moment's gravity as he was, however. She looked jolted by his words and grabbed at his shirt. Her slim, sweet bare body was already making him dizzy with lust again.

"I don't understand. She had a different name?"

"Apparently so." He removed her hands from his shirt and reached for his jacket, attempting to shake out the wrinkles, but it was already rumpled from too many recent nights of being slept in.

"Where do you expect to find him?"

"There's a hobo stuck in the Central Police Station's tramp room who he did a favor for, and I expect the favor was returned. I'm going there. And after that, I'm going to find the men who made the bloody mess in this house."

"What do you mean?" she asked, rising hatred and fear on her face. "The people who beefed Dander and Higgins? They deserved it!"

"I despise what those two did to you, but murder is still murder, and I'm not going to let a gang of killers high-tail it back into Saint Paul unscathed." He gave her a brief kiss, but he felt her pull back and then force herself to return his affection. *Does she resent me for wanting to find Peach and Kilbane?*

"Please don't tell Karoline about what happened between us. I'd like to tell her myself."

For an instant he thought he saw a look of cold disgust cross her face, but she turned somber instead.

"Go and complete your business, Detective Queen," she said. "She won't hear a thing from me, I promise."

Although they shared the destination, the police wagon driver was still grateful to be rid of Queen when they arrived at Central. Despite getting a dollar for his extra help, a suspicious look was the only thanks the driver gave in exchange for Queen's generosity. *The hell with that*, Queen thought.

Krumweide chewed on a hard-boiled egg as he opened the door to the cell full of sleeping tramps. *Jesus*, Queen thought. *It's eleven in the morning and they've all decided to take a nap together on the floor. Anyone that thinks the life of a tramp is romantic needs to get a whiff of a roomful of them together.*

"Wake up, Jim," Krumweide said, standing over a snoring heap of flesh, its face half-covered by a tilted, wrecked stove-pipe hat.

"He's a hard one to raise," the sergeant said. "This always does it." He grabbed a pinch of the egg with his stubby fingers, and sprinkled bits of crumbled yolk into the hobo's mouth. The hobo sputtered and sat up, looking around, and then up at the two policemen.

"No salt," Milwaukee Jim said disgustedly. "You should be ashamed of yourself."

"Get your lazy carcass up and out. This detective wants to talk to you."

"Another one," Jim muttered. He rubbed his eyes and adjusted them onto Queen. "You're the short chap's friend. The one who stood there when these fellows swiped my shoes."

"And I'll take your shoes again, if you don't get your miserable ass up and tell me what I want to know."

"I can always get another pair," the hobo crowed, waving his soft hand in a flippant fashion.

With both mitts, Queen grabbed Jim by his dirty collar and yanked him up, pushing him through the dank sea of slumbering tramps and into the corridor.

"Will this take long? Lunch will –"

"God damn your lunch. I want to know what you told Detective Cahill yesterday."

"Well, good day to you too, sir!" the hobo exclaimed. "A pity the rules of polite society have gone the way o' the dinosaur."

Queen poked him in the forehead. "Shut your gob, chum. None of this foolishness. Tell me where you sent him before I prick that round tummy of yours like a balloon. You're a dull-sounding bag of wind who needs a good deflate, I think."

"Not the way to treat someone who has something you need," Milwaukee Jim returned, self-importantly.

Hell, Queen thought. Time was wasting, and he was going to have to treat him with kindness. Certain that his flask still held a few long sips of whiskey, he willed himself to pull it from his pocket. While the thought of this half-shaven three-chinned beggar sucking on it was repugnant to his very soul, he still, reluctantly, showed it to him.

The sight was met with glistening, teary eyes.

"Very good, sir," Jim said, licking his cracked lips. "We absolutely have a deal." He looked around for a moment, making sure no one could overhear. "There is a man. He is in fact a tramp, but of the lowest order of tramps. The young detective asked if I recognized his name. Of course I had." He shuddered, peered over his shoulder into the dark, and then returned to meet Queen's gaze. "Gottschalk."

Queen didn't recognize the name. "And why was he important to Detective Cahill?" he asked.

"I don't know," Jim whispered. "But I do know this: Gottschalk doesn't have a shadow. I swear on my ailin' mother he doesn't. I've seen big bucks, brutes who aren't afraid to pick fights with anyone, clear a path around him like skeered kittens. He has a satanical cast, and that's the God honest truth."

"Sounds like a scary fellow," Queen replied dismissively. "Tell me what goose chase you sent my detective on now."

Jim pointed hopefully to Queen's flask. "Perhaps a taste?"

"You'll get it all when you've answered my questions."

The hobo gave a dejected nod. "Gottschalk never, ever speaks to anyone unless he can help it. He likes to be left alone, and we're all happy to oblige. But at night, in his sleep, he speaks."

"And what does he say?"

"Terrible things. Truly terrible. What he's done. People he's hurt. People he's taken."

"Taken?"

"Don't you know?" asked Jim, incredulous. "I thought that's why you were here. The young detective already knew."

"Keep talking."

"Gottschalk has … a preference for little boys. He takes children from the bosoms of their dear old mothers, and brings them on the road, on the rails, to do with as he will. He even carries candy in his bag. I think it reminds him of all the little ones he's hurt. Men of that ilk, and I assure you, detective, they hold the bottommost rank among us travelers, call the children they kidnap 'prushuns.' It's trampdom slang." Jim twisted his hat's brim anxiously and looked down. "It just doesn't sound right, saying all this out loud."

The chocolate candy he found on the buggy's floor. Ollie. This was the man Trilly had warned him about, and he had simply brushed her words away. What a fool he was.

"So where is he?" Queen felt the agitation in his voice. The realization that Ollie truly had been in danger, and not just skipping around town, tore a hole in his heart. He had to find him.

"He kept saying the name Nininger, over and over. Old Slim and I talked about it afterwards. It was a real town once, but abandoned now. A few miles west of Hastings, the other side of Saint Paul. He'd say the word like a chant, and keep us all awake and shakin' under our blankets."

"Have you been to Nininger before, Sergeant Krumweide?" Queen asked. "I've never heard of it."

"Neither have I," Krumweide said, appearing shaken.

"I know it intimately," Jim said, nose slightly upturned. "Back when I was younger, there was a house I'd knock on that had the most exquisite handouts. The woman there was simply superb at baking peach cobbler. She'd give me two pieces and wrap it with cold fried chicken and I've got to tell you, with my most serious face," he took off his hat and put it over his heart, "that in all my days since, I've never smelled anything that has tickled my nostril hairs like –"

"Hobble your lip," Queen told Jim. Jim put his hat brim into his mouth, wearing the hurt expression of a child.

"Krumweide." Queen turned to the sergeant, still looking queasy over what he'd just heard. "Get Mr. Milwaukee Jim his belongings and have him at the ready for when I return. Make sure he gets his lunch first."

Jim's head shot up and he stared wild-eyed at Queen. "Whatever do you mean?"

"You want this?" He held the whiskey flask up, like a carrot to a mule. "Then you have a little more work to do. I'll be back in a couple of hours."

Col. Fred Ames's office sat directly next to his brother's, and it was there that Detective Harmon Queen entered, interrupting the police superintendent from some paperwork and a roast chicken sandwich.

"We need to talk," Queen said brusquely, closing the door behind him.

"I've been wondering where you've been hiding," Ames replied with a cold glare. He put down his pen and leaned back in his chair. "Unless you sent Tom Cahill to rescue Mother Mary herself, you had no business countering my direct order. You spat in the very face of my authority, Queen. It is the last straw. Give me your badge."

With a toss, Queen sent it skittering across the desk and into Ames's lap. "I don't give a damn about your goddamn police force anymore. What do I care, anyway? I can get paid more money as a private detective." He took out a cigarette, struck his match with a quick flick of his wrist, and inhaled hard and fast. "I've been thinking this morning, about how Sheriff Anderson was waylaid last night outside on the corner of Third Street and Fourth Avenue. Right in front of the Dandelion Saloon. It seems odd, doesn't it, that the owner of that shit hole was on the list I turned in to you just yesterday afternoon?"

Queen put his hands on the Colonel's desk, cigarette hanging from the corner of his mouth, and snarled. "You pulled the trigger on a mitt game without my knowledge."

"I did."

"And a good man is in the hospital. It didn't go the way it was supposed to, did it?"

Colonel Ames's thin lips turned to a frown. "I had instructed Detective Norbeck to escort him out of town. Evidently the former sheriff didn't comply."

"Norbeck? This was his doing?" Queen couldn't believe what he was hearing. Everyone knew Chris Norbeck could be volatile when pushed. An operation like this required a man with a steady, calm head. He was going to give Chris Norbeck the beating of his life when he saw him next, with or without his badge.

"And, you, Queen, usurped my direct command. If Tom Cahill had been with him, watching him, perhaps I wouldn't have felt the need to go to such extremes. I wanted Sheriff Anderson out of this city if I couldn't get a direct line of information regarding his doings. I felt I had to act."

"Well, for your knowledge, Detective Cahill didn't listen to me either. I asked him to look after the prostitutes from Dander's brothel. He never went."

Colonel Ames's mouth dropped. "The hell you say."

"The hell I say."

"Oh, Lord." Ames's expression swung from hostility to distress in the blink of an eye. His shoulders collapsed and he released a crestfallen sigh. "I feared this might happen."

"Feared for what?" Queen was flabbergasted at Ames's transformation. The man always looked so formidable, but the mention of his protégé, out on his own, seemed to have cut the life right out of him.

"Sit down, Queen. Please."

Queen took a chair and sat. "You need me to send for a doctor?"

"No, no, no," he replied, shaking his head. "I don't need a doctor, and if I did, my brother would insist on doing the honors himself." He looked up at Queen with deep lines on his brow, fumbled for the detective's badge and slapped it down on his desk. "Please take it back. I spoke in haste, and I regret it. We both have the interests of Mr. Cahill at heart, wouldn't you say?"

Queen nodded. "We do," he said.

"He's in trouble, I just know he is." Ames wiped perspiration from his forehead with his handkerchief. "You know he looks up to you, don't you? He says you're often harsh to him, but only because you want him to do better. In his words, to learn the ways of the streets."

I already owe Cahill an apology, Queen thought. Now he felt guilty, treating the kid the way he had.

"I didn't know he thought that way about me."

"Well, he did. He does," Ames said. He reached for two glasses and a bottle of scotch, an expensive brand, from a cabinet behind him and poured. "I think we both need a drink for what I'm about to tell you. I'm going out on a limb with this one, Queen, but only because I think you're the only one who can help with this. God help me, but I never thought I'd ever say that to you."

"I never would have expected it, either," Queen replied, taking a quick swallow. It burned sweetly in his stomach, and he felt his nerves relax a little with the sensation. Ames emptied his glass, his tension seeming to release as he leaned back in his chair.

"Tom Cahill protected me, during the war. Did he tell you that?"

"A little, but no details."

"There was a situation, a serious one. I had sent out a squad of scouts, but ordered them well past enemy lines. Mistakenly, I might add. Only Tom Cahill survived. His sharpshooting skills saved his life, and when he returned, he saved my career from ruin."

"How so?"

"My commanding officers accused me of poor judgment, and blamed me for needlessly putting my men in harm's way. Tom Cahill testified that my decision was justified. He lied for me." Ames's eyes widened at the memory, and he reached for the bottle again, filling his glass to the very top this time. "And later, when I came down with a grave illness and attempted to pull myself from duty, he vouched for me again, even when others accused me of cowardice. I owe him my career."

"And you feel honor-bound to protect him now."

"Of course I do, Queen. But I worry about him for other reasons too."

"And what are they?"

"Take another drink, Queen. You'll need it for this." He poured another round, but poorly this time. Ames's hand shook as he handled the bottle. Is it the alcohol that's turning the colonel into a bowl of oatmeal, Queen wondered, or the burden of this secret?

"That's better," Ames said, draining another glass whole. "Here is the plain deal, Queen. Cahill doesn't have aspirations for marriage. He isn't attracted to women like a normal man. When we were in the Philippines, I found him, late one night, in his tent, cavorting with a native boy. They were in an embrace, without clothing. I left in a hurry, I will tell you right now. It was very upsetting."

So Cahill is a snipper-snapper, Queen thought. A little Miss Nancy. Another little gem of information to make his life that more difficult.

"When I confronted him about it the next day, he broke down in tears. He swore he would not do it again. Actions such as these simply cannot take place in the Army, and it horrified me to even contemplate such sin, but he was remorseful. I gave him another chance, as he had given me. We developed a bond of secrets. Now, you've been let in on them."

Queen was at sea. "What does all of this have to do with your concern for him now?"

"Weeks ago, before he officially joined the force, I was given a message from a fellow officer who had served with the both of us. This man frequents resorts in this city with regularity. He claimed he saw Tom fawning over a boy and was sure it was more than a simple friendship between young men."

"Well, Colonel, if what you say is correct—and don't get me wrong, I don't condone such goings-on—but if in fact it's true, I don't see a reason to come down hard on the kid. I don't personally give a damn what he does, as long as he keeps it to himself."

The police superintendent's face drooped into a sloppy mix of sadness and anxiety. "Queen, he was spotted at Emil Dander's brothel. I fear, now, that he may be mixed up with that girl's murder. I tried to keep him from that case, and to dissuade you from involving him, but I don't know now. Everything is spiraling out of my control. He's like a son to me."

Son of a bitch. This was not a turn Queen had expected.

"What kind of rifles did your men use during the war? What did Tom carry?" Queen asked him, the words tumbling from his tongue.

The colonel blinked. "Trapdoor M1889s. Rotten pieces of equipment."

"Why is that?"

"They still used black powder, not like a good smokeless Krag. When you fire one, it kicks up a thick white smoke that an enemy can spot. Those damn rifles are no good for firing from cover."

"What kind of cartridge does it use?"

".45-70. Why do you ask?"

Queen felt in his suit pocket for the bullet Norbeck had given to him, the one he hadn't returned to the morgue. He touched its tip, blunted from impact, and then held it out at the Colonel.

"This was the bullet found in her chest. Could this have been fired from Cahill's rifle?"

Ames stared at it, transfixed, and then slowly nodded.

Could it really have been Cahill? The little boy he had encountered near the dead girl's body had mentioned a cloud, but Queen had thought he was gibbering about seeing white smoke in the middle of the night sky. Maybe it had been the puff from a military rifle? Cahill was an expert marksman, after all. More pieces came flowing from his head, fitting together like a diabolical puzzle.

The only boy Dander employed had been Ollie. Who else could Ames's officer friend have seen with Cahill, except for Ollie? The dead girl had been found wearing Ollie's jacket. Could Tom Cahill have been trying to kill Ollie in a fit of jealousy? Had the dead girl been the victim of mistaken identity? Of all people, Cahill seemed to have a firm head on his shoulder; not prone to anger like Ames. Or like himself. It seemed so damn far-fetched, but the evidence was saying something different.

And here he thought Cahill had been searching for Gottschalk, but perhaps it was Ollie he really wanted.

Christ Almighty.

He stumbled from his chair, and the liquor shot up to his brain to stoke the coals of his already raging headache. He slid the badge off the desk and dropped it into his pocket.

"I know where Tom Cahill is going," he told the dumbfounded colonel, slamming the door as he left.

CHAPTER 13

IME WAS SHORT, BUT QUEEN didn't care. He stalked through the police assembly room like a caged tiger, backing officers against the walls, until he fixed on a sullen-looking figure at a desk in the corner, applying carbolic acid salve to his nose. The man screamed as Queen kicked the chair out from under him, then held his hair, backhanding him again and again until a couple of brave patrolmen stepped in and yanked Queen away.

Norbeck stared up, aghast at the surprise attack, and limply put up his fists. Queen was already a safe distance away from him, his arms gripped tightly by the officers.

"What in God's name were you thinking, Chris?" Queen barked, bits of drool flying from the corner of his mouth. "You beat up an old man in the street!"

"Hell, Harm." Norbeck grinned. "You hit like a girl."

"I hit you like that because you can't take a full lick." Queen wriggled his arms free from the officers and wiped his hands on his shirt. "You and that disgusting shit on your face. I got it all over my hands."

"I can take care of that," Norbeck said. He relaxed from his crouch and took out his handkerchief, extending it towards Queen. Queen, with a resigned sigh, grabbed it and wiped it on his shirt.

"It's eating through my goddamn clothing."

"Sorry, Harm."

"All right, Chris. Get up."

Norbeck stood, turned his chair upright, and promptly plopped back down in it. "I shouldn't a' done that, I know. I just got carried away with myself. He's old for certain, but tough as nails. Look what he did to me!" He turned his head to reveal a swollen cauliflower ear.

Queen raised an eyebrow. "That's impressive," he said.

"I know," Norbeck replied with a nod. "And I went too far on him. Something just snapped in my head when he wouldn't come with me. Is there anything, you think, I can do to make it up to the old bag o' bones?"

"Yeah," said Queen. "Return his pistols and apologize. Offer your help. Whatever he needs. Wipe his ass if he wants you to."

A ripple of laughter came from the onlooking officers. Norbeck winked to the room and grinned widely.

"I'll bring him back his guns, Harm. Maybe a bottle of something strong too, to ease the pain."

"Good," Queen said. His head was clearer now, and this was one more thing off his chest. He slugged Norbeck hard on the shoulder as he passed him, wiped the dribble of spit from his chin, and made his way out into the Minneapolis afternoon, first to get the hobo Milwaukee Jim, and second to go to Nininger, wherever the hell that was.

It had been so easy, snatching it as it slept, and now Gottschalk carried his new love and joy under his arm, along the river's edge. He indulged himself in the sensations of the slashing winter wind, blowing off the water against his skin. Everything was going according to divine plan, slipping deliciously into place. He brushed its hair with his hand as he moved, feeling the soft curls with the tips of his fingers. He hadn't tired, because he knew Christ and Odin held him in their highest favor, and graced him with abilities normal men didn't possess.

He'd reflected with great seriousness on whether to dispatch the two other things that lay there by the fire, next to his prushun, by slicing their throats or hammering their skulls until their brains seeped out and crackled in the fire. Their restful little naps had not been disturbed, though, because the men who ground the flour were still moving atop the bluffs, and he didn't want any screaming to draw suspicion. So he simply whisked away the thing called Petey, covering its soft pink lips with his hand so their world might stay quiet. They could peacefully undertake their pilgrimage to a place of rest, soon to be theirs only, as it once was his before, a long time ago.

Their journey was not without complication, as men wandered along the banks at inauspicious places, impeding their progress, but he moved as if celestially shielded, even in the daylight's cold glare. The path to his rebirth was clear, as it had been during times past. This time it required the purity of youth. This rebirth was especially significant because it was connected by brothers. One to die and the other to live anew. Both were in his possession, and now only the home of his childhood and the words of the Sage were required for his transformation.

One step after the next he went, over rocks and logs and icy creeks emptying into the river, through jagged branches that reached out to claw at their bodies, but never quite touched. He had chosen to walk the entire way, perhaps twenty-five miles or more, and had not required a moment's rest, except to give water to his prushun, cradling the liquid in his hand and saying a prayer before carefully pouring it in its mouth. It had cried softly for the first few miles of their journey, but he had never worried. They always cried at first, once they realized the lives they knew were about to be swept away in favor of a holier existence. It was so, too, with this one named Petey. Now, as he glanced down at its face, it slept, lulled to its slumber by the soft movement of their travel.

The sun was in the west as he approached the woodlands surrounding their home, and made his way through the leafless trees and across the soft, white ground. All was blessedly silent, save the wind, still harsh but steadily lessening its power. The cold wind energized him and he reveled in its wicked beauty, but he remained intensely aware of the boy. He wanted it to continue its sleep until his arrangements were laid.

They went up the road through what had once been the village's main street. A few houses still stood, remnants of long ago, back to the time when he had played with his sister in the wide roads. The houses had been neglected, entangled with trees and brush and weeds. Allowed to challenge his memories of what once was.

The one house still intact and cared for, untouched by time, was home to the Sage. It stood like an oasis in the desert, a beacon in the wilderness. Glorious, God be praised.

It stood alone, separated from the other houses, surrounded by a majestic grove of trees. He climbed the steps to its broad veranda, caressing the door handle before turning it and entering the hallowed space.

It was a house out of time and place, a refuge for those who desired to learn and advance in their spiritual cultivation. His refuge now. Artifacts gathered from the far reaches of the earth were displayed in cabinets, in jars, on tables. Oval portraits of historical figures dotted the hallway walls. Passing those, he climbed the staircase to a small bedroom. It had been layered with dust when he'd arrived on the First of January, but he had meticulously scrubbed it clean for his

little one's arrival. With great care, he laid his precious possession onto the bed, careful not to disturb its sleep. There.
It could slumber in oblivion until the night came, and with it
the time for its holy transformation.

Silently he descended the stairs, listening to the house's
comforting hum. It vibrated through the walls and in the
floors, and he wanted its sensation to flow through his body.
Everything about the house was sacred to him. It symbolized
rebirth. It was where the Sage had once, as an idealistic young
man, thrown his very soul into what everyone believed would
be Utopia on Earth, but ultimately became a doomed cause, a
catastrophe of epic proportions.

Gottschalk's family had been sucked into this abyss, and
suffered a financial undoing they never recovered from. Stark
and lonely years followed, filled with poverty, transiency and
painful hunger, but his father always forgave the past. Gottschalk, however, was a boy whose cold, hard resentment ripped
through his heart. His father, a faithful Lutheran, sensed his
anger. He tried to explain how Christ taught to turn the other
cheek, but the bitter young man wanted nothing of it. He
wanted the vengeful God of the Old Testament to teach him
how to express his fury over the lot life had cast him.

He had left home at fourteen for the true guidance he
desired, and quickly learned the dark ways of man. One night,
soon after setting forth on his own, he hopped a train and
found himself in a boxcar with four hoboes, who told them
they wanted to use his body for the vilest of purposes. When
persuasion didn't work, they simply tore off his clothes and
followed their filthy urges to take what they wanted from him.

For many boys, such an experience might have sent them
back home, weeping and broken. But for Gottschalk, he had
learned his first terrible lesson: You can take what you want
from this wretched world with force. And so his mortal edu-

cation began. Begging became lying, lying became stealing, stealing became hard drinking, and hard drinking became assault. Arrests led to prison, which led to chain gangs and splitting rocks, which led to a muscled, hardened body that imposed its will on whatever came across its path. The experience of inflicting unrelenting pain whittled down his conscience, notch by notch, as each day passed.

While the warm blood emptied his body in favor of cold, and the things his father taught him about right and wrong ceased to matter, he was still a boy with an education, and his hatred for the Sage continued to simmer underneath his skin. So he kept studying and preparing with steeled focus, reading about the man in whatever Minnesota newspapers he could get, or books that mentioned the misdeeds of the "little demagogue," so called by the man's legions of enemies. The Sage was a fraud, a humbug, and a swindler of cunning skill. Every published attack Gottschalk read reinforced what he already knew. He devoured information about the Sage's great manipulations and plotted his revenge wherever he could: in boxcars, under sheltering trees in pouring rain, from the dark innards of jails and in abandoned barns amid desolate fields.

In November of 1882 he finally found himself back in Minnesota, at his father's funeral. He had spit on the man's dead face, called him a coward, and raised all manner of hell in the church where he lay. Walking away from the funeral, he saw a pasted bill touting a speech by one Mr. Ignatius Donnelly.

The vision of his dead father had lowered his spirits to a dull, despairing ache, so it was in that place that his idea formed. He had dreamt in his head of the most monstrous ways of snuffing the Sage's light. He'd considered kidnapping him and locking him in an empty boxcar, shunted on an unused sidetrack, to die of starvation as his family almost had. In another moment of inspiration, he'd hatched an idea to tie him to the back of a steam engine in a snowstorm, fantasizing over the image of the Sage's body wracked by freezing cold as the train rumbled for hundreds of miles over bridges and through mountains until finally, when it came to a stop, he would be nothing more than a frozen mass of beaten flesh, blue and stiff and dead, dead, dead.

Here was an easy opportunity that might never pass again. The Sage was scheduled to give a speech in Minneapolis, and he could walk up to him with a pistol and kill him cold, as Charles Guiteau had murdered President Garfield the year before. While it wouldn't match his years of imagined torture, his retribution could be here, and now. He took a newspaper from a blithering little newsboy, tearing it open to confirm the news.

MAKE WAY FOR DONNELLY

Donnelly, the "pestiferous little demagogue," is billed for a speech at Turner Hall tonight to close the Democratic campaign. The TRIBUNE sincerely hopes that he will not fail to come, and that the hall will be packed with mechanics and laboring men.

So once he finished pilfering a respectable-looking suit and hat from a store and forced his way into a bathhouse for a hard scrub and a shave, he found his way to Turner Hall, where a group of Democrats had gathered to assess the party's victories and defeats in the recent fall elections. Public tickets had been sold and seats had been filled in anticipation of Donnelly's address, but the bastard didn't show.

Gottschalk's disappointment far exceeded the crowd's. He seethed with hatred as he looked for a saloon. His first objective was a drink. His second, to pick out a victim to smash to the ground with his hard-knuckled fists. The first barroom he saw, he went into. And there he saw him.

The Sage, at the head of a table, standing firmly over an enthralled group of men, his deceptively innocent, babyish face fiery with passion, words rolling off his tongue like the sweetest music he had ever heard.

The gun never came out of Gottschalk's pocket. He sat and listened like a hypnotized snake, charmed by the diminutive man's lilting musical voice.

The Sage castigated the state's mill lords and lumber barons, accusing them of sucking the land dry without giving back in return. He denounced them with fire and brimstone and likened them to robbers and cutthroats. Gottschalk sat entranced. He had never heard anything like it in his life. Anti-trust, anti-monopoly, anti-railroad. Every newspaper article he'd ever read about the Sage had relayed these same ideas, but they had been lifeless without the speaker. To hear them in person, to be present with such bewitching power, was a greater thrill than he'd ever experienced. He felt faint with the moment's enormity. It was as if the scales had fallen from his eyes. It had been his first rebirth.

Normally Gottschalk made no room for shallow reminiscences, which he knew misused his time in the present moment, but he did keep room for such sacred memories as his first awakening. Now, the memory bound him to the momentous occasion about to happen. He moved through the house as though dancing on air, satisfied that everything would soon be coming to its conclusion. The house's voice now spoke to him, drawing him to the Sage's Sanctuary, where a great desk stood among shelves and shelves of books, stacked from floor to ceiling.

This was the library where the Sage had created his masterpieces, far-reaching works of scientific, revelatory writing that would outlive the ages. Living here, basking in the Sage's aura, would help catalyze his own transformation into higher consciousness.

He felt the room pull him closer, this enchanted den where words once flowed like magic from a pen, writing the very script of humanity's tragic performance. He wanted to sit in the Sage's chair, hold the great man's pen, and write the last chapter to *Ragnarok*. In this final chapter, he imagined, humanity would face its sins in the flaming form of a Second Great Comet. The one that would put the world, once more, into chaos.

Slowly he descended into the soft leather chair, and spread his fingers over the desk's smooth surface. Its energy washed over him, like the blood of Jesus, entering his being with a palpable, unrelenting bliss. The time was drawing very, very near, and he was the only one who had deciphered the message, the only one now alive who could save humankind once more from oblivion. It was he who would make the preparations.

And it started with the sweet darling upstairs, the joyous bundle that would purify Gottschalk. It would finally crown him the Prince of a new world, free from the greedy clutches of the wealthy and corrupt. It was marvelous to imagine, a cleansing of astronomical scale. The new shall rise, and the old shall perish.

Then he flinched, with the pain of a forgotten task. He had to prepare the filthy prushun Ollie for the ceremony, and best to do it now. Sitting atop the great desk was a silver machine that made flame. This was the Sage's personal gift to him, as it had been left with the understanding that he would come to claim it. It was the weapon that would spark the transformation, and he kissed it lovingly, aware of the power it would soon wield him.

Across the wintry-white yard was a special hiding place, and it was there that he needed to go, to fetch it, bring it forth, and drain its blood. So he went, his long steps making the barest of imprints in the snow. But to his bewilderment, he noticed erratic footprints around the old stone well. Two sets of prints, neither of them his. He followed the tracks with his eyes into the dark grove of trees. He looked down into the icy water, to the far-below bucket where he had tied the body of the prushun Ollie. Moments ago, he had expected it to be barely breathing, clinging to life, stripped to nothing but a shell, safe and secure in the depths.

But he hadn't expected him to be gone.

Queen's flask was empty, and Milwaukee Jim in high spirits, as they bounced on the train towards Hastings. The detective was fully aware that what he was doing was outrageously irresponsible, hauling this hapless fellow across the Twin Cities, but he needed someone with intimate knowledge of the place they were headed. His plan was to have Jim lead him to the old town, point out where he thought Gottschalk might be holed up, and get the hobo the hell away from there. Then, he would play a lone hand. It wasn't a very good plan, he knew, but bringing lots of Minneapolis officers out far past their area of authority might draw attention, and he didn't want Mayor Ames to face more negative press. Better that it was just him, dressed in plain clothes and with a traveling companion, although Milwaukee Jim's tattered clothes and stench were attracting unwanted attention that he hadn't considered in his haste.

"When was the last time you bathed?" Queen asked him.

The hobo scratched his ear, deep in thought. "God's honest truth, I've got no idea. Water has never been my boon companion. I don't like it. Don't like to bathe in it, don't like to cross it when I'm being chased, and I certainly don't like to drink it. Speaking of which, you aren't carrying a second flask on your figure, perchance?"

"No."

They let the train rumble beneath them for a few moments, before Jim spoke again.

"He's a bad, bad man, this Gottschalk."

"I've figured as much."

"No, he's worse than you've figured. I am only a model of cheeriness because of the whiskey you gave me. Otherwise I'd be shattin' my pants."

"No offense, Jim, but either way you would still smell like shit."

Jim bit his lip and tried to look hurt, but Queen was having none of that. His concern was about a violent German lurking in the darkness. Anyone willing to murder children was a vile soul, and he had no doubt that he'd done just that to McCartan. The kid had been killed, after all, not long after he and Ollie had departed his company. This Gottschalk was crazy enough to push a hole through somebody's neck, and that was something to goddamn think about.

"You're the treasurer of a company when you own a prushun," the hobo suddenly said.

"What?"

"When you have a little boy under your hand, it's like being treasurer of a company."

"How is that?"

"Begging's a sight easier when you can send a sweet-faced little boy up to the door askin' for food." As soon as Jim mentioned food, his eyes danced happily. "It's a guaranteed bundle of goodies. Every hobo wants a prushun."

"They do?" Queen's eyes narrowed at Jim. "Do you?"

"Well, certainly!" The tramp's grin showed a half dozen of his teeth were missing, and the others were a queer brownish-yellow color. "You live like a king with a prushun."

"And you would expect to have unnatural acts with him?"

"Lord, no!" Jim exclaimed, a look of horror on his face. "I would never do anything like that, and neither would the men I call my friends. But one'd be awful handy to make meal-time easier. A few like Gottschalk do use 'em in despicable ways. They know where to get them and how to snare them."

"How does that work? Enslaving boys?"

"A revolting business," Jim said, taking out a rotten-looking twist of tobacco and tearing off a piece. He held it out for Queen, but the detective swatted it down.

"There aren't any spittoons in this car, Jim, so if you're going to chew you can't spit on the floor."

He nodded and put it in his mouth anyway. "This is how it works," he said, moving the wad around in his cheek. "Imagine, if you will, a man, recently fresh from his travels, wandering through the city, looking for trouble. He walks up to a rickety ol' tenement building, where a handful of boys sit, nothing to do, and he greets 'em with a wave and a smile. 'You fellas look like you could use a story to liven you up!' he might say. The boys gather 'round him, eager to hear of his travels, and he proceeds to excite their senses with tales of the road. 'Ghost stories,' we call 'em. Great adventures, makin' most of it up, I might add. Now after a while, the boys are all peetrified, we call it, or hypnotized. As he goes on tellin' the tale, he'll find one boy that he likes especially, and he'll give him a wink, or a little smile, more than his share, and make him feel like he's extra special. That's the beginnin' of how a jocker snares a prushun."

"A jocker?"

"That's what we call these fellows who catch the boys. Once you have a boy, you've automatically got three squares a day. Good food, too. Nice fat bundles, not just bread and butter."

"How long do these boys stay?"

"Well, some, like the one I'd seen with Gottschalk on an occasion or two, scatter as soon as they have a chance. A few don't mind the road so much, and they look to their jockers kindly, like fathers. But those are few and far between. Jockers'll loan, trade and sell their prushuns. The market price is high."

"And when they grow up?"

"They might go home, but usually they're all messed inside their heads. We call 'em ex-prushuns, and they don't know any better than to go get their own boys, so they can abuse 'em just like they were abused."

Queen was certainly getting an education. He moved his hand into his suit coat, suddenly wanting to feel the cool comfort of his revolver's handle. Trees and houses passed by as the train chugged towards Saint Paul, and Queen's thoughts of his enemies turned from Gottschalk to ones closer to home. Once this was over, he would make it hot for that Irish bastard Kilbane, especially now that Fred Ames was equally incensed and on his side, albeit for different reasons.

The whistle blew as the train approached a curve, and a swirl of gossamer snow tickled the window, thawing against the warm glass. Soon it would be night, which would pose difficulties in navigating through the dark forest and into Nininger. In anticipation, he had telephoned his friend Peder at Dania Hall, who promised to have one of his men in Hastings waiting with two horses and a map. Having Jim as a guide made him feel more secure on their little expedition, as long as the tramp didn't slip off the horse, or worse. It wasn't a full moon, but it gave enough light to see through the bare trees, so he figured they should be okay.

When he asked Peder about the women, his friend had tried to ease his worry, reminding him of Big Snorre and the other strappers camped in the yard, but still promised to check on them when he finished work. Queen also wondered if Trilly had mentioned to Karoline what had happened between them. It wasn't something a polite lady would discuss, but Trilly definitely wasn't a lady. She was a cocked pistol, ready to fire at anything and anyone in her way. This left him more than worried about hurting Karoline, if Trilly were inclined to spill the details of their rendezvous. The poisonous look Trilly had given him just before departing now filled his head with doubt, and he pondered his standing with her.

He looked over and saw Milwaukee Jim sound asleep, chin touching his chest. Christ, what a life of freedom he had. No responsibilities, no appointments, and no pressure. He envied him at that brief moment. Then he noticed a dribble of tobacco juice run down Jim's chin, and the aura broke.

"Jim, wake up. Spit that shit out before you get it all over your clothes and on the floor."

The hobo stirred, and nodded amiably. "I must say, I haven't been this warm since last July. What a toasty ride!"

"Better than a boxcar, I'd wager."

"Most definitely." He stood and stretched, his gut sticking out as his arms went back, and then wiped his brown chin with his sleeve. "Perhaps I'll take a quick jaunt to the back rail."

"And the washroom while you're at it."

Jim gave a short, clumsy bow, and began whistling "Camp-town Races."

Through the window, Queen watched the scenery passing by. Little houses rested snugly in rows, smoke drifting from snow-capped chimneys. The warm maize-colored lights from their windows flashed by in a comforting blur. Now approaching Saint Paul, soon they'd reach Hastings, then Nininger and finally, God willing, Tom Cahill and Ollie, safe and sound. He got lost in his thoughts, wondering what he would do once he stood face to face with this Gottschalk. Would he bother to arrest him, or just shoot him dead like he really wanted to?

"Detective Queen! An interesting night you have planned for yourself."

Queen turned to see Jack Peach sitting in the seat beside him, lighting a cigar with a steady, easy hand. As always, he was dressed to the nines, in a suit as fine as cream gravy.

"This is the smoking car, isn't it?" he asked, as he leaned to his side and put his matches in his pocket.

"You lied to me," Queen growled. "You paid their bail and then cut them down to shut them up. I should put a bullet in your head."

Peach chuckled and made a tut-tut sound, shaking his head disapprovingly. "That would certainly be standard fare for the notorious Harmon Queen we all love to read about in the newspapers. He loses his temper and shoots some poor soul in the middle of a packed train."

"When I've finished my current investigation, your boss is next. Nobody comes into Minneapolis and does what you did and gets away with it. Especially not from goddamn Saint Paul, Jack."

"We're still not friends," Peach reminded him. He blew smoke lazily into the air, and then pulled out his watch and feigned surprise as he looked at it. "Speaking of Saint Paul, it is, in fact, the next stop. Home, sweet home." He patted ash from the cigar over Queen's shoe.

It was everything Queen could do not to take Peach's head and slam it into the seat in front of him. Who does this bastard think he is? He knew the answer a moment later, as Peach, with blazing speed, put his hand under Queen's lapel and yanked out his pistol.

"Too easy," he laughed. He flipped it over in his hand so he held the barrel, then tucked it in his jacket. "I've got my own, too, in case you're wondering." The train was slowing now, grinding its way into Saint Paul's Union Depot. "This is where we get off."

Feeling a deeper humiliation than he ever remembered feeling in his life, Queen buttoned his jacket and nodded. I guess I'm taking a little unexpected side trip to visit Jiggs Kilbane, he thought.

The smell still lingered in the air, the smell of sweat and fear. Gottschalk inhaled the salty stink, memorizing it and cataloguing it in his mind, for use one day when he wanted to relive this moment's thrill. The prushun's disappearance was unexpected and unpleasant, as the sun was setting and the time of reawakening getting close. Both boys were necessary, but only one lay comfortably in his possession.

This will require another death, he decided, of the man who let the filthy Ollie free. He also realized he needed nourishment to complete his purpose. He reached into his haversack for a chocolate, and placed it slowly on his tongue, allowing the bittersweet bite to dissolve with his warm breath. He encased it in his mouth and let its sweetness fortify him. He reached for another, and another, gorging himself like an animal until his mouth was full and the chocolate oozed from his lips onto the snow, splattering like dark blood. He felt his eyes burst from his head and his fingers tremble. And then he heard the faintest of noises behind him.

Cocking his head slightly, he turned, and was met with the bucket from the well, swung hard and into his face, shattering his teeth. His head snapped back, then upright in an instant. Blood and chocolate mixed into a stream that poured down his neck. A short man met his vision, wearing four eyes and a desperate expression.

Gottschalk could smell the fear on this one.

The man drew a gun, but Gottschalk reached out his long arm to grab his wrist, twisting until he heard the bones crack. The man screamed and Gottschalk twisted harder, grunting with delight at the splintering sound. He had done the same to many a rapist who'd dared approach him in his youth, leaving them crawling on the ground for mercy. So it came with great surprise when the man's healthy hand formed a fist, and in a dazzling burst of movement, landed a blow under Gottschalk's chin. It was a strong blow, and the German dropped to his knees with a whimper, surrendering to the spectacular, all-encompassing pain. The man tried to pull away but Gottschalk kept hold of his wreck of a wrist, tightening it like a light bulb as he stood up, drawing a bloodcurdling shriek from the little man that echoed through the river valley.

"Let it go, please, I beg you," he now pled, teary-eyed and appropriately regretful at his folly in striking the Heir to the Sage.

The wolves will devour the sun and the moon.

Gottschalk laid the man's broken hand against the well's stone edge. He admired its purplish color. The fingernails appeared translucent in the moonlight. He reached into his bag for his claw hammer, and extracted it with pleasure.

"Where is it?"

The little man's throat choked, and he couldn't answer. Gottschalk repeated the question, this time using the hammer to smash the man's thumb into pulp. He waited for the scream to subside, and then raised the hammer again.

"Wh-wh-where is what?"

"The thing called Ollie. The thing you came to rescue."

"I-I don't know. I c-couldn't find him. I looked everywhere. I went into the house –"

Another solid strike from his hammer ended the man's index finger. More sobbing, more groaning, more gnashing of teeth.

"You contaminated my sanctuary," Gottschalk said. His blood boiled at the thought of his sweet little thing breathing foul air.

"I-I-I didn't realize. I'm telling you I don't know where Ollie is. I came to free him, but he must have already escaped." His eyes dropped to the mouth of the black well. "Th-this is where you put him?"

Gottschalk bent his fleshy, fishy face into a smile, and nodded. "I'm sad to say, my friend, that his departure is now your misfortune." With that, he hauled the man up, to make ready for the sacred transfiguration.

CHAPTER 14

*Q*UEEN WAS WILDLY OUT OF HIS ELEMENT in this city. He felt not just like a fish out of water, but one that had already been skinned, filleted and fried.

Saint Paul was the enemy, and he thoroughly hated the place. Police Chief John O'Connor ruled the city like a tyrant, ran his police force like an army, and his detective squad was composed of pucker-lipped thumpers who thought much too highly of their own mediocre sleuthing abilities. He knew he would find no friendly faces in the crowds of people hustling home from their long work days. No sympathetic patrolmen would help if he were to try to get away. Better just to see it through, Queen told himself. Perhaps Jiggs had some kind of deal he wanted to propose. Queen would listen, agree like a simpleton, and then depart as quickly as he could for Hastings. He'd probably meet Milwaukee Jim sleeping on a bench at the station and they could be on their way.

Peach nudged him forward. They walked under the massive glass and iron train shed, which spanned nine busy tracks. The Union Depot was, without question, a grand piece of architecture, but Peach was in too much of a hurry for sightseeing, so they sped through the building and into the Saint Paul dusk.

There were no stars; just swollen gray clouds ready to unleash a blast of snow from their bellies, and softly shining streetlights ready to illuminate its descent. A few fat snowflakes fluttered from the sky, creating a tranquil scene as they settled on the shop awnings, despite the hurried pedestrians packing the sidewalks underneath. Queen and his escort made their way to the broad pavement in front of the station, tangled with hacks of all shapes and sizes, angling for a spot near the doors. After weaving through the wheels and horses, Peach marched him up to a buggy with black curtains hanging from the windows.

"Is this the undertaker's wagon?" Queen asked under his breath.

Peach laughed. "Just get in, Queen. The sooner we get to Mr. Kilbane, the sooner we can just get this over with."

"Are we heading to his gambling house?"

"Where else?"

Where else indeed, Queen thought, as the rig lurched forward. It was dark inside, except for the little light that shone in the cracks around the curtains. Peach had one leg folded over the other, and his arm up on the seat, appearing disinterested. They said nothing to each other, and the ride was uncomfortable as they turned onto Wabasha Street and toward their destination.

"It's too dark," Queen complained, and he pulled back the curtain, letting the soft electric streetlamp light dapple the cabin. He half expected Peach to protest, but the man's eyes just glittered with humor.

The heart of Saint Paul's business district was along Wabasha, and it was busy with shoppers and commuters scurrying in and out of shops, trying to keep their balance on icy sidewalks. A slumped-shouldered sales girl with a tired face trudged past a pack of bright-eyed newsies, who screamed their headlines from a corner.

He watched a gentlemen in a top hat and long wool coat, cane placed firmly in hand, stride with regal confidence across the street. A dignified woman with a hat of peacock plumes held tightly on to the old coot's arm for support, her ankle-long dress brushed wet at the hems. The couple was oblivious to a fist-shaking wagon driver who was forced to rein his horses back to prevent an accident.

They continued to clop along in their carriage past steam laundries, meat markets, saloons and furriers. Queen recognized the towering block-long Schuneman and Evans Department Store, where he'd once bought something called "eau de toilette" for his sister on her birthday, long before he'd been declared unwelcome in the city.

Past West Seventh Street they went, through the very heart of the city, where streetcar tracks and wires crisscrossed in a teeming, confusing intersection of horses, rigs and people. They were moving up Wabasha Street, north towards Rice Street and then University Avenue, where Kilbane kept his little hideout, away from the city's distracting noise. As they ascended the gentle slope, businesses became homes, and the bustle outside began to subside. Queen realized he liked the activity, as it pulled his mind away from the seriousness of his situation.

"Nice night for a ride, I guess," he said, to fill the silence. Peach rubbed his eye with his finger and looked out at the street, still uninterested in small talk.

They reached Rice Street and veered left towards University Avenue, and Queen was momentarily awed as he saw, to his right, the brand-new State Capitol, a massive, gleaming, white granite block that lorded atop the hill. The building was almost complete, save the enormous marble dome, barely a third done. Scaffolding still clung to the sides, and a crane towered over the top. Large winter-beaten boards with advertisements for Gold Medal Flour, Happy Durham Tobacco and Hires Root Beer bordered the street, fencing off the worksite. The pop ad reminded him suddenly that his throat was beyond dry, and he regretted again that he had given his last few precious drops of whiskey to an indolent tramp.

Peach inspected his watch, and then shifted in his seat, a twinge of anxiety on his shadowed face. He pounded on the ceiling and a moment later the buggy jumped forward. Queen knew they must be late. Satisfied with their surge of speed, Peach put his hands behind his head and leaned back.

"Almost there, Lieutenant," he said.

And they were. Queen recognized the two-story brick building in front of them from prior visits. To any upstanding citizen walking by, it was nothing more than a commercial block, matching dozens just like it nearby. The driver yelled "Whoa" when they arrived, and the rig jerked to a halt.

"You first," Peach said, motioning with his revolver. It was a British Bulldog model, with a short nose and an ivory handle, the kind sneaky people hid in tight places like coat pockets. He still had Queen's pistol tucked in his waist, too.

"I see you've got your pocket advantage. Does that shoot a big bullet, Jack?"

"Get a wiggle on," Peach replied, waving the gun toward the door.

They both stepped out and crossed the sidewalk into a non-descript storefront with "Acme Slot Machines" lettered across the door's glass. The room was well lit and lined with one-armed bandits, shiny new and ready to move into loving new homes. A "clerk" stood in their way when they entered; big, ugly and mean-looking as hell. Queen knew he wasn't there to help him buy a slot machine, either. The brute moved aside as they strode past him and into a back room; this one rigged-out, with a thick plush rug, comfortable chairs, and gold-framed scenes from Greek mythology. Queen had been here many times before, but those had all been in pursuit of plea-sure. While he was intimately familiar with this room Kilbane called "the Lounge," he assumed he wouldn't be enjoying complimentary drinks or free chips for the casino tonight. He wasn't surprised either, when Peach opened a door to the side, partially blocked by a palm tree, to the staircase leading to the second floor and Jiggs Kilbane's office.

Peach went first, Queen following. To make sure Queen didn't have any second thoughts, the ugly bruiser from the front room brought up the rear, carrying a double-barreled shotgun. At the top of the stairs, Peach rapped twice.

"Enter!" a sharp voice barked.

Peach gave Queen a knowing little wink.

"A little hot-tempered today. Let me go in for a minute and talk to him."

He left Queen on the steps with Big and Ugly. The guy's breath was rancid and he had a lazy eye that was staring at a spider on the wall. It gave Queen the willies.

"How'd your eye get like that?"

"Screw," the man replied, and killed the spider with a swat of his hand.

"Gentlemen," Peach said, opening the door. "Please come in." First Queen, then his guard, entered the bare-bones office. It was dimly lit, and a far cry from the lavish décor they had just left downstairs. A dusty chandelier hung from the ceiling and ancient wallpaper peeled from corners of the wall.

And there he sat, in all his potato-eating glory, Jiggs Kilbane, the pride of the Emerald Isle, with his wire-rimmed glasses, hooked nose and slicked-back orange hair. He sat on the edge of his desk in a nobbish green suit, and gave Queen a needle-pointed stare. They had a history together, most of it genial, but now things had changed for both of them.

"You're lookin' to get me, I hear, Queenie," he said with a smirk. "You want to take care of me, huh? That's the message I got."

"Who gave you that message, Jiggs?" Queen already knew it was Peach, but was ready to play coy as long as the gangster had such a firm upper hand.

"Over there, Queenie. You got blinders on or somethin'?" He snickered and pointed to a camelback loveseat, and at two young women sitting on it.

Queen adjusted his eyes.

His heart dropped into his stomach.

There sat Miss Trilly Flick and Miss Edna Pease. Trilly met his gaze with indifference. Edna, with horror. He looked for some sign from Trilly that she was in danger, held captive and against her will, but her glassy expression directed at no one in particular dashed his hopes into the rocks.

"These young women were being guarded," Queen said, turning back to Kilbane. He felt his face go hot, and clenched his fists to keep his hands from shaking. Grief, shock and anger at this betrayal hit him all together like a trio of bricks to the forehead. But he knew he couldn't let Kilbane see this affect him. You have to remain composed, he told himself, but Christ, oh Christ, he and Trilly had been so intimate just this afternoon! She'd probably sent a message to Kilbane the minute he'd left.

"What did you do to the men at Ulland's house?" he asked, trying to keep himself from looking at the girl he'd thought he could love.

"We didn't do nothin' to those stupid fish eaters, Queenie boy. These whores left on their own free will, didn't you?" He grinned toward Trilly, who yawned and glanced away.

"So, what now?" Queen asked. "She told you I was coming for you, and now you want to talk, right? What are you willing to offer me?"

Kilbane started laughing so hard he blew snot from his nose. "Money? You think you're going to get money? Remember, you owe me goddamn money!"

"If it's not that, then what?"

Kilbane took a moment to catch his breath and took a drink of something clear from a glass on his desk. "This is not a negotiation, Queen. You think just because you're a police detective, and a famous one to boot, that you're safe from harm's way?"

"As a matter of fact, yes."

"You do, huh?" Kilbane gave a little laugh, which transformed into a sinister smile. "Ask me a question."

"What?"

"You heard me, Queenie. Ask me a question. I'll answer any question you goddamn want."

"Why did you kill Dander?"

"Easy," Kilbane said. "I didn't want the dandified gump to drag me down with him once he got his day in a court of law."

Queen understood what was going on. Kilbane was humoring him. There was no way he would willingly blurt out his misdeeds to an officer of the law unless he wasn't planning on letting him out of this room alive.

He still wanted to know.

"What did you two have going on, that you were so scared about somebody finding out?"

"I heard through the vine that your superintendent of police was going to tear Dander apart on the stand. Make an example of him, as a white slaver, who kidnapped young girls off the street and ripped them apart until they obeyed his every word and deed. A real crucifixion, but with my name at the tip of his lips." Kilbane straightened his tie and then snapped his head to his shoulder twice in quick succession, trying to make it crack.

"Actually, Colonel Ames doesn't care much about Dander at all," Queen said. "He was planning on sweeping the whole thing under the rug. Just waiting for it to blow over."

"Nonsense!" Kilbane lashed. "I got my ways of knowing what I know. And you want to know the reason I'm a little jarred about the whole thing, Queenie?"

"Why is that, Jiggs?"

"Cause Dander had nothin' to do with it! He worked for me! Every goddamn girl at that dump he ran over there was mine. I loaned them to him. Even that stupid whore that tried to tear out and got a bullet for tryin'." He held his hand over his heart. "Which I didn't do, for the record."

"So what happens from here, Jiggs? You know they'll come looking for me if I'm not back by tomorrow. I'm famous, to quote you in your own words."

Kilbane scoffed. "First, nobody knows you're here. Second, nobody cares. And even if someone was to have seen you step off that train, no Saint Paul cop will lift a finger to help you." He hopped down from the desk and shook out his spindly legs. "Face it, you're fucked."

A twitch of fear suddenly jerked at Queen's heart, but he forced a steady expression. He was, in fact, alone in this city, and Kilbane was fully aware of it. "Answer another question for me, then," the detective said hastily, not wanting to leave a lingering pause.

"Sure." Kilbane grinned. "Why not?"

"The dead girl. Her name isn't Maisy Anderson. Who is she, really?"

"Somebody from some other city, connected to someone much more powerful than certainly you, or even me."

"You can't tell me?"

"Naw," he said, running his tongue over his teeth like a lizard. "We still got other ears in the room, and I want them around a little longer." He spread his hands towards Peach, Big and Ugly and the girls, as if Queen didn't already know who in the hell he was talking about. "She was one of the few girls I ever employed who came willingly. She begged me for work, in fact."

"But she fled on New Year's Eve," Queen said.

"Because of that prick Dander. Ain't that right, honey?" He looked at Trilly, whose eyes flashed darkly. "See, she hated the fucking bastard. I have to say, I should've put an end to his antics a lot sooner than I did. But we all make mistakes, ain't that right, Queenie? You made a mistake when you threatened me, and too bad for you. After all of our recent trouble, you just ain't worth keeping around."

"And why was she called Maisy Anderson?"

Kilbane's eyes lit. "That's an interesting story. We don't got a lot of time, but I'm in a charitable mood, since everything's going my way today. Maisy was a girl in my employ, and let's just say she wasn't satisfied in her job. She was one of those acquired girls that had to be cajoled a little before she went to work."

"You're talking about her in the past tense."

"Yeah, I am. She was. She didn't last long. A customer of hers cut her up one night while she was bein' belligerent. Some whores, you know? Just don't go easily. They gotta make a big stink. Anyway, she and the dead girl on the fence, well they was mighty good friends, and when Maisy died, the other 'un took her name in loving memory. I figured it was okay, as long as she wasn't going by her real name. That goddamn last name is more well-known than Christ!" Kilbane sniggered at the thought. "One of the richest men in the country, and he doesn't know his own kin is dead."

Queen felt his lips go dry. "So, the real Maisy is dead, too."

"Ain't that just what I said?"

And there it was. Sheriff Dix Anderson travels to Minneapolis with a heavy heart, discovers his granddaughter still might be alive, only she really isn't. How was he going to tell him this? I'd better figure out a way of making it out of here alive first, he decided, and worry about Anderson later.

A soft sob cut through the air, and all eyes turned to Edna. Her face was contorted into something truly disturbing, as if a demon was letting itself loose into her brain. She grasped her hair and began pulling out tufts, eyes darting around the room, at the walls, the floor, the ceiling, at Jiggs Kilbane. Then they darkened and fixed on Queen. Her sobs increased in halting gasps of air and tears.

"Jesus," Kilbane said. "She's fucking bughouse."

Her eyes stayed locked on Queen and they pled for help. Queen had never heard her say a word, but she was silently begging him to do something to help ease her mind, appease her terror. Even Peach looked spooked, and he wasn't one to ever lose his polish.

Then she stood up.

Trilly tried to take her hand and pull her down, but Edna refused, and instead slapped Trilly across the face with a furious, malevolent burst. For a split second Queen saw the pain on Trilly's beautiful face and felt his heart melt, but her expression turned villainous, a thin crack of an evil smile, and he looked away.

Edna moved toward Kilbane, who stumbled back. She hissed, reaching out with hands in the air, and then whirled around to Queen. He held his ground and grabbed her by both shoulders, gently shaking them.

"Edna, what is it? Are you sick? Send for an ambulance!" he hollered at Kilbane, who only looked back at him in disbelief.

Then she spoke. She *spoke*.

"Lies. All lies. Maisy Anderson is alive. I know where she is. I know where she is."

Queen stared at her and she stared back, both equally awed at her breakthrough. She looked overwhelmed and relieved, and then the tiniest smile flickered across her face.

"I just spoke, didn't I?"

"You did, Edna." Queen put his hands softly on her neck. "Where is she now?"

Her mouth opened to finish, but the bang of a gunshot closed it.

Edna Pease slumped forward into his arms. Queen looked over her shoulder and saw Jiggs Kilbane pointing a smoking pistol at her, standing behind his desk with the side drawer open. Queen held her up as Kilbane pulled the trigger again and he felt Edna's body convulse with the bullet's impact. He knew by her face and her touch that she was dead, and he would be, too, if he didn't act fast.

"I'm so sorry," he whispered, and he threw her body forward onto the desk. Her head flopped back on its surface, staring straight up. Kilbane jumped back, disgusted, and the gun slipped from his hand and onto the floor. Queen whipped around to whop Peach with a hard slug. Peach took it square in the jaw and thumped against the wall. Queen was already past him, bounding down the stairs, showered with plaster from a shotgun blast inches from his head.

He'd never moved so fast in his life. He leapt down the last few stairs, feeling a sharp pain in his knee, and skidded to the door, pausing only to frantically paw at the lock. He got it unlatched, wrenched the door open, and made tracks down the street as fast as his forty-year-old legs would carry him.

More gunshots behind him, and he twisted his neck back to look. Two men were chasing him: Jack Peach, running in a long, casual gait, and Big and Ugly, carrying his shotgun out in the wide open. A woman screamed and people scampered out of the way, clearing a direct path to Queen. Out of shape and already breathing hard, Queen knew immediately that he couldn't outrun them. He looked around for a possible escape.

A streetcar was stopped at the intersection ahead, the destination sign reading "Rice & Concord," and he made a dash for the rear of the car. The conductor stood on the platform, wearing a navy blue uniform and pillbox hat, watching the unfolding chase anxiously. He waved his hands in protest as the detective charged up the steps, but stepped out of his way when Queen brandished his badge. Policemen rode streetcars for free, and fishing around for a nickel fare would only slow his stride.

Queen felt relief when he finally passed through the sliding doors. Safety in numbers, he thought. He apologized his way to the front and knocked on the window of the front compartment's partition, making the motorman at the controls turn as he smacked his badge against the glass.

"Police detective," he yelled. "Make tracks!" The motorman nodded and edged the car forward, and Queen leaned against the door to catch his breath. Neither Big and Ugly nor Peach had managed to follow him on, he thought, satisfied.

A couple of well-dressed ladies who must not have liked cocky policemen shot rotten looks at him, but most of the passengers looked grateful for the increase in speed. It was fully dark outside, so the motorman had turned the interior electric lights on, and the coal stove next to him heated water pipes along the base of the car's wall, making things warm.

He felt relaxed now. This car would head back the way he'd originally come with Peach, south to Wabasha Street and a few short blocks away to Union Depot and then Nininger. He glanced at the window, to make sure Peach and his friend weren't still running alongside, but the windows were fogged up and impossible to see through.

An elderly gap-toothed fellow in the front seat gave him a knowing smile. "I know who you are. I read the papers."

Queen forced a smile back, and gave him a nod, hoping the man wouldn't announce it to the world. The man instead reached into a pocket in his coat and pulled out a bottle of something dark, and held it out to Queen. It looked delicious, swishing around in a seductive swirl, mocking his dry throat, but he shook his head. Nothing to draw attention, he thought. Once this night was over, he'd go home, sleep tomorrow away, and mark his survival from Peach, Gottschalk, and sobriety with an all-night whiskey-fueled celebration. Then, after sobering up, he'd go to Dania Hall, and ask permission from Peder to court Karoline. That was the proper way to do it, and he intended, after all of this had passed, to try being proper for a while.

A loud bang behind him and the rush of wind suddenly interrupted his happy thoughts. He whipped around in time to see through the partition the motorman's door being opened on the front platform, on the right of the car. A man held onto the grab irons from outside, and with a swing pulled himself in. It was Big and Ugly, and he had somehow managed to shove the shotgun between his shirt and a suspender loop. It hung, clumsily, like a toy sword on a boy. The motorman fell back in surprise, only inches from Queen but separated by the glass. Big and Ugly pushed him aside, and threw the partition door wide, staring down at Queen with red-hot hatred. He came forward, and Queen fell back. Passengers on either side erupted in shouts and cries, some cringing in their seats, others covering loved ones with their arms or torsos, defending against what might happen next.

The man only had eyes for Queen, though. He grasped the shotgun's stock, ready to draw it out. Queen decided in a snap-instant to bull rush him. Like a star Gopher tackle, Queen sprang, and managed to wallop him with the brunt of his weight. They both fell back through the partition door, sending the motorman sprawling against the stove. Big and Ugly's head bounced against the floor, then buckled forward, slapping his chest, before resting again on the wooden boards. He wore an expression of stupefied mush; his lazy eye shot straight up and almost out of his head, blinking like an owl caught in the sun. The motorman dragged himself up to the controls to slam on the brakes, throwing everyone hard against the rattan benches. Queen heard the conductor shout something from the rear, and the passengers scrambled towards his voice and the exit, pushing their way down the steps and through the wire gates into the winter night.

Queen looked over to the motorman. "I've got a handle on things," he said, giving the man on the floor a rough kick with his boot to the head. After a soft moan he fell silent. The detective reached down and slipped the shotgun from the man's suspender loop, hoisting it to his own shoulder.

The motorman, instead of congratulating him, however, stood frozen. He was looking past Queen, and Queen followed his gaze to the rear of the car. There stood Jack Peach, grinning, and pointing his Bulldog pistol.

"Fun and games," Peach remarked, "make for a memorable evening." He fired, and pieces of wicker flew from a nearby seat.

Queen instinctively covered his eyes with his elbow to avoid the debris. With a fast flip he bumped the shotgun from his shoulder into his hands, pointing it towards Peach. But the gangster was already gone. What the hell, Queen thought. What kind of trick was the dandy up to? He didn't care to find out, and turned and waved his hand at the motorman, who stood close to the coal stove, frozen with uncertainty.

"Get us out of here," Queen shouted. "Fast."

The motorman clenched his teeth and shook his head.

There's no time for this, the detective thought. Peach has got to be planning something, probably with more men. The more time I waste in a stationary streetcar, the more time he has to rally his soldiers. He looked down at Big and Ugly, motionless, and concluded the car needed to cut dirt, and quickly, before it was him on the floor as a bullet riddled corpse. Queen rushed forward and the motorman recoiled at his approach.

"If you aren't going to help me," Queen growled, "then sit down or get out, for God's sake. But we're going, whether you like it or not."

The motorman, thin-shouldered and gaunt-faced, slipped past him and sat down in a seat, made the sign of the cross on his chest, and put his hands on his lap, seemingly ready to meet his fate.

Queen rolled his eyes and studied the controls. With no idea how to operate the machine, he grabbed a lever and pushed. Nothing. Looking back, he saw darkness, but imagined Peach with a pack of henchmen emerging from the darkness and opening fire through the platform's wire gates. He pictured Peach with his meat knife, strolling through the gun smoke, ready to slice his throat from ear to ear. That's not the way he wanted to die, standing at the controls of a goddamn trolley, bleeding all over his wrinkled tie. Queen grabbed the lever and pulled it this time, finally making her move. The car creaked forward, accelerating gradually at first, but picked up speed as it began its gentle descent down the hill and towards downtown Saint Paul.

Queen began to relax again. This wasn't so hard. They were definitely burning track now. He looked back to the motorman smugly, more confident in his ability. The motorman looked back, again past him. For someone so silent, Queen decided, the fellow could twist his face with more expression than an actor in a nickelodeon drama. He followed the motorman's gaze out the front window, and saw the turn in the distance. They were moving fast now, but the change from Rice Street to Wabasha meant a forty-five degree veer to the left. They wouldn't make it at this speed.

"How do you slow this goddamn contraption down?" Queen burst out, panic setting in.

The motorman disappeared behind the seat. Holy son of a bitch, Queen thought, and madly turned back to the controls. He examined all the levers, valves and gauges, attempting to make some identification of the brake, but a noise made him crank his head back. He saw with alarm that the ugly man was on all fours. He'd somehow managed to turn his big body around to the front, and was reaching for his weapon, which Queen had placed standing up, in the corner of the front seat. Queen clawed at the dashboard, shaking, turning and pushing every movable part he could lay his fingers on. Finally, he released a lever and the brakes slammed on with a squeal, making the car shiver and creak and sending the ugly man sprawling again. Queen tripped and fell on the man's back, slipping on his fleshy folds as he scrambled for the shotgun. Queen's searching fingers found it first, caught hold and hauled it out from under the bench. He stood and leveled it at the man, who was fighting to regain his feet.

Then Queen saw the second streetcar hurtling full-chisel down the track behind him.

He tossed the shotgun to the front and rushed to the controls again, dived into the compartment, and managed to release the brakes with a tug. The car behind him was gaining fast, though. He hurriedly pulled open the controller handle, launching the car forward. The pursuing streetcar's fender, a steel-pipe and wire net used to catch pedestrians who got in the trolley's way, looked like a metal mouth, and the single headlamp a yellow eye. Its sharp light filled Queen's field of vision as he looked back to gauge the distance, which was rapidly closing. Above the car, sparks sprayed as the trolley pole cut across the ice-covered wire. The detective lifted his hand to block the headlamp's blaze. Through the rear window he barely made out the figure of Jack Peach, a glowing cigar in his teeth, in the motorman's position, focused intently on his task. Staring at Queen, Peach tipped his hat with one hand, and with the other swung the controller handle with a violent pull. The second car heaved forward, building speed on the downhill, and smashed hard and fast into Queen's car. Glass showered from the windows, around and into the ugly man, who, finally back on his feet and about to move at Queen, fell backward from the impact. Queen hit the divider, but regained his footing like a cat, throwing his controller all the way up to the top notch. As the trolley surged ahead he glanced back, only to see Peach's car hot on his heels.

It was a hell for leather chase.

Both cars raced through intersections, narrowly missing wagons and horses, hurtling much faster than trolleys should go. Queen figured it at forty or fifty miles an hour. He yanked on the leather pull cord and the streetcar's bells clanged weakly. Worried that someone would get hurt, and his instinct to get out of Saint Paul at the forefront of his mind, he knew he had to stop this thing soon. With any luck he could reach Fifth, dart out into the shadows and hope for the chance to escape by foot to Union Station, just a few blocks away.

Back again he glanced, over the ugly man lying stone-cold quiet in the aisle, to Jack Peach, less than fifty feet behind. The guy is off his nut, Queen thought, but then he remembered that he had started this ridiculous chase, and it was his own damn fault. Peach inched closer, gave Queen a mocking salute, then raised his gun and fired. One shot, then two; more shattered glass; splintering wood exploded around him.

Behind him he heard a groan, and he turned back at the sound. It was the motorman, forehead bleeding, pointing ahead.

"West Seventh is next!" he shouted. "Stop ringing the bell, it's only for signals! Hit the gong with your foot! Blow the whistle!"

Queen immediately understood. A streetcar barreling straight through a major intersection such as this one would surely result in a gruesome, mangled wreck of horse flesh, metal and death. He needed to warn whatever was ahead that they were coming.

As his trolley careened wildly into downtown, past a blur of tightly packed shops and mesmerized onlookers, he searched with his foot until he found the pedal, and struck it hard. The gong's boom echoed down the street.

"The wooden handle in front of your face! Pull it!" cried the motorman. Queen wondered for a moment why he didn't just move his ass up here to do it himself, but there was no time. He jerked it down, and a long, deep whistle cut through the winter air. It was barely enough warning, and as they whizzed past Seventh Street he watched horses rear and people dive for safety. He managed a relieved smile, but the motorman abruptly wiped it away with his next words.

"Straight head! We're going too fast! Stop it now!"

And there was Saint Paul City Hall, on Fifth Street, straight ahead, beyond a two hundred foot, snow-cloaked lawn. Just before it, the track swung sharply to the right. There was no time to stop, but only to avoid jumping completely off the rails, skating across the lawn, and smashing into the door. One last time, he twisted the lever hard to the right, and the brakes slammed on with full, brutal force. A hideous squeal and the sound of grinding wheels erupted from beneath him, the entire streetcar shuddering from the strain. The cold wind through the broken windows whipped at his face, and he gripped the control, with nothing more to do but watch. The turn was suddenly before him, City Hall's massive stone exterior looming. The impact would kill them instantly, he knew. Queen gripped the control and closed his eyes. He felt the floor beneath him tilt to the left, and suddenly the wall was the floor, and he was on it, his body tumbling and slamming as the car moaned, careened, and finally with a horrifying, savage jolt, smashed into the sidewalk. Then the lights cut, and he knew the pole had separated from the wire. A foot hit his back, and he saw the dim form of the shotgun whip through the air and narrowly miss his head. Thin shards of glass pricked at his face, and he reached for something to hold onto, with wild hope that he might survive this hellish ride in a single precious piece. He heard cries from outside as the overturned car skidded across the lawn, shaking and banging as darkness drowned his senses. Snow from the open windows beneath him sprayed up in icy pellets, stinging at his blind eyes. With the hideous cracking of wood, and a last, final, terrible groan, the streetcar slid to a stop, on its side, and lodged against a tree, fifty feet from City Hall.

He lay for a moment, stunned, and then slowly lifted himself up, wiping the cold from his eyes. A single streetlamp flecked its faint glow through the windows, which were now on the ceiling. The coal stove in the driver's compartment was separated from its chimney, and smoke seeped through the exposed hole. The motorman wasn't moving, and neither was Big and Ugly. He pulled back the motorman's sleeve and felt for his pulse. It was there, faint, but steady, and he sighed in relief. Big and Ugly hadn't been so lucky. He was near the back of the car, his sticky hair matted with blood. Queen grabbed the shotgun and his derby, and crawled for the rear exit, noticing as he passed that Big and Ugly's head was cracked wide open.

He hadn't wanted anyone to die, not even one of Kilbane's bruisers, but he was mostly concerned for himself at this moment. He stumbled from the back, eager to be clear of this death machine. As his eyes adjusted to the bite of more cold, he noticed, probably a hundred feet back, Jack Peach's streetcar, battered but still upright, sitting neatly on the track behind.

"Even here, he has to goddamn show me up," Queen mumbled to himself as he put on his hat. He staggered along the sidewalk, looking for a place to hide. People were nearby, he sensed, but standing back from the accident. Luckily there were also hiding places, and the only plan he could think of was to find a dark one, fast. He tried to hurry, as the last thing he wanted to hear was Peach's familiar, taunting voice.

But he knew it would come.

And he didn't have to wait very long.

"Queen, I'm out of ammunition!"

The detective looked around, weakly raising the shotgun.

"That sounds like trouble for you, Jack. Your man's dead inside, by the way," Queen said.

"Those things are part of the risk, I guess," Peach replied, with an unaffected tone. "Let's call a truce. I'm waving my white handkerchief. You don't want to be here in a few minutes when this place is bursting with police."

A pistol plopped into the snow, directly in front of the streetcar's entrance. Where the hell did that come from, Queen wondered.

"Well, that's your gun, Peach. How about mine? Toss it over, so I know where you are."

He heard Jack laugh loudly, and located the gangster's voice from behind the overturned trolley's smoldering wreck. "I thought you might have forgotten in the heat of the moment. I don't have your piece, Queen."

"You don't have it?"

"Mr. Kilbane does. Remember the cooked wag-tail from a few minutes ago? I don't remember her name, and she wasn't much of a looker."

"Of course I remember…the one your boss murdered."

"Not to my recollection."

"He shot her in cold blood."

"It's your Smith and Wesson that did the shooting, Queen. Your gun. I slipped it to Mr. Kilbane while you waited outside. You're a murderer, Queen. You're finished."

"If I'm finished, then why are we talking?"

Another chuckle from Peach, and then he stepped into Queen's sight, arms raised, a cigar in his right hand.

"Good point, Queen. Let's discuss this."

"What the hell is going on here?"

"Kilbane wants you rubbed out. Put in a domino box. Taking your gun was just a precaution, in case a situation like this one materialized." He motioned with his head to the marred, smoking ruin. "Sometimes, Queen, I don't much care working for him. His grammar is rot, and he's Irish of course, which isn't ideal either. But one thing he is absolutely tip-top at, is back-up plans. He had you dead in his sights, Queen, from every angle."

"I feel like you're about to give me a way out."

Peach gave a personable smile. "I happen to like you. I think you might be able to help me out in a pinch one day, as well. I'm just going to tell Kilbane you cut a dash."

"He won't go off his rocker on you with that little favor to me?"

"He'll be furious, but I'm too valuable to him for him to take out his frustrations on me. He'll still be gunning for you, Queen."

"I still have it in for him, too. He just killed an innocent girl in front of my eyes."

"I know."

"Answer me this, Jack."

"What?"

"Trilly Flick. I thought she and I were, well, friends, as it were. I never expected a blindside like that."

"You seem to have more than an informal interest in her."

Queen's cheeks burned, and he looked past Peach into the City Hall's shadows.

"I've known her a lot longer than you have, Queen. Who you saw on that sofa a few minutes ago, that's who she really is. As for her friend," he threw his cigar in the snow and stamped it out, "she didn't deserve that in my book, either. Let's just say I've got my eyes on jolly old Jiggs Kilbane now. I never made him for a woman killer."

"Edna Pease, the one he shot. She said Maisy Anderson isn't dead."

"The hell if I know, Queen, although I'm pretty sure she's not here in Saint Paul. I've met all of his ladies in this town. But Kilbane still has a dozen disorderly houses all over the Midwest, and I haven't been to all of them. She might be in Chicago or even Kansas City."

"I'll take your word for it."

"Please do."

A sea of black derbies was gathering across the street, moving closer, their owners ogling the accident. Peach flipped his head in their direction. "Best time to go now, Queen. Get back on the train. Go back to Minneapolis. I'll make sure nobody follows you."

"How will you do that?"

"Kilbane and Police Chief O'Connor have a little arrangement worked out. I can smooth things over with the cops."

Queen felt himself extending his hand, warily at first, but to his surprise Peach took it and they shook.

"Thanks, Peach."

"Any time. And call me Jack," he said with a cheerful wink.

CHAPTER 15

─────────

*Q*UEEN GALLOPED DOWN NININGER ROAD alone under the open sky, a yellowing map in hand. Somewhere in the mangled streetcar he had lost his gloves. He was keenly aware of the dropping temperature as he alternated his frozen hands on the reins and under his arms, attempting vainly to keep them warm.

It was getting late, very late, and he was worried. Worried about whether his side trip to Saint Paul might have cost someone's life. Worried about carrying a shotgun with only two shells. Worried that despite the clear road, he would have difficulty finding Ignatius Donnelly's house. After parting ways with Peach, he had crept back through the darkness to Union Depot. There was no possibility that he wouldn't finish what he started tonight. Once he got off the train in Hastings, he'd half expected to see Milwaukee Jim in the station, lying cozily on a bench and, fresh from his nap, ready to guide him to Gottschalk. But there was no sign of the hobo. Considering their destination was fraught with peril, he wasn't about to blame him.

Peder's man hadn't been there with the horses, either. The march of time was weighing heavily on his mind, so to speed his journey to Nininger, he lowered himself to the basest of crimes: horse theft. The black mare had been tied to a post outside the depot, and he'd just mounted her and ridden away, with nary a blink from anyone passing by.

The curled moon was no longer visible, smothered now by a vast silver quilt of clouds. He rode past white-blanketed fields behind rough fences and the odd wrinkled cornstalk that nudged its head through its powdery cover. A lone squirrel scampered across a fence rail. Under other circumstances it would have been a beautiful winter's ride, but he was focused on the task at hand, eager to find this Gottschalk character and end this business as quickly as possible.

His thoughts were suddenly interrupted when a figure came hobbling along the roadside, shivering in a thin shirt. His mop of hair was messy and his eyes glazed with exhaustion.

Queen stopped his horse. "Ollie," he said.

The boy halted and looked up, eyes not registering any recognition.

Queen jumped off his horse and approached the boy. He took off his long coat and put it over Ollie's shoulders. "We need to get you in front of a fire."

Ollie looked right through him as his legs gave out, falling into Queen's arms.

The detective gathered some scattered cornhusks and a few dead branches from a withered oak tree that hung over the road. Starting a fire was difficult with wet wood, but Queen had spent boyhood summers with his uncle in the north woods, and had learned the art of campfire making. He had matches, and searching his stolen steed's saddlebags, found a dry copy of the *Journal*. The newspaper was enough to get a nice blaze going, and after a few minutes under the heat, Ollie seemed to loosen and come to.

He stared at Queen gratefully. "You came for me," he said.

"Listen, Ollie. I want to tell you how sorry I am for leaving you alone with the buggy."

The kid nodded. "It's not your fault, sir. There was no way of knowing. I thought I was finished with him." His face was older than it should be at fifteen, with hollow cheeks and sad eyes. "But he came back."

Queen pulled out his empty flask, forced some snow through the narrow opening, and placed it on the fire. The melting water hissed and steamed, and Queen took out his cigarette case for a smoke.

"Can I have one?" Ollie asked, a hand outstretched and trembling.

He pulled one out for the boy and lit both. They sat for a few minutes, him on his haunches and Ollie slumped forward by the fire, smoking their cigarettes and listening to the silence. Once the water was hot, Queen wrapped the flask in newspaper and handed it to Ollie. He sipped at it as he thawed.

"He's up ahead, right? The man that kidnapped you. Gottschalk."

Ollie looked down into his cup and said nothing.

"I'm going to get him."

The boy kept sipping the warm water.

"What did he do to you, son?"

Ollie sat silent for a few seconds and then slowly scanned the direction he'd come from, as though he expected the German to materialize on the horizon.

"He had his way with me, sir. For five years he had his way with me. I thought I'd finally finished with him, and then he came back. Burned me first. Then tied me up in the bottom of a well." He pulled back his sleeve, and showed the detective the blistered, crumbling skin on his forearm.

Queen shook his head, sickened by the sight.

Ollie finished a last swallow of water. The heat seemed to be giving him life, and he stood and began circling the fire, stretching his legs. "He's been planning, for years, over what to do when the end of the world comes. He's got a book that tells all about it. Once the comet hits, he always said, we'd be the only ones left. A king and his prince, is how he put it, but that was a long time ago. This second round, all he's done is look at me with dead eyes. He was trying to break me, I think. Leave me in that well until I couldn't do nothing. But he couldn't." Ollie looked proudly into the detective's eyes. "I got out before he came back. I escaped. On my own."

"That's mighty impressive, kid."

"He needed me for something, though. He kept saying it." Ollie looked back the way he'd come, and shook his head. "I think he's got my brother, too."

"Your brother? Are you sure?"

"It's just a feelin' I got. He says he doesn't want a tainted boy no more." Ollie hung his head in shame. "He's the one that did it to me in the first place." He looked at Queen. "I don't want what happened to me to happen to Petey. You can't even imagine it."

"Is Gottschalk there now?"

"I don't know, but I don't think so. He wasn't when I left. I haven't seen him on the road, but he doesn't use roads when he travels if he can help it."

"Where is this well you escaped from?"

"In a town, just up ahead, sir. 'Cept it's not really a town, 'cause there's nothin' in it besides ghosts and run-down old houses. There's one house though, it's bigger than the rest and in good shape. It sits away from the others, in a bunch of trees, close to the river's edge. The well's in the yard. Just follow this road. You'll see a signpost that points to the right. Follow it to where the houses sit."

Queen figured from his map that Nininger was still a good three miles away. At Ollie's slow, stumbling pace, it might have been two or three hours since he'd left. Gottschalk could well be there now. Perhaps Tom Cahill, too, but the thought of mentioning his name to Ollie made him pause. The poor kid had already been through hell, and he didn't want to add to his misery by mentioning Cahill's infatuation with him. Still, Cahill was a murder suspect in Queen's mind, and he needed to know where he was.

"Ollie, was there anyone else at this house?"

The boy frowned and wagged his head. "Someone like who? It was just him and me."

"Listen, Ollie. There was a man who visited you at Dander's place in Minneapolis. His name is Tom Cahill. I know he… well… was affected by you."

Ollie cracked a big grin, the first Queen had seen that night. "Sure, I know Tom. He was real swell to me, and sometimes brought me sandwiches and bottles of pop."

"Do you know he's a detective now?"

He shrugged. "Nope, but it's hard to believe. He seems too nice a fella to be a policeman."

"When was the last time you saw him?"

"Maybe three weeks ago? It was a busy night, and he wanted to talk, but I didn't have time. He just left, and that was it."

"Did he ever try to make any unseemly advances?"

"Yeah, sure," Ollie said with a sad little laugh. "Said he'd give me money and buy me things if I laid down with him. That happened every night for two weeks. Then it just stopped and I didn't see him no more."

"Does that bother you? Getting attention from men?"

"Lots of men that liked boys came to the house, and they'd try to give me money and touch me, and have me touch them. But the hell if I'll do that for anything but love."

"So you never—"

"I don't feel like talkin' about this no more. I like girls when I've got a choice in the matter."

Queen winced inside at Ollie's words, but kept his expression neutral. He didn't want Ollie to think he would judge the kid, but his stomach turned sour at the idea that a fifteen-year-old boy could take this conversation so lightly.

"Was he jealous?"

"Of what? Of me? I guess I never gave it a thought. Maybe, but I don't know why. Maisy was the girl for me." His smile turned wistful, and he whistled a bar of something sweet. "She liked it when I whistled that song."

"Ollie, her name wasn't really Maisy. Did you know that?"

He showed genuine surprise. "No, what was it?"

"I was hoping you might know, but evidently you don't. It doesn't matter right now. What's important is that you scoot out of here and go home. You need to check on your brother and your mother." He took out his notebook and a pencil and wrote in it, tore out the page and handed it to him. "This is an address of a friend of mine, named Peder. If you get into any kind of trouble, or need a place to sleep, I want you to go here. He's ace-high, and sound as a goose. Do you understand?"

"Y-yes sir, I do."

"Good." Queen took the horse's reins and handed them to Ollie, along with five one-dollar bills from the roll in his pocket. "Ride this horse back to the Hastings depot and tie it on the north side. Buy a ticket with this money and a good dinner when you can, and don't let anyone stop you. Can you do it?"

"I can." Ollie stepped in the stirrup and swung himself over.

"Ride safely, Ollie, and don't stop for anyone. If someone tries to get in your way, ignore them and just go past." Queen slapped the horse's rump to send it on its way. Ollie nodded, turned, and galloped off towards Hastings.

The stars were out, and with them blackness. Queen followed the road, alternating walking and running for the next three miles. He paused only to catch his breath and battle the bite of cold that lashed at his lungs and made him wheeze and cough. Finally, with both relief and a little dread, he saw the faded wooden sign pointing to the old village of Nininger, just as Ollie had promised, and turned down the narrow road.

And as Ollie had described, a few dilapidated buildings lined an overgrown street. A grove of tall trees stood at the end, and under them the shadow of a large house. He could make out the river farther on, and even the bluffs on the opposite side were still visible in the darkness. Queen stepped cautiously, shotgun in hand, and crept along a sloping hill for protection, even though he felt confident the night would hide him. He made for the trees and the house. As he got closer, he noticed lights on both floors, smothered by curtains. Someone is home, he thought. And it certainly wasn't Ignatius Donnelly.

He circled the home, watching the yard for signs of life, but saw nothing moving. He crossed a line of footprints and followed them to an old stone well. This must be the same one Ollie mentioned, he thought. He strained his eyes into the black hole, looking for movement.

Empty.

And then he noticed blood smeared on the well's edge. The bucket, still on its rope, lay on its side in the trampled snow. He picked it up. A streak of blood on it, too. Curious.

Queen was cold without his overcoat, and the gun's metal stuck to his palm. He wished to God he had a nip of whiskey to take away this chill. His head was already pounding from forced abstinence. He moved as quietly as he could towards the house, trying to keep crouched, watching intently for the slightest movement in the windows. Listening for the smallest sound, he heard only the whistle of wind and a crow's far-off cackle.

Suddenly, from the corner of his eye, he caught the tiniest flicker of light. It wasn't coming from any house or building, but seemed to originate near a hulking black mass. As he approached, the shape became clear. It was a huge pile of wood, arranged in pyramid fashion. The light came from a greasy lantern sitting nearby. He pointed the shotgun and moved toward the pile, watching for the jump of a shadow that might spell danger.

The oddly-shaped mound of wood had been stacked dry, and a maze of footprints was mashed into the snow around it. Somebody has been working hard on this recently, Queen figured. He crept around its perimeter, searching for anything resembling a clue.

Circling back around to the lantern, he heard a muffled sound. First, faint pounding, then a low-pitched wail. Someone was crying from inside the pile, he was sure of it. He listened for where the sound was clearest, and began pulling off chunks of wood, tossing them behind him. Christ, he thought, as the crying got louder. Somebody is buried underneath here.

The next few pieces he threw off revealed a box's wooden edge. A few more chunks gone and he was looking at the face of Tom Cahill. Small boards were nailed across the box to prevent his escape but let in air, and Tom blinked back at Queen, his eyes wet and his glasses gone.

"Who is it? I can't see! Who's there?" Cahill cried out.

"Harm Queen, kid. What the hell is this?"

"He plans to set it on fire. It's a funeral pyre, I think. Can you smell the kerosene? He poured it all over me, along with the rest of the woodpile. He talks in riddles and gibberish. He's much stronger than he looks." Cahill's eyes darted from

Queen to the blackness behind him. "He'll be back soon. He carries a claw hammer, sir." Queen noted Tom's bloody fingers sticking through the cracks and grimaced.

"Aw, hell, Cahill," Queen muttered, shaking his head. He kept removing the firewood, hand over shoulder, until a good third of the box was uncovered. It wasn't actually a box, he began to realize, but a pig trough. With the shotgun's barrel, he tried to pry off a board, but it wasn't budging. He set the gun down and grabbed the end of the trough, pulling as hard as he could. It was just too heavy, no give at all.

"I'll get you out of here, kid, as quick as I can." The shotgun back in his hand, he tried again to force a board loose.

"How did you know I was here?" Cahill asked. His teeth chattered as he spoke, and his eyes were moist and earnest.

"Your hobo friend told me." Queen leaned hard against the shotgun's stock and heard nails squeak as they loosened. "Once I get this one off, let's try and slip you out."

A footstep fell behind him, soft like a cat, barely audible, and Queen yanked out the shotgun from the box. Cahill screamed, staring at whatever was behind him. Whatever it was had the upper hand.

The hammer ripped down just as he twisted around, missing his head by inches, but smashed into his knee instead. The pain seared his flesh and made him fall backwards. The man bearing the weapon had fleshy lips, and ears that looked too big for his head. His brow creased with predatory concentration, which forced his eyes into savage slits. Queen knew this was Gottschalk. This was what Queen imagined a demon might look like, from the pictures in his children's Bible from Sunday school. The hammer rose again and came down ferociously, but Queen willed himself to roll out of the way. He felt the air and heard the buzz as it missed his ear. As the weapon fell, Queen lifted the shotgun, reaching for the trigger while aiming, a difficult move he thought he could manage, but his adversary was much too fast. Gottschalk kicked the shotgun hard, and it flew from Queen's hands and into the darkness. Queen grabbed the lantern by its handle and swung it wildly at Gottschalk, who bent back with ease to dodge the blow. The lantern hit the woodpile, its glass chimney shattering. The flame leapt onto the kerosene-soaked wood, instantly igniting it. As the fire caught the breeze it swelled with a roar, skipping across the pyre. Black smoke rose through the licking flames and smeared the air.

"The fire was mine to start, minion of despots!" Gottschalk cried. "It must be done by me for the effect to be complete!"

Queen saw the kick coming and tried to cover his face, but the boot's hard toe slammed through his arms and into his head. He sprawled backward next to the burning woodpile, his face next to the pig trough where Cahill lay.

The man pulled off his shirt, exposing a grizzled, muscled body of what Queen guessed might be a man of fifty. Gottschalk whipped the shirt over the flames, putting them out while snarling under his breath.

Queen saw his chance and dived towards the discarded shotgun, ignoring the pain in his knee and ear, but the man saw him move and kicked again, this time in his shoulder, knocking him hard to the ground. The snow and ice stung at his hands and face. Gottschalk snatched up the shotgun and tossed it atop the woodpile, then pulled from his pocket a small brass box. He lifted open the cap and turned the screw on the side. After three clicks, the flame from the lighter erupted, and he held it under his chin so the orange light lit his face like a monster from the pits of hell.

"From the prophetic writings of the great Sage," he recited, eyes dimmed but still intensely alert. "When the Age of Ragnarok arrives, a great battle shall play out before the world. The halls of Valhalla will empty and the gods of Asgard will fly down from their thrones and stand at the right hand of Jesus Christ. As the battle to end all battles ensues, the world shall be engulfed in a fiery inferno, for a Great Comet from the heavens will bear down on the world to snuff its pernicious, damnable sins."

Gottschalk took the lighter and tossed it onto the wood-pile, and with a burst of light, the fire began anew. He lifted his hands into the sky and faced his pyre.

"Once this life ends, a new one begins. I am the man who will entwine with my partner in sacred alliance, and enter the dawn of a new world!"

He laughed, a dark, rumbling laugh that seemed to catch wind in time with the flames, and then rose in pitch to something maniacal and otherworldly.

Queen gasped and then mustered his strength. He tried desperately to pull the box that held Tom out from under the burning pile. He could feel the fire's heat now, growing in intensity, and heaved with all of his might. But still, nothing.

Gottschalk seemed in a trance. He turned, ignoring Queen, and looked toward the house, raising his eyes to meet the upstairs window. Son of a bitch, Queen thought, he's got someone up there. That's where he's going, and someone else is in danger. Gottschalk took a single step forward, mesmerized at what lay inside the bedroom. Queen lurched forward, stumbling onto his bad knee but somehow forcing himself back up, and grabbed the man's legs. The fishy-lipped man looked down at Queen, as a sadistic child with a stick might look at an injured dog, and hit him again. Queen tried to hold on but the pain was too great, and the man simply stepped through the detective's locked arms.

Oh, hell, no, Queen thought frantically. Tom is about to burn to death, and this man is readying to do God knows what to whoever is in that upstairs room. He felt a tear stream down his cheek from pure frustration. He couldn't stand up. He couldn't see straight. He had no way to stop him.

"Don't move a muscle," came a voice from the black night. Queen strained his neck towards the sound, and watched Sheriff Anderson step into the firelight, arms hanging loose at his sides, the very image of an old West gunfighter.

A blast of cold wind suddenly swept through the yard, lashing the hems of Anderson's long Mackinaw coat, which whipped behind him like a cape. Gottschalk turned to look, awestruck by the sight of the old sheriff. The wide hat pulled over his eyes didn't hide his grim expression, long and drawn.

"It is harsh in the world," Gottschalk croaked with a broad, horrible smile. "Whoredom rife, an axe age, a sword age, shields are riven, a wind age, a wolf age. Are you here to stand beside me, before the world goes headlong?" He held out his hands, open, to embrace the man before him.

"I told you not to move," Sheriff Anderson said, and in an instant a revolver was in his hand, its barrel glinting against the flames. And it blazed.

Queen counted six shots, with Anderson pulling the hammer back faster than he could follow with his eyes. Six bullets peppered Gottschalk's body almost simultaneously, throwing him back and into the flaming pyre. He shrieked with a hellish reverberation, writhing and shaking as the fire engulfed him. Queen watched, transfixed and aghast as Gottschalk's skin blackened and crackled, until Anderson's voice snapped him back to reality.

"Detective Queen. Let's get him out."

Anderson sheathed his weapon and his lanky outline withered into something hunched and old. He grabbed at his ribcage and hobbled toward Queen, and together the two silently gathered their fortitude. With all their battered might, they pulled at the trough that held Cahill. The scalding heat blasted their faces and Queen knew Anderson was in as much agony as he was, but still they tore at the wood like men possessed, until finally it gave.

They stumbled back as the trough slipped out and Cahill kicked at the boards from inside. Queen and Anderson yanked from the outside until he had enough room to slip through and escape. Cahill toppled out, landing in a heap, cradling his mangled hand. The three lawmen sat, panting and looking at each other, under the roaring fire's brilliant light.

"My god," mouthed Queen. "That was something."

Anderson had difficulty rising. He could feel the bandages around his side slipping off, and the throbbing ache from the cracked ribs. It hurt like the dickens to breathe in and out, and Anderson rubbed his side in a futile effort to erase the pain. The night was cold, and the air in his lungs felt like fire as he marched towards the house.

Queen limped, groaning, behind him, using Cahill for support. The three struggled up onto the veranda, past benches and chairs overlooking the river, and through the door.

It was a curious house, for certain. Anderson had never imagined he'd enter the home of such a famous man, and despite his exhaustion and pain, he was intrigued. The rooms, he noticed, were cluttered with oddities, what appeared to be treasures from far-flung places in every corner of the world. African masks, carved animals, pottery and other rarities dotted tables and shelves. It all gave the house the feel of a charming museum, one where things were left out to touch instead of being locked away behind glass.

Anderson looked through each room on the main floor, finding each empty, before climbing the staircase. In the first bedroom at the top of the stairs, he found Petey.

The boy was dressed in a white silk nightgown and sleeping peacefully on his side, his little hands tucked under his cheek. Candles burned on the bureau, table, and along the headboard, wax dripping over the wood, but what made Anderson grimace was the candy. Candy was strewn across the linen sheets. Chocolate creams, cocoa balls, burnt peanuts, toasted marshmallows, almond nougat and lemon buttercups, and a dozen other varieties the sheriff didn't recognize, lay around the little boy in a sugar heaven.

He heard Queen struggle up the stairs behind him and say something foul when he entered the room. Anderson laid a hand on Petey's shoulder and gently shook him until he awoke, a big smile spreading across his drowsy face at the sight of the sheriff.

"The man with the strawberry gun!"

Anderson helped the boy to sit up.

"You'll be with your mother soon, young man."

Petey's cheek was still red with the bed's warmth, and his blueberry eyes looked solemnly into Anderson's. "Did you get that man? The one that took me and Ollie?"

Queen sniffed and turned his head away. Anderson ran his fingers through the boy's hair and tickled his ear. "I got him, son. I got him."

The old man looked bushed. He labored past them and towards the door, almost staggering, as if the weight of his burden might buckle his knees and drag him to the floor. Queen wasn't ready to tell him what he had learned about Maisy yet. Better to let the sheriff sit and rest for a while. He waited for Anderson to step outside, and then motioned to Cahill to take a seat. This would be hot conversation, he knew, but a necessary one.

"I saw Ollie as I rode in here. Your friend from Dander's place."

The kid winced, as though he were dodging a clout to his face. He looked at the wall, deathly quiet.

"Listen, I know what you're all about. You're a goddamn snipper-snapper, Tom. A prancing *molly*. And while I personally don't give a flying rat's ass whose rump you slap around, it is bad for the police force. Bad for *business*."

Cahill looked horrified. He started to speak, stopped, and then opened his mouth again. Words stuck in his throat.

"Do your parents know?" Queen demanded.

He shook his head.

"Who else have you tried to mash with besides the boy?"

Another shake. Cahill shaped the words with his mouth, barely squeaking them out. "No one."

"He's fifteen goddamn years old, Tom. You're twenty-three."

"He told me he was older. Said he was eighteen." Cahill's eyes pled to Queen, desperate and honest. He's telling the truth, Queen thought, and frankly he wasn't completely surprised. Gottschalk had dealt Ollie a bad, bad hand. He'd not only raped the boy but he'd also scrambled his brain. Ollie had no doubt learned how to use his handsome, boyish looks to get what he wanted on the open road, and had plenty of experience fending off rough-handed sex fiends. Cahill didn't fit that bill, though. He was just miserably confused.

"Of all the stink holes in Minneapolis, why were you bumming around that one? Hell's Half Acre? What kind of an addled dolt are you?"

"It was a poor choice, but that's where Ollie was." He wiped his eye with his sleeve. "Mr. Queen, I'm so sorry. For everything. Bringing you out here, wasting your time. I'm not fit to carry a badge, I know. I'm better off just going back home. You won't say anything about any of this, will you? About Ollie and I? I really didn't know he was so young. I never meant to cause this trouble."

"Just shut your pie hole, Tom," Queen said, exasperated. "You've got the police superintendant behind you, and he already knows everything. Go find a fresh bandage for that hand. You need a rest, kid."

The sheriff, cheeks flush and frozen, tapped his boots steadily on the plank floor, keeping time with his heartbeat. His hands held pieces from his pistol, the cylinder in one and the frame in the other. It was still again, and as he looked at the curve of the land in front of him, barely visible in the night, the rolling gray bluffs and scattered skeleton trees, momentary peace consumed him. The rhythm from his boots reminded him of a song, and it rose to his rusty throat as the words came to him, forlorn and soothing.

> *Oh my darlin', oh my darlin',*
> *Oh my darlin', Clementine,*
> *You are lost and gone forever,*
> *Dreadful sorry, Clementine.*

He croaked out the melody and while it reminded him of his granddaughter, it comforted him, too. Someone else, at some moment in time, had written the song over the loss of a loved one, the same as him.

He wanted to keep singing, to clear the dust from his pipes, and fought hard to remember the words to the verse. Then he stopped, forgetting the song, and looked up.

Anderson first saw an orange glow in the distance, moving like a fat firefly in the darkness, and as it got closer he saw that it was attached to a man. He was dressed well, his derby rakishly cocked, and he sauntered towards the front porch, finally stopping to toss his cigar into the snow.

Anderson raised an eyebrow in surprise. The man tipped his hat and put his finger to his mouth, cocking his ear towards the door.

"Shall we keep our conversation quiet?" he asked the sheriff.

"Depends on what it's about, son."

"Well, a beautiful night, for one. The temperature is dropping precipitously, but I can still feel my fingers and toes." He wriggled the fingers on the hand that wasn't pointing the pistol at Anderson's head. "Thank heavens for fingers and toes," the man said. He smiled a little smile, and glanced up to the sky reverently.

"Are you lost?"

The man's eyes twinkled, reflecting the yellow light from the veranda windows. "Quite an evening you've had." He looked past the well to the smoldering pile of blackened wood. Anderson followed his gaze, and could make out the German's charred remains, contorted in a mound of soot.

"Somebody had a bad night," the sheriff said.

"I can see that," the man said, with a wincing grin.

"So you're here for Detective Queen, then?"

The man nodded. "If you left right now, I wouldn't care. I saw your horse tied to a tree back towards the road. You can take it. No ill will." He took a step forward and Anderson could make out his short-nosed companion. The Bulldog was a gambler's weapon, five shots, but good enough, especially at close range. It had felled President Garfield, and he was special. Nothing special about Anderson, and at ten paces it might easily be over soon if he wasn't careful here.

"You don't know my name," the man continued, "and we can part ways without any unpleasant attachments, sheriff."

There. He said it. Anderson wasn't wearing his star, and not dressed like any city law in his wild Mackinaw coat. "You know who I am."

The man cleared his throat and his eyes almost imperceptibly narrowed. "I read the newspaper," he said.

If he knows who I am, why would he think to let me ride away? Anderson answered that himself, as soon as he thought it. He wouldn't. Anyone familiar with Anderson's dogged personality already understood that letting the sheriff walk would be one hell of a bad idea. Perhaps it was a ruse to draw him away from the house, to kill him out of sight before taking Queen and Cahill by surprise. Maybe he was simply a coward and preferred a man's back as his target. The man was dressed fancy for a common killer, and acted affable, although the gleam in his eyes told Anderson's gut something different. There was something too natural about him. Too cool to be believed.

"You don't seem particularly surprised that I'm here," Anderson said. "I would think it strange if I stumbled upon someone like me in the middle of nowhere, sitting on a porch on a winter's evening while a German burned in the background. You take it in like it's all part of a day's work."

"Well," the man laughed softly. "If you only knew the work I do."

"Why don't you tell me?"

"No more questions, friend, or you'll be in a bad box."

"I think I already am."

The man sighed. "You're right. You are."

"So why don't you tell me why you're here, then?"

"Don't press me, I said." His voice strained, and Anderson could make out a hint of displeasure. An idea came to him.

Perhaps if he pushed a little more, he could get the dude flustered. Put him off balance, and somehow get a pull on him with the one good Colt in his left holster.

"You're not dressed for weather such as this," Anderson said. "Those clothes are sore on my eyes."

"Now that's the pot calling the kettle black," the man chided.

"Are you one of them dandified rump roasts that cad about town dressed in fine get-ups and make asses of themselves on Saturday night?"

"Do I look like that to you, old man?" His derby had slipped down over one eye and he glared at the sheriff with the other. "You'd best stop with the jests, and think for a moment about your situation."

"What am I to think about, if you don't tell me anything? If I don't have anything to think about, I just let my mind wander, and consider what's in front of me at the moment. At this moment it's you, with your gasbag mouth and your gay cat clothes. Why don't you just vamoose, boy, and leave me be?"

The pistol in the man's hand shook, and he peered over it, in fiery rage. "My name is Jack Peach, granddad, and I work for Jiggs Kilbane. You know who he is?"

"Afraid not."

"Well, here is a name you might have heard of. Martin Baum?"

Anderson's toes began to tap, faster than before.

"I would have been satisfied to give you a quick end, old man, but I don't feel sorry for you anymore, insulting my suit, so instead I'm thinking to give you something else instead."

"How do you know Martin Baum?"

"Well, that's his formal name, yes. He also goes by *Uncle Martin*. By a certain young lady."

Panic rippled through the sheriff's body. He suddenly didn't want to hear the rest. The man scoffed at the sheriff's stunned expression.

"You've been looking in all the wrong places. She's much too pretty to be knocking about low-case joints. Only the best resorts for Maisy Anderson."

"W-w-where?" Anderson sputtered. "Where?"

"Right under that crooked old beaker of yours. In Minneapolis, all along. She's holed up in a tip-top resort. It's the cheese, old man. Hot stuff, so don't you worry. She's got men lined up to grind her, night and day. She yowls away like the two-bit whore she really is."

Anderson's head went down into his thick hands, the pieces of his gun clattering to the floor. His head swelled with sudden dizziness, and he fought control of his senses. *She is a prostitute.* He'd known it all along, but to hear it, now, confirmed, hurt worse than he ever expected it would. Every ounce of pain was being squeezed out of his heart.

"I, for one, don't think she deserves the goose feather pillows and perfumed sheets, but my boss, Mr. Kilbane, thinks she's prettier than the Gibson Girl."

Anderson lifted his head slowly, and met the man's eyes. "Tell me where."

"That would be a good question for your friend Baum. You've been wondering all this time who stole your little girl away, haven't you?"

"Th-th-that's impossible."

"Impossible?" scoffed Peach. "God's own truth. Martin Baum was waiting for her at the railway station. He promised to escort her to college, but sold her into a different kind of education instead."

Anderson wouldn't hear another word. He glowered with a hatred that blasted from his soul, come up like the devil to kill the man standing in front of him.

Unfortunately, though, the man he wanted dead had *him* dead to rights. Peach's British Bulldog, steady again, was pointed at his head. One of Anderson's pistols was pulled apart and scattered around his feet. His other thumb-buster was still holstered on his left hip, but the way he was sitting the gun's grip was bent up at the back of his chair. Even if he went for his six-gun, it wouldn't be smooth, and the man would draw a bead and bed him down.

But he had no choice. It was for Maisy.

Anderson's left hand dropped to the gun on his hip. He closed his eyes, knowing that in this first exchange of bullets he would be the second fastest, but if the man missed, he would shoot him dead with his eyes closed.

The old sheriff had actually managed to unshuck the pistol halfway out of the holster. He was surprised he had been that fast, and then the bullet slammed against his forehead.

The sheriff's eyelids fluttered for a moment and then stopped. Jack Peach had made his jack, and the lights were doused.

Neither of them knew what to think when the shot rang from outside. Both stood up together and started toward the door, but it opened on its own before they reached it.

Jack Peach stepped in, as handsome and toff as you please, his hat cocked jauntily and a fresh cigar in his fingers, his gun pointed at them.

"Hello, Queen. We're back to last names."

"Where did that shot come from, Jack? Was that you?"

"It was, and I'm sorry to say I had to put old rusty guts out of his misery. He's been through enough, hasn't he?"

"You killed him?" Queen's heart almost leapt into his throat. The double-dealing bastard. He four-flushed me. Tricked me into trusting him and got us out here alone so he could knock us off one by one. The detective took a step back, bumping into the armchair behind him, his head exploding with anger over how he could have been so stupid as to trust this two-faced swell in front of him.

It seemed as if Peach could read his thoughts. "I'm here because of you," he told Queen. "It's much cleaner to kill you here than on a busy Saint Paul street. I got lucky and found grand dad, too." He turned his head to Cahill and gave him a reassuring smile. "It's the way the world works, pal. No hard feelings."

Cahill's face collapsed, devastated. Peach saw his expression and gave him a patronizing pat on the shoulder, taking care to keep the gun aimed in Queen's direction.

"Don't look so black, chum," he said. "Anyone else creeping around here?"

Queen searched the fringes of his vision for a weapon, any kind of weapon. Peach wasn't going to sit down for a bottle of fizz with them before using that gun. He was methodical and efficient, and Queen knew the end was coming soon for them all, unless he could think of something fast.

The stickpin. It was still in his coat pocket.

"There are more detectives on their way, Jack." Queen said. He took a step back, trying to draw Peach away from the room, as he hadn't yet noticed Petey curled up under a blanket by the far fireplace, deep in sleep. "Your best choice might just be to burn the breeze and get as far away from the Twin Cities as you can go. You've just committed murder."

"I know, I know," Peach said. "I've been doing a lot of that recently, it seems. Dander and Higgins? That was my work. I also take responsibility for Ellie Van Allen, and her unfortunate tumble."

"Ellie Van Allen?"

"The *real* name of the murdered whore who has led to this most unfortunate situation in front of us. Kilbane thinks I don't know her history, but I know much more than I let on. She was the granddaughter of the Pennsylvania Van Allens, the family that owns Columbia Steel. A naughty, naughty girl she was. She came willingly at first, and enjoyed being Mr. Kilbane's girl and escaping her tight-fisted grandfather's grasp. But eventually she caused just too much trouble, and he sent her to Minneapolis and Dander to pummel her back into place. She didn't like it much, and who could blame her? Having to live under Dander's whip had to have been unbearable. She threatened to leave and go back to her family. *That* couldn't happen, of course. I didn't pull the trigger myself, but Kilbane wanted it done, so I gave Dander the order." Peach leaned against the door as he continued, one knee pulled up casually, foot resting on the door's frame. "And I was there to make sure it happened."

"I'll bet you were on the corner smoking a cigar too, with a big old cloud of smoke circling your head."

The mouthy little boy at the crime scene had seen Peach, not Cahill after all. He checked Tom for his reaction, but the kid just clutched his smashed hand, still reeling from the sheriff's death. And here stood Jack Peach, admitting everything, because they would all be dead in a matter of minutes. Even slumbering little Petey, who had been through too much already, would continue sleeping for eternity, once this dude in the flash suit put a bullet into his brain.

Slowly, Queen reached into his pocket, and grasped the stickpin in his fingers.

"Go ahead, Queen. Take whatever you have in there out for me to see. Let's have a little fun. You aren't a very good gambler, though, let me remind you." He chuckled, dropped his cigar on the carpet, and stamped it out.

Queen's legs pushed against the chair behind him, and he stepped to the side of it and then back, toward the library. He hoped Peach would move forward out of instinct, as the aggressor, and he was right. Peach closed in, still waiving his little British Bulldog pistol, and then Tom was no longer next to him, but behind.

"Walking with a bit of a limp, eh, Queen? Somebody hurt you? That burned corpse out there, perhaps? You think I was wrong to kill the old man, but you set someone on fire."

"Tom, paste him!" Queen shouted. Peach stared at Queen for a half second, stunned, and then whirled around to face Cahill, who faltered back, equally surprised.

Queen ripped the stickpin out of his pocket and lunged at Jack Peach, almost tripping over the carpet in his rush to get to him. He plunged the pin into Peach's arm, and Peach let go of his gun. Queen felt the pistol land on the carpet next to his foot.

The gangster gave a soft grunt and glanced at where the stickpin stuck inside him like a needle in a pincushion. His eyes blinked mild concern, as though the hole in his suit disturbed him more than the hole in his arm. Then he gave a wry little smile and brought his fist up with a fast, brutal uppercut to Queen's chin. Queen staggered back and Peach moved forward, giving the detective a vicious kick to his already injured knee. Queen's leg collapsed under him and he fell onto Peach. He grabbed ahold of the gangster's lapels for support and then dragged him into the library. They wrestled for the upper hand, knocking books from shelves and breaking pictures with their heads as they bounced like billiard balls from one wall to another. As they tussled, Queen took every chance he could to slap and tug at the pin, adding to a spreading patch of blood on Peach's coat.

Queen knew, though, that Peach could sense he was tiring fast. Peach wore an expression of mild amusement as he flung the detective across the room and into a corner lamp, sending bits of colored glass onto the floor. Queen tried to rise and Peach shoved him back again, hard into the wall this time. The gangster was maintaining his strength, while Queen's was draining quickly, but the detective still managed to stand. He lifted his arms and his hands formed shaky fists, which made Peach chuckle.

"I told you before that you're too damn old," Peach said and moved towards him with a snake's speed. Queen balled his hand but Peach was already behind him, his forearm tight around the detective's neck in an iron lock. The gangster grabbed a glass paperweight from the desk and slammed it into Queen's side, and the detective squeezed his eyes shut to contain the pain that exploded through his kidney. Finally, with a great heave, Peach pushed Queen, face down, onto the massive desk, sending an inkwell and an ashtray crashing to the floor.

"I've got you now," Peach laughed, face bright red from the exertion. "First a streetcar chase, and now this. You've really given me something to remember you by."

He held Queen down with an open paw around the detective's neck, and with the other hand extracted the stickpin from his arm. He examined it with a quick grin.

"I don't know if this'll sting or not, but since you insisted on prolonging this, I guess it's about what you deserve."

Queen managed to twist his head enough to see Peach raise the stickpin, ready to bring it down hard into his back. He also saw Tom Cahill come up from behind, Peach's Bulldog pistol in his good hand.

"Shoot, Tom, shoot!" he shouted.

"I can't see without my glasses!" Cahill screamed back.

"Shoot!" Queen screamed so loud his voice caught in his throat, and the word ended in a whisper.

Jack Peach was never, ever one to lose his head, even in life and death situations. But now, for the briefest of moments, Queen saw with satisfaction, Peach's face showed fear. Pure, unadulterated fear. Then a single shot cracked, and Queen felt Peach's full weight fall on him, pinning him to the desk.

With his one good hand, Tom pushed Peach's corpse off him. It hit the floor with a hard thud. Cahill was holding back tears. While once, not long ago, Queen might have berated the naive, confused kid for showing weakness; he didn't blame him now, not in the slightest.

"What the goddamn deuce just happened?" Queen asked, and he wondered it with all of his heart.

EPILOGUE

*I*T WAS ONE OF THOSE resplendent January days in Minnesota when the sun shimmered in a golden glow against an azure blue sky, flooding the world with light intensified a thousand-fold by the drifts of white snow. The biting cold and glorious sunshine combined to lift Harmon Queen's mood, but nothing could lift it higher than having Karoline Ulland's arm in his.

They strolled through Loring Park and around the lake, enjoying the sun on their faces and each other's company. A group of bundled-up children threw handfuls of hard, powdery snow chunks at each other, and sent one ricocheting across their path, breaking at Karoline's feet. Queen roared and bounded through the snow after them, leaving them scampering and screaming in delight.

"You're a big bad man, Harm, scaring little children like that." She chided him with gaiety in her voice. "You'll injure your knee again with your antics."

"And get put on a desk duty like Krumweide? Not for me, thank you."

They continued their promenade under the naked gray trees, past a statue of a man with long hair and a charismatic smile, holding a violin in position and a bow poised for a melody.

"That's Ole Bull, Harmon. He's beloved by all Norwegians, both in Norway and America. I was here four years ago when the statue was unveiled. My brother helped organize the event from Dania Hall."

"I was here as well," Queen said. "But looking for pick-pockets."

"He was the greatest Norwegian violinist who ever lived. Did you know he started a community in Pennsylvania called New Norway? It failed, however."

"Tom Cahill told me Nininger had the same story," said Queen. "Gottschalk, the man who kidnapped the boys I told you about, was the son of a musician."

"How is Mr. Cahill, now that you mention him, and the young brothers?" Karoline asked.

It had been weeks since everything had happened, but Queen hadn't had much time to digest it personally, as there had been much to do. He'd taken time to arrange for Dix Anderson's body to be transported to Bemidji, where he'd heard that the sheriff would be buried next to his wife. Sheriff Roy had telegraphed him with a reminder that there was another plot in the cemetery already bought and paid for next to theirs. As telegrams cost green, it was left to Queen to infer what that meant.

He took Karoline's mittened hand with his glove and squeezed it tight.

"Ollie and Petey are living with their mother. I had a talk with her, and told her to find me if she was ever swamped for money. As for Cahill, he cashed in his chips and quit. Colonel Ames tried to talk him into staying, but he wanted to squaddle back to New Ulm to help his father on the farm. I think he's had enough of Minneapolis."

"He saved your life."

"He did."

"How could you let him go? You always talk about how few people you can trust in your position."

"He's his own man. I can't stop him if he's set his mind to it. He's got a head for figuring things out."

"I hope so. I worry about you, and the mysterious people you associate with. With the exception of that obnoxious Detective Norbeck, who disturbs me greatly, I've yet to meet any of your police department friends."

"I worry a little, too. My reputation has always been rank."

"You've promised to cut back on your drinking. You've admitted that it was the culprit for much of the nastiness written about you in the papers."

"And I have. I need to be clearer from now on. Colonel Ames was grateful that I was able to save Tom from a terrible end, so grateful in fact that he gave me something."

Karoline turned to him, breath drawn in. "What?"

Queen pulled out a badge from his coat. The gold plating caught the sun and glistened as he let her look at it. "I'm Chief Detective, now, Karoline."

She looked at it with admiring eyes and gave him a big hug. "This will include a larger salary, I assume?"

"Of course. Not only is it a promotion for me, but also my bank account. Why do you ask?" he laughed.

"You know why. I've set my cap for you. I expect that you plan on courting me properly, Mr. Queen. One day we'll need a home together."

"And a closet-full of new dresses as well?"

"Shame on you, Harm." She hit his arm hard. "I'm not one to put on frills."

"And what of my sister? What shall she do, living all alone?"

"And what of my brother? Perhaps we need to push those two together!"

"It's a future to think about, Karoline. There is something I have to do first, though. It might take me away for a while."

"Yes, you've told me before, Harmon."

"Dix Anderson was the last family she had. There is no one else."

"Except you."

"Yes."

"But she doesn't even know who you are. And you expect to swoop in and scoop her up and take her away?"

He took Karoline's hand and squeezed it. Despite her protestations, he knew she understood. She was the one with the selfless heart.

"I expect to find her and get her out of whatever situation she's found herself in."

She leaned over and kissed him lightly on the cheek. "I agree with you. She needs someone strong and noble to rescue her, and there is no one better for it than you. That is why I love you, Harmon Queen."

Photograph Credits

CHAPTER 1—Abandoned house, Minneapolis, 1890s, Hennepin County Library—Special Collections

CHAPTER 2—Nicollet Avenue looking north from Fifth Street, Minneapolis, circa 1895, Hennepin County Library—Special Collections

CHAPTER 3—Minneapolis Police Officers, early 1900s, Hennepin History Museum

CHAPTER 4—Central Police Station, Minneapolis, circa 1901, Minnesota Historical Society

CHAPTER 5—Chicago, Milwaukee and St. Paul Railroad Station (Milwaukee Depot), Minneapolis, circa 1901, Hennepin County Library—Special Collections

CHAPTER 6—The Bohemian Flats, Minneapolis, circa 1901, Hennepin County Library—Special Collections

CHAPTER 7—Newsboys Parade, Minneapolis, circa 1900, Hennepin County Library—Special Collections

CHAPTER 8—City Hall, Minneapolis, circa 1901, Hennepin County Library—Special Collections

CHAPTER 9—Stone Arch Bridge, Minneapolis, circa 1901, Hennepin County Library—Special Collections

CHAPTER 10—Union City Mission, Minneapolis, circa 1901, Hennepin County Library—Special Collections

CHAPTER 11—Bismark Bar, Minneapolis, circa 1902, Hennepin County Library—Special Collections

CHAPTER 12—Class of 1901 and 1902, Swedish Hospital School of Nursing, Minnesota Historical Society

CHAPTER 13—Chicago Great Western passenger train pulling out from Minneapolis railroad station, circa 1900, Minnesota Historical Society

CHAPTER 14—Saint Paul streetcar, circa 1900, Minnesota Streetcar Museum

CHAPTER 15—Ignatius Donnelly's home, Nininger, circa 1900, Dakota County Historical Society

EPILOGUE—Ole Bull Statue, Loring Park, circa 1900, Hennepin County Library—Special Collections

Notes and Acknowledgements

My purpose in writing this book was to bring to life the vibrant backdrop of Minneapolis at the turn of the 20th Century, and weave in characters both real and imagined. It was a book I had envisioned for many years, starting back to the mid 90s when I gave historic crime tours of the Twin Cities and first learned of the Mill City's seedy past.

Harm Queen is loosely based on real-life Minneapolis police detective Norman W. King. When I first discovered this historic, hard-boiled cop, I was floored by his larger-than-life personality. From the 1880s and on he was a regular and popular subject of the local rags. Newspapers would alternately congratulate King on his sleuthing abilities and condemn him for his drunken, irresponsible behavior. My detective's personality is similar, however I've allowed him to operate outside of the confines of marriage, and engage in some fictional casework.

Both Alonzo "Doc" Ames and Col. Fred Ames were real men, both eager to capitalize on Doc's profitable return to City Hall. Controversy surrounded Doc Ames wherever he went. He was absolutely beloved in the city by the less fortunate; freely giving time and medical service to whoever required them. He was also egotistical to an extreme, and bathed in the adoration of his followers. Colonel Ames served in the Spanish American War and suffered bad press from what many suggested was real or feigned illness at the moment his command became most needed. When Doc Ames's mental prowess began its decline in his final term as mayor, his brother Fred began calling the shots behind the scenes with cold calculation.

The Big Mitt game was very real, and documented in stunning detail through various court trials as the administration came crashing down in 1902. True too, was the mass firing of half of Minneapolis's police force in favor of more "flexible" officers, many of whom did have very unsavory backgrounds. I would encourage anyone interested in finding out what happened before my series ends, to start with Lincoln Steffens's famous expose, called "The Shame of Minneapolis." It appeared in *McClure's Magazine* in 1903 and summarized the rise and fall of Doc and his cronies for a national audience.

Many of the historical figures I touched upon briefly will play larger roles in upcoming books. Fred Connor, Doc Ames's personal bodyguard, was one of the few African-American police officers on the force in Minneapolis, and highly respected for his abilities. Coffee John Fitchette owned the most famous seafood restaurant in Minneapolis and plays an important position in the corruption to come, along with Doc's medical office assistant, Irwin Gardner, and his loyal secretary Tom Brown. Billy Edwards was also real, and continues in his role as steerer for the big mitt games. Even Freddy Bonge, the enthusiastic newspaper reporter, found himself in hot water as the Ames administration came tumbling down and will do so again in further stories. And then there was Chris Norbeck, as odd in real life as he is in the novel. He'll play a pivotal role in things to come.

I've always been fascinated by the notorious killing of Kitty Ging by Harry Hayward. It remains one of the most famous, publicized murders in Minnesota history. While Harry's brother Adry was indeed part of the foul plan, he never shacked up on the Bohemian Flats levee with a cadre of prostitutes, as I have fictionalized. The historic figure of Ignatius Donnelly was as eccentric and extraordinary as I tried to portray. His house stood lonely in the abandoned, ruined town of Nininger for years after his passing on New Years Day, 1901.

Tom Cahill, Emil Dander, Jack Peach, Jiggs Kilbane, Milwaukee Jim, Gottschalk, Peder and Karoline Ulland, Edna Pease and Trilly Flick are all fictional, and the murder of Maisy Anderson was my own invention. As for Dix Anderson, he is a melding of two men. The first was a deputy sheriff named Andrew Johnson, who among his many escapades took a bullet while shooting it out with a couple of yeggmen on a railroad bridge near Bemidji in 1909. The other man is my grandfather Dix Coffin, who will turn 100 in March of 2014 as I am writing this. He wore no flamboyant clothing and carried no six shooters on his hips, but he is as fair and just and moral a man as I've ever met in my life. Sheriff Johnson, later on in life, would perform my grandfather's wedding to my grandmother Arvilla Halverson.

I want to give special thanks to a number of people who have helped me with this book. My family has been enormously supportive, starting with my sister Alison, who immediately read every chapter I wrote and gave me instant feedback and encouragement the day after I emailed it to her. My mom Gail and sister Jen acted as beta readers and assisted my story while rallying me forward, and if I could bottle and sell my mom's enthusiasm for the characters I would be a rich, rich man. I spent hours with my father Phil going over many, many pages, and his talent for appropriate vocabulary and turn of phrase was much appreciated. I'm also blessed to have great support from Teri Hansen Anderson, who kept up with each chapter to offer praise and advice. Spence Johnson, long time Hastings stalwart and teacher, helped me with some of my Nininger questions, and historic weapons expert Chris Fischer helped wade me through an understanding of period rifles. I have a excellent editor, John Meyer, who kept me on track with accurate history and language, going far beyond his duty to help the story stay true and sharp. A special thanks to Lieutenant Chris Hudok, Minneapolis Police Historian, who not only stood by to answer any historical questions I pestered him with regarding the MPD, but took time from his busy schedule to check my manuscript for accuracy. Another man I need to thank is Aaron Isaacs of the Minnesota Streetcar Museum. He gave me lots of great advice on structuring the streetcar chase, and also wrote a superb book on the subject called *Twin Cities By Trolley: The Streetcar Era in Minneapolis and St. Paul*, which I highly recommend. Rebecca Snyder of the Dakota County Historical Society and Jack Kabrud and Susan Larson-Fleming of the Hennepin History Museum also offered their assistance to me, which I appreciate tremendously. I owe much of my love for history to Jerry Fritsch, longtime Cottage Grove teacher and "Colonel Snelling" at the Historic Fort, whose knowledge of Minnesota's past is extraordinary. We had many great conversations over cold bottles of Summit IPA. A very special thanks to Emily, who is there every day to keep me focused on writing, when I would rather be standing in line at Dairy Queen for a cherry sundae with Wei.

And finally, a wonderful friend from England named Nikk Bond, who when very sick still urged me forward and boosted my spirits with her encouraging words. I drew inspiration from her, even after her passing, to complete the book and make it available to all.

The next Harm Queen book is already in the works, and the brand new Chief of Detective's search for Maisy will continue, even as he gets sucked farther into the Ames brothers' web of corruption and deceit.

*For more information
on the Big Mitt series,
visit my author page at:*

www.ErikRivenes.com

www.ingramcontent.com/pod-product-compliance
Lightning Source LLC
Chambersburg PA
CBHW030546260626
47157CB00006B/2208